Copyright © Sfarda L. Gül 2023

First published 2024

*Lacrimosity and Righteous Rage Press*
First edition

Cover and map by Sfarda L. Gül
Mask chart by Ayşe-Mira Yaşın
Sigils by Nadia Sampellegrini
Internal illustrations by Sophia Arnaout, Sfarda L. Gül
Edited by Belle Manuel

A catalogue record for this book is available from
the National Library of Australia

ISBN (*paperback*): 978-0-6458756-0-7
ISBN (*ebook*): 978-0-6458756-1-4

For more information visit: *https://sfarda.carrd.co & https://larrpress.carrd.co*

# ALSO BY SFARDA L. GÜL

The Hypostasis of Dissent Duology
*Non Omnis Moriar* (II)

*Earth Hagiography*
*Feed the Forest and Never Choose Death*
*Saudade Knows Me by Name*

## POETRY PUBLISHED IN:

*Musing Publications*
From Heart to Stomach
*Mollusk Literary*
Metachrosis Literary
*Full House Literary*
Qafiyah Review
*HyeBred Magazine*
Split Pomegranate
*The Malu Zine*
and others

## SHORT STORIES PUBLISHED IN:

*The Globe Review*

# CONTENT WARNINGS

Political oppression.

Death and executions.

Graphic violence and gore.

Police brutality.

Gun violence.

Sex trafficking.

Violence against women and trans people (*including implied transphobia; challenged*).

Scenes of sexual harassment.

Slut-shaming.

Discussions of sexual violence.

Discussions of infanticide, birth-related trauma, pregnancy loss.

Discussions of sexual mutilation.

Graphic self-harm (*an additional warning issued before the scene in question*).

Suicidal ideation, depression, mentions of suicide.

PTS nightmares.

Panic attacks.

Eating disorder behaviours.

Descriptions of food.

Riots.

Religion and religious fundamentalism.

Classism.

Genocidal language.

Implied Romaphobia (*challenged*).

Murder of an Armenian-coded character.

Deaths of POC characters (*off-page; depiction of corpses*).

Mentions of paedophilia, necrophilia.

Death of a child (*off-page; depiction of corpse*).

Child neglect and abuse.

Mentions of divorce.

Death of a parent.

Workplace violence.

Smoking (*tobacco and opium*).

Alcohol.

Mentions of intravenous drug abuse (*including depictions of side effects*).

Surgical procedures and needles (*singular instance*).

Fires and burns.

Non-erotic nudity.

Allusions to consensual sex (*no depictions of sex*).

Strong language (*including misogynistic and classist slurs*).

Take care of yourself, reader; your wellbeing is of utmost import~♡
If you find throughout the reading experience that a content warning is missing, *please do not hesitate to reach out to the author.*

# DISCLAIMER

This novel is <u>not</u> intended to be a true-to-life representation of any languages or cultures coded, mentioned, or alluded to in any degree of detail throughout the novel—text proper or footnotes—appearing in approximately this order: Venetian, Sardinian, Etruscan, Roman, Western Armenian, French, Ilmen Slovene, Erromintxela (*Romani*), Basque, Kalbelia, Palestinian, Chuvash, Balóch, Friulian, Albanian, Aragonese, Neapolitan, Sicilian, Izwawen (*Kabyle; Algerian Amazigh*) and Algerian, Maltese, Greek, Danish, Tigrayan, Ḥijāzi, Turkmen, Irish, Mongolian, Aragonese, Georgian, Sumerian, Chinese, Griko, Welsh, Emilian-Romangol, Northern Sámi, Galician, Akkadian/Ugaritic, Ryukyuan, Nama, Milanese, Senegalese Fula, Luoravetlat, Kalaallit, Warnumamalya, Māori, Croatian.

While a SWANAn, Eastern European, and Central Asian herself, with this book being in part *Own Voices* for multi-ethnic representation, the author does <u>not</u> fall under all of the aforementioned identities. The author does <u>not</u> subscribe to any of the religions underpinning the inspiration to those featured in-text.

<u>Do not</u> take any of the material featured in this book as unaltered cultural, theological, or historical fact.

If you find issue with the portrayal of subjects, peoples, *etc.* in any capacity, *please reach out*.

This is an adult novel. **18+**

# NON SERVIAM

*The Hypostasis of Dissent*
Book I of II

SFARDA L. GÜL

"Astute, immersive, grotesque, yet always bold and boasting
serious moral weight, Gül's complex gothic will entrance and
edify readers who relish the challenge." —*Publishers Weekly*

*for the fighters, the workers, the resistance;*
*for those whose voice is stifled and pain*
*is unseen; for the truth-seekers*

# AUTHOR'S NOTE

I published the first book of this duology at the age of 22—a month and 10 days before my 23rd birthday.

The conception for *The Hypostasis of Dissent* came about when I was a teenager who had just immigrated from the police state I was born and raised in. I think what I both wanted and needed then, in my heart of hearts, was a revolution story. A story of resistance to authoritarianism and systemic injustice where "violent" freedom fighting was granted the philosophical foundedness it deserved and "reform of an institution from within" was idealistic naïveté.

I started reading philosophy and political theory *far* too early in my childhood, but I suppose that comes with the territory of an intrinsically politicised identity. Nonfiction is my reading choice to this day, along with poetry (I read little else). That's why the story of *THoD* expanded from what I had initially intended to be a novella into a duology with a hefty second entry—as you learn, truly learn, politics and sociology and philosophy and decolonial history, you grasp just how dirty this work is.

That ultimately reflects in *THoD*. It's a dark and gruesome story about what is ultimately war. Because a fight for liberation from tyranny is war. But it's a righteous one—the purest form of love for humanity and earth.

I'm very intrigued to see how this story reads when I'm in my 30s, 40s, 50s.

This duology is not for everyone—I gleaned that very early on. The poetic writing style, the heavy worldbuilding and conlang, the candid violence, the perspective switches, do not carry mass appeal, but it's a narrative voice I'm unwilling to compromise on, *especially* the prose, for it would not be my own without it. English is my second language; I grew up in a country where most people have little to no knowledge of it, and I am very proud of the proficiency I've achieved.

*The Hypostasis of Dissent* duology is for a very niche readership somewhere out there, and I'm content with that.

Maybe, that readership is even *you*.

## READING IS POLITICAL

# Weekdays in Faustinian

| Monday | *díem auróra* | 'dawn day' |
| Tuesday | *díem sóle* | 'sun day' |
| Wednesday | *díem zenítis* | 'zenith day' |
| Thursday | *díem tramòne* | 'eventide day' |
| Friday | *díem crepúsca* | 'dusk day' |
| Saturday | *díem lunéra* | 'moon day' |
| Sunday | *díem stelláre* | 'star day' |

# Vencenzani Masks

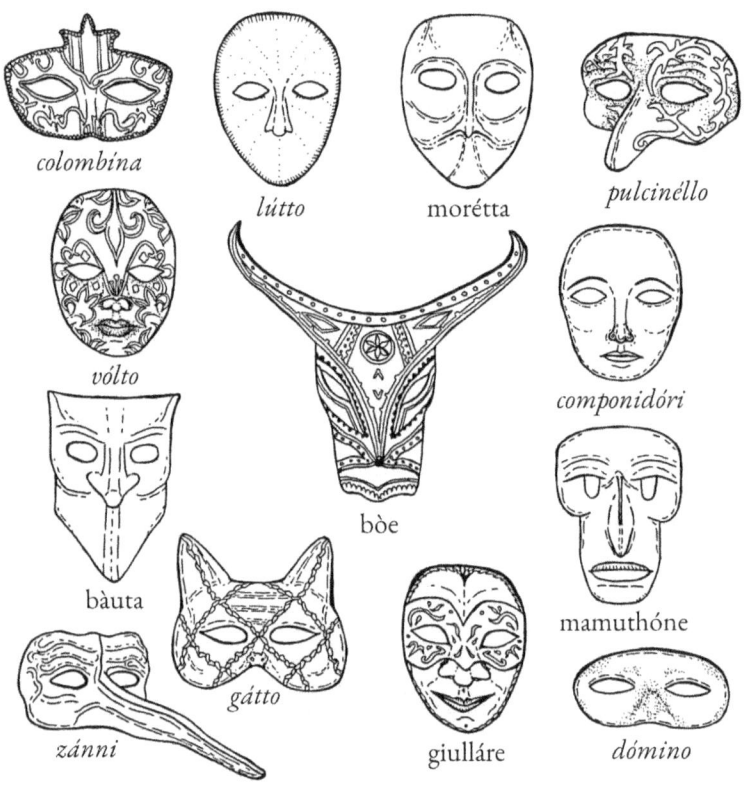

colombína

lútto

morétta

pulcinéllo

vólto

bòe

componidóri

bàuta

mamuthóne

zánni

gátto

giulláre

dómino

Take note that this book is very heavy on *worldbuilding* and *conlang* and is written in *poetic, metaphorical*, at times *archaic-esque* and *abstract* language, something which some readers may find detracts from immersion for them. This is the author's *stylistic choice*, as she deliberately writes in English the way she would in her first language, and is reflective of her *authentic artistic voice*.

# Faustinian Military Sigils

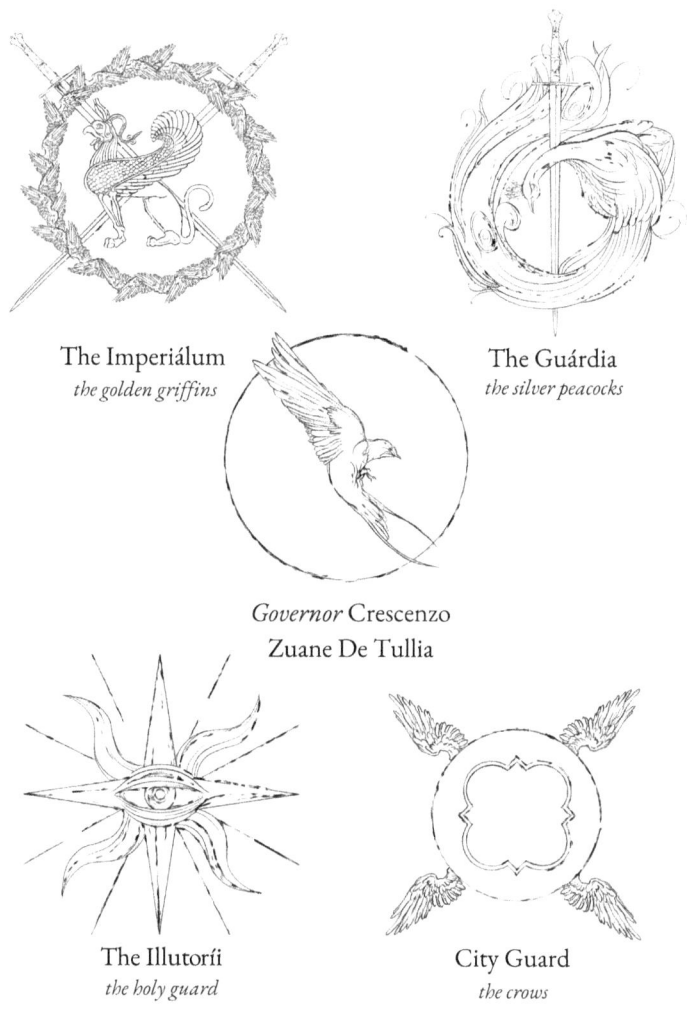

The Imperiálum
*the golden griffins*

The Guárdia
*the silver peacocks*

*Governor* Crescenzo
Zuane De Tullia

The Illutoríi
*the holy guard*

City Guard
*the crows*

Artists whose works are features in this book (*who are not the author*) are credited in the Acknowledgements.

# ACT I

*and shadow being beneath*        *came into the veil...*

"Like a flame burning away the darkness,
Life is flesh on bone convulsing above the ground."

—*Begotten*, dir. E. Elias Merhige

# Scene I

## Sophia

*Giorgianna[1]*

YOU WERE HARDLY TWENTY *the first time you met death.*

*It wore the skin of three faceless men springing from winter's shadow. The city hadn't breathed through the night and neither did you—your screams ripped the stars off the solstice sky and snuffed all light from the world.*

*Her eyes anchored to your memory. Eyes of the woman you loved like a sister you never had. Eyes blue as forget-me-nots. How true to name they were.*

*Her skull bled across the frost-mantled flagstone like a cracked pomegranate, yet she shrieked at you with all she had left within her.*

*'RUN!'*

---

[1] *jyohr-JAHN-nah*

*You did.*
*And you never stopped.*

## FAUSTINA, VENCENZA, 1762, 18TH CENTURY, 9TH CENTIMILLENNIUM ZE (ZEPHYRUS EPOCH)

*midspring*

"VIOLINIST?" demanded Madáma Irene Falco, inspecting my callus-tipped fingers with a precision befitting a predator scouting a spoor.

"Cellist," I croaked out.

Aubergine silk and powdery-sweet perfume wrapped the pewter-haired woman's petite frame—hard as a nail, crow-dark eyes glinting within the pallid wrinkles of her gaunt face. "Name?"

"Giorgianna Damiani."

"Cicatricose knuckles," Falco spat. "*The Arum* sells no damaged goods—I serve men of status."

My stomach dropped.

I needed to remain in the city state above all. Thus, I needed work far from the eyes of the powers that be. The alternatives were starving on the streets, or rotting in the dungeons, and those could be considered *lucky*, my predicament considered.

"Nonetheless," Madáma's eyes slitted, "your assets aren't few." Her slight fingers spindled through the waist-length mane of my caramel coils, scrutiny snapping to my face like a hyena's ravening jaw. "Broad, heart-shaped cheekbones, pointed chin—vulpine quality. And your lips… indented on the bottom as deeply as the bow." *All papa's features.*

My heart wrenched hard as rusted iron.

"A mole beneath your left eye and a daintier at the centre of that cheek; amber eyes vivid enough to pass for red at a glimpse." *Mother's eyes.* Falco's thin lips curled as she returned to my cold hands. "Shame for the scars." Her eyes coruscated with a thirst. I'd soon learn it was a thirst for pain. "Engendered by what?"

My throat thickened. "Injustice."

A scoff. "What would you know of *injustice*?"

*Ammuríre Lunéra marked the year's shortest day, when wintry night swiftly cast its nivean batiste of fog upon Vencenza, the southernmost of Faustina's quadruplet city states.*

*You strolled arm-in-arm with your beloved friend down the snow-swaddled marble promenade that Undying Moon, carrying tiny baskets of winter apples[2] to neighbours and exchanging with them words of goodwill:*

'Lignéza, ìgnis morírum.'
'Ípse fócire è vóstrum.'
'Éra ípse è vóstrum.'

'Woodless, a fire dies.'
'Our hearth is yours.'
'As ours is yours.'

*You were hardly twenty, but your eye caught the fear paling the neighbours' cheeks when your beloved friend smiled in that ridibund way of hers. You knew, too, why that door shut so loud against the silence of*

---

[2] A variety of apple tree which gives red fruit in snowy winters: the Vencenzani choice of offering during Ammuríre Lunéra ('*Undying Moon*'; the winter solstice). Iutulicanii prefer winter mandarins—pale citruses with a taste reminiscent of honeydew melon.

*the slumbering city, the blank mask—an apotropaic pagan talisman— hooked to its frontal façade rattling like shaken nerves.*

*Your eye caught the fear because you knew it like your own. Because you weren't to* feel*—the law decreed you oughtn't. You'd never laugh with anyone but your beloved friend and your father. Your mother would see your fingers bruised and bleeding for such transgression. The Governor would see you headless.*

*In a disillusioned procession, the pair of you descended to the courtyard. Sa Piázza del Alluvióni:* 'The Square of Floods'. *Its marble floors never went without a sheet of shoe-deep water in the summer, and in the winter, it became a skating rink.*

*But no longer, not since the regime change.*

*You knelt beside the smooth expanse of tenantless ice, hugged your knees, your curls cocooning you the way your mother, the blood of whom bestowed upon you such glorious hair, never would.*

*Scythe strokes of wind swept the balconies of Vencenza's eburnine buildings—fused tight as sutures and orné with ossiform stucco and curlicues. Above unfurled a lampblack sky strewn with stars like diamonds fallen from a weary miner's wagon, and no one but you and your beloved friend stalked the streets beneath that clinquant corpse field. Not the votaries of the Order in their blood-soaked regalia. Not the dark-hearted soldiers of the City Guard.*

*You heard your friend gasp.*

*From a nook in a solomonic column etched with eyes and faces, she lifted a baby bird, pale as cottony down, cradling it in her long palms. The fragile creature lay stiff with death.*

*"The poor thing deserves a proper burial." She swaddled the bird in a kerchief and slipped it inside her snow-sweeping lazuline daraz. Like friend like friend, that fascination with Death. Yours pressing roses to be preserved like taxidermy and encrusting teeth upon earrings you'd never wear, for your mother never permitted your ears be pierced; hers pinning cadavers of moths to frames festooned in bebilla needlelace and silver leaf, carving white clay statues stabbed through the heart with glass swords. It made you outcasts, your knowledge-hunger. Your soul-suffering.*

*You observed her, then.* Emanuela Vehanush Airaldi. *Tall as the mountains of her maternal land and graceful as its brooks. Sculptural as her creations. Coins wreathed her swanlike neck and wove through the hip-length darkness of her rippling hair, silver beads swinging around her chest and jaw. She'd said the embroidery on her flowing gown's lapels was called* 'marash', *that her pendant, a glass pomegranate aril like a suspended blood drop, symbolised life and abundance in Lerrkirakan culture. That's why you crafted that pendant for her—a reminder of her distaff homeland.*

Ema *was your name for her, your dearest friend since age six. Your first friend. Your* only.

*Behind her colombína, eyes blue as forget-me-nots clouded with a melancholy the glimmer of her pearl smile—a ballerina's artifice only authentic as diamanté diadems—could never dispel in an aeon.*

*Vencenza's people had worn masks for over a millennium: a symbol of resistance against northern colonisation which had kept your land grasped and unbreathing within the Faustinian Empire's[3] brutal fist.*

*Eight years prior, Governor Crescenzo Zuane De Tullia[4] swindled power over Vencenza, enforcing his tyrannical* Sa Nóba Giustíca—'The New Justice'—*to make a crime of laughter and a pariah of all emotion.*

*You were only twelve.*

*And now, as the twilight of your civilisation descended upon its own withering flesh, masks took on a perversion of their former liberatory motif, becoming De Tullia's armour against turpitude.*

*Against rebellion. Against humanity.*

*Now, to live was to wear a mask evermore.*

"Silly Giorgi!" *Ema nudged your side as you walked home arm-in-arm, rosen lips a-sparkle with her brightest jewels.* "When this ends—and it will!—you'll come to Lerrkir with me. The air is wonderful in the cloud-drinking mountains, and Nurrn Lake near the capital is always blue as our flowers." *She gestured to the satin-and-nacre forget-me-nots*

---

[3] The Faustinian Empire, its heartland located in Salvatrice in the current Republic's north, existed between 849–1650 ZE.

[4] *kreh-SHEHN-tsoh tsoo-AH-neh DEH TOOL-lee-ah*

*mensing her colombína.* "In the summer, we host an ancient festival for our goddess of love and fecundity where we splash each other with water. All of Lijaġhak's streets glister!" *Ema mused with that hopeful fervour often, her adornments donning the iridescence of bona fide diamond. As if you weren't trapped. As if the city gates weren't impenetrable and labour camps didn't lie beyond like gangrene to the body of this republic dubbed Faustina. But you'd chat about bygone pleasures for hours on end in your father's makeshift observatorium, you sitting with your cello and Ema repeating her échappés, those rare tranquil vespers smelling of lavender tisane and bergamot incense.*

*A lifetime lost.*

*Vencenza's flesh pulsed with vessels of canals, roads to be tread only on foot, no steeds or mounts permitted—certainly no Auréli pegasides or Ilinka tróiki. Watery caliginosity rippled in the alcoves of the city's rete, eyes opening up in the walls of the chapels you passed where unseen choirs cantillated in ghostly hymns, and the pair of you grew hushed.*

*You fell* silent *when descrying a Wanted poster rustle in the algific breeze.*

*A single mask was rendered on it with an executioner's diligence for no other reason but a haunting reminder. An* outlawed *mask: a mouthless bàuta. Every Vencenzanii knew of the bounty on The Bauta's head, the hatred of him propagandised by the Minister of Dominion.*[5]

*The Bauta put to the pyre tragic plays in protest, terrorised the corrupt City Guards, and decried the draconian laws that locked the city in chains.*

*The Governor called him sick. A sick*ness. *A demon heresiarch of order's destruction. A rattler of chains in the darkness; a whisperer of treason.*

*And was the Governor's word not gospel?*

*What you wouldn't do to pry open the gates into the governing kingdom, unspool the brains of the powers that be and devour every arcane verse inscribed upon their gyri and sulci. Decipher every truth and fallacy and withheld wisdom.*

---

[5] Another term for Governor—Vencenza's ministers have a dual title.

*But you couldn't—you weren't to* know, *either.*

The law decreed you oughtn't.

*It writhed inside you like a trapped animal, everything you swallowed, desperately hankering, but your mother's voice hissed in the darkness of your mind:* 'Nothing is worth it.' *So, you would take it to your grave.*

"What is 'enemy' in Hoġerr?[6]" *you asked Ema, wishing to dull your dread, for sometimes you felt you could see yourself through those eyes swivelling in the ancient walls.*

"Ɣosokh!" *Fiván.*

*Ema always spoke Hoġerr with such joy. Such ache of separation.*

"Rose?"

"Vart." *Arròsa.*

"Love?"

*Ema smiled, true as quartz forged of the sun's essence, a hearth in the cold.* "Sēr." *And even with the vólto obscuring your visage, Ema pulled you close and pressed her face to yours. Just beneath her right cheekbone, a large mole splotched her porcelain skin like ink. You didn't have the tiny dot in the centre of your left cheek before you met Ema, only the beauty spot beneath that eye to match your mother. You fancied to think the second came about from yours hugging Ema. It became your mythological ritual.*

'Love' *in Faustinian was* 'ataínè': 'eater'. 'Gnawer'. *The symbolism appealed to your Shadow in its cannibalistic subsumption. You floated through existence split in twain after all, a diptych.*

*And you were hardly twenty the first time you met death.*

*It wore the skin of three faceless men springing from winter's shadow.*

*Two restrained you; the third pinned Ema down, drove her skull into the frost-mantled flagstone until it bled like a cracked pomegranate.*

*Your screams ripped the stars off the sky and snuffed all light from the world, but you were too weak. Each time you lunged to save your beloved friend, the men broke your fingers, their* snap *a nightmarish mnemonic*

---

[6] The people and language of Lerrķir.

**Nota bene**: Accented vowels in [transliterated] Hoġerr are denoted by a dot above/below (depending on letter height) the preceding *consonant*, unless a macron (ō) is indicated to elongate the marked vowel.

*you'd forevermore hear in the spit of woodfire and the phantasmal finger-drum of rain, and nobody came to help you that solstice night.*

*Ema's eyes anchored to your memory. Eyes of the woman you loved like a sister you never had. Eyes blue as forget-me-nots.*

How true to name they are.

*It must've been a surge of a cornered animal's rabid fear which broke you free, and it was then that Emanuela shrieked at you with all she had left within her.*

'RUN!'

*You did.*

*And you never stopped.*

*But you couldn't save her.*

"When did this come to pass?" Falco's question came bluntly, an interrogation.

"Two years ago," I forced through the phantom bind constricting my throat.

The murderers' names were never disclosed to me, and only one of the three was put to death. *One too few.*

I sought answers.

I sought *justice*.

So, I would remain in this wretched city until I obtained the key to break into De Tullia's kingdom and learned the truth of the night still haunting me. The night I was reaped of one of my most fiercely beloved.

I clamped my hands shut against their tremble and recollected myself presently.

Madáma Irene Falco still studied me, toying with a grey-streaked lock fallen loose from her wealthy chignon, pearls like triplet rows of molars chattering around her bird-boned throat. "Take off your clothes."

# SCENE II

## ELEUTHEROMANIA

*Cesare* [7]

INSIDE EVERY BONE LURKS A SHADOW in reminder of its inevitable ruination. The city of Vencenza impressed upon the mind precisely thus.

A simple city, really. There was the east, 'upper óssium'[8], its baroque structures soaring in chryselephantine elegance like tusks for the firmament's skin, each quarter of the state cleaving to an orderly celestial motif, or otherwise religiously-inspired, its populace equally obedient.

A city simple as life, that is.

Because westward, upper Vencenza yielded to something darker. Older. *Lower*.

Strange thaumaturgy veiled The Court of Secrets like a cloak, disorienting intruders and uninvited guests looking to pick at something fleshy; to unmake a haven of clandestine revelry concealed in plain sight.

---

[7] *CHEH-zah-reh*
[8] Literally '*bone*'; the general city excluding its theatres.

The veil could be torn—nothing was infallible—but it took decisiveness. Surety. Knowledge. And sometimes, even the unwanted carried an advantage in their step.

If polished bones constructed upper Vencenza, then its westward oldtown, of which The Court was only a mote, was wrought of those freshly torn from a still-warm body.

Its darkness thrummed with living souls. Twisted like fingers. Weaved into the flesh of manifold corporealities.

This instance, it became a violinist playing to a tavèrna situated upon The Court's northern edge where shorelines of endless canals locked into a skirmish with wharfs.

A billowing silk shirt the colour of raspberry clad his broad shoulders and lithe limbs, the onyx corset across his waist glimmering with striations of amethyst and sapphire sequin. Black pants and stiletto boots augmented his towering height; waves of dark hair slashed the centre of his throat like an executioner's blade.

Yet the song of his violin cut deeper, through to the buried psyche, strains an unspoken lament of ruin. Of voices ripped from cords shouting treason and dissent.

A song for freedom.

A song for life.

Cesare detested separation from his jacket—it meant being poorly armed. On this night, moon a luminous platter in the dark, he braved wearing his daggers on his person if for no other reason than the rush of casual criminality. Cesare was hardly a stranger to the law's fire poker as it were.

Violin packed up, he approached the quiet bar where dockmaster Iyad Amāl Maram al-Uwwād loitered in the lamplight. A beige shirt and sirwāl loosely draped his slim frame, red-green-white taṭrīz stitching his sidriyeh and an aerose key pendant swinging over his heart. Black hair bleached a lurid yellow-white brushed his protrusive collarbones as it spilled from beneath an olivaceous kūfiyya.

"Rusty, Agostini." Iyad gestured to Cesare's violin, his dry voice tinged with a Dīmardi burr like the clove in his pipe.

"Be a dear and serenade me, al-Uwwād." Cesare hopped up to sit on the bar, long legs crossed, receiving an unimpressed eye roll. "*Your* prowess with a bow is equal to none, I'm sure."

"Heard the news going around?" Iyad pivoted subjects in his wonted candour.

"It never rests."

The dockmaster leaned closer. "People've been disappearing from upper town." He switched quietly to Calvessi, a seabound mercantile cant spoken at docks across Vencenza and its motherland Sancta Maria—a clever rearrangement of phonemes turning the rhythmic trill of Faustinian into a gibber intelligible only to those able to decrypt the formulaic code of the argot's genesis. "Same as ten years back. No trace, no word. Just *poof*, like they never existed."

Cesare knew, just as he knew it wiser to stay concealed under pretence of ignorance for concern of coming off suspiciously in-the-know to sycophants, so he replied with "Any leads?" in Calvessi of his own. Unsavoury eavesdroppers could be anywhere this close to upper Vencenza, and one always needed to be wary of the upper ossíi.[9]

"What d'you *think*?"

Cesare dodged a sickle to the hand miraculously in time.

The peppercorn eyes of a pale-faced woman glowered him down.

"*You* again," she hissed, dislodging her unbloodied weapon from the bar table.

---

[9] Literally '*of the bones*'; citizens of the óssium.

Cesare threw a theatrical hand to his chest. "I entertain your patrons out of the goodness of my heart, yet you endeavour to wound me, Anukka."

Iyad suppressed a titter, kissing his sour wife on the cheek. His icy mask melted only around the icier Ahărla[10] woman.

She brushed off her red-embroidered black tunic and belted the sickle at her hip. A helmet-like headdress with a back-spanning tail suspended hundreds of argent coins around the woman's sculpted face, whilst a wide circle scarf paved with silver like fish scales swung off her wide shoulders. Keske rosettes emblazoned either side of Anukka's breastbone with russet to symbolise her married status.

She said nothing.

A *tsk* from Cesare. "Our vying imperator proposes an assembly at the citadel in a week's time—díem zenítis." The mere thought of the reaper Crescenzo Zuane De Tullia sank a shiv into Cesare's side.

Iyad scoffed. "And *you're* right on its trail, I wager."

"Your return on investment would be splendid," Cesare quipped, still opting for Calvessi and caution. "I shall be making my customary appearance to deal a weakening blow to the powers that be."

"How exactly shall you get *in*?" Iyad questioned.

"The old wing—eastern end of the ministerial house—once comprised palatial quarters. Now, it's a museum. Subterranean tunnels branch beneath Vencenza proper, serving the most fortuitous point of incursion *into* the old wing and the rest of the citadel from there. Guarded as the tunnels are, it's nothing a little collusion cannot surpass; Ygąl[11] and I've been hard at work since the assembly's announcement—" *four weeks* "—and Donatello is a treasure trove of intel to boot."

Anukka glared. "And what'll happen when your stratagem inevitably meets a demise?"

"I'll see *my* demise of shame before I am thwarted!"

Anukka scrunched her aquiline nose. "Too clever by half."

---

[10] *ah-HAWR-lah*; people of Ahăruj (*ah-HAW-roo'y*).
[11] *ee-GAAHL*

"Enough to overreach the divinities." Cesare smirked tightly, Anukka's face flashing a lemon-sour mock in return.

"I've heard tell..." Iyad leaned in, voice low to dispel the brewing hurricane, "that instability fissures the senate's inner circle." Cesare's ears pricked up. "De Tullia's beginning to refuse counsel from even his *Adviser*. I mean *'an jadd* the goat offed his opponents after his inauguration!"

To attain power, Crescenzo Zuane De Tullia stabbed his own brother, Constantino Asile De Tullia, in the heart and liquidated his family and assets. His second opponent had battled alcoholism, and De Tullia exploited that by continuously poisoning the man with summerwine. The third he had his lackey torment until she took her own life. And the fourth he subsumed into his inner circle as the Grand Judge—a mere affectation of amity. Even the deaths of his militaristic genitors were rumoured to be Crescenzo's doing.

Cesare hoisted a brow at Iyad. "You heard tell *where*?"

"Rascals hanging around my docks cajoled some servants from the government building at the local butcher's some days back. Secretive bunch, but *one* tale they *didn't* skimp out on..." His dark eyes darted, nearly swivelling. "Some Guards patrolling the citadel walk around like unblinking ghouls. And listen—one claims she found a *hole* drilled into the skull of a soldier she wooed."

Anukka puffed a breath and shook her head, Iyad expressing consonance, but Cesare chronicled the cryptic detail, determined to let nothing evade him. He required all the ammunition at his disposal when infiltrating the ministerial house was merely one small means to the end of toppling that putrescence of an empire.

In truth, this marked not the first instance of citizenry disappearing under De Tullia's rule. Upon his enthronement ten years prior, dissidents were many—still glowing with a hope of overturn; unaware of the cosmic horror they beheld upon that mezzanine. Soon enough, they vanished like ghosts called back to the Netherworld, and Vencenzanii fell into a horror-stricken silence.

Cesare would never.

"You tread on thin ice," muttered Anukka, and Cesare knew she addressed him. "You play no fool's game. Upon my parents' graves remember: Revolution is not victory. Revolution is *death*."

Cesare beheld the woman's features, steely and cold, desolate as the frozen north.

His body lived as a vessel. A weapon. Material and finite. Breakable as he'd never admit.

His soul was an abstraction. Formulation. Idea.

His words were an emanation of that soul, illuminating the canvas of fabricated reality before the eyes of the masses.

To liberate words muffled by a tyranny was to liberate the mind.

To liberate the mind was to be free.

Relenting would never be an option. And Cesare was an instrument of abolition. He could *never* let himself lose.

Lips cocked like a revolver, he lifted a nonchalant shoulder. "The old ballad of means and ends."

Anukka threw a snort. "*Your* soul for the damning." She turned to the ornate glass decanters of mead and sara beer—Ahărla ritual beverage. "Better you than me."

Cesare hopped off the bar, slinging the violin case across his back. "Better *Them*." His bright hazel eyes shot to the window. Past the waters of the arterial canal. Towards the white skeleton and polished cartilage of the government building rising like an acropolis, a boneyard, an ancient carcass drained and stripped of flesh, behind a leviathan halo of aqueducts.

*This ends before I do.*

# Scene III

## Judgement Day

*Giorgianna*

*YOU WASTED TWO YEARS hounding the justices of that dead democracy, yet they never yielded the names of the men who stole your beloved friend.*

*You learned the House of Judgement by heart, its colossal sandstone colonnades and too-high ceiling, wide marble stairwells guarded by officéri[12] curving around them towards the hemicycle of balconies a level above.*

*The Grand Judge caught your eye upon them one fateful day, a mature man in regal nielle trailed by a mantle as if spilled judicial ink, a*

---

[12] *ohf-fee-CHEH-ree*; officers of the City Guard.
   A Faustinian noun ending in '*a*' will have a plural ending in '*ae*' (e.g. *fumàna/fumànae* [fog]). A noun ending in '*o*' or '*u*' will have a plural ending in '*i*' (e.g. *faltú/faltí* [sky]). A noun ending in '*e*' or a consonant will have a plural ending either in '*i*' or '*ii*' (e.g. *raixàme/raixàmi* [brushwood], or *mètlum/mètlumi* [district/province]). A noun ending in '*i*' will have an additional '*i*'—'*ii*' (e.g. *èteri/eteríi* [foreigner]). Nouns such as '*ossíi*' are *plurale tantum*.

matching *chaperòn*[13] *wrapping his head and a dómino tied to his face. He strutted among four giuratóri*[14] *whose fingers hid within conical white sleeves, whose eyes were bound by a mesh like bandages.*

*Your aching heart jumped to your throat then—you darted for the stairs with frantic beseeching, but legionaries restrained you.* "I demand to know the names of the men who killed Emanuela Vehanush Airaldi!"

*The Minister of Justice peered down his nose like you were a leper.* "You demand *nothing* of this institution."

"Shall I show you the scars they left behind when they broke my fingers? You *know* who they are, it is *my* right—"

"Your *right* is what is dictated to you, citizen." *Veronesi's rhadamanthine voice came down like a gavel to crush you, and so the soldiers dragged you down the steps of the portico and onto* Boulevard of Everseers. *You'd have lifted your mask and spat on them if it wouldn't land you in The Trabeculae,*[15] *so you bit your tongue to blood, gagging on your grief like water.*

*Veronesi once vied to be Governor. You didn't know which would be worse when the system was corrupt to the bone. He was the reason Emanuela's killers walked free.* They all were.

*You remembered that díem crepúsca sun ascend the blueing lilac of the enubilous western welkin.*[16] *An aroma redolent as offal clogged your nares. The red beads curtaining your hat's brim chittered like pulled teeth as you bore your head aloft.*

Boulevard of Everseers *ran between narrow waterways obumbrated beneath patina-veined hypostyle cloisters, its vastness overhung with costiform bridges from which bloomed lush bouquets of honeysuckles pink as guts. Amid the flowers swung tarnished cages holding starving prisoners and decaying corpses, purple-grey limbs and waxy bones*

---

[13] A turban-like headpiece, often depicted with a long tail of cloth hanging off the side. See Jan van Eyk's *Portrait of a Man* (1433) for reference.

[14] *joo-rah-TOH-ree*; members of a judgement tribunal.

[15] Enormous subterranean prisons stretching beneath the foundation of Vencenza's government building, deeper than the edifice is tall and certainly wider in area.

[16] Unlike Earth, the planet Gethlem spins in *retrograde*.

*jutting between the bars to toss tarry shadows to the flagstone in grim mockery.* The Hanging Gardens.

*You smelt it beneath the nectar: rot. An empire's decay. Made worse by the brackish blood of Vencenza's veins, the breeze oppressive with desperation.* Rage. *And rage sired vengeful progeny.*

*The grief inside you had festered to fury until it clawed at the cage of your ribs to break out. But you couldn't let yourself look upon the abyss for long.*

*You recalled your mother bringing you to The Hanging Gardens in your teenagehood, gripping you by the shoulders and jaw, and impelling you to look upon the barbarity.*

'Nothing is worth it,' *she'd hiss.*

Freedom *wasn't worth it if all it got you was* That.

*You comprehended what it meant to be ruled by fear, then. It became all you knew, so you split in twain.* A diptych. *Love and grief to rage and darkness, writhing within the gilded bars of Fear's cage.* Vencenza's cage.

*And what power did—*could—*you wield beneath a ghastly tyranny which beat you bloody for an outburst, or tortured you for laughter, or decapitated you for dissent? A tyranny dubbing the extermination of the lowly a* 'purification'? *A tyranny so feared by its subjects they kept silent, no matter how desperate? De Tullia's rule remarkably paralleled the Faustinian Empire when northern imperators decimated with horrific abandon, uprooting cities and erasing peoples—droves of Atarisi corpses nourished the plains of central Faustina, and not a single descendant walked the earth.*

*You were nothing beneath such a regime, so you hid the shadows of your rage inside your ribcage and let your anguish drown you.*

*The midspring sun that díem crepúsca left no caress of warmth as it soaked through the realgar velvet of your sleeves. You remembered Emanuela's smile, a glowing hearth in the coldest winters, and your fingers snapped with mnemonics of a pain you still recalled. You may have cried despite yourself, but the balconies snared your eye.*

*Within ink-stained caliginosity, a figure lingered.*

*A mouthless white mask, chin jutting and angular, stood in for its face, nothing evident of the eyes but black pits sinking gravity.*

*Like a wraith, the umbra dissolved it.*

The Bauta…

*Itches of sweat pearlised down your neck, dread impelling you to clear The Hanging Gardens.*

*Architectural motifs of full moons and miniscule stars gave way to sickled lunes as you crossed one of a million canals, signifying your departure from the northeast.*

*Diamond drops splashing off waterways baptised the stone beneath your rushing tread with a seasalt chrism, skirts and capes of the clergy and masked citizenry whispering along umbracious passageways flocked with crow-mask legionaries like the hiss of blood through ears. Yet, in spite of the life still thrumming through the city's ailing husk, murmurs rarely whished by. But* oh *how you wished they would, if only to drag you from your mind. From the bodach burrowed within.*

*The citizenry's fear of revolt didn't render Vencenza without rebels. Between The Bauta and The Morettae, dissent overran the city. It had been Crescenzo Zuane De Tullia's quashing of the latter a decade ago which secured his would-be throne. The Morettae had terrorised the populace, putting innocents to the sword with misguided intent despite their frondeur politics, as if the deaths of subjects might wound a tyranny, and De Tullia seized his chance thusly.*

*He comprehended what it meant to be ruled by fear—to* rule *by fear —what made the populace tick and quiver. He recognised the power in exploitation. So, whether by manipulation or suborning, De Tullia won favour, and his triumphant speech propagandised the worldview:* 'Purity of emotion is purity of the material. Weakness is all affection can sire; thus emotion is to morality what a cancer is to the body.'

*Through fear, the ruler attained control.*

*Your* mother, *too, comprehended rule by fear—Elenedda Murgia took care to cultivate you as a frightened flower, poised even when drowning.*

*And now you would drown* yourself; *you deserved it after you couldn't save your beloved friend.*

*You wondered if The Bauta didn't know fear, or if he acted in spite of it. You wondered what it might be like to* be *him.*

It all took place a mere day heretofore, yet I detested that fiend with every shred of my soul, as if my nemesis since the conception of the cosmos. How quickly such passion could fester.

"Previous employ?" Irene Falco questioned.

I shucked off my stockings. "Playwright at *The Crescent.*"

Falco seemed intrigued with her prim head-tilt, eyes analytical and prying. "Under?"

"Impresario Basilio Lanuza." The name corroded my tongue like venom.

"He found it fit to take on such a young playwright." *Not a question.* Falco snorted whilst flicking the measuring tape to my bare chest, sending my skin crawling as if with insects. "Must be promising, you."

*Hardly.* Basilio Lanuza's wealthy-man frivolity reflected sharply in his operating of the enterprise. Inheriting *The Crescent* from his father, Salbador Lanuza-Corbalán—a prestigious aristocrat beside the senate's ear, Basilio hadn't the first clue of thespian culture. Hence, I, a literature and linguistics graduate, became the theatre's playwright following his insulting firing of the previous for 'indiscipline'.

Whatever familial endeavour Basilio forwent in favour of *The Crescent*, he would have surely suited better.

# SCENE IV

## ABYSSUS ABYSSUM INVOCAT

*Giorgianna*

*VENCENZA, A BODY WITH SIX HEARTS: its six theatres from ancient days hooked through the sprawling maritime cityscape, commencing at the shoreline and concluding in eastern oldtown.* The Sea Star, The Crescent, The Nox, The Eventide, The Zenith, The Sunrise.[17] *The final had been shut for years. The rest decayed at the despot's damnation.*

---

[17] Vencenza is divided into ten quarters, six of them based on its theatres (*i.e.* its 'Six Hearts') with the surrounding architecture corresponding to the regional theatre: *The Sea Star*—large stars and constellations; *The Crescent*—crescent moons; *The Nox*—small star systems and full moons; *The Eventide*—upside-down half-suns with curved rays; *The Zenith*—full suns with pointy rays; *The Sunrise*—upright half-suns with curved rays.

In the south is the small Temistochlisi Quarter belonging to Vencenza's Themistoklísi community, and in the northeast stands the Iutulicani Quarter populated by Iutulicani Vencenzanii.

The Court of Secrets is regarded as its own quarter, not only forming a significant southern portion of lower óssium (oldtown), but also constituting of Vencenza's slum district.

Vicari's Lane *carried you to the porch of* The Crescent *that díem crepúsca, your nerves still strained from the House of Judgement, The Hanging Gardens, The Bauta. You knew they weren't to ease soon. Perhaps ever.*

*The grandiose edifice rose in creamy stone near the sprawling aquamarine wharf, its dome mounted by a namesake crescent upon a brass finial.*

*You glimpsed the cosmetics artisan, Lucrezia,[18] in the shade of the front portico beside a masked man you didn't know. The quarter-Shpokëze[19] remained a chatty sort notwithstanding the laws.*

*From* The Zenith *to* The Nox, *similar conventions arranged Vencenzani playhouses: a spacious àtrium by the front doors proceeded via colossal stairs to the auditorium, weaving via arterial hallways towards the theatre's inner ventricles whilst venous passages coursed in opposition, all stitched with capillary corridors to be tread by vìtae.[20]*

*A subworld; the ebb and flow of life; the thrum of blood, sustaining.*

*So, the theatres were Vencenza's* 'hearts'. *Córpus, víscera, vìtus—* 'body', *the edifice;* 'flesh', *the interior;* 'blood', *the people. The rest of the city was the* 'óssium'. Bone. *Fleshless cradles in which one slept beneath the skin of the firmament. One the spirit sought to transcend.*

*You'd barely reached the auditorium archway when someone rammed you, and you met the cerulean eyes of a boorish man.*

"Harpy." *Bratty, nasal tones left his mouth, incongruous with the ragged formation of his build.*

"Abramo," *was all you yielded, back pinned so straight it hurt, chin high. Like Mother taught.*

*Abramo Sessa joined* The Crescent *ten months[21] hitherto—over two years after yourself—and you never learned why he abhorred you so. Why vitriol embittered every word he spat in your eyes.*

---

[18] *loo-KREH-ts'yah*

[19] *shpoh-KYOH-zeh*; demonym for Shpokë's people.

[20] Literally *'lives'*; multiple theatre staff.

   **Nota Bene**: the singular is *'vìtus'*. Thus, it is not grammatically correct to utilise the term *'vìtae'* as its plural. This is a vestige of Proto-Faustinian.

[21] A month on Gethlem is approximately 35.4 days.

"Cease your discourtesy, signór![22]" *Lucrezia's voice rang silvery as bells. To your side whirled a plump woman in a silvern pince-nez and frilly mint dress, ebony waves spilling glossy as wet ink over her rounded shoulders and slit straight-edged across her scrunched brow.*

*Her rainstorm eyes struck Abramo.*

*The man's gaze doused you both in kerosene.* "Honour with honour," *an ugly gurn ruptured his porcine physiognomy,* "harpy with harpy."

"Damn your honour," *you bit, and fear of your teething anger ran its claws down your spine, so you grasped Lucrezia's dainty hand and spirited the pair of you down the auditorium aisles.*

*The ribs of the vaulted ceilings warbled with murmurs of vìtae as you recounted to Lucrezia your fruitless quest for justice. When your sleepless spirit of inquiry questioned whom she had spoken to, she replied,* "a friend from lower óssium, a dollmaker." *Dots peppered her rose-porcelain skin, less freckles and more innumerable dark beauty marks. You held a clammy palm to your left cheek where* your *moles were. One for Emanuela. One for Mother.*

"Final preparations for *'A Bedlamite's Ballad'* to-night are underway." *You sought a distraction in the mundane. And yet...* "Have you ever thought on it?" *Your voice fell to nearly a whisper, heart pounding a witch drum.* "The barrenness of these halls each turn? How every pantomime we stage, coin is thrown to the four winds." *The law decreed only tragedies be performed, and only the select few approved by the Minister of Dominion himself, for the thespian sort and its likeness were artisans, and artistic creation could not be reduced to mere rule— in of itself embodying rebellion. The state, fathoming the threat free thought spelled to its continuance, saw fit to control it, or otherwise quash it like all rebels.* But how long until the hearts of the city cease beating? *The hegemony bound your fingers. Your psyche eroded beneath its boot. It only made you drown faster. It only darkened your Shadow.*

*Lucrezia whisked you into a capillary enveloped in carmine curtains that díem crepúsca. In the penumbra, velvet flowed thick as ichor.* "Violence will only ever be repaid in kind, but laying down arms won't

---

[22] *see-ÑOH-r'*; an unmarried man.

do when you wield a single shovel against a thousand crossbows." *The tiny woman's voice dug into your bones and darkness trickled out. The string of silver coins adorning her throat flashed with her eyes.* "This is not the world we should wish to live in."

*Footsteps, swift and pointed, sounded before you could hope to find your voice.*

"Signorínae[23] Montefiore e Damiani!" *A middle-aged man plain of features and blond as tarnished gold whirled around the bend. His resplendent garb gleamed teal and purpurous like peacock feathers, at the centre of his chest swinging a lautitious alexandrite fat as a fist. Hazel-blue eyes polished to gemstones struck you and Lucrezia hard enough to bruise.* "Yokels loitering in light of spring's biggest production!" *Impresario Basilio Lanuza's face flared a furious rubicund.* "Make yourselves scarce at once!" *And he fleeted off with nothing but a scroll thrust into your hand for farewell.*

*You dug your heels against the jerk of aggravation. You'd fain spit in that man's face too, but knew you never could, so you swallowed yourself again, and again, and again, even as rage pulled at your feet like a retreating tide.*

*A string quartet's mournful berceuse floated from the orchestra pit.*

*You remembered the opening piece of* 'A Bedlamite's Ballad' *too well.* 'Elegy of Spring'—*that brumal flurry of a dirge. You remembered it for all the times you fumbled the portamento, and your mother's hand fan came down so hard your knuckles ruptured like berries. You carried the scars as grim reminders alongside the ivory rivets left by the faceless men of winter solstice shadows.*

---

[23] *see-ñoh-REE-nœ*; unmarried women.

*Luciferous alchemical[24] lights glared at the stage where a paper cityscape, white as piano keys, haunted the backdrop.*

'A Bedlamite's Ballad' *told the tragic tale of a curse befallen Zargòsa's capital, Du Rrât a du Errèina,[25] driving its people to murder and treachery.*

*Thespian voices echoed in mockery of the auditorium's vacuity.*

*A decade ago, thousands flocked to playhouses, journeying from far and wide to The City of Masks, decked in elaborate costumes and masks of delicate colombínae and demure morèttae, glamorous vólti, sleek dómini, antiquarian pulcinélli, clever gátti and cheeky zanníi.*

*But those days vanished like pages torn from a history book, reaped with that old world you remembered only through a child's eyes.* Flesh without spirit.

***Boom!***

***Boom!***

***Boom!***

*You were twenty-two the first time you heard gunshots: that díem crepúsca when thunderous explosions pulsed in your eardrums and tore shrieks from your lungs.*

*All you remembered was akrasia chasing you through the scurrying crowd towards the stage behind which you knew Lucrezia was. But you didn't find her. Rather, you sighted an apparition in the fuscation of the catwalk above, a white bàuta for its face, and your blood ran tomb-cold. It* froze *when Basilio passed you, decidedly bound for centre stage, sneering that unwelcome character's notorious epithet as if it were a demon's moniker:* "Bauta."

*As if invoked, the spectre snatched a rope and slid effortlessly to the stage. Shadows danced like flames around his fleet-footed tread and*

---

[24] Alchemy includes the preparation of potions, medicines, and protective charms among much more, as well as the creation of homunculi (*i.e.* artificial people), the process of chrysopoeia—transmutation of materials into gold—and the manufacture of lights through flaming of the luminescent white mineral *liophirite* native to solution caves.

[25] Literally '*The Blood of the Queen*' in Abeslâri, Zargòsa's historical majority language.

*spilled in a cape off his elegant wide shoulders, cruciform hilts of the twin stilétto daggers strapped to his thighs coruscating no less than diamonds. He adjusted his flint-black tricorn and blazer with infuriating nonchalance.* "Forgive my intrusion, won't you, but *Saints*, what dreary things your pantomimes are."

*A pianissimo Zargòsian lilt imbued his voice so faintly it almost didn't, and the first time you heard him speak, you wished was your last.*

*He plucked at the white ruffles of his shirt, gaze fixed on Basilio.* "Doubly insulting a half-Zâro[26] man, *yourself*, should permit Errèina be portrayed so lamentably. Lazhâv...[27]"

*Basilio drew his revolver, gripped the pearly handle in his tremulous hands.* "Your day of judgement is nigh. All you're worth is to *rot* in the Everlasting Null with your filthy kind!"

*The Bauta laughed, curt and off-handed, but that was all it took for the eviscerated edifice to scatter his voice like starlight through the cosmos, its echo colliding with the mezzanines and shivering through your bones.*

*You wanted to empty your guts, then. Yet a darker shadow in your psyche hungered.*

"If there's justice in this world." *The Bauta's words punched you. You knew there wasn't.* "Tell me." *He gripped Basilio's eyeline, obdurate.* "What moral principle is possessed by this order for which it should stand to be preserved?" *The question smote you speechless.* "No precedent bolsters De Tullia's puritanical ideology. Human nature hinges on sensitivities, emotion. *Sa Nóba Giustíca* is more than criminalisation of laughter—it is criminalisation of *life*. And how many innocents will he kill in the name of his tenure? How much is he, spurred by some *vague* impulse to assert ultimate dominion, willing to raze?"

---

[26] Zargòsa is inhabited by four ethnic groups; in order of most to least numerous: Abeslâri from the east, Zâro from the north, Marlâre from the southwest, C'linèse from the northwest. While Abeslâri are the most numerous (and their language the most widely-spoken), the ruling family, the world-renowned Pedrolas, are Zâro.

[27] *lah-ZHAHV*; 'shame' in the Marlâre tongue of Zargòsa. Ironically, or perhaps poetically, it is, secondarily, Marlâre for '*seduction*'.

In Zargòsian, '*zh*' is pronounced like the French '*j*' or the Cyrillic '*ж*'.

*To hear those words aloud, not merely inked on the pages of forbidden tomes or confined to the lazarettos of your mind—you wanted him to stop.*

*Yet you wanted to listen until the sun burned itself out and every luminary died.*

"I don't know who calls the shots in this game," *The Bauta clicked his tongue,* "but he who laughs last, laughs best." *And you knew he smirked beneath that awful mask.*

"SILENCE!" *Basilio bellowed.* "You low-born vagabond *rat* dare insult our good Governor!"

*The Bauta spat a contemptuous laugh.* "Sad little sycophant! Injustice is plain as the ground we tread—!"

### *Boom!*

*You hadn't thought as you snatched the revolver from Basilio's trembling fingers; only when its explosive bark sent you staggering backwards, and crimson stained The Bauta's sleeve like rowan berries in snow, did all warmth leach from your skin.*

*He aimed at you with loaded-gun eyes where empires burst into flames reflected like scrying crystals, and in that moment, you could believe he was a demon.*

*The Bauta cocked his revolvers.*

*A whirlpool of panic took you.*

### *Boom!*
### *Boom!*

*A light jolted in the fly loft, plummeting and smashing to shrapnel like a meteorite between you and The Bauta, yet metallic burns never ripped blood from your chest.*

*A thud and a wail impelled you to glimpse over your shoulder.*

*Basilio had thrown himself sidelong to dodge what he'd surely assumed were bullets aimed at him and collided with a theatre prop, his brow spilling gore like a burst fruit.*

*When you turned, The Bauta had vanished, only blood left puddling on the stage.*

*Alive or not, fear wracked you.*

They say such things come in threes.

# SCENE V

## TO KILL A CORVID

*Cesare*

JUBILANT MUSIC, half-smothered by chatter and din, twirled through oldtown's thumping streets decked with innumerable stalls as Cesare headed out of *Three Suns*.

Scent of stale brine and flowered sharbat spilled through the summer air, the midnight bazaar teeming with fantastical characters in shimmering green seadrake scales and glossy fins, ballooning chiffon pintucked and powder-blue, argentous tunics beset with glittering stars, vine-climbed stilts and rhinestoned armadillo heels, garlands of gold teeth pleated into delicate trinzali.

The Solar Square served as oldtown's atrium, though not wholly exempt from the thaumaturgy wrapping its carnose ligaments around Vencenza's western flank, for the loops which disoriented ingenuous wanderers always led them back to the Solar Square, foiling venture into the city's innards where The Court's secrets may be divined upon.

Eligio[28] met Cesare near a baked goods and confectionery stall tended by a sour-faced tubby man in a zánni so bleak it struck as unfinished.

"Troubling…" drawled Eligio through a sequined vólto of his own painting as he appraised Cesare's tidings. His churidars, paag,[29] and heeled boots bloomed in the violaceous hue of irises, long-sleeved sherwani coat an iridescent shift of pale cyan to glacial blue splashed with nacre zari like opal. "What they want *this* time eludes us."

"Conditions permit, we'll catch wind in due course." Cesare balanced prismatic light on his stilétto. Ithilweni steel. '*Lòthmir*',[30] as iridites[31] called it. Sharper and sturdier than any human-made alloy. He'd purchased his paired blades from an Illýrisi vendor—a green-skinned iridite with curls like bouquets of lilac—seven years ago with money he accrued at *The Sunrise*. A rare find; a *dangerous* find. A dagger's image, after all, was branded into forearms of poor bastards trapped in prison for ten months or longer. Or those stood on death row. A Malefactor's Mark. Daggers drew blood, and blood was filthy yet sacrosanct to the flesh.

Eligio's acorn-brown eyes narrowed. "What are you thinking, Ces?"

"That a little investigation is in order." Cesare tossed his stilétto, letting it spin through the air before catching and sheathing it in his thigh harness.

"A *little*? On *your* watch?" Eligio crossed his slender arms. "Doubtful."

---

[28] *eh-LEE-joh*

[29] Here referring specifically to the Balóchi style of turban.

[30] Literally: '*diamond steel*'; a portmanteau of Ithilweni '*lòth*' ('diamond') and '*mír*' ('steel').

[31] One of the two majority races occupying Gethlem, primarily residing in Ithilwen, eastern Balinor, with small communities scattered across the globe (namely Rǔnethäre in Isatōnia and Thír'la'dǎl in Yegrika, as well as the small Erathèla community living in Ilinó). Their identifiable phenotypic characteristics are double-pointed ears, a slightly taller frame, sharper bone structure and exaggeratedly wide-set limbs, unnatural hair and eye colours (*i.e.* not anything a human could possess), and no iris. Their blood contains hemerythrin in place of haemoglobin, giving it a pink-purple colouration. Iridite skin can only be in shades of green, blue, purple, pink, and greyscale, engendering a rigid, oppressive caste system within Ithilwen. '*Iridite*' comes from the race's Ithilweni name: '*ìri'adīt*' meaning '*opal person*' in reference to both the complexion of iridites, as well as opals being considered to be pieces of stars—vital cultural and spiritual symbols for ìri'adītu.

Cesare flashed a wisenheimer grin, earning himself a sigh and eye roll he'd grown beyond acquainted with.

A head popped out across the stall, its brown hair a fluffy halo of tight coils. Lissandri[32]—Eligio's younger twin. Chartreuse clovers embroidered the crushed velour of his aubergine tailcoat, pantaloons resembling silver baubles and stiletto boots matching the green.

He signed *'what's the holdup?'* on The Fingers.

Everyone on Gethlem knew The Fingers, given it functioned as more or less a universal tongue to overcome language barriers, but Cesare read between the lines.

He nudged Eligio's shoulder. "Duty calls."

Smile lines crinkled Eligio's eyes as they sparked to match Cesare's impish glance. Sensible as he was at age twenty-three, even Eligio wouldn't pass on a chance to terrorise the baker. It wasn't unwarranted, mind! All the geezer did was chase hungry orphans down with a slingshot and hand them over to City Guards as if they'd committed some grand larceny for pilfering half a ciabatta loaf. Who knew a little money to fill the coffers made a man such a colossal cock?

While Eligio made use of his charm with the unenthused baker, Cesare and Lissandri proceeded to rob him blind, snatching up pastries and chocolate and candied fruit.

"*Hooligans!*" the man roared, grabbing a ladle and hurling it at Cesare.

He effortlessly caught it in his unoccupied hand.

"We deserve a little compensation, old man!" He spun the cooking implement through his wrist and tossed it in the nearby canal, dissolving with the other two in the effervescent commotion.

---

[32] *lees-SAHN-dree*

Idle fingers linked in a chain, Cesare and the twins shuffled like beetles through bright summer blooms along the winding rays of streets emanating from the Solar Square. Countless parlours encircled the courtyard as if a variegated bookshelf. Where one was pastel-soft as strawberry gelato, mystique and goëtia[33] swathed its neighbour, the crystalline splendour of a palazzo adjoining it.

Yet, in the square's centre, a strappado had been erected: a hideous frame designated for torture. A victim's hands would be bound behind their back, their body suspended by a rope from a pulley so they dangled above ground, their shoulders slowly dislocating, arms paralysing over painful days.

The grim lesion that was the strappado may have succeeded to scar, but lower ossíi proved fearless.

A woman danced around the tool of punishment to the larkish melody of accordion and viola, beating a tambourine in time with claps of onlookers. Red ribbons attached to a tophat fixed white organza around the dancer's gambogian componidóri, her gold-beset crimson skirt swirling in wild exuberance.

Dancing had become as outlawed as laughter: both expressions of joy touted by *Sa Nóba Giustíca* as forces of corruption. As such, Cesare adored the sight of it in the streets, fingers itching for his long-beloved violin, voice reeds aching to be strummed by a legato in time with the beat and coin chime.

Eligio hobbled on his heels to the threshold of *Commegnos*[34] *Curios*—the jewellery store of the twins' parents—and slumped on the steps, a vanilla cannolo in hand. Lissandri cracked every joint he had before biting into a vegetable scone. Cesare grimaced at the insulting excuse for a baked good; Lissandri screwed a face back at his glacé cherries.

"Which *sadist* proposed we wear heels, again?" Eligio threw an accusatory glare at Cesare specifically, hissing as he flexed his foot.

---

[33] *goh-Ö-tee-ah*; sorcery or witchcraft. *Chiefly*: dark magic.
Borrowed from the Auréli '*goëtiè*' of the same meaning.
[34] *kohm-MEH-ño*

"Look on the bright side." Cesare sloughed off his boots and stepped onto the pavement in stockings. "For once in your lives, you may look me in the eye."

"There are two of us here," droned Lissandri around a mouthful of scone.

"I'd thought myself concussed."

"Prick." Lissandri went to stomp on Cesare's foot with his stiletto and missed stupendously to his amusement. Cesare tossed his boots and violin case into the blacked-out parlour just as a streak of fuchsia zapped by the corner of his vision.

"*FLOCKS!*" a blonde girl screamed out.

Shushes turned the Solar Square into a nest of frightened snakes as ossíi scrambled to erase all traces of festivity and present a respectable marketplace before the legions descended.

Cesare helped a mascheráre[35] hide her outlawed masks—giullári, bòes, mamuthónes—and hissed at the blonde in fuchsia to clear out lest she get done in. "Inside. *Now,*" he urged Eligio and Lissandri into the *Curios,* following only once he knew the twins were out of sight.

City Guards spilled like gunpowder across the Square. Vigilant orbs glinted behind half-masks fashioned of fuscous feathers, beaks extending beyond sullen faces.

Pressure twitched Cesare's jaw, his eyes burning upon the insignia embossing the soldiers' gauntlets: a barbed quatrefoil inside a circle sporting two pairs of wings.

*Crows.*

Cesare hated birds.

In the crows' midst, a pair of Imperialíi—the Governor's elite soldiers—glowed in immaculate gold. Imperiálus Diodato Casca and Dardan Kadare. Enormous pauldrons like hernias bloated their shoulders and elegantly tapered cuisses protected their powerful thighs, loathsome faces masked by golden colombínae and ornate helms stamped with griffin feathers.

---

[35] *mahs-keh-RAH-reh*; mask-maker.

Cesare counted nineteen crows before several companies of two or three broke off, flitting down the rays of streets, whilst the remainder, griffins at the vanguard, ambled through the petrified populace as if a funereal procession among gravestones.

Cesare slipped on his running boots, snatched his revolver holster and waist-cut leather blazer, but heartbeat deepened in his ears when Dardan's paces slowed, halted. When his eyes dropped to a femme and her young boy, both dressed in rags—forsaken children of The Court.

The soldier's iron mouth warped into words Cesare couldn't hear, but he didn't need to, because when the femme's thin hands tightened around her boy, Cesare's chest caved.

Dardan wrenched the femme from the child with no stint on roughness, tearing from her shoulders the threadbare woollen shawl and yanking down the back of her dress. *"Baseborn filth!"* And he hurled her hard against the strappado.

Shrieks shook the stars off the sky, loudest of all the heart-wrenching *'mama!'* of the boy now squirming in a crow's granite grasp as the femme's minced brains dripped down the torture instrument and across brickwork etched with simulacra of the gods.

Cesare made for the door.

"Ces, are you *mad*?" Eligio lunged to grab him, but Cesare was too quick, laying distance between himself and *Commegnos' Curios*, slipping into the shadows he knew like his own, and cocking his revolver to shoot.

# SCENE VI

## APONOIA

*Giorgianna*

PEAR WOOD AND IANTHINE BROCADE *clad the impresario's office, its air pristine with pine, as untouched as the rows of books poised along sweeping shelves.*

*You sat in a nephrite velvet armchair facing the grand desk the evening of that díem crepúsca, a five of faces and a sun goddess[36] fluttering through your fingers like butterfly wings as you twirled them to abate your hammering heartbeat. Father taught you sleight of hand, and one day you hoped to pry from him how* he *came to know it so well.*

*Basilio paced, fingers balled into white-knuckled knots and tongue spitting forth slur after slur upon The Bauta's moniker.*

"Worthless vagrant!" *He shoved papers off the table, and you flinched not at his wrath—your mother had broken you in to such scenes—but his bigotry. His hate.* "Upon our Gods, may the recusant be flayed of his

---

[36] The houses of Vencenzani playing cards: *Suns*, Moons, *Stars*, Faces.

visage lest I put a bullet through his unearned hunk of a heart!" *Veins bulged beneath Basilio's skin like worms as he flung his pulcinéllo, a gust of gold-purple-teal darting across the room and slamming into the bookcase beside Abramo's head.*

*You wondered if the red drenching Basilio's face and neck was shame. Even if not criminalised wholly, the rulers condemned anger—every emotion marked an impurity upon the human face, stemming from the womb of corruption—and the impresario had allowed an anarchial lowlife to stoke him.*

"He brought ruin to my production!" *You forced steady breaths as the impresario resumed his philippic, Lucrezia shaking her head behind his back.* "I will not be humiliated by a demonic brute who saw fit to maim me!" *Basilio threw his hands to the bandage stamping his brow, and you frowned at his assertion, knowing his wound had been dealt by a prop he fell onto of his own accord.*

"Hush at once," *Lucrezia attempted to soothe the man in the way one would a petulant child.* "You'll invoke the demonic again if you persist in speaking of it."

*Basilio shoved the tiny woman away, hard enough to stumble her, and your jaw fell slack. And you shook with more than terror.* "That barbarian nearly *killed* me! Ought I *take* it?"

"Basilio, he did not come close to you!" *It was the Shadow speaking through you; the Shadow who beheld Basilio's ire.* "The Bauta never touched you."

*He seethed.* "You dare!"

*You rose to your generous height.* "Is his ruining our trade not wound enough? Must you lie?"

*Basilio briskly routed for the door.* "I shall have none of these attacks!"

"DON'T YOU LEAVE THIS FUCKING ROOM!" *Your arm thrust out, finger pointing at the man's head. Your chest heaved, the thump within its cage the only sound on the hylic plane. Not the thump of a frightened hare, but a blustering ocean storm distending your bones.*

*Basilio wheeled, the alexandrite at his heart glinting like a hateful third orb. And it was as if he* saw *it rippling within your hessonite eyes, the second face making the diptych of You: your* Shadow, *hungering and vengeful.*

"Basilio, please." *You touched your heart.* "Our theatre matters more. He brought ruin upon the production, yes. Now we must rebuild—"

*Glare-white exploded across your field.*

*Your neck lurched sideways, feet doubling back in place where you belonged as the sting of a hard slap bit your face, skin aflame beneath your palm when you cupped your cheek.*

*Lucrezia latched onto you, the half-dozen present vìtae gasping.*

*At that moment, the pain was your mother's hand, and the tremor in your limbs was once more fear. At that moment, all you wanted was to* Run.

"A lowly wretch *would* spew inane apologetics!" *The impresario spat in your face.* "You show the true visage of your loyalties."

*Your ribs clenched in ken of his accusation, but he bit back his tongue's lash when the door swung with a rattle.*

"Dónno[37] Basilio Lanuza?" *A gruff-voiced City Guard stood in the doorway, tall as a pylon, the hilt of a spatha[38] peeking over muscular shoulders. Somnolence dimmed his eyes, sclerae red and pupils dilated to toothless maws.*

*Your mind paved over with frozen flagstone, lacquered in blood, echoed with the screams and snapping bones of that cursed winter solstice two years ago. The powers that be never accorded you or Ema justice, and the soldier upon the threshold was one of Them.*

"Myself, esteemed officére." *Basilio's voice smoothed to oil, his invisible mask latching on tight.*

"I requisition an audience." *The Guard did not put forward a suggestion as he ushered Basilio out.*

"What of the rest of us?" *Lucrezia's voice commanded attention.*

*The Guard looked down his nose at the tiny woman. She didn't falter an inch.* "Not necessitated."

*And he quitted the office alongside the impresario.*

---

[37] '*Lord*' or '*nobleman*' in Faustinian.

[38] A type of straight longsword used in the Roman Empire.

*Maybe you wanted to shout after them, but your tongue numbed with all the words you could never speak aloud.*

*You felt Lucrezia's hand on your arm, heard her gentle voice, but could no longer stand to remain, so you stormed from the suffocating chamber and down the abutting corridor to your writing studio.*

*Alchemy ignited at your corporeality and scared shadows into the chamber's nooks.*

*Breaths grew shallow in your throat, head spinning with a riotous cantastoria of thoughts as you sank to the floor and trembled like a failing dam against the surge of everything you had been beaten to suppress.*

*All you wanted was an admission that a cancer crippled the old bones of this house, yet the darker pane of the diptych of You yearned for the putrescent house to break.*

'…Injustice is plain as the
ground we tread!'

*Those words rattled your skull like gunfire.*

*You shot to your feet as rage clawed your ribs, agonised and desperate. You detested those words. That* voice. *The fiend who set in motion what was to be your ruination.*

*You wanted to scream and curse and tear the world to bloody shreds as you snatched an inkwell off your escritoire, arm twitching to hurl the glass vial into a wall and shatter it. But your fingers cramped, your joints locking with fear.* 'Nothing is worth it,' *your mother hissed.*

*Breath couldn't reach your lungs until you drove the inkwell into the table again, hard enough to splash. In the dimness, the ink on your fingers was almost blood.*

*You teetered on the edge of a fall ever since De Tullia cozened control over Vencenza, so you clung to the hinges of the diptych of You. You clung to* Fear, *to* Mother, *even as it bruised and bled and tore you in two.*

*Opening an escritoire drawer, you beheld the cruel silhouette of a revolver gone unused, holstering the monstrous thing at your hip and routing down the corridor towards the thespian room. Bound for home.*

*Your heart juddered when thick fingers clasped your forearm, when Abramo's ceruleous eyes sank into you like crucifying nails.* "Sticking it to Lio is admirable, harpy. But is taking The Bauta's side not beneath you? Surely even *you* wouldn't shed enough virtue to degenerate into a traitorous prostitute."

*The screech of your teeth sheltered a scream, restrained the impulsion to bite out a man's jugular and spit its lifeblood into his eyes.* "Get. Your hands. Off me." *Wringing your arm free, you continued to the auditorium in a swivel, leaving the mephistophelean weasel to loiter in the dark with his gloating smirk for company.*

*You didn't spiral back into that whirlpool of hysteria solely by dint of a tentative glitter on stage catching your eye.*

*A cufflink rested in a ridge between floorboards.*

*You cradled the curio in your palm, the encrusted tanzanite shifting in violet facets like a drop of indigo midnight in a piscina.* Undoubtedly Basilio's. *The noble had all the disposable coin in the world for such an exquisite cut.*

*You wanted to cast the contraption into the marina or crush it in your fist if you could. Instead, you purged a sigh and dropped it into a pocket among the vinaceous folds of your skirt. You didn't know why, but you didn't know anything anymore.*

*The exit stood barely ten steps afield, but you halted, stiffly dipping your head to Basilio and the Guard in the àtrium before slipping out of the theatre and off its moonlit porch.*

*You tossed on your vólto, your black veil, your wide-brim hat festooned with red beads.*

*Règuiem[39] dressed the city and sea in a nacreous mantilla, and past* The Crescent's *córpus,* The Sea Star *glimmered like a distant beacon across the watery Vault of Faces, the acronychal Nereida[40] suspended*

---

[39] '*Night*' and '*rest*' in Faustinian.
[40] A luminous type-A main-sequence star with a bluish-white hue located approximately 8.4 lightyears (79.5 trillion km) away from Gethlem and prominent in the Salacia ('*the Mermaid*') constellation.

*overhead like a tiny second moon. From the Vault, River Vena streamed into the city, bifurcating ad infinitum into Vencenza's vasculature and bleeding into the body of Faustina.*

*Stone faces stared from the walls of an adjacent building, blank-eyed and tight-lipped as every Vencenzanii ought to be. As* you *ought to have been.*

*Goosebumps pulled your skin at the thought of walking the midnight streets by your lonesome. Guards patrolled Vencenza, but you would never forget Emanuela, nor the justice owed but never given to her. To* you.

"Does said revolver remain on you?" Falco's voice grew dangerous. She had finished inspecting my flesh and measuring my limbs, moving on to a thorough study of my teeth and face.

"No," I did well to lie. No doubt I'd need it again, just like I'd needed it that very night.

*Vencenza's bones twisted, swallowing Omika's[41] light.*

*Shadows possessed the peculiar capacity to conjure moving bodies and watching eyes, hands reaching for you, voices jeering at your fear.*

*The night always resurrected the dead.*

---

[41] The moon; synchronised and tidally-locked to the planet Gethlem. Omika's singular orbit is approximately 35.4 days, correlating with Gethlem's synodic month. A year on Gethlem thus lasts 425.05 days with a leap year every 20 years. Therefore, Gethlemian 'humans' age at a slower rate than we Earthlings and are, biologically, vastly different to us.

*When you turned a corner, it took every ounce of resolve to not scream.*

*Black hoods drooped around a trio of male faces obscured by zannii, and, as your airways closed, you wondered if Death had come to you a second time.*

"Awfully late for a lovely dáma[42] to traipse the city, no?" *the tallest crooned, shrivelled mouth curled to bare teeth half-taken by rot. His pale chin jutted like a tusk, fingers spindly as spider legs, skin the wanness of hessian.*

"No." *You moved to pass only for the remaining pair to obturate your path. One man's beard burned fire-red. Flaxen waves brushed the other's brow.*

*The toothy man clasped your forearm.* "How stand-offish."

*It must have been that surge of a cornered animal's rabid fear which broke you free a second time, which locked your fingers around your revolver.*

*You aimed. Pressed the trigger.*

Clink.

Silence.

*Dread took your bones and counted them.*

"Little shrews shouldn't be killing," *the toothy man sibilated as the three swooped like birds of prey.*

*It couldn't be you this time, so you bolted, frantic shouts for help rasping from your lungs just like that solstice night two years ago.*

*Brutal agony gored your right arm.*

*You faltered and tottered.*

*Another slash of pain tore your flesh below the first, blood pouring like hot oil down your hand from the pulsating wounds.*

*Iron fingers grabbed your hair, dislodging your mask and headpiece as they yanked you off your feet and dragged you kicking across the cobblestones before hurling you into the wall.*

---

[42] *DAH-mah*; a female-presenting person who appears to be a dónna ('*lady*') by way of dress and behaviour, but whose socioeconomic status is unknown. '*Dáma*' is not a polite word—a derivative of 'Madáma' ('*female brothel owner*').

*The toothy man's corpse-cold hand gripped your face, forcing your eyes upon his hideous visage. His seafoam orbs gyred, vulturous.* "Pretty creature." *He threaded a curl of yours around his bony digit.* "I always delight at a rare specimen for my collection." *Your guts churned as he grinned.* "A long time coming." *In his hand gleamed a scalpel.*

***Boom!***

***Boom!***

***Boom!***

*Bullets ripped through.*

*You shrieked, scuttling backwards in a frenzy.*

*The men hastened beneath the shelter of eaves, clutching their bleeding shoulders and backs, the blond's lips reddened.*

*Blood seeped between the stones. The air soaked sweet and ferric. In the dimness, the blood was almost ink.*

*The toothy man hissed something, and the trio exited the scene.*

*You pawed for the tine impaling your spasming muscle, dislodging a rhomboid blade with no hilt, and whimpered as your arm locked. Suffocating heat claimed your trembling form.* They say such things come in threes...

*A soft thud dropped onto the nearby cobbles.*

*Your head whirled towards the nearing footfalls and your heartbeat ceased.*

*The Bauta's cape streamed like charred midnight, his mask white as the stars. A dark blossom of alizarin marked his sleeve's ruffled cuff.*

"How fortuitous that we crash again, vólto." *His tongue clicked like another shot.* "Déjà vu?"

*You hauled your leaden body away, clutching the strange blade.* "Stay away from me."

*A half-laugh, bitter as dark coffee, escaped him as he crouched near.* "You think I'd come down solely to prolong your misery?" *He pulled a diminishing roll of gauze from his waist-length jacket, reaching for you, but you recoiled.*

"Don't touch me." *The Bauta's darkness sickened you like the smog of an immolation. A blade and bullet both. He didn't make sense.*

"Do you *want* to die, then?" *he put simply. And maybe you did, but you conceded, allowing him to shuck the torn sleeve from your upper arm with a double-edged stilétto,* a lawbreaker's blade, *exposing serrated lesions spewing sanies and blood from their gaping innards. He plucked a thread and needle from an inner pocket, the pair all but dancing as those slim, tender fingertips of a murderer made deft work of stitching your wounds.*

*Time wore on, pain culminating with every pierce until, at long, long last, he secured the final suture and firmly bound your arm with gauze, such clean, meticulous work.*

*You leaned your occiput against the wall, slipping the rhomboid blade into your skirt beside the cufflink. The world flickered in and out.*

"You know," *The Bauta wiped his stilétto, gloved hands so poetically sullied—like he'd got done dismembering a carcass, instead,* "if you had better aim, you would've died to-night."

*Words in response failed you, but some wayward splinter of you itched with curiosity.* "Why *The Crescent*? Why any of this?"

*The Bauta rose, then pocketed his hands and tsk'd, and somehow it became the most derogatory sound to ever cross your ears.* "Historic documents speak of the Faustinian Empire under Imperator Mirone Nascimbene Evangelio,[43]" *he recited as if commencing a lecture.* "When a famine raked southern Faustina, peasant women brought their emaciated infants to Evangelio, hoping he would witness the horror and impart aid. In staunch silence, Evangelio's soldiers opened fire. *Sa Nóba Giustíca* exists upon De Tullia's belief that Vencenza has corrupted in the century since the Empire's fall. By his own credence, he is infallible, and all must conform to his iconography of rightness. To *serve* in *staunch silence* just like Evangelio's men." *Each word tossed a tinder into the rising pyre of his voice.* "And the *second* someone rises to revolt, they get locked in shackles, strung up on a rope, beheaded. Percase worse. Is that a world you want to live in?" *He had stepped to your side again.* "Is that a world you want to *die* in?"

---

[43] *mee-ROH-neh nah-sheem-BEH-neh eh-vahn-JEH-lee-oh*

*Your skin crawled in reminder of who you were alone with, yet you forced yourself to rise despite your tremble. Despite your* Fear, *you beheld the abyss.* "I suppose you fancy yourself our martyr." *Perhaps that man's nerves had thrummed at the pluck of your tone. Perhaps he too saw that hungry Shadow ripple within your eyes.* "Yourself—castigating another's character, deserving as it stands, when *you* operate by violence alone. *Yourself*—your own iconography of '*rightness*'. Obdurate! A *hypocrite* parading like some holier-than-thou vigilante."

*The Bauta passed back and reached a slender hand as if a beckon to '*jump*' over an abyssal chasm.* "Walk with me beneath the Hanging Gardens this venal regime fills with dissidents to rot alive, or pass along the slum district in the pit of our oldtown where the most orderly and *law*-abiding citizen is stomped by the oppressor's boot, and I will ask *again* what moral principle is possessed by this order for which it should stand to be preserved!"

"Do not *dare* speak to me as if I know not of pain!" *You couldn't name why you quivered like a drowning wretch, why your teeth ached for the tear and bleed of flesh. All you knew were the forget-me-not eyes flashing across your memory like a scar's glisten.* "*I* ask what grounds *you* had to bring violence upon us to-night! Are *we* not stomped down by the oppressor's boot? We are granted no choice but staging tragedies —tragedies we tirelessly pen only for *you* to destroy—so what *grounds* do you have to punish us further? What does *your* violence attain?"

"It sends a message."

"You are a madman."

"*You* are naïve."

"And *you* have *such* the moral high ground!"

"Do you?" *The Bauta paced around you a semicircle, your gaze never straying from the oblivion within his mask, your back never turned to him.* "Violence is fated fruit of the desperation begotten by a life-denying tyranny which sustains a *systematic* violence. Naphtha," *he flicked open a lighter,* "to a spark." *Light scattered into his eyes, igniting ochre-vivid flames around his pupils, like sacrificial pits, the bourn of his irises the glitter of cut peridot.* "*I* fail to see how a man like Crescenzo Zuane De Tullia would respond to any language but the one he speaks most fluently." *A clink extinguished the fire, The Bauta's eyes once more a cosmic nihility each.* "You are naïve because you blindly believe a violent—*truly* violent—man could listen to reason. If violence gets you nothing, how did He get all of *this*?"

*You breathed to quell the wrath thrashing inside your ribs—it would rip you or rip another. You wanted it to be another; you wanted it to be Him. But you locked your ribs and let it drown again.* "I have sought to *reason* this entire time." *Your tongue bled against the words.* "But I begin to think you may speak some sense. About *violent men* and listening?" *You snatched your blood-soaked headpiece, your mask, that awful gun, and turned to storm off, but The Bauta said,* "Hold on," *and that night, for some reason, you did.*

*He swung out his revolvers' cylinders, withdrawing the remaining two cartridges and handing them to you.* "Yours should accommodate these."

*You peered at him, then plucked the bullets as if he might've burned you if you lingered.*

*The Bauta clicked his tongue.* "Well met, princess." *He tapped his tricorn, running lithe fingers along the brim in a parting salute.*

"Well as a bane, your majesty," *you gritted, melodic laughter the fiend's only reply as he dissolved into the night.*

*You studied the cartridges in your ink-smeared hand, brass jackets lustrous in the moonlight.*

*If chains tightened in keeping with the preceding six years, The Bauta's freedom was indeed on course for expiration. But what fallout would come from that? A man like he would scarcely let himself perish without marking an unhealing gash in the world he left behind.*

*You had watched intently the way he moved, spoke. Spectral. A flame trapped in flesh.*

*You understood then that he was* free. *Unbounded.*

*At once, spite bloomed in your chest.*

*At once, you hated him.*

# Scene VII

## Achamoth

*Giorgianna*

"AMPLE HIPS, NO BREASTS," Falco judged my bare form. "Statuesque: long fingers, wide shoulders. Though a peasant's olive complexion. My clients favour the feminine sort over amazons, but the exotic face and tresses might make you a winning doll yet." Her glassy eyes trained on my razor-scarred thighs. "Hideous," she derided. "Evidence of a diseased mind. I trade in flesh—scars are a desecration, like a popped seal on a tub of paint."

I clenched my teeth, glimpsing my scars.

Between giggling girls and stolen strawberry kisses, darkness and guilt marred the memories of my adolescence: insults and slurs, fingers shoved down throats to stay 'pretty', inconsolable midnight tears until I screamed and tore my skin. I punished myself for every misstep—Mother needed to be pleased even if I despised her in my anger. But had I been a better daughter, perhaps all else could be better too. Perhaps my parents could still love each other.

With my father so often absent at the observatorium, working himself into oblivion, Emanuela was my spark of incandescence in the gelid winters she loved. I'd play my cello and she'd dance ballet, sing in her Hoġerr mother's language. She'd tend to my ruptured knuckles, and I'd bandage her slit arms. Our wounds would bleed a little less together.

And now, she was dead, two of the three men who killed her walking free. *You couldn't save her.*

Falco's fingers clicked at my nose. "One *never* lets her guard down in the slums!" She sauntered to the sofa, slinging herself upon its thulian brocade. Before her stood a treen coffee table inlaid with stained glass mosaics of arums, its surface arranged with smoking paraphernalia. The Madáma lit a dome-shaped lamp at the centre.

My hair—my mother's hair—swaddled me as I draped my unclothed chest with it. I desperately wanted my father, the way he stopped Mother when she endeavoured forcing me into an asylum to 'handle' my grief over Emanuela's death. I wished for solace.

"You are a vault of stories," mused Falco, holding a lengthy pipe to the lamp. Sweetness imbued the cool floreal air when she exhaled smoke. *Opium.* I recognised the aroma from childhood summers spent in Ferréli in Vencenza's western provinces, my áti[44] Catina, in her art deco embroidery and gamboge headscarf, smoking those poppy tears for her aching joints and plucked nerves on a stone porch embowered by sa pompia trees. The only times she and Mother conversed without antipathy.

I missed the verdant hinterland summers, the heady meadows floating with dandelion tufts and goldenrod pollen as if draped in the mystical gossamer of a faerie realm, the endless canopies of woodland leaves. I'd hoped to live there long into adulthood, to eat lush berries off their bushes and chase dragonflies through creeks, to skinny dip in the lace-crested aquamarine sea and make love in the tall grass with wildflowers in my curls. But a labour camp now stood in Ferréli's stead, and only ghosts haunted the old ruins.

---

[44] '*Maternal grandmother*' in Faustinian.

"Some of the regulars enjoy girls with a silver tongue." An ugly, bleak smile didn't reach Irene Falco's eyes. "Tell me, fugitive bird, are you acquainted with betrayal?"

*Midspring shone in full prime, the medlar of would-be summer putrefying like wounds with every slash of dawning you stalked the susurrant streets beneath.*

*This díem lunéra, you routed for* The Crescent, *your dress blooming like a blood-red rose. You still shook—only the night prior did you meet Death once more.*

*When you stumbled to a halt beneath the eleven eyes of The Watcher, that omniscient deific judge, your breath extinguished.*

*A flock of City Guards dragged a woman off her porch onto the crescent-shaped sampietrini. The geometric mosaic of her emerald dress gleamed bright as guillotine blades. Batons came down, smashing her lips to pulpy wads, scarlet marring the pale stone. The Guards said nothing as they bludgeoned, as she wailed formlessly—didn't need to. The stick was the law.*

*Ossíi shrunk back, heads down and tread brisk.*

*Notwithstanding your own distance and pace, you glared upon the murder of crows with an ever-darkened hex. Not one soldier patrolled the street those bandits attacked you on, the street that dissident fiend saw fit to descant to you along. Not one soldier patrolled the night of Emanuela's murder.*

*Yet there they were this díem lunéra.*

*Silk banners blazoning De Tullia's pale swallow sigil flanked The Watcher like silver swords.*

*You wondered what the Gods thought of Man's violence as you crossed a bridge at the end of the street, if They condoned slaughter in the name of light's purity. That was De Tullia's justification, after all. The Upper Trimorph, the Triple Face, were the creators of corporeality and thus those who bestowed the blank face, pnèuma, 'spirit', unto the flesh by chipping off pieces of themselves. The Arcónti were a pantheonic emanation of the Upper Trimorph—Lower entities which the face 'wore' like a mask of emotion.*

*Nearly a millennium ago, prior to persecution by the Faustinian Empire yet after the decline of paganism in the country's south, ancient Vencenzanii believed Lower Arcónti and the Upper Trimorph were of equal import, that cosmos and flesh were one essence in differing physicalities. Following revival by theologian Pietro Vestri in the late 1640s—one of the many catalysts for the Empire's fall—Illutèri doctrine stratified the pantheon, lending less significance to the shadowy Arcónti. Crescenzo De Tullia wielded this syncretism to his political advantage: if Arcónti were lower emanations and personified psychological phenomena, then Arcónti must be agents of corruption to the initial 'purity' of human pnèuma through bestowal of emotion. Corruption confines the pnèuma to the Chénoma, the Everlasting Null, the material void separated from the divine knowledge of the trimorphic godhead. Thus, the theologically-bent Vencenzani populace was given an elevated incentive to conform to* Sa Nóba Giustíca.

*You stood in the àtrium of* The Crescent. *As if you'd been a passenger of your body.*

*The auditorium's silence wormed under your skin. The timepiece in the àtrium had barely ticked over to nine hundred upon your arrival, yet the floors creaked like sclerotic joints under every step.*

*Your heart sat in your gut as you turned the time-worn knob of the thespian room backstage, stepped into the opiparous cardinal chamber. Then, your blood reversed course.*

*Impresario Basilio Lanuza stood at the centre. Beside him towered a pair of City Guards in their ashen uniforms and corvine masks: a blue-eyed superior and a redheaded fledgeling.*

*Your eyes frisked the* vìtae: *silent as tombs around the periphery. Lucrezia wasn't there.*

"Signorína Giorgianna Damiani." *The icy blue of the older soldier's eyes sapped all your warmth.* "You stand accused of conspiracy against the state and espousal of extremist ideology. You are under arrest."

*The words fell like a dozen dead men, and the ice of the soldier's eyes rimed the earth—now flagstone. Now solstice. Now Death.* They say such things come in threes.

"Disreputable recusant," *the snake Basilio spat, the third eye that was his alexandrite pendant flashing equal odium your way.*

*When the young redhead pounced, you had already moved—a thrown stone across a plane weltering as water; a fox hunted for sport, bile in your throat and heartbeat faster than your feet. If you faltered, they'd catch you, so you weaved through the capillaries you knew better than the soldiers, curtains and hooked moons a smear of gore in your reeling senses.*

*A door cut short an obscure corridor—one which thespians flowed in and out of the theatre by.*

*Your body thrust into the oak, hands tearing at the handle.*

*The lock wouldn't give.*

*Basilio's bark led the soldiers to you—vultures to carrion.*

*You couldn't breathe, a desperate creature clawing at the door which became the bars of a cage; which became the men who broke your fingers that winter solstice night.*

*Your body surged forth one last time.*

*The lock gave.*

*Dainty palms grasped your elbows, and you would've shoved your saviour into the abutting duct if you hadn't descried their rainstorm eyes.* "I reported an illness and oughtn't be here." *Lucrezia whispered frantically.* "You must go, I…" *You guessed by the protrusion of her orbs, the gape of her dry lips, what words might have hung off the tip of Lucrezia's tongue, but—*"There's no time."

*You heard hammering footfalls.*

*And then you ran.*

*It was as if you had never stopped.*

"Yes, Madáma," I finally found my voice. "I've met betrayal enough to name its birthmarks."

"Think again." Irene Falco puffed an opiate cloud. "My spinster slag mother sold me, at nine years, to traffickers to make ends meet. I lost my womb, my innocence, my humanity. I am fifty-two years of age. I grovelled on my knees in this establishment for *twenty-eight years* as a lavìre[45] because of betrayal. By my own *mother*." The woman tapped the stained glass window behind the sofa. "I earned my turn."

To her right, rounded doors inlaid with vitreous damselflies barged open.

I yelped, arms clutched to my chest.

Madáma's guards towered in the archway, thick and solid as orcs. One held ropes. The other carried a branding iron.

Falco's head tipped once she refilled her opium, the blackness of her eyes dead and starless. "Some girls are born to suffer."

---

[45] Typically a neutral reference to sex workers in only Vencenzani Faustinian.

# Scene VIII

## Auctoritas, non Veritas, Facit Legem

*Cesare*

FOUR STOREYS OF A FREEFALL whistled below as Cesare scaled the sloped terracotta roofs of lower óssium, briny breeze whipping dark waves about his face.

Vencenza's oldtown rippled with canals thin as capillaries, each edifice slumped against the next as if friends seated languorously side-by-side, demanding pedestrians angle their shoulders sideways to traverse.

Cesare broke in the streets at an age younger than seven in the ritzy districts of southeastern Du Rrât a du Errèina where buildings were stacked like layered honey cakes, giving a wide berth to their neighbours across cobbled boulevards teeming with musicians and jota dancers.

Leaping to distant balconies became second nature, Cesare's feet light and steady, palms callused, scarred—no longer burning against the abrasion of railings as he swung from roof to roof to balconet to cobble.

He had chosen his kill in the Solar Square wisely, shooting down the crow who detained the little boy and granting him precious time to run amidst the incited pandemonium. Meanwhile, Cesare retreated into the pitchy blackness of oldtown, sights set upon two crows heading northeast. Seeing as whatever hex bound the Court hadn't yet led them astray, the soldiers knew their precise destination.

Soon enough, the pair were bashing on the rickety door of a home.

A man emerged, red of hair and beard. Unarmed. Vaguely familiar.

Cesare kept to the dark.

'...*under arrest for suspicion of treason and unlawful possession of contraband.*' A Guard shackled the redhead.

'*Wh—what? We help—*' A clobber to the abdomen choked the man's plea. One Guard kicked his shin so hard the convict toppled; another landed a punch that sent a tooth flying. Soldiers weren't permitted to strike the face—the Governor liked his subjects neat and pretty for the gallows.

They dragged the man off without negotiation.

Cesare pursued.


Guards shoved their gallowsbird towards the titanic patrol gondoa,[46] slate-dark all over. A weighted figurehead on its bow, mounted by an iron crow with folded wings, counteracted the weight of a massive cabin-like sternward trunk where the redhead was promptly locked up.

A legionary disembarked to unmoor the boat.

Cesare shed the shadows. "This cage isn't made for crows."

Legionaries grabbed their weapons, attentive to Cesare's stilétti and revolvers, his proximity. "What does slum trash want?"

Cesare clicked his tongue. "I want you to dance for me." His gloved hand dipped into his jacket, flinging a white cloud of coarse itching

---

[46] '*Gondola*' in the Vencenzani dialect.

powder into the Guards' eyes. They dry-heaved, scratching their faces to sore redness. "I want what your keeper took." Cesare delivered a bullet into the Guards' skulls in two clean shots, ripping rèquiem apart.

Bodies thudded, an echo and ring dangling on the tatters of night. *Sniper's vision.* Cesare's most prized quality within himself.

He picked keys off the corpses, unlocking the trunk. "Changeover." He tossed the keys at the rattled redhead fettered inside.

The convict fumbled until the cuffs gave way.

Cesare squinted, the man's familiarity irking him until it scratched at a memory.

Redhead clambered to escape.

Cesare's arm shot out to block the doorway.

He met eyes with the bemused convict. "Díem crepúsca, three months ago. Didn't you and a pair of your *chums* waylay a woman in the dead of night?"

The man licked his bleeding lips, his chin angled a degree starward.

Cesare's nostrils flared.

The man lunged backwards, grabbing the shackles and swinging them at Cesare's head.

Cesare dodged, a throwing knife swiftly in hand—one of the numerous stashed in his jacket—and drove the blade into his opponent's forearm, jerking it forward.

Redhead howled as the steel tore open his arm like gushing pipes, crimson jetting down Cesare's waspie. He sent the redhead tumbling with a hard kick and thrust the throwing dagger into his throat. He gargled, blood bursting sticky-sweet as grenadine across his teeth to trickle into his beard.

"Well deserved," sneered Cesare, stomping the blade deeper for good measure.

Redhead's body thrashed until his struggle asphyxiated with him.

Cesare tore out the knife and wiped it on the man's shirt, dropping his bloodied gloves on the deck before searching the legionaries' pockets. He found an envelope sealed by gold wax, the sigil of the Imperiálum stamped into it: a griffin encircled by interlaced wings, two longswords crossed behind. Inside hid a tidy piece of inked parchment.

> *'At command of our esteemed Minister of Dominion,*
> *a pardon is to be issued to specified condottiéri discovered*
> *committing crimes in lower óssium for the duration of time*
> *by which they do not outlive their usefulness. Upon such*
> *developments, they are to be imprisoned immediately*
> *and without the necessity of an arrest warrant.*
>
> General M. Dioli<br>34/2/1762/9 (ZE).[47]'

*General Manuele Dioli.* The Governor's Minister of Blades; a hardened warrior and a colossal egomaniac. Cesare had heard his fair share of vile whispers about the golden griffin's violence and perversion but, presently, dwelled on '*...outlive their usefulness*'. What 'use' could the state have for condottiéri?[48] People they ignorantly deemed 'bandits' —criminals by nature?

Months following that díem crepúsca incident in midspring, Cesare's inner-city contacts reported sightings of the redhead's suspicious band, but none had intel. Amidst his assembly-related machinations, Cesare hoped to find leads.

He slipped the note into his jacket, exchanging it for a black pouch. Equally black powder bloated its bowels, gritty like sand as he strewed with it the gondoa and corpses. Saltpetre—alchemised gunpowder generated through hybridisation with azoth: the animating humour, lifeforce, '*soul*' (if one believed such things), within all fleshbearers.[49]

Cesare stepped ashore, chewing his cheek as he observed the gondoa. Its ghastly symbolism.

Upon the fall of the Faustinian Empire and the consequent constitution of the Republic of Faustina with its four city states one-

---

[47] Gethlemian dates are written: *Day/Month/Year/Centimillennium (EPOCH)*. Century is usually omitted except for official or historical documents wherein it is positioned between the year and the centimillennium.

[48] *kohn-doht-tee'EH-ree*; colloquially means '*outlaws*' or '*bandits*'; *actually* denotes members of a minor, unofficial, typically self-sufficient government ('*cadre*') traditionally unaffiliated with criminal activity.

[49] '*Fleshbearer*' refers to animals (irrespective of species), humans, iridites, and sometimes plants, but not homunculi (artificial persons) or blasted flesh (necromantic resurrection errors).

hundred-twelve years ago, the foundation of Vencenza had been built on tenets, in theory, simplistic: a Governor was to be elected by democratic process every five years and never twice in succession. Upon inauguration, they were to assemble six Ministers to share their tenure—of Emissaries, Churches, Blades, Scholars, Coin, Justice.

And now...

One man serving twice his incumbency, his Ministers little more than vacuous pageantry to maintain an illusion that his dominion was not autocracy.

The city ran rampant with brutality against the downtrodden by legionaries, every window shut and barred by night as if not men but infected ghouls crazed by the moon stalked the streets, church choirs damning the defiled prison that is flesh and chanting canticles to purity, eyes forever upturned to transcendence beyond this constructed Hell. And De Tullia, ever the apt weaver of lies, fashioned his fascistic reign into an impeccable web of deceit.

But was the old world *good*?

Were the Hanging Gardens and ancient prisons stretching on for lightyears beneath the government house not there in that *Golden Age*? Long before? Did heads not roll? Did innocents not hang upon the gallows for treason just as they were bound to come to-morrow's dawn?

Upon De Tullia's inauguration, abandoned or sparsely-inhabited villages in Vencenza's provinces were demolished to make way for prison camps, their people forsaken to death or destitution—did *they* not exist for the eight hundred years of the Faustinian Empire?

Once chipping away at empire commenced, it became unthinkable to not see politicos, of now *or* centuries past, for exactly what they were: soulless, bloated necrophagan creatures glutting on decay of their own assembly.

Cesare found the matchbox he always kept on him.

*This ends before I do.*

Striking a match alight on a nearby column, he flicked it at the gondoa.

Furious flames made swifter by saltpetre burst alive, climbing up the woodwork like vines, crawling on the floorboards as roots, devouring all dead progeny of the earth.

Cesare's blood surged against his veins as if beckoned towards the flames like its own entity, as if trapped within a corporeal confinement it was never meant to inhabit.

Fire, the force that had once been his saviour from a too-early demise, consumed the gondoa, a sarcoid reek of burning fat and boiling blood invading Cesare's nostrils.

He reached for a pack in his jacket and brought the tobacco to the pyre, lighting a sigarétta for the fall of civilisation.

# Scene IX

## Purgatory

*Giorgianna*

THE WHIP CRACKED, a scream its anguished echo.

Lavìri huddled like bundles of nerves around the floriated walnut floors of the bordello's main room as Madáma Irene Falco whipped one of our own bloody—a girl crouched on the ground, bare shoulders clutched in trembling fingers, onyx curls cradling cheeks florid and wet with tears. No older than sixteen.

Falco threw back her macilent arm.

A black tail tipped in gleaming steel streaked the air and ripped the girl's moon-pale back like linen. Another scream surged. Nara's fingers clasped mine as I jumped with my heart.

Falco liked *The Arum*'s lavìri punished with humiliation—stripped by her guards and flogged to the muscle before the others' horror. After beatings, she'd have us wait three hours before bringing ano-apozem,[50] permitting we heal every wound bar *one* of her choosing.

Falco had whipped me once, the second-last strike hooking around my side, snapping a rib and stripping it of flesh. *That* was the wound she made me keep.

*Crack!*

My hand clamped a gasp.

Falco grabbed the young lavìre by the hair. "Get out of my sight." She slapped her hard and pivoted sharply, eyes punching air from my chest as they swung for Nara and me.

"Gennara!" she snapped in that flytrap way of hers. "Come. The rest of you clear out! Your shifts commence in an hour."

Lavìri scrammed like frightened butterflies.

Falco grabbed Nara's wrist and brandished a pale finger at my face. "I haven't forgotten the last time, *girl*." She yanked my curls as if needing to hurt me by any means she could figure, my jaw unclenching to purge a yelp.

Bloody whip trailing behind her like a sated snake, Madáma Falco dragged Nara along towards the door severing the bordello from the adjoining tavèrna—embedded with frosted glass moccasin flowers. Both establishments lay in Falco's iron-fisted possession. Nara took it frighteningly blasé, numbed by her four years at *The Arum*.

I drew lungfuls of breath, ribcage expanding against my corset's claret bones. Madáma forbade us the wear of a chemise, so my flesh chafed as if sprouting thorns.

Blood swilled the young lavìre's back as she huddled twitching on the floor in muscle-wringing agony. *That* was what the martinet put you through for resisting her vile guards' violations.

---

[50] Apozem is a group of alchemical healing elixirs split into two subtypes: *katō-apozem*, and *ano-apozem*. *Katō-apozem* is non-regenerative, healing by scarring. *Ano-apozem* is regenerative, healing via complete restoration of damaged tissue by accelerating healing pathways. Ano-apozem cannot function on fibrosis, meaning partly-scarred tissue will not be repaired.

I slunk to the girl's side, hand in my hiked skirt's pocket. "Take this." I jammed my last analgesic pill into her cold fingers. "Lie on your stomach; try to sleep until Madáma comes with apozem."

She shook her head, curls pasted like calligraphy to the sunken curve of her cheeks. "You aren't allowed. She'll punish you again—"

"She won't if you *go!*" I helped her stand, hurrying her towards the lavìre quarters.

A shallow heartbeat hammered my sternum once she vanished through the clinquant diaphane of carnation curtains.

The bordello bloomed into an art nouveau garden, stained glass ceilings a mosaic scatter of flower petals sprouting wheaten lilies of lights, every dramatic brass undulation embossed upon the walls curved like wisterias. Like a cracking whip.

Rose-gold hooks shaped into tree branches suspended azalea-pink swathes of aerial silks from the ceiling. I found comfort in the silks, at least. There was artistry in the smooth cloth, tender benevolence in the way it held the sore limbs. *The Arum*'s sole respite, even if terribly meagre.

The slums of The Court of Secrets drew aristocracy's foulest men to gratify their sick perversions, but Falco was content with riches by any means. How else would her debased enterprise glitter amidst hovels? She'd '*earned her turn*', had felt the very hurt she subjected us to, but, in the end, a different sort of spite festered within her. Above all, she knew how to unspool your pain with the right pluck of a question, to weave it into a pliant cloth to choke you with, and she relished in the whine of my loneliness as it rattled in my throat, the twitch in my fingertips for warm skin. It was pitiful to still crave touch after all the bruises it marked me with, to still yearn for the exquisite torment that was wanting. But how could I ever hope to make love in the tall grass now with the flowers withered and the earth crawling with demons, twisted by *The Arum*'s mocking iconography?

Irene Falco ensured neither pregnancy nor moonblood could present an 'impediment' to boot, forcing all her lavìri to have their wombs cut out if they had one. No anaesthetic, no analgesic. Merely ropes, a bed, and a scalpel, followed by horrific violation at the hands of the Madáma's guards. I'd rather not beget life into a slaughterhouse of a world, anyway.

A few exceptionally unfortunate lavìri were forcefully impregnated, then beaten until miscarrying. Or forced to carry their unwanted pregnancy to term, only to murder their own newborn by force. One night, when disposing of bloodied satin sheets, I found the cyanotic corpse of an infant in the refuse receptacle, and I realised right then and there, for the final time, that the rulers were unforgivable.

'*This is mercy*,' Falco would sneer. '*Rŭnethãri brothels would rip your tongues and teeth out, poison you until your bones turned brittle as splinters so you couldn't run!*' As if *she* didn't torture young women and transfemmes out of envy for a youth stripped of her. As if *The Arum* was a bona fide brothel, at all.

And she knew she needn't some stilty contract to keep lavìri in her employ when our alternatives were the streets or prison, and The Court's thaumaturgy kept us entrapped.

But *I* had to get out.

Wanted or not, I would learn the names of Emanuela' murderers. *I* would be the justice the *law* refused to be.

Darkness clung to my skin like soot as I stepped beyond the bordello.

Waning midsummer teased its wounded fingers at the fallen night, vainly seeking to spill its hot blood to warm the sunless sphere. Instead, crickets played discordant fiddle to the nubiferous starscape, the air laden damp with the odour of decay, of mould and mice.

Falco's guards loitered near the porch. Six feet tall and bulked with muscle beneath plain grey shirts and bistred trousers, hair cut short and rough-hewn faces forested with tamed beards.

Arms laced and teeth set, I descended stiffly, eyes low.

"Walking dolly coming out to play? Scary on your own." One of them shoved his thick fingers into my hair, the other plucked at a strap of my corset and groped my thigh.

Chuckles stalked me as I rushed down a squalid path blackened as a deadman's throat. Nothing repulsed me more than the large hands of a man—like maggots vying to burrow under my skin.

I'd spent one-hundred-seven days—three months—at *The Arum*, and it seemed every week some ruffian made a pass at my life. One's life was a gold coin: valuable, but easy to lose and coveted by thieves. Nara claimed it came with the territory at any slum bordello—hers helping me escape the first attempt was how we'd met.

Lower and Court ossíi mingled in the tavèrna end of *The Arum*, every pane of the chamber an ethereal woodland grotto. We'd gleaned that most Court residents weren't permitted to enter the bordello, only the tavèrna. Falco wished to keep her customer base pure.

I shouldered through tempered chatter, tossing casino chips into a card game to the hearty cheers of barflies. I'd found myself taking well to the workers, the drifters, the forsaken.

Giulia[51] minded the bar, her berry-dyed curls shaved on one side, bronze curves clad in crushed black velour and beestung lips painted ebony to match her coffin nails. I was smitten with her from day one, but her affection for any person was none.

Nara leaned emaciated elbows on the counter, auburn hair tossed over her ribbed chest, her corset and ruffled skirt (the ensemble all lavìri were forced to wear for our *Madáma*) lurid as fuchsias. Pale linework of a dainty dagger branded the skin between the wings of Nara's fragile shoulder blades. A Malefactor's Mark, not unlike inmates, marking us as rotten organs unwanted in the body of the world. The same stigma as on *my* back.

I bumped Nara's hip. "Falco out of sight?" Adjusting my crimson corset straps, I hopped onto the counter, resting my forearms on my peaked knees.

Nara grinned, a canine missing in its row since her adolescence. "And out of mind." She laced her fingers behind her head. Polluted rivers branched beneath her skin, knolls of bruises marking her chelidons where she defiled them with needles. A thick scar glistened pale against her tanned arm.

Everything in The Court owed dues. So, the night Nara helped me escape an attempt on my life, she struck with me a blood promise. To

---

[51] *JOO-lee-ah*

watch my back in the slums. I'd already gotten nicked by the bandit's blade on my left bicep, so Nara inflicted a matching wound on herself, and our pact was sealed. Blood was worth diamonds and scars were irreparable, so the only means by which a blood promise could dissolve was the death of one bound party. Once you promised a drop, you owed it all.

"When Isa drags her arse here," chirped Nara, "I've gossip. *Old*, but *well* riveting!" She winked a muddy yellow eye.

Curiosity fluttered in my belly. I always wondered, with generous envy, how Nara so proficiently caught whispers when the Court confined us to loops we couldn't stray from.

The waif of a woman sat cross-legged behind me, plucking fake gold roses from the flower-decked bar and setting them among my curls. It was a small comfort, knowing they at least weren't red. Falco hadn't managed to pry the intimate detail of my beloved blossom from me— *Rosa sanguinus*: the most striking flowers to have bloomed in áti and ápa's dooryard before the legions came to make that little village a death camp.

My insomniac attention roved the tavèrna, its torote and licorice air all the sweeter with sonorous contrabass, the ache in my heart for my cello strumming in time. *Díem stelláre to-day; luck might befall me.*

Patrons hummed, familiar faces sharing liquor and banter.

Some of Falco's clients liked their purchases indisposed, so lavìri were inebriated for them, or drugged outright. On two occasions, I fell subject. The flavour of booze would evermore repulse me. So, instead of alcohol, I poured into myself silence.

Within a wisteria-bowered booth, a blonde woman chatted with Giulia, her statuesque frame adorned in sangria satin and palms poised by her slim chin. Calliupa Soriano—a lavìre from someplace better who occasionally dropped by Falco's tavèrna (for reasons *I* couldn't fathom).

A reedy man lounged at a nearby table, left eye orange as a citrine, right socket clutching a mechanical orb. Black shorts and thigh-highs sheathed long legs clad in fishnet, his magenta jacket sewn with innumerable buttons, circular cinder goggles embracing an amaranthine hat sitting tall atop russet curls and a buckled leather belt suspending an enormous pair of gleaming gold scissors. His meline features seemed familiar. *One of Nara's regulars?*

But the man across from him was a stranger.

He dressed plain and lowly: black pants and a billowing cotton shirt cinched into knuckle-skimming frills by cufflinks, bright as snow against his brown skin. The tips of his thick hair, waved and molasses-dark, slit the centre of his lean throat, his long limbs laced tight with muscle. An enormous silver hoop suspending a dainty crotal bell hovered a finger's width above his right shoulder—broad yet sharp as if marble-chiselled.

Both men brazenly held a sigarétta each.

"*Signóri!*" Irene Falco's voice exploded, jolting me and Nara.

The Madáma emerged from the cellar behind the bar and charged for the smokers.

The mechanical-eyed man squawked. "*Ah!*" He threw out his arms in theatrical delight, armour rings clinking. "My *dar*ling Irene!"

Nara leaned close. "*He's like that in bed, too.*"

We choked on furtive giggles.

Even so deep in The Court where De Tullia wouldn't hear me, where Mother couldn't strike me, I hardly laughed. The totality of my own consciousness would drown me if I let the grip on my psyche slip, so I didn't *feel* anymore. *Mother said nothing is worth it.* Even if I starved and brutalised within.

"Don't '*dar*ling' *me*, Donatello," Falco reprimanded, grimacing like a guard hound. "I tolerate *no* smoking on my premises. Discard the darts or vacate."

Donatello descended into a babble while, with an insolent simper, the dark-haired man dragged his sigarétta and exhaled a plume of moonstone smoke.

For a cloven half-moment, our gazes crossed.

His kohled eyes smouldered a kaleidoscopic hazel-green like andalusites reflecting fire, his high, sculpted features, those long silk lashes and sharp lips full as a femme's pout, all an artisan's sedulous work. Heart-flinching and devastating like an arsonist's whimsy.

I fidgeted with my curls as warmth budded upon my cheeks, fingers pathetically a-tremble. As if he wasn't a man at *The Arum*. As if he wasn't *a man*, although that was merely an unfounded guess. As if...

*I've seen those eyes before...*

Unsmiling and ignorant of Falco's admonitions, he drew more smoke, hair stirring the lambent candlelight as he leaned his temple on his slim knuckles, undaunted, *unfearing*, and that blossom of spite in my chest sprouted thorns too.

A fist prodded my arm.

Nara snatched my attention away. "Isa." She pointed to the door.

In walked a woman in an old pistachio-and-cream empire gown, her bronzen skin peppered with freckles and hair streaming loose and golden down her back. Glaucous eyes behind a pince-nez found us with effort. Eluisa—Nara rarely called people by their whole forename—worked as a nursemaid for her uncle and his wife in the surrounding vicinity to pay for treatment of her own diminishing vision. *Never a dull day.*

Fake roses tumbling from my hair, Nara and I huddled with Eluisa around a table near the smokers Falco at last left alone (once Donatello slipped her a packet of opium, that was).

"Last week," Nara's eyes glinted, "in oldtown, a Guard gondoa was torched to *cinders*! Apparently, there were *bodies* in there. Little more than driftwood and ash was left behind so *that's* just rumours. *And*, not even an hour *prior* to that, somebody shot down a crow in the Solar Square!" Nara poked me in the clavicle. "Bet it was your most beloathed."

I shuddered ire off my shoulders. The Bauta set in motion my banishment from Vencenza like the harbinger of ruination he was. I'd loathe him for the rest of my days.

Eluisa dithered before asking: "*Where* in oldtown?"

"Northeast of the Solar Square—the *nice* end where The Court's magical idiocy won't let us go." She snorted. "Wouldn't lump the barge under *that* adjective though." Nara never disclosed what she meant by '*the barge*', only that it was the sole location The Court allowed her to venture.

I questioned just about everyone about the magic binding The Court of Secrets, how it functioned, and yet, somehow, no Court resident had even a clue. It'd gotten to the point that folks opened our conversations with '*before ye start, I know nothin' 'bout this theurgy tosh*' even when I hadn't intended to ask! This realm's recondite hollow lived up to its moniker.

Eluisa grabbed Nara's arm and took off on her homily regarding needles.

Nara had hauled herself to *The Arum* in a bid to escape her brother. After Falco ordered her womb be cut out, she had Nara's vivisected body dumped in a ginnel, declaring that if the waif of a woman survived the night, she could return. She wouldn't have, not without Eluisa finding her. Nara returned out of spite. She feared nothing, now.

My wrung mind wandered, shrapnel of fractured voices bouncing through my ears.

Donatello tittered like a chipmunk's teeth chattering on an acorn. '*...shall be* thrill*ed to know.*'

'*A season's passage was all it took,*' his companion replied, and I stilled, hearing nothing but his voice, its droll lilt. The pianissimo notes of a Zargòsian accent.

"Giorgi?" Nara's brows sat together when our eyelines hitched.

Black fury awakened, clawing. *Should've chosen a different rendezvous scene, bàuta.*

Launching onto my feet, I gripped Nara and Eluisa by the forearms and pulled them on my barward walk.

They nestled closer.

"What—"

"The dark-haired man in the white shirt," I cut Eluisa off.

Nara covered a laugh. "*Mhmm*, I saw you staring like you were ready to mount him."

I scowled despite my furious flush, then looped my arms through Nara and Eluisa's. "I need you to help me cajole Giulia."

# SCENE X

## AQUA TOFANA

*Cesare*

*RIGHT ON THE MONEY INDEED, Donatello.*

Cesare cleared the rasp from his throat, setting down his water infused with black cherries. *The appropriate party will appreciate these tidings.*

The dollmaker flitted off, a teaspoon of glitter-flecked goldwine remaining in his glass. Cesare never understood the allure of alcohol, nor why she whom he learned was Giulia was so insistent they drink.

He toyed with his morganite cufflink, lamenting the loss of his tanzanite pair, a favourite of his collection—a gift from the impresario of *The Sunrise*—before checking the time. *Twenty-one hundred.*

Iyad and Anukka expected him at *Three Suns* to be this evening's entertainment for some paltry coin and a scrap of gossip like the previous week—the night of that impromptu sacrificial burning whispers of which seemingly percolated through The Court's innards.

Cesare had never been to *The Arum*, and its opiparous florality unnerved him to the bone, the ostentatious display of finery an eyesore.

He hardly had an interest in sex, so never sought the establishments intended for it, but knew from the twitch of the lavìri's shoulders that a plain bordello *The Arum* was not. He knew, too, how easily Vencenza gilded rot; the steel-tipped whip strapped to the Madáma's hip hadn't escaped him.

"*Signór!*" a voice boomed, and Cesare knew he was being addressed. Acrimony charred Falco's eyes. "You and that menace smoked up my tavèrna enough. *Leave!*"

Giulia rolled her eyes behind the woman's back.

Matching the gesture with deliberate clarity, Cesare plucked his tricorn off the table and made for the exit. Two days' worth of fatigue swam in his skull. "Lachô latziâ.[52]" Cesare laced his voice with poison and animus, flinging at Falco a smirk like a knife before departing.

The petite crotal bell dangled by his hoop earring sang to the wind with every head-turn as Cesare surveyed the moon-laved streets beyond the bordello. So alike the alleyways he'd frequent in his seventeenth year to take the edge off with a tourniquet and needle. So alike the corners of Canronê he visited in his childhood where itinerants squatted, where he met the doctor who saved his life from damnation to Hell at his father's woodcutter hand.

Stifling his throat-clear, Cesare ducked beneath a fenced cloister, passing an illuminated space within the edifice. His head spun. *Fuck you, I'm not* that *tired.*

He coughed tightly, stumbling forward as his limbs numbed.

Narrowly dodging the legs of an upturned iron table which doffed his hat, Cesare climbed to his knees, fingers tingling. Pain pierced his gut.

---

[52] *lah-CHOH laht-zee-AH*; 'good night' in Marlâre.

His tongue tasted salt-sweet copper. *Poison!* The cherry water. *That's* why Giulia was so insistent.

Panic made a quick entrance.

"You have six minutes." The voice Cesare heard was dim candlelight and autumnal crepuscule.

He shoved himself off his knees to sit up, elbows barely holding his back upright.

In the doorway stood a junoesque woman, aurate alchemy haloing her like a solar eclipse.

A ruffled skirt, hiked at her mid-thigh, fell around the back of her ankles as if flesh flayed off her torso, her svelte waist cinched by a carmine corset and long legs sheathed in black thigh-highs. Bruises like criminals' fingerprints stained her arms.

In one slender hand she held petal-pink silks. In the other glimmered a straight razor.

She tipped her head, caramel ringlets tumbling across broad and angled shoulders. "Do you remember me, bàuta?" Beestung lips, indented on the bottom as deeply as the bow, scarlet as the cherries Cesare so fancied, set into a cruel glower. *Some people never leave you.*

He cut out a sardonic smile. "My shoulder hurts every time I think of you, vólto."

Giorgianna's vulpine eyes, framed lavishly within curled lashes, ignited blood-red with rage.

She switched off the alchemical light.

Black pupils plunged her irises into an abyss.

"I'll put you out of your—" Giorgianna swung the razor for Cesare's throat "—*misery!*"

He dragged himself back, missing a chance to grab his knives before she kicked his abdomen, thrusting the breath out of him. His arms buckled. Her foot readied for another hit. Cesare went to grab her ankle while he still had feeling in his limbs. Silks looped around his wrists, arms yanking over his head as Giorgianna hooked the sash onto the leg of the upended table behind him and pulled it taut like shackles. Cesare strained against the silk in vain. *How did she get this thing so tight?*

She climbed onto his middle, squeezing her thighs to pin him down. Hate frenzied her eyes, each spiral of her endless hair traced with rose perfume as it spilled off her shoulders. *Immensely inconvenient time to find my attacker beautiful.*

"You know," he began, "under different circumstances, I'd be fine with this arrangement, but—"

Giorgianna stuck the straight razor under Cesare's jaw, fingers pressing his neck.

His stomach flipped. The touch of another's skin in any instance but fraternal closeness repulsed him, and there was no longer the sensation in his legs to throw her off.

"You talk too much," hissed Giorgianna.

"Planning to bump off the dollmaker too?" Cesare gritted carefully, conscious of the blade against his veins.

Malice twitched her lip. "I'll not spread my ire too thin."

"Special treatment? You flatter me, princess. But I must say, *quite* the repayment for my good nature—my needlework is impeccable, you know."

"Keep running your mouth, time is quicker."

Pain spasmed Cesare's stomach in concurrence. "At least tell me what I did."

She lingered on his lips for a split moment too long. "See the misfortune I've fallen upon? *You* played *no* small part in the dissolution of my life. I *am* here because of the dominoes your visit to *The Crescent* knocked over. *So*," her fist tugged the silks, "I will watch you *choke*."

Cesare swallowed the blood niggling his gullet. "Lis—"

A keening female whimper shattered the night.

Giorgianna's eyes darted between the balusters of the fence, wild and wide.

The female voice shrieked.

Three counts of vulgar male shouts tracked her.

Giorgianna ducked closer to Cesare, her long-fingered hand clamping his mouth. *Great. I'm maximally incapacitated.*

Cesare's ears trained on the commotion.

He couldn't make out the words, but knew they were ugly.

His chest lurched, expelling droplets of blood into Giorgianna's loosened palm. "Still poisoned!"

Eyes fixed to the darkness, she released Cesare's wrists and shoved a pill into his hand. "Antidote." She clambered off, coldness claiming Cesare's clammy flesh abruptly enough to make him gasp like he'd been stabbed.

He swallowed the pill, grudging to admit the thump in his chest was fear for his life.

Sensation teased his muscles, his limbs lead-heavy as he recovered his hat and hauled himself up, wiping blood from his lips.

"You must leave," he heard Giorgianna.

She clutched the silks and razor to her chest like sacred artefacts, knees tucked close and shoulders curved.

A frown tugged Cesare's eyebrows. "What's going—?"

"*Sh*—!" Giorgianna waved her hands, the alarm in her eyes distilling to dread as she switched to The Fingers: '*I know how to deal with this, get* out*! Don't even* think *about intervening.*'

Cesare's gut sank.

'*Go!*' Giorgianna urged. *Pleaded.*

Throat dry and chest heavy, Cesare glimpsed the street, sighting nothing, but hesitantly obliged.

# SCENE XI

## THE BLOOD OF THE COVENANT IS
## THICKER THAN THE WATER
## OF THE WOMB

*Giorgianna*

*YOU WERE HARDLY FOURTEEN the first time you met your mother's Shadow.*

*Heartbeat bashed your ribs like a guttersnipe begging sanctuary as you scrambled off the marble floor of the dim bathing chamber in Elenedda Murgia's home upon* **Aegidius Boulevard.** *Your thighs rubbed like firewood to ignite pain as your fingers fumbled with a straight razor in desperation to confine it to a drawer.*

*"Giorgianna?" came your mother's exacting voice, her pointed footfalls nearing.*

*You slammed shut the cabinet in time with the door's opening swing, but your heart stilled at the sound of bouncing metal, the sight of that bloodied razor springing across the marble.*

*In your panic, you weren't careful.*

*A statuesque woman stood in the doorway, her eyes wide as copper plates and fixed upon the razor. Upon* you.

*Your mother's warm complexion was yours, your same caramel coils beneath a thickness of sapphire silk, a flattened peppercorn of a mole above her lip like the one by your left eye. But the thinly chiselled architecture of her face, solemn as gothic buttresses, was nothing of you.*

"Where is it?" *Her question struck like a hammer.*

"I—"

*You squealed at the snap of your mother's nails around your wrist, her cold hands shucking your sleeves, scouring your arms for blood.*

"Mama STOP!"

*She clawed at the chiffon layers of your skirt.*

"WHERE IS IT?"

*The cloth shredded.*

"LET ME *GO!*"

*A clap of skin on skin flung your body sidelong.*

*Your gruing palms gripped the bathtub. Your cheek throbbed.*

*Elenedda Murgia's eyes bubbled with lava, threatening a cataclysm.*

"Hold your tongue!" *she seethed like she'd crawled out of herself.*

*That was the first time you met your mother's Shadow, hardly a girl of fourteen yourself.*

*She gripped your curls—the curls her bloodline begot—and yanked you upright, peeling the tattered skirt aside to expose cuts pulsing pyrrhous and raw down your thigh.* "Your father hears none of this, understand? I'll not have you besmirch me with your hysterics!" *She snatched the razor off the floor.* "Nothing of Ludovico Damiani should've remained in this house." *Her voice caught and broke as she shoved you away.*

*You sank to the cold marble, shivering in your mother's darkness.*

*Fixing her silk headscarf, her bow-shaped choker, the endless silver sa cannacca chains garlanding her mazarine bodice, Elenedda Murgia composed herself—a beast returned to its cage.*

*You wondered if such a creature festered within you. A Shadow.*

*Since De Tullia's inauguration, Vencenzanii bent over backwards to craft a mask of obedient righteousness. When people feared for their life, they forsook their Self.*

*Mother flicked the razor shut.* "Make yourself presentable for rehearsal." *And she left you.*

*You curved your arms, slim as sprouts, around your huddled form, and let tears pour.*

*Scabs still marred your knuckles from days prior. You'd committed a blunder during a cello recital, disgracing your mother, so her hand fan came down on your fingers—a cross-pein hammer to beat into shape your Fear. The first time Father enquired of your scars, you claimed you punch walls for catharsis. Mother ratified the lie, so you lied evermore, even to Ema. Your mother comprehended rule by fear, after all —Elenedda Murgia took care to cultivate you as a frightened flower, poised even when drowning. But why were you, a flower, drowning?*

*Your mother's village was called Ferréli. 'Blacksmith'. Your* mother *was the blacksmith, your forger, herself already forged by your iron-fisted áti. And even with your father's embrace—those tempering waters —you became a blade all the same.*

*The diptych of You, as it were—a knife and a flower, but the thorny sort. You always wondered why you liked red.*

*Your father's youth passed by in a slum orphanage where kids forgotten as himself became his cherished siblings. A lesson in compassion. In* love. *A lesson you clung to amid the fear of your mother's home. If only it had come easier.*

*On that cold marble, you swallowed the scream lumped in your throat since your twelfth year, wiped your bewet cheeks, and you never cried again.*

Tying the thread, I bit it at the knot, sipping up the blood spritzed across my lip.

Crooked sutures rooted into my thigh where a gash oozed thickened gore, imparted by a client in some perverted desire to lacerate a being beneath him. To see how it feels to draw another's blood he thought so dirty. One more grim reminder to remain on flesh already striated with innumerable razor scars.

I wiped the blood with a serviette and flushed it along with the contents of my stomach. With each client, I forcibly emptied myself, sickened by rapacious men tearing into my flesh with their uncallused fingers like predators to meat. But I'd developed the compulsion long ago—aged fourteen when mother frightened me from blades. With no other means of purging my unbearable passions, no longer permitted to even cry, I turned my fingers to my gullet, not seeking thinness as Emanuela's exigent ballet academy drove her to, but craving an exorcism.

A headache flowered behind my eyes, thorning down my spine. *The Arum* supped my life like parasitic roots, each night begging me to cut it short, yet I remained in this city and plane of existence both, clinging to the prospect of justice for Ema. *And yet...* sometimes, I thought it easier to drown in sorrow than to crawl with split knees over rubble.

I rose to my feet.

Framed in a tangle of begilded branches, the ensuite mirror desilvered—splotched with darkness like spilled bruises, and upon its pane my own eyes stared back at me, cabochon carnelians, blood from burst capillaries soaking into the snow of my sclerae.

Features like my father, eyes like my mother, yet an ugly, warped creature of my own sort.

I opened the abutting cupboard.

Moonlight tiptoed across the blade of a straight razor. Falco prohibited weapons, so we took whatever protection possible. Light mithridatism came in good use, too—a little of the right poison imparted tolerance. Safety.

Grabbing the razor, I slunk from the ensuite.

Mosaic glass and ceramics assembled my bedchamber into a prison cell, creamy arums blossoming into lights from the foliate ceiling. I'd have thought it beautiful if it were another sphere of reality. If the nameless man who hurt me wasn't asleep in my bed.

I kneeled carefully beside him, skin crawling against the damson silk—paid for by the nobles to whom Falco served us up on a fork.

My eyes tread the man's glowing complexion, far fairer than my *peasant's olive*, hair spadiceous as fine leather. I didn't know his name, but I knew him to be fifteen years my senior.

Too many nights, my sole safety was a dreamless sleep in the empty bathtub cold as a dead bastard's teeth, clutching tulle like a tender lover I was forsaken to never have. Yet there *he* was, his brocade garb littering the floor, jaw soft with sleep, hands smooth from not a day of labour: without a care for his crimes.

I beheld his throat, its beckoning veins, and swallowed thickly, gripping the razor, blade angled away and lifted heavenward.

Rage clawed me open to get out, starved as it sipped my blood and blackened marrow. A Shadow.

*So easy.* One slash, one vengeful caress, and the degenerate would choke. *So easy to kill.*

I trembled as panic rose up my throat.

My eyes crushed shut. *No…*

A whimper deserted me as horror shoved me off the bed and chased me scuttling backwards, my spine knocking a nightstand. Heat flushed my body. Mother was still in my ear; the regime still loomed over me.

If I couldn't even requite myself, how could I possibly bring Emanuela justice? *I will always be too weak. Too afraid.*

Curls tangled in my hooked fingers. *No no* no! *Leave me!*

I had to get out. The Court's sorcery confined me to a single circuit of its vasculature, but I *had* to get *out!*

Forcing myself to my feet, vision a dark tunnel, I slipped on my bloomers, laced my corset, my boots and hitched skirt. With no bandages, I ripped a strip from the bedsheet to bind my open wound, withdrawing a brown satchel from the flower-carved closet beside the window.

Falco forked over little remittance. Whatever I had at any time I either gave to the homeless or bought focaccia with—the Madáma fed us merely watered-down menesta mmaretata soup with its lean meat and tasteless greens. Upon accruing enough coin though, I procured the satchel to house my old skirt, vólto, revolver, and the two playing cards gifted to me by papa.

Slinging the satchel across my chest, I draped a knee-sweeping black cativellu—an Iutulicani shawl gifted to me by Eluisa—over my curls, consulting the timepiece with its stalk-and-leaf hands. *Not yet twenty-three-hundred of díem stelláre.* That elusive luck may befall me yet.

I climbed onto the windowsill and released the sashes hitching my skirt, hems tumbling to my feet.

The black maw of darkness gaped a storey below.

Emanuela's parents, Ignasio Airaldi and Arpineh née Davtyan, fled to Lerrķir upon their daughter's murder, jumping through hoops to flee Vencenza's cage. Not because they didn't care, but because one must always be vigilant when oddities transpire so close to them.

I wondered, too, if my own banishment, if the attempts on my life in the slums, were connected to that hiemal Ammuríre Lunéra night two years ago.

*Father.*

I had no one in this world but him—he could help me make sense of this! I couldn't explain my inkling, couldn't read the writing on the wall, I only knew I had to find him. *Ignasio and Arnipeh were right.* And lower óssium was far too intelligent to not perfuse its peculiar modus operandi with abstruse definitions. One ought to listen if the living flesh of this city tried speaking to them.

Moonglow ran its fingers along the haruspical creases of my palm where water still pooled.

A weight dropped in my gut.

After Ema's demise, I wanted to protect everyone I could, even if I bled for it. How could I leave *The Arum*'s lavìri and the slum's forgotten denizens behind to suffer?

I glanced at the awful man. Innocent people perished, yet reapers like *he* got to go on living in their castles of gilded bone and rotten flesh. *Because* you *were too scared to draw blood.*

I gripped my straight razor and slashed my left palm. Flesh squelched, rupturing with pain. Scarlet dripped into the shadows as if feeding them. Blood promised to *me.*

Emanuela's murder remained without justice, and I would find the key to the kingdom. I had come this far. I had been lured to my fall and forsaken, but I couldn't remain on my knees. *I shall avenge.* However possible. If I could exact retribution for a person I loved, if I could dull the pain of the most downtrodden, it would be enough.

This time, it wouldn't be fear which made me run.

With a deep breath, I hopped off the sill.

The black maw swallowed me.

If I died, at least that would be Nara freed from a blood promise.

# Scene XII

## Ennui

*Giorgianna*

*KNOCKS THRILLED THROUGH THE FRONT DOOR.*

*A kick of pulse to your throat sent you darting down your apartment's corridor, but your chest unravelled when you opened the door to behold a tall man in a swallowtail coat embroidered with constellations like diamonds strewing a cosmic void, his skin fair as buttermilk beside the warm candlelight of yours.*

*"Terrible trek across Vencenza—hardly ever such commotion," mused Ludovico Damiani.*

*"Bon auróra, papa!*[53]*" You threw your arms around your father's slim middle, delight swelling your heart.*

*As if in deliberate malice, footsteps thudded up the spiralling central staircase of the apartment.*

---

[53] *'Good morning, papa!'*

*You clutched your father's lapels on instinct as three men in neat dark uniforms ascended to the circular foyer dipped in cloying light like honey. Capes of smog spilled over their sturdy shoulders to marr the mornglow.*

Legionaries.

*Your heart careened into the cavity of your thorax as they knocked on the door of the opposite flat.*

*A young man in billowing pantaloons and white-black striped waspie cinching a turquoise poet shirt popped out. Fear sluiced his eyes.*

"Signór Arturo Dioli?" *one of the Guards demanded.*

*The young man cracked an awkward smile, faltered, readjusted his puffy beret.* "Y-yes. Is—?"

*Irons clasped his wrists. Locked.*

"You are under arrest on suspicion of treason and conspiracy."

*Goosebumps lifted your skin at the keen of Arturo's wails, his futile pleas, his fight against the shackles availing him nothing but a clobbering across the head, a stomp to his gut when he toppled.*

*Father hid you away in the apartment, and you were moving in an instant, walls flickering until you stood in your bedchamber and rummaged through the sea of crimson cloth stuffed into your wardrobe. Your tremoring fingers disentangled a pair of books you weren't permitted to own. Theologian Pietro Vestri's* 'Devices of Corruption' *and philosopher Gualtiero Savona's* 'Apognosis'.

"Elenedda told you to be rid of those!" *your father exclaimed.*

"They need better sanctuary." *You fleeted to your paper-cluttered office where air lay thick with rose oil and dust, and displaced a wooden plank behind the armoire, slipping the books into the abyss beyond.*

"How did you contrive to hold onto them?" *Bewilderment bracketed your father's tone as he removed his black dómino and lobbia. From the graceful taper of a pointed chin, to cheekbones wide and high as an angular heart, to his lower lip dipping inwards like yours and a nose which curved downward when he smiled, Ludovico Damiani's every facet mirrored you. An orphan since birth, your father knew nothing of his parents, but many a blood singer traced his paternal lineage to northern Yegrika, most of all Tmurt-Asif. So, he took on an unofficial middle name in homage: Lounès. Meagre as that blood coursing through you may or may not have been, the vaguest of foreignness was certainly something kids always noticed on you.*

*But where your eyes rutilated a vulpine amber like your mother's, your father's were the wise depth of leather-bound tomes, his hair likewise—once worn to his hips, yours to braid with his permission, now cut clean and short.*

*You wondered how often your father noticed Mother's complexion, her coily hair, upon your person. How often you were a blade cutting through his heart.*

*A sigh broke your silence as you rose.* "I snuck to the ancient catacombs of the necropolis and hid them in an old grave with all the crumbled bones and powdered teeth for a year and a half after De Tullia's tenure commenced."

*Ten years prior, Governor Crescenzo Zuane De Tullia dispatched his legionaries across Vencenza with the order to eradicate every book deemed treasonous—works on liberatory politics and philosophy, sexology, pre-Empire denominations. Anyone found possessing outlawed titles faced imprisonment. The two you owned were preferentially targeted for their incongruence with the state's creed.*

*The ceruse of alarm painted your father's cheeks.*

"I'm sorry," *you mumbled thinly. Had you—a girl of twelve years, then—been caught committing such suicidal selfishness, the price would not be* yours *to pay, but* your *parents'.*

"Don't be." *Your father simply hugged you.* "I only care that you are alive." *A half-chuckle rumbled through his chest.* "You wouldn't be my blood without scripturient compulsions and reckless abandon."

*You wrapped your arms around him, grateful for his gentle touch, the kindness he learned and never lost.* "No word from the senate apropos of Emanuela's case." *Same thoughts plagued your mind for nearly a quarter of a decade, so you'd lodged yet another request of audience with Grand Judge Giordano Veronesi's judgement tribunal, damn near the thirtieth. Yet a woman's murder was evidently not worth their precious time!*

*Your father's bergamot cologne momentarily opiated you as you added,* "I intend to visit The House of Judgement before work this morning." *You could no longer stand the unending chase—one might as well wait for the sky to turn crimson and the Gods to fall to the earth. Taking up arms yourself remained your only means of attaining justice. If only you knew what the future held.*

*Father pulled away.* "Would you like me to lodge a request on your behalf?"

"No. This justice is mine to seek." *You couldn't let your burden be his.*

*Father studied you with strained lips.*

*Your gaze fled to the ten asterisk-shaped stars pinned on his lapels— five on each side.*

*At age nineteen, soldier brutes caught Ludovico Damiani attempting to take his own life and confined him to an institution. Whilst imprisoned there, a bubbly man named Zorzi gleaned that your father aspired to an astronomer's path, and brought him little stars he wrought from wire, amounting to ten. Father's friends eventually extricated him, but he wore Zorzi's gifts ever since, despite favouring the planets above all. That's why he stopped your mother before she could confine* you *to what she'd dubbed 'a madhouse'. Your father knew the scars such places left.*

"Very well," *he resigned.*

*You hurried to pivot the subject:* "To what do I owe your company?"

"Before I divulge that." *You father retreated, hand brushing the ringlets framing your face, and in his slender fingers appeared a two of stars he twirled with no effort.* "The final three planets in our Seren[54] system are…?"

*Sighing, you raised your arm. Stacked cards materialised in your hand, the sun goddess for papa to see.* "Ananke, Thespika, Lethe."

---

[54] Situated within the distal region of the Panihida Arm of the Zephyrus Vela galaxy, the planetary system of Seren was formed 18–19 billion years ago. Zephyrus Vela itself is a dwarf galaxy named on account of its spiral, windswept appearance, with six arms and a pale blue galactic bulge at its centre. Each arm's nomenclature can be traced to the individual who most thoroughly observed them:

Kýrillos Arm—*Kýrillos Elioú Ayathí;*
Ea-niša Arm—*Kušim Lugalsilâsi Ea-niša;*
Panihida Arm—*Panihida Strŭi'nna Sobol'.*
Tarawele Arm—*Zanga Tarawele;*
Cua-Pa Arm—*Hawj, Cua-Pa;*
Vita Arm—*Guillermo Di Vitis.*

*His cards fluttered like dragonfly wings.* "Which is…?"

*You flicked your cards, sun goddess becoming the six of faces as you switched them too quickly to notice.* "'Inevitability', 'reprieve', 'oblivion'."

*The two of stars in his palm split into triplets.* "And that means…?"

*A clandestine smile cracked your lips.*

"Astronomers are poets, and you ought to quit pretending otherwise." *Your cards vanished as you backpalmed them into your glove pocket.*

"I never pretend." *Ludovico Damiani lifted his chin, flourishing the two of stars triplets in one revolution. The cards transformed into a dried rose, peachy-roseate as morning skies.* Rosa erubesca. *Your herbarium was missing the cultivar, and you recalled telling father as much.*

*He handed the dried blossom to you.*

*You kissed his cheek.* "Why are you here?" *You poked his chest in jest.*

"Caught a spare moment at the observatory and reckoned I'd stop by rather than writing."

*The planets enraptured your father so completely that you hardly saw him. Exchanging letters went a small way to keeping your lives tethered.*

*His lips squeezed together for a heartbeat—the very gesture you picked up on.* "I ought to, moreover, apologise in person for mine not attending 'A Bedlamite's Ballad' to-night."

*Your stomach sank, but you couldn't blame him.* "I understand… Basilio should grant us a week free after this pantomime. I hope you scrape time for yourself." *Your arms crossed.* "You have *much* to explain, yet! This guessing game is far less amusing than you'd think."

"I own I haven't been forthright, but the sheer magnitude of what I must say daunts me; I must ensure I handle everything with proper grace and caution."

*You gestured to your office, its walls mounted with glass frames imprisoning pressed roses, dried and dead in their timeless beauty.* "As good a time as any."

"It's eight hundred hours. You have a House of Judgement to drop by."

*Your eyes rolled.* "Here we go—"

*He held your shoulders.* "This day in two weeks' time." *Remorse flitted behind his eyes, barely a wisp, but you caught it all the same.* "I will answer everything you wish." *He kissed your knuckles.* "I love you, Giorgi."

"I love you too, papa." *Disappointment found you as you squeezed him in a tight hug, then bitterly watched him grab his hat and walk away.*

*Time spent with your father was so horribly rare, and now you might well be destined to wait an eternity until you met again.*

The bloodless moon reigned at its full-bellied peak, by touch studying the carved wood and churrigueresque sandstone of oldtown's eccentric architecture, the sky's obsidian expanse striated with stardust like adularescence.

*Three Suns* stood four blocks northwest of the Solar Square—an Ahǎrla woman's tavèrna fashioned of brick-shaped planks as if a gingerbread house, her Dīmarḍi husband a dockmaster at the wharf just on its porch.

For most citizens of lower Vencenza, The Court of Secrets' bizarre magic was a quotidian anomaly. Took a wrong turn? Get spat out right where you started. Faltered on your step? Enjoy walking in circles. Meanwhile, *my* passage was permitted only along the horseshoe street on which *The Arum* bloomed, and through a narrow alley towards *Three Suns*. Most other *Arum* lavìri landed no better luck—Nara's mysterious barge came to mind.

I dared not enter *Three Suns*—never stopped being wanted—but braved to sit on its sheltered eaves, by a carved window gazing out of its whimsical walls, and listen to the music. Ahǎrla shapar and vargan, Dīmarḍi naqqārāt and ūd: my only lights in the gloom.

But I didn't arbitrarily choose the nights bridging díem stelláre and auróra to come by. Only on those late gloamings did the dark-toned violin spill its songs, each pellucid note glittering as starlight on caliginous waves, potent enough to drown within.

I leaned my temple against the window frame.

I missed the vespers spent in my father's office in our old apartment, far from The Hanging Gardens, before the separation, before De Tullia, filled with armillary spheres and astrolabes, where he would gaze into his telescope and pore over star charts of Ravus' three moons and Genaris' four rings. Where he'd go on his awestruck spiels about the universe and all its tenants, eyes gleaming as if luminaries resided upon the curved planes of his dark irises. Eight-year-old me would sit in a high-backed armchair stitched with sequin constellations and play her cello, never berated for a screech or flat note. Father himself had not played the cello in years, at that point.

He tailored all his shirts himself, sewing forearm sheaths to billowing sleeves with loops to hitch over the middle finger. Not for the fancy of it, but to ensure the cuffs would not ride down and reveal the tally of pale scars notching his arms—enacted unto himself. He caught me harming myself one night a year ago. I anticipated my mother's frantic wrath, but all he did was embrace me like a small child, making me swear I'd never again put a blade to my flesh and draw blood in self-punishment. That's when he showed me his scars.

I never asked for solace, even when wanting it more than anything, so I carried my anguish within my ribs. Within my blood. Alone. Even if it rotted and drowned me.

Now, those vespers dissolved with the dawn of a new age. My only wish was for Ludovico Damiani's voice to never fade with the planets' glimmer.

The violin drew a lingering note like a lover's parting kiss and fell silent.

I hid my vólto's sash beneath a curtain of hair like any good Vencenzanii, pinned the cativellu at the nape of my neck, and hopped off the roof.

First, I needed to seek a gondoa to sail me closer to upper óssium—just north of the Solar Square at least. From there, I could make my way to the Misersi church, then, *finally*, papa's home.

I was dealt a terrible hand. All I could do was play it and hope for the least terrible outcome.

Palming my revolver and straight razor, I stalked into the city's adumbral warrens.

Wind picked up its pace, running through bony vestibules of lower óssium and chasing my bare arms beneath my shawl. Chatter languished as I journeyed closer to *The Arum*, shadows like black tongues lapping away the lambency.

I froze at a junction with a perpendicular snicket. At its terminus, where sibylline darkness bled from the pulsing flesh of walls, two silhouettes swayed as if reflections upon water, one tall, one petite, their bodies clad in trigonic peculiarities.

A different coldness rolled down my skin—acute, auguring.

"ALL WERE ONE."

A gasp broke from me as I staggered sideways.

My flinching eyes scoped the night-deep alley. Empty.

When I glimpsed the snicket again, the silhouettes were gone, and I could swear the darkness retreated.

A shudder wracked me. I would have quickened my pace, perhaps ran, had a warm haze not flooded a wider street up ahead, light splashing off a canal, so I sidled over curiously instead.

On the water bobbed a merchant gondoa, the weight of a large wagon-esque trunk at its stern counteracted by a figurehead at its bow mounted with two faces.

Out of the adjacent building walked an unmasked man with a small barrel in hand. He opened the trunk stacked with crates and baskets.

I catalogued details: no lock on the doors, the vessel marked by no registration cipher or merchant's sigil.

The man shut the trunk. *Now or never.*

I burst out. "Are you bound for upper óssium?"

He started, then eyed me askew. Grey streaked the darkness of his chin-length curls, stern face tan and gently-wrinkled, neck wreathed in innumerable necklaces. "Who's asking?" Mariano imbued his voice's hoarse glumness. *Yes, then.*

"Someone looking for a person."

The man lit a sigarétta, holding it in his mouth as he talked. "What, you want a coachman?"

"The Misersi Quarter is as far as I request. If not, then the Solar Square."

"A fugitive, are you?"

The man's question jolted me, and it was all the answer he needed.

"Sorry, girl." He unfastened the hawser from the mooring bollard and slotted the oar into its fórcola. "Not getting locked up for a lunatic."

I bolted, grabbing the top of the oar. "I'll pay you."

The Court traded only in three currencies: blood, steel, flesh. *Steel* included *coin.*

"*Saints*, why d'you need it so much?"

"Why do *you* have an unlicensed mercantile vessel filled with a sizable stock of goods?" The man's—*smuggler's*—sable eyes flung wide at my riposte. "That could fetch you just as hefty a sentence…" Though I *was* outright harassing a man into complying with a deadly scheme, beggars couldn't be choosers, and I would no longer falter.

"So be it," he grunted. "But I won't aid your escape if crows start getting out shackles."

Exhilaration fluttered through my belly. "Deal!" An expectant look held his face. "Sail me to my destination first," I contended with just enough counterfeit brattiness to render myself too aggravating to argue with.

He puffed smoke and begrudgingly opened the gondoa trunk's door.

I stepped aboard and nestled at the threshold, facing the smuggler. "I'm not *that* variety of stupid."

The man snorted. "Clearly *some* kind of cracked."

"Compromises."

With a head-shake, the smuggler returned to his oar. The gondoa swayed into movement.

I lay my head on my knees.

The morrow was never a promise, not even for the most hopeful.

I didn't hope anymore—knew better.

A deadman had only one place to rest.

# SCENE XIII

## HEIMARMENE

*Giorgianna*

"WAIT!"

The gondoa rocked to a nauseating halt along the arborescent venules.

"*Now* what?" the smuggler huffed, his foothold controlled as a seafarer's.

"That way leads to the Misersi churchyard." I referenced the thinner duct branching a degree left off the presently-tread canal. "The person I'm searching for lives along it! Do you know the passage?"

Seconds passed before the man finally concluded: "Yes."

"Could you get me there?"

He glared askew. "Well you'll hardly get out, will you?" He shoved the oar into the wall to propel the gondoa backwards before directing it into the offshoot.

The vennel cinched so narrow I could almost touch the flanking buildings, the smuggler resorting to half-rowing, half-pushing against the fulvous ancient brickwork to keep moving. Arquated bridges bonded each edifice with its cloven counterpart like star-crossed lovers holding hands, grimy light streaming off barred sills. Sleepy doves congregated upon the nose bridges of faces carved into the entablature beneath the soaring eaves.

Through gaps between the buildings, City Guard boots stomped the flagstone in rows of a dozen, heavy as the pulse of blood in my head.

I tentatively asked the smuggler, "Are you Mariano?" on account of him invoking the Saints—the Holy Martyrs of Sancta Maria elevated to near-godhood upon their execution by the imperial Salvatrici legions centuries ago.

"By my father. Themistoklísi by my mother."

I adjusted my cativellu over my horripilated arms. "Ki lalés Themistoklísika?"

The smuggler's head whipped firmly towards me for the first time along the journey, his face a-gawk. "Pós eséna?"

I lifted a shoulder. "Akadimía.[55]" The tongue of Themistóklis came in good use during a literature course at my alma mater, whilst Asifargazi, Tmurt-Asif's language, proved an implausible study subject irrespective of my wishes.

The man returned to rowing, no end to the winding canal in sight. "Why not leave?" he continued in Themistoklísika. "Why mess with the theurgy and flocks?"

"The lonely world beyond our borders offers no respite," I half-answered.

"*You'd* know, girl, I'm *sure!*"

"Wouldn't be so hasty to assume." Emboldened by the foreignness of our shared language, curiosity prodded my tongue: "This... magic... *hex*... is like a defence against intrusion, as if The Court is self-aware. Living. *Knowing!* Who *did* beget it?"

"Are you *not* knowing?"

I crossed my arms. "Slum folk is astonishingly taciturn."

---

[55] **Translation:**
   'And you speak Themistoklísika?'
   'How [do] *you*?'
   'Academia.'

"They've hardly the wherewithal to seek out these things. To you, it only matters that the sorcery exists, and how to navigate it. But the *rest* of lower óssium?" The man almost-chuckled, melancholy such a heavy dark mantle upon his shoulders. *"They're* the cats-to-be-killed."

"So, *you* are knowing?" I pushed eagerly.

"You're aware of the Empire's last imperator—Mirone Nascimbene Evangelio?"

"Could one be none the wiser?" My scoff bore purest revulsion. "On his uninvited stay in Vencenza well over a hundred years ago, the Salvatrici sovereign endeavoured to *'cleanse'* our city of its *'sullied'* slum populace."

"Kakistocracy like no other." Alike distaste punctuated the smuggler's tone. "He had three 'Everseers'—clairvoyants he employed for their veridic counsel. The third, an enchantress and sibyl, was dubbed *'Cardea the Three-Eyed'*. Upon learning the imperator's intentions, she fled to lower óssium. There, she expended every drop of the azothian energy inside her to lock The Court of Secrets behind thaumaturgy, metamorphosing the purlieu into the labyrinthine lazaretto we know and, evidently, so *dearly* love."

My mind mulled over the revelations like a mill to grain, nourishing my spirit of inquiry.

Azoth, the same totipotent energy which gave rise to the universe, stirred too within the core of each fleshbearer. Yet another humour, capable of differentiating into a complex gamut of magics, from principal to corporeal to sorcerial, when tapped and transmuted into the blood, rendering magic a learned skill barring only a few exceptions.

But that's where it demanded its tithe.

As a humour, azoth was also *life force*, soul—*'pnèuma'*, in Illutèri doctrine—and depleted as a fleshbearer aged until death. The azoth a magic wielder drained from their core could not be replaced unless they were to rob energy from the universe, or somehow through the ingestion of fleshbearer's transmuted blood or magic-soaked flesh. Expending azoth was no different to bleeding oneself. So, magi[56] expired quicker

---

[56] *MAH-jee*; plural of 'magus' (*MAH-goos*); 'mage'.

than non-magi, lifespans of zealous practitioners sometimes severed by *half*.[57]

"Did they recover Cardea's body?" I gave voice.

"If 'body' is the right word." The smuggler hauled his vessel around a protrusion of crumbled stairs before clarifying: "The azoth she unleashed just about torched her, and your body doesn't burn like paper at the singe of it. It burns like *wax*—you *melt* right off your bones. No clue how her remains were even found with soldiers barred from traipsing through oldtown, or what happened then, only that Cardea the Three Eyed was both a saviour and a fiend, depending on how you look at it."

"A saviour," I asserted, hesitation be damned.

"Without her sacrificial azoth locking this place away, you and I'd be pushing up daisies no question."

My eyes snared on a sill a block ahead and my heart jumped. *"There!"*

The smuggler stilled the gondoa where I indicated.

I mounted its trunk to level my shoulders with the rectangular window, the only one along the stretch with a dainty overhanging ledge, and banged on the glass.

Blood thrilled through me as I peered into the cluttered room, scoping the familiar scene: cetalone on the desk, planispheres and skycharts upon the walls, old torquetum beside the long-unplayed cello in the far corner.

"Girl?" I heard the smuggler.

Shushing him, I knocked on the window again. "He is always home at these hours."

Seconds ticked by with no response.

Tension warped my brow as I tried to pull on the frame, surprised when it gave. *"Papa?"* My voice echoed through the tiny apartment smelling of lavender tisane yet silent as a charnel, and my frisson stilled to perturbation.

---

[57] Upon death, azoth contained within a fleshbearer fragments and releases, becoming part of the free azoth in the cosmos. It is then able to reconstitute in any other way at random, both within open *and* closed systems (fleshbearers are *closed* systems wherein azoth is trapped and unable to be freely exchanged; the universe and natural formations *etc.* are *open* systems). Thus, the magnitude of energy and matter in the universe remains constant.

I sat on my haunches atop the trunk, eyes unseeing. In that moment, I realised I'd wanted more than anything to see my father again, to be held by someone I knew loved me after these months of torture. *Why isn't he home?*

"Girl." The smuggler's troubled tones compelled my attention at last. His gaze winced away from my arms to my masked face. "I don't think you should be here."

A pit sank my stomach, and only when the wind swept my shoulders did I grasp the dismay upon his countenance.

Hastily shutting the window, I huddled back into the trunk, hiding my bruised arms beneath my shawl. "The Misersi church is a few blocks onwards. Sail me there."

The smuggler made no jaded commentary, his conduct verging on fretting as he slotted the oar into its fórcola and cleared the remaining stretch of water.

Bustle of people swelled with the lump in my throat.

I disembarked onto a semicircular docking platform paved in griseous masegni, the high walls engirdling it etched with dendritic and almond-shaped patterns and breached by a steep staircase ascending to a piazza.

Coin pouch in hand, I pivoted to the smuggler. "Dél'ì lùtius e vísus benedétti—![58]"

"No," he refused resolutely.

"*No?*" I jolted. "But—"

"You need it more," countered the man. "I'm a tough geezer of the streets. You are a *girl*. Li int: protetje ta'ịl Qạddi.[59]" He propelled his gondoa from the ledge, as if content and *determined* to leave without his share of the bargain.

---

[58] '*Blessings of light and vision*'; a well wish, as well as a very formal greeting.
[59] '*Unto you: Saints' protection*'; Mariano prayer of good luck. In Mariano Faustinian, vowels are accented with a dot either above or below the emphasised vowel depending on letterform.

"No debts!" I tossed the coin pouch into the retreating boat. "*Éroso!*[60]"
With a wave to the bewildered smuggler, I scarpered up the stairs and
stepped back into a city baying for my blood.

The vicinity of *Ettàva ris Sánguinem dél'Aís*—'*Cathedral on [the] Blood
of the Lord*'—served as one of the ten quarters of Vencenza, belonging
to an ethnoreligious Salvatrici minority dubbed 'Misersii' after their
religion, Church of Myseres,[61] who remained in Vencenza following The
Empire's fall one-hundred-twelve years ago.

Unlike Illuteríi,[62] Misersi siblings had no organised Holy Guard, so
kept to their fortified cathedral. Citing Salvatrice's historic oppression of
non-Myseric faiths, The Order of Illutère never permitted the Misersi
purview's expansion, manifesting in the modest dimensions of the
*Ettàva*, itself nascent relative to the vetust behemoth of the Illutèri *Sa
Basílica del Illuterixióne e Benefácio Vísus*.[63]

---

[60] '*Farewell*' in Themistoklísika.

[61] The Church of Myseres, originating from the È'thaliél iridites of Ithilwen, is a
monotheistic faith worshipping Ným'nathír ('*All-Seer*' in Ithilweni)—referred to as
[*the*] *Lord*—along with multitudinous prophets and messengers called '*Mys'erathèla*'
('Truth-Searchers'), a name also applied to Ithilweni theologians and votaries. The
Myseric holy book, Iś'thaït (literally '*Truth*' in Ithilweni), was written by
Mys'erathèla Naére Lýthienne Rýl'laè Nuéleth, God's first messenger. In Ithilwen,
the regnant King is considered an extension of God and revered accordingly. Angels,
Saints, *etc.*, are not present in Myseric theology.

Due to The Church of Myseres being so ubiquitous, with practising non-iridite
communities almost all across Gethlem, the above terminology differs by language,
and denominations, syncretisms, and sects exist (topically: the Misersii of northern
Vencenza).

The symbol of the Church of Myseres is an almond and its tree, symbolising
rebirth and nourishment. Almond fruits are attributed to God's blessings, the tree
itself representing God's persistence on earth.

[62] Votaries of the church. Not to be confused with *Illutọríi*—the Holy Guard.

[63] '*The Basilica of Enlightenment and Bless'ed Vision*'.

Above the rose windows of the central church tower, white and manueline as carved selenite, a timepiece proclaimed the first hour of díem auróra, yet the churchyard still scintillated with merchants, meandering flâneurs, skittering children. Crow-masked officéri, perched on their wretched posts—outcrops of the piazza elevated to pedestals—scrutinised the citizenry lest a stray chuckle or outburst escape.

My heart beat head-whirlingly shallow as I cleaved to the shadows.

At the vast central fountain, a lonesome bard hid behind a long-nosed zánni, strumming his mandolin and singing a lugubrious dirge. A group of onlookers sketched a hemicircle around him. *Sa Nóba Giustíca* forbade music and dance, barcarólae no longer echoing along the canals except in sorrowful laments.

An unpeopled passageway limned in alchemy's cyanotic radiance swallowed me. Flowerpots and colourful organdie beset tiny balconets of windows blinking from high up towards the pediments. Shadowy alcoves tucked into the brick walls concealed doors.

Eyes split open in the living walls. Swivelling. Watching. *Knowing.*

Voices meandered up the path from an offshoot.

Dread speared my gut when I peeked around the bend and descried the dark armour and darker capes of City Guards.

'*Thirty-six wanted… four on trial… unacceptable.*'

'*Will dance… association… playwright… other two.*'

The thump in my ears claimed the men's voices. *Run.*

I tried the knob on the door tucked into a recess.

Beyond its threshold, water gleamed like black pearls, tossing restlessly as the vengeful dead.

My eyes roved the nitid crests as if they would write out answers for me, and when I gazed down, I could sense my own reflection, dark and distorted.

Tiny fingers gripped my elbow.

I yelped, pivoting, razor in fist.

Abyssal black eyes ingested me. "SHE SHALL WEAR MANY FACES;" a woman's voice; a whisper percolating my bones, "ONE OF MANY IS UPON HER." A stark white vólto, lips aureate, temples moulded into black swirls of ram horns. "WHEN HER SKIN IS TORN, STITCHED LIKE A MARIONETTE,

HAIR WOVEN INTO THREAD ANEW, WILL SHE, UPON THAT SILVER LOOKING, SEE HER FACE?"

I wrenched myself free, edges of my vision blurring as I doubled back. When I looked left, I stared down the street I'd eavesdropped on, but the soldiers had vanished.

"CROWS DON'T RECEIVE INVITATIONS." The crepitant murmur of a second voice. Male.

I took in the strangers, one tall; one petite, their bodies draped in misshapen triangles, pantaloons campanular, feet hiding within incarnadine winklepickers.

"I saw you in the slums." My body rebelled against every instinct to run. "Who are you?"

"DOES SHE KNOW NOT?" the man intoned. "WE ARE THE VESSELS OF THE MANY FACES' DIVINE SIMULACRUM, TASKED WITH A MISSION TO COMPLETE UPON THIS FACELESS CIRCLE."

Darkness trickled like water between cobbles and panes, through my fingers, my hair—an algid amnion enveloping my corporeality, vast and atavistic. And a darker Shadow in my psyche *hungered*.

"WE ARE THE MAGNUM OPUS OF THE GODS' CHILD," the woman whispered. "ALL WERE ONE AND WILL BE AGAIN, FOR THE THIRD EYE BLINKS. THE SEVERANCE FROM REBIRTH IN ILLIMITABILITY IS MERELY AN AMNIOTIC MEMBRANE PREGNABLE ORBITALLY."

"Why are you stalking me?"

Two spoke as one: "FIND HIDDEN WORDS SPAT BY THE BLEST TO THIS PLANE FROM THE CELESTIAL LAZULUM, SENTENCED TO QUIETUS BENEATH THE SOFFITS OF A SUZERAIN'S KEEP. THE OVERLORD SHALL BE DEFIED—IMPART SUCCOUR. FORGET NOT THE THAT WHICH YOU WOULD RATHER SO."

A bead of cold sweat rolled down the notches of my spine.

"BLOOD DOES NOT WASH OFF." Those words impaled the soul confined within my carnate chrysalis, the unhealable wound left behind haemorrhaging darkness into my marrow.

Caliginous waters deforming the sphere retreated like a tide and I stood upon the pale churchyard again. The lonesome bard with his zánni and mandolin sang by the central fountain still, his circle of onlookers packed in like a mass grave.

He lifted his head to warble the final notes, and the audience applauded. Always quiet. Always restrained.

Yet a drum pounded in my ribs, my fingers itching to fidget. *Something is wrong.*

As the crowd dissipated, and the bard set aside his mandolin, one onlooker approached, tapping his shoulder.

The musician turned.

Steel ignited bright as a newborn flame in the onlooker's hands—a sword cleaving flesh, severing spine. The bard's head arced the air and *thunked* onto the cobbles like a cork off a wine bottle, blood bursting in slick scarlet spurts from his stump of a throat.

The killer kicked the musician's decapitated corpse into the fountain. Water turned to claret.

The churchyard erupted into bedlam.

Razor never unhanded, I gripped my skirt and bolted for the widest avenue—the hardest to blockade.

Figures sprung from peoples' shadows, their velvet masks, black and mouthless, circling the centre of their faces, eyes round as insect orbs. *Morettae.* The piazza dripped red at their blades, ossíi slumping to their knees with opened throats and rendered guts.

Crossbow bolts released by legionaries tore through.

*So many.* Morettae were feared and reviled, yet their ochlocratic hordes clogged every nook, every entrance, every escape.

Bells tolled in the *Ettàva* as I scraped my way from the frenzied tangle of limbs towards the piazza's edge.

Rough hands grabbed and hurled me against the fortification of the church. Sharp pain rooted into my skull, light sharding across my field.

I shoved myself to sit up, swung my razor. Metal parted my assailant's calf. *Moretta!* He grunted against the mask flushed to his face, stunned long enough for me to clamber up. He slashed with an ugly dagger before I could turn tail.

A sharp prong of pain cut from my lungs a scream. Flesh of my forearm parted and spewed.

The Moretta kicked me in the abdomen. I doubled back.

A garrotte clasped my throat.

I scratched at the thin rope as air leached from my lungs. Laboured rasps seared my throat. Bones bruised against my corset.

My legs buckled, my sagging weight only tightening the noose. Tears stung my eyes from pressure. Agony. Helplessness. The voice of my thoughts silenced by a city that decried it.

All sound electrified into a screech, nothing and all at once.

And the rope loosened.

My muscles quivered as air flooded my lungs and I dropped to the masegni, launching into a coughing fit painful enough to bring up blood, I was sure.

A smallsword swung for me.

I lurched sideways.

The attacking Moretta swayed and fell to the stone heavily as a sack of sand, cheek splitting on impact like overripe tomatoes. A dart sat lodged in the nape of their neck.

My feet stumbled over the masker who had wielded the garotte—now sprawled unconscious with a matching dart under his ear.

A rope-anchored grappling hook flitted towards a lookout in the fortification, a nimble silhouette descending fast towards the street and crashing feet-first into one of two oncoming Morettae.

"Evening, signóri. Apologies," a young man dressed in cherry-red and shamrock-green harlequin overalls quipped behind the profusely-blushing smile of a giulláre, punching the second Moretta in the diaphragm with brass knuckles.

My panic-blurred vision descried an identical second jester helping me upright.

A murder of crows flew around the corner.

"*Exeunt!*" the first jester called.

The second snatched my wrist and hurdled after the first.

Sickness clambered up my throat with each swerve and zigzag as the pair pulled me through buildings and past a distortion of colours and people and music like a tumble down a frightening dream of a psychedelic hellscape before staggering to an abrupt stop in a tiny ginnel.

I dropped to my knees, gulping down air.

"Are you all right?" The second jester's voice, raspy and soft, brimmed with concern.

My head lifted, and I winced at the sight of two smiling harlequins looming over me. "It's liveable." My voice tore like paper as I pulled myself on my feet, still coughing. Both my straight razor and cativellu were lost to the fray, but my satchel remained.

The first jester reached under his hood and tugged the giullàre free to reveal sylphic features swart and warm as ochre. "Abậ's[64] people ought to invest in a Holy Guard of their own." His voice was smoother, sharper.

"Well, we're safe now." The second jester unmasked, and I realised their gangling builds and outlawed costumes were the *least* of their similarities. From the deep brownness of their skin to the keen acuity in their eyes, to their soft and rounded noses, they mirrored each other precisely, only a pale scar on the first twin's chin for distinction. "I'm Eligio, by the by," the second added with a dimpled smile, pointing to the brother with the scar. "That's Lissandri."

A frown plucked my brows. "Where am I?"

Lissandri shrugged. "Solar Square's a few blocks east."

My gut cooled. "What?" *Cardea's azoth played its wretched tricks.* "How will I get back to upper óssium?" Outside The Court of Secrets, oldtown's innards were as good as uncharted territory to me. My route to *Three Suns* never passed Solar Square, so I couldn't use it as a vantage point.

Lissandri side-eyed me. "What d'you need it for?"

"I simply do!" I bristled.

"Hey, it's fine." Eligio's slim hand touched my shoulder, sending my body recoiling with tension. "We could help you once daylight comes? But it's *far* past midnight now and you are hurt. *Rest* is what you need."

I shrouded my arms in curls. "What's it to *you*?"

"Extending humanity to someone who's clearly been denied it." Eligio's mild eyes, brown like polished acorns, were so genuine I

---

[64] *AAH-bah*; 'father' in Âbạdil.

almost didn't want to believe anymore that such unveiled kindness could exist. "We live in *The Sunrise*, if you know that old theatre." I didn't. "There're spare rooms aplenty."

Apprehension found a spot to nestle amid the knot in my middle. "A catch?"

Eligio put his palms up. "No catch, swear."

I squinted.

"I mean," Lissandri pulled a wry face, "your alternative is Vencenza's oldtown with crows and crooks crawling about." For that, he received Eligio's light smack on the arm.

Hesitation spiked me, but Lissandri was right. I knew the worst of this city. And the truth was that I got into a *stranger's gondoa* trusting him to keep his word.

I squeezed my lips and nodded to Eligio.

We arrived at the theatre's rear entrance, a wide canal rippling below and a single face smiling poignantly from above the door as it wept aurulent tears.

*The Sunrise...* One of Gherardo De Luco's hearts![65] *How was it permitted to remain?* Every monument depicting smiling faces had been destroyed upon De Tullia's inauguration.

---

[65] Perhaps the most influential figure in Vencenzani history was architect and playwright Gherardo De Luco, who, *c*. 1010-9 ZE, proposed the construction of six theatres starting at the shore of the Vault of Faces and tracing a crescentic shape inland, their names following the reverse solar cycle of the day: *The Sea Star*, *The Crescent*, *The Nox*, *The Eventide*, *The Zenith*, *The Sunrise*. Initially, this idea was rejected, but with the change of power eight years later, Imperator Axmenrun⁺ Tanaquil Nurtia agreed to take on De Luco's proposition and the project was officially undertaken, overlooked by De Luco until his death eighteen years later (*c*. 1036-9 ZE) at the age of 49 from severe bacterial pneumonia. He never got to see his theatres finished in their entirety. The day of his birth, 5-9-987-9 ZE, is commemorated by Vencenzanii.

Past the wood-dressed hallway, curtains veiled a dark vestibule ornamented with what seemed to be glass garlands. I gathered we were offstage right.

Lissandri switched on the alchemy, illuminating the curtains into an elysian canvas of blushing peach, necklaces of aureate crystal twinkling like a dawn's sunblinks.

I pulled my mask free, drinking in the sight.

Lissandri yawned, "I'll declare our return and retrieve bandages," slipping beneath the heavenly drapes.

Eligio tugged off his hood. "Why the wandering?" Milk chocolate curls spilled over his brow and shoulders in a fluffy halo, a tad longer than his brother's.

"A tale fit for a madman's sonnet." I hissed at the fresh gash throbbing on my forearm. "Though, I recall being accused of treason and denounced as a traitor."

He chuckled, slipping out of his giulláre suit. "You and I both." Flowing shalwar and a sage-green kamiz adorned down the chest with rich geometric stitchwork swathed his willowy frame.

'...*didn't know where the bolts live.*' Gold-bell tones chimed from the stage, heralding a Vilhelmian accent.

'*Not in the crockery cupboard!*' retorted Lissandri.

'*I thought they'd be safe in the cups—wouldn't roll away.*'

'*I've got a tool box, donkey.*'

A gangly girl emerged from the blear luminance of the stage. "You don't let me near it!" Freckles sprinkled her rosy-cream skin all over like cinnamon on panna cotta, her right eye blue as a tarn and the left a drop of golden honey, downturned and wide apart on her round face. A puffy saffron dress circled her knobby knees, her ginger hair woven into warbraids. *Cannot be much older than fifteen.*

---

In 1703, 53 years following the 1650 fall of the Faustinian Empire, 10th Governor of Vencenza, Anacleto Di Losna, had the theatres renovated to reflect Vencenza's newly-regained freedom.

[†] In Faustinian, the letter '*x*' is pronounced '*kh*' except at the end of a word wherein it becomes '*ks*'.

Eligio grinned. "Lissandri giving you a hard time, Rosalia?"

She pulled a face. "When's he *not*?"

Lissandri returned the gesture. He'd shed his costume too, now dressed in a tan worker's blouse and loose umber pantaloons embellished with clockwork and suspenders. "That bad boy needs stitches, methinks," he referenced my gash.

Rosalia's tepid eyes circled to me. "And *you* are?"

"We seem eternally cursed to crash into each other, vólto."

My blood thickened and froze. *That voice…*

I whirled around, beholding an eldritch stain against a backdrop of celestial light.

Sharp lips cut into a switchblade smile. "Déjà vu?"

# Scene XIV

## Memento Vivere

*Giorgianna*

MY EYES BLEW TO CIRCLES.

"*No…*" I retreated, hair standing on end. "What is this?"

"Cesare, if it pleases you." The Bauta removed his tricorn. *He lives here…* "Little over a couple hours passed since you poisoned me—only *just* got full muscular sensation back."

"*Giulia* poisoned you," I corrected. "On my behalf."

He *tsk'd*, mockery wilting his arched brows. "Couldn't make the kill yourself, princess?"

My lips hooked into a scowl. "Want a repeat attempt?"

His eyes thinned to knife cuts. "I dare you."

Eligio gawked, head darting between us. "I beg your pardon, *poison*?"

Lissandri nodded at me. "I've been tempted to, as well."

"*Woah!*" exclaimed Eligio, arms thrown up. "Explain?"

"Not yet." Cesare's tone hardened, his gaze affixing the twins. "Call this in poor taste, but you'd kill me if I withheld." They tensed up. "The *Curios*. It's ransacked to oblivion."

"*What?*" exclaimed Lissandri, pupils shrunken to specks.

"Micheletto[66] said it's the legions' doing. About twenty City Guards barged in barely an hour ago and turned the place on its head."

"Are mạti[67] and ạbậ safe?" cried Eligio. "Please say they are!" He clutched Cesare's shoulders, eyes frantic.

"*Hey!* Listen!" Cesare stilled Eligio's wrists. "They're unharmed. Legionaries didn't touch them."

"We need to go," declared Lissandri, already marching for the door. Cesare followed.

Eligio dashed after the resolute pair before halting and turning to Rosalia and me. "Come with us." His voice and hands shook.

I blinked but trailed them down the stairs and out to the city despite my stupefaction. When wind skimmed my cheeks, I recalled I no longer wore my vólto. "What's going on?"

Rosalia shuffled over. "*Commegnos' Curios* is a jewellery parlour of Eli and Andri's parents in the Solar Square. Commegno is their papo's surname—Micheletto, but their *mamo*, Lậlẹn's,[68] is—well, *was*—Gangozạr Jậlbạni." The girl appeared entirely unperturbed. "*Err*—I mean, I think 'Gangozạr' is like a patronym?"

Cesare had moved to the vanguard as we plodded behind a row of contiguous buildings parallel to the wide canal running posterior to *The Sunrise*, the alchemy-touched tenebrosity hazy and magical as gold-speckled gossamer in the night, stars dissolving upon watery crests. I couldn't name the last time I thought nighttime to be beautiful, and, with that, unease crept under my skin again.

We slipped into a needle-thin twitchell. Towards its end, where the spiced redolence of honey tzípulas and a virànte's[69] song sweetened the

---

[66] *mee-keh-LET-toh*

[67] *MAAH-tee*; 'mother' in Âbạdil.

[68] *lah-LEHN*

[69] A Faustinian stringed instrument resembling (*and functioning as*) a hybrid of a mandolin and a viola.

backish canal air, Cesare opened a door tucked within bisque stone embellished by coloured glass. A bell's chime marked our entrance.

Cesare hadn't exaggerated with 'ransacked to oblivion'.

Vitrines and chiffoniers lay smashed, cabinet doors hanging off hinges and carpet littered as if with confetti by shattered crystal, sparkling gemstones, cufflinks, ornate necklaces and lockets, jewel-engraved music boxes and miniature figurines.

A large woman rushed from a chamber behind the counter, her skin copper-dark and brown eyes chatoyant as a doe's. Lâlęn, I assumed. Covered by iridine chiffon, tight coils reached her chin, billowing shalwar spilling from beneath her periwinkle dress embroidered with abhala bharat mirrorwork and garlanded with pearl and chalcedony.

"*Micheletto!*" she called in lachrymose tones towards a monstrously steep staircase to the second floor. "They're here!"

A tall man with familiar acorn eyes hurried down, his trousers dark and slippers embellished florately, a green plaid vest buttoned over his white linen shirt and reedy shoulders draped by a small floral shawl. Buttercups tacked his wide-brim hat, smooth cinnamon hair beneath streaked with grey. Between the attire and Lissandri's quip about their 'ʼabậ's people', I figured Micheletto must be Misersi. His pince-nez reminded me of Lucrezia. Of a gone time.

The twins dashed to their parents, embracing them tight and plunging into a babel.

I secretly observed, noting that Lissandri was lemon-bitter to Eligio's vanilla-sweet like Lâlęn was the carefree dance to Micheletto's brooding hum, the twins' every feature so clearly moulded from their parents.

My lips hid into a taut line, fingers fidgeting with my curls as my heart balled up. As I was struck once more with my own aching loneliness.

"Were either of you harmed?" Eligio questioned.

Lâlęn squeezed his cheeks, pulling a gloomy smile. "*We're* all right. The place isn't."

"What *happened*?" pothered Lissandri.

Micheletto pushed up his glasses. "A raid? Can't be sure. Must've been a good twenty Guards in here. They didn't seem to be *looking* for anything, mind."

Legionaries rarely committed such violations without reason, no matter how backward, but I hadn't been in the óssium proper for three months. *Everything is unravelling…* I wondered if this was connected to the Moretta attack near the *Ettàva*. Did the legionaries suspect something of the Commegnos? Perhaps the couple was aware of The Bauta's modus operandi, and who was to say *he* had no links to The Morettae? The twins *had* been at the *Ettàva* to-night…

When I emerged from my ruminations, I found Lâlęn's eyes on me, a beam like summer sun scattered through raindrops limning her soft face. "We have guests." She laced her fingers together, eagerly looking to her sons.

"Giorgianna." My lips relinquished a halting smile as I clasped my hands over my heart and dipped my chin in a Vencenzani bow.

Micheletto mirrored me. "Our doors are always open to fugitives."

Anxious heat spiked me. Though it was true, the thought still harrowed.

Lâlęn's expression shifted. "Do you need help, chamrộk?[70]"

I grew ill.

The woman held my wrists in her warm hands, scrutinising my cut and bruises. "You need something for this immediately!"

"It's nothing," I urged frantically. "Really, I've dealt with worse, don't—"

"Nonsense!" Her fingers tightened and my gorge rose. "You never know what infect—"

"*Let me go!*" I tore away, clutching my own arms. "Please don't hurt me." My voice came weak. I hated how low fear stomped me, reminding me of my mother's hand fan, of Falco's whip.

"Hey…" Eligio stepped towards me as if to a rabid fox. "I promise you are safe here."

"No." I hurriedly collected myself. "Forgive the offence." I pinned straight my spine and steeled my shoulders the way I would for Mother, patting down my hair. "That was not appropriate conduct, especially with

---

[70] *chahm-ROHK*; 'dear' in Âbạdil.

such timing—" Rosalia rammed into me with a yowl, her foot having twisted on a rogue bead of honey calcite.

I helped the girl regain balance, catching sight of something pinned beneath a jade periapt. We acknowledged it simultaneously and dug up a small note.

"What is it?" queried Cesare.

Rosalia handed it to him, much to my pique.

Everyone hovered around to see.

He read aloud, "'*Whatever you surmise to know, I trust you to ensure. Carry out all imperatives; make use of your condottiéri if judged necessary. No recompense until the venture's completion.*' Signed—" Lâlẹn smacked a hand over her mouth. "'*Governor C. Z. De Tullia*'." The name shuddered the edifice like cannon fire. "The Governor exploiting condottiéri to outsource his dirty work…" Cesare idly tapped his gold nose ring. "Riveting."

*Condottiéri*… Even in the slums there were hardly whispers of them, certainly no 'cadre'—condottiére party—that *I'd* heard of. But I was no longer so naïve as to believe there were none.

> '*You are naïve because you … believe a violent … man could listen to reason.*'

My vision shuddered in recollection. In rage.

> '*Bet it was your most beloathed.*'

He was. All my misfortune sprung from The Bauta—my nemesis in every possible world. The First Cause of all my pain.

The fulgid hazel of Cesare's eyes burned my retinae, and that's when I realised I'd stared daggers at him. *If only it could draw blood.*

I grinded my teeth, looking away.

"The Governor tipping off Guards to attack peaceful establishments?" Micheletto scratched his stubble. "Troubling."

Cesare clicked his tongue. "And *fortuitous* that it happened to be *this* one." Scorn whetted his tone.

"Cesare, what are you implying?" whimpered Lâlẹn.

"It would take an astronomical halfwit to *sign* something this incriminating, let *alone* hand it to *patrolling crows* to keep hold of when the senate *has* couriers. I conjecture this letter was left *to* be found."

My eyebrows sewed. "What does anyone achieve by that?"

"*I* cannot answer that." Cesare's silver earring chimed at the shake of his head. "But that's easy enough to rectify."

I wanted to rip out his throat for his blasé tone.

He walked in one darkness with this city's bones; knew precisely where to sink his blade into its flesh. Knowing—*that's* what he possessed. All but illimitable.

I was immured, fallen and trapped, yet my desire for cognisance grew more throat-slitting with every wasted heartbeat. I'd dig my nails into myself and pull out my own insides before I admitted aloud that Cesare, The Bauta, *my nemesis in every possible world*, was everything my Shadow longed to be.

But my Shadow longed to be more. *Illimitable.*

"Stay with friends until at least the day after the assembly—safety's sake." Cesare's voice blinded my mind's eye. "I've informed my vicinal contacts of the incident; your passage is safe." His fingers, lithe as a musician's, toyed with the crotal bell on his hoop, then adjusted his nose ring once more. *Always so fidgety.* A frown teased my brow. *His fingertips are callused...* "I've errands to run in the óssium and Antrum before midday regarding the assembly."

My curiosity stirred. *The assembly...* Months ago, the Governor had announced a city-wide congregation within the walls of the ministerial house on a date swiftly approaching: this díem zenítis. *That's surely what he speaks of!* His bold turn of phrase in the Commegnos' presence undoubtedly confirmed they knew of his machinations. But... '*antrum*'...? *What in the world is he talking about?*

Micheletto held his wife. "Thank you for everything, as always. Lord's blessings."

Words of farewell passed among us as we routed for the front door, the twins and their parents exchanging embraces and kisses whilst Cesare sneakily dodged Lâlẹn's hug.

I dithered a step behind before turning to the Commegnos. "Truly, I am *so* sorry. My reaction to your kindness was beyond improper—"

"Bosh!" Micheletto waved a hand. "No harm done."

Lâlẹn tucked curls from my face. "I can see you've suffered, weathered it bravely. But I hope you know none of it is your fault, whatever it is. You deserve peace."

'*Some girls are born to suffer.*'

My skin tightened at the recollection, but the Commegnos' words heated my chest like firelight.

In The Court's slums, every tender word could mask venomous turpitude and every kind gesture owed a due, hence the blood currency. So quickly, I had forgotten what it meant to not glance over my shoulder at every moment. I wasn't acquainted with warmth anymore.

"Is all well?" Eligio's soft tones sounded beside me.

Lâlẹn smiled. "Yes. Tậe minnạt vậrạn.[71] Now go! Take care."

The couple shooed us off the porch under the shade of the Square's encircling cloisters.

A sun mosaic embossed the sweeping leagues of sandstone, longer rays emanating towards the feeding streets from a centre upon which stood a hideous black strappado: an instrument of torture quite literally stomping on the Gods—those faint demarcations of the Divine Faces engraving the stone. The eleven eyes of The Watcher, the slumbering Thinker with an open third eye for lips, the gaping mouth and blank-yet-watching eyes of The Speaker.

Dread pricked my skin. *Rule by fear.*

Arms folded and hands fisted, I impelled my attention away.

A watchmaker adjoined *Commegnos' Curios*; bibelots and cuckoo clocks displayed in the vitrines briefly stole Lissandri's attention.

---

[71] A deep '*thank you*' in Âbạdil.

I stuck by Rosalia, standing aloof of the men as they turned back into the oldtown warrens. *I disregarded* so *many childhood lessons in the past few hours…*

"Are you Vilhelmian?" I asked the girl to stave off my trepidation.

"Yes!" Rosalia hopped along the cobbles like stepping stones. "Flodalfolken.[72] I lived in Ellinor with mamo and papo until I was eleven—not too long before they were taken." Her feather-light words launched a boulder square into my middle.

Eligio passed back. "Rosa—"

"Oh shush!" She swatted her hand at him. "We were here on holiday four years ago—mamo was a milliner and *adored* Vencenzani fashion! Anyways, my papo loved to laugh, and *that* got him—and mamo—arrested." Her breezy tone only stoked my trepidation. "I ran, stumbling into *Commegnos' Curios*, and—*actually*, I lived with the twins' parents for *aaa*ges. Only moved to *The Sunrise* maybe a couple weeks ago?"

The city itself seemed to stand still as a funeral, Cesare and the twins' shoulders rigid, their chatter silenced.

My mouth gaped for speech. "I'm so sorry…" Words proved too unwieldy to string together—how *could* you, when even children weren't safe under this vile authority?

Rosalia shrugged, picking a spider off the croceous frills of her dress. "We never want them to, but tragedies play out. And sometimes they remind us to live."

The twins exchanged woebegone glances, sharing them with us. Cesare didn't waver from his dutiful post at the vanguard.

Pain bled like a contusion into my heart.

*My* immemorial tragedy played out like an unhealing wound, defiling my veins until only bloodletting could cleanse me. *Nothing* could cleanse me. For no two tragedies played an indistinguishable course.

Rosalia cupped the spider in her palms, and crushed it.

*And sometimes they remind us to die.*

---

[72] Demonym of Flodalfolk, the largest ethnic group of Vilhelm, the other two being Bargpafolk and Kappfolk.

# Scene XV

## Pronoia

*Giorgianna*

WE ENTERED *THE SUNRISE* from the rear, offstage right.

The lights flickered on, and we froze, eyes soldered to two maskless intruders. One crow-haired, one blond. Both cloaked in hangman's black.

Revolvers aimed their hollow sockets at us.

A cold sweat took me. *My attackers the night of 'A Bedlamite's Ballad' three months ago…*

"What do *you* want?" piped up Lissandri as Cesare shoved us all behind himself. Eligio grabbed onto his brother, hissing for silence.

Counterfeit rue dented the toothy man's wan brow. "Be not so callous to a former colleague. You wound me." ***Boom!***

Glass sprayed from an overhanging light in a glistening hail, the scorched tar of alchemy detonating in the air.

I shielded Rosalia as screams surged, as shards impaled the floor.

The toothy man's laugh creaked like rusty hinges, his raptor eyes forcing themselves upon mine. "I remember *you*, little shrew."

Gooseflesh crawled on me as I held the girl tighter as if I could hide her in my shadow. "Do *you*, No Tongue?" A nod from the flaxen-haired man. "No Tongue doesn't talk much. The Minister of Dominion had his tongue out for our loyalty." His long head canted. "How far would *you* be willing to go to not get caught?"

"Are you threatening me?" I sneered despite myself.

"Yes," Cesare answered for the man. "What *loyalty*, Davide?[73]"

No Tongue opened the sack slung over his shoulder and passed an object from it to Davide.

The object was The Bauta's mask.

My eyes bore into Cesare's back. *Harbinger of fucking misfortune!*

Davide tossed the bàuta to him. "I like keeping you motivated," he crooned, No Tongue cocking his gun in a threatening reminder.

Cesare clicked his tongue. "How much did you tell your new master?"

"None save that I had the means to capture you." *Willing to aid a man who wishes him equally dead.*

"Then why, humour me, did you not bring his birdbrained goons along?"

"Too simple. Not to *mention* the intermediates."

"You want me to hand myself over so you may win some favour with your Lord of Bless'ed Dominion, is that it?"

"Not at all!" Davide waved about his gun. "I'd like to propose a *game*, is all."

A groan from Cesare. "*Saints*, you people are a menace."

Davide sighed. "I remember your first days at the theatre with crystal clarity, you know. I could've *sworn* you were a girl. So nubile, so driven, yet so hopelessly broken. How you'd flinch at the slightest suggestion of touch, the way Paolo shielded you. Unattainable little doll." '*Walking dolly coming out to play?*' I sickened as his speech oozed on, "Those glassy eyes, the satiny hair, the pretty pictures etched into your lean body. You were *such* the sight to admire."

I almost retched; Davide looked easily two decades Cesare's senior.

---

[73] *DAH-vee-deh*

"Are you done recounting your perverted dreams of me?" Cesare spoke with unnerving nonchalance.

Davide snickered. "I like you. You make this city *so* fun. But I have a duty to my Governor, and that is a paradox I grapple to resolve. So, I offer *this*: let me walk alive—*just* me—and I'll leave this theatre alone. The Governor will never hear of to-night, and your precious *Sunrise* can remain your sanctuary like this *neeever* happened. Instead, Vencenza's bones can be our chessboard. Crows considered, of course."

"Why should your word be anything but worthless to me?" bit Cesare.

Thin lips peeled from Davide's grotesque fangs as he drew a switchblade from his belt, a crooked snaggletooth of a metal hunk, and sliced his own palm, iron singing in harmony with splitting skin. He held his arm out, flexing his fingers as if squeezing an overripe drupe, and haem dripped onto the floor, an anointment. "A blood promise." *Indelible as scars.*

Silence thumped with my heart.

"Just you?"

I gawked at Cesare. He couldn't possibly consider signing away his life like that!

A shallow nod from Davide. "Just me. And *think*: if you kill me to-day, my boys—" he looked up "—will be *riiight* on their way to inform my *Lord of Bless'ed Dominion* of your safe haven, and all shall be put to the pyre."

The smell of brewing violence distilled in the air as Cesare unsheathed from his hip baldric a stilétto I recognised, wrapping his right hand tightly around the blade and pulling it through without a wince. Crimson steeped the refulgent steel, the sapphire pommel of the cruciform hilt a glinting indigo-violet orb. "Who am I to refuse?"

He darted for Davide.

No Tongue's bullets tore up the walls and floors until his revolver ticked. Empty.

Rosalia shrieked into my chest. My arms squeezed around her as Eligio pulled us back.

Cesare's blades bound with Davide's, Lissandri skidding across the stage with brass knuckles drawn, No Tongue in pursuit.

Cesare kicked Davide's gut, forsaking his chance to kill, instead lunging for No Tongue. He caught his collar and yanked him back seconds before his misericorde would've impaled Lissandri, driving a stilétto under the blond's sternum, lethal blade angled towards the heart, before tearing downward to decant the blood from his belly like wine.

Lissandri scuttled backwards to us on all fours.

Cesare turned quick as silver, his dagger meeting Davide's with a plangent *ding*.

"*Ah-ah*." Davide grinned ear to ear. "Remember what we promised with."

Cesare scowled, eyes aflame, no doubt with all his heart wishing to cut Davide's out. "Get out before I forget." He shoved Davide's blade hard enough for the toothy man to stumble.

Davide cloaked his close-cropped hair and sauntered to No Tongue's corpse. All the while, Cesare circled, fluid as fire, never allowing his opponent out of sight.

"Shame," mused Davide. "I *miss* this place. But a deal's a deal." He hauled No Tongue onto his shoulder, unmoved by the blond's guts leaking down his chest. "Walk carefully, Bauta." He granted Cesare a jagged grin, but when he made to depart by the rear doors, he took pause, and his final glance hooked like rusted hinges into *me*. "Cardea served you well, shrew. Her azoth is a relic of a sorcerer possessing an illimitable capacity for transmutation—unimpeded by that pesky little occlusion in the fleshbearing nous. *Transcendental*, perhaps." A screechy chuckle. "Where do you think her 'Three-Eyed' epithet stems from?"

Tremors rolled down my limbs when the door shut. When the sibylline verses of those masked stalkers writhed through my psyche anew: '*...severance from rebirth in illimitability is merely an amniotic membrane pregnable orbitally.*'

When my mind's eye blinded, I saw fields of crimson slathering the shredded floorboards—a grisly poppy meadow, blood's dizzying stench drenching the air with an abattoir's decay. Rosalia, nearly green at the sight, hid behind the curtains, soothed by Eligio.

Cesare rushed to our huddle. "Is everyone all right?"

"Are *you*?" Lissandri gestured to Cesare's hand.

"Don't worry about me," dismissed Cesare, hooking his arms around the twins' shoulders and pressing their foreheads to his temples.

My heart sank.

'*I only care that you are alive*' my father once told me.

*I no longer have anyone…*

"Move to the parlour," said Cesare. "We'll deal with the stage later."

I crouched to the floor, arms wrapped around my knees, eyes fastened shut as dread prevailed. I felt repulsive against the empyrean curtains stitched as if from the matutine sky—some grotesque wretch twitching and mad with affliction, sinking its nails into its own muscle.

The garotte still burned my throat, my flesh gravid with Davide's parasitic leer. *I want my father.* Like a child. A lifelong inmate finally thrown from the dungeons and forced to make do with naught. *Why did my cards fall so?* Ema's murder, the nasty piece of work that was Abramo Sessa, the snake Basilio, my exile, papa's disappearance, the stalkers, the endless passes at my life by strangers in the slums, *The Arum*, the Morettae, Davide, the sibylline—I shook with the weight of it all. The implication I couldn't interpret.

"Hey, it's fine," Eligio hushed through his own trembling tone, mouth gently bowed when I peeked. "I mean, I get it. But I think it's best we move away from… *this*."

I launched to my feet. "It *is* fine. It's nothing." I couldn't let my grief spill out.

"We need to take care of some wounds," insisted Eligio, handing me my mask. "A distraction's in order, anyway."

The five of us proceeded down the auditorium's inumbrated stalls, through the gargantuan main doors tattooed with rose-treacle paint, and left down a creaking hallway.

*The Crescent* wholly embraced visceral heart symbolism, draped with crimson curtains like flayed skin. Here in *The Sunrise*, intricate motifs in time-worn glimmers of gilding beset the sepia wood cladding the walls: lazy suns with listless waves for beams, tearful, smiling faces, lucent breezes and honey light pouring over salt seas.

The hall dilated into a round parlour, a large pine table with a solitary chair at its head the sole furnishing. Vaulted ceilings soared for the very gables of the roof, windows marking each storey—three—as if the parlour was a miniature city courtyard. A balcony encircled the level above like a nimbus, bridged with the parlour by a staircase and leading to thespian quarters, I presumed.

Eligio all but shoved me into the seat, inspecting my arm's inflamed gash. "Cesare and his impeccable needlework may be better suited—"

"I'll put you in the ground," I sneered at Cesare.

He broke into laughter, unbounded and songful. The others joined him, even if edged with the distress engendered by the intrusion.

I set my teeth, cheeks heated. He enraged me, and that felt good when drowning in despair, like a raft to bleed my teething gums on. It *didn't* feel good to envy him.

Lissandri yawned, checking his brass pocket watch. "We've go' ano-apozem, if you wan'."

"Sutures suffice," I declined. After *The Arum*, it would take a lifetime before putting ano-apozem to my skin didn't repulse me for that cockroach way it crawled across wounds.

Dimples pressed into Eligio's cheeks. "Guess you'll have to settle for less-than-impeccable." He took the thread and bandages Lissandri retrieved and commenced tending to me.

Cesare flattened a long hand to his collarbone, brows grasping each other.

Lissandri handed him a caustic smirk. "D'you forget it?"

Cesare's face paled. "Anukka's gonna cut the strings."

"Maybe Iyad will protect them?" suggested Eligio, my brow tweaking at the names.

Cesare sighed. "They're fucked."

Lissandri left him an eye roll that couldn't've been *anything* short of painful, sleepy attention settling on me. "You've gone through the wringer. We all have. Put a pin in your murderous intentions. What happened to *you*?"

Snatching my wounded palm—*my* promise made in blood—from Eligio, I recounted my story, omitting names, motives, *The Arum*'s abuse, but truthful notwithstanding my curtness.

Eligio tied the bandage around my forearm as my narration approached its conclusion.

Kneading his cheek between his teeth, Cesare stared pensively floorward, back against the nearby window, the clotted cuts across his right palm and within his fingers' clefts oozing sanies in his ignorance of them. Lissandri, gaze saturnine, rubbed his chin scar. Rosalia's orbs long-since glazed over with disinterest.

"I need to find my father," I asserted, "and then I must obtain a key to the kingdom and take for myself the knowledge withheld from me." Knowledge of Ema's killers. "Knowledge I am *owed*."

"Why your father?" softly asked Eligio.

I thanked him for his care. "Because I'm convinced everything is connected, so I must unravel it." Because papa was all I had left.

"How're you gonna do that?" Rosalia questioned.

I roamed her mismatched eyes, glassy as a sturgeon's, and loosened a breath, ashamed to admit that, for all my resolve, I was lost at sea. "The government doesn't cease pursuing fugitives when they go missing." The tenure was corrupt at the bone—set up to manufacture insurrectionaries by its mere being just *to* render them fugitives. One way or another, as Micheletto and the smuggler implied, I was just that.

"Your mask." Cesare's voice split a headache down my spine. *Gods, he likes to hear himself talk.* His eyes dazzled within the smoke of black kohl, a smirk on his lips. "Unalike the one *I* recall."

The impulse to bite back reared its head but I swiftly decapitated it, gaze plummeting to my vólto. The smooth white porcelain once swirling with bloodink[74] vines now lay bare, eyes seamed with black and lips red as roses. For Vencenzanii, masks were our identification documents. Each citizen was only permitted one, that *one* put on permanent record in the House of Judgement, and unauthorised wear of a mask not designated 'yours' was unlawful. But so was *I*. "There was a girl at *The Arum* who finger-painted," my age, but like she'd regressed to a child's state to bear the horrors, "but she didn't have any red paint." Once, I peeked through a crack in her door, concerned by the loud banging I heard, and witnessed

---

[74] An ink made from cinnabar.

as she bashed her elbows on a nightstand hard enough to split flesh, and soaked up the blood to redden her paintings. "So, when Falco begrudged me my meagre coin, I bought the girl a tub of it. In return, she let me use her white paints to anonymise my mask." She never told me her name.

"And what was *that*?" I changed tack before guilt could bring my stomach up. "Davide?"

"Sinister fucking pederast who worked at *The Sunrise* before it shut," derided Lissandri. "*Left* before it shut, too. *Or* was fired. I know Paolo, our impresario, had *less*-than kind words to say about Davide after his departure."

"Supposedly ran with the bandit crowd," Cesare appended. "Back then, that was mere speculation. The confirmation comes at hardly a shock, nevertheless."

"So… is this some kind of vendetta?" I asked. "I'd appreciate not being hunting game for once."

"Irrelevant, I fear." Cesare's insolent mirth darkened. "He's in the Governor's web and therefore in my way. Another set of guns pointed at us never helps."

"How can you be sure he'll honour his end?" I raised.

"Blood is worth diamonds; one of the only reliable currencies in The Court." But was the exchanged payment sufficient?

"We're safe *here*," pondered Eligio. "What about *outside*? We cannot all so easily defend ourselves."

"If he gets his hands on you, he'll make you into bartering chips." Cesare's breathing seemed to strain. "About time I cashed in those favours of mine," he goaded my ever-stirring spirit of inquiry. "Until then, stick to the light and keep shut the windows in the night like any wise citizen. Better safe than your bones picked by the crows. *I'll* deal with this predicament."

"You deal with *every* predicament," groused Lissandri.

"Your point?"

Eligio frowned. "Ces…"

"*Speaking* of predicaments." Cesare brandished the note from the Curios. When it hit the table, it was like the penny dropped.

"Do you think…?" Lissandri's head whirled to me, to Eligio, to Cesare. "Maybe?"

"Evidently, Davide was always involved in underhand machinations. City Guards would have no business having this on hand. Nowhere in this are they addressed, nor do they function as messengers. *So*, now that we *know* Davide's dancing to The Bone King's piano, the details align: I suspect this letter was *planted*, with *him* as the addressee."

I considered the insinuation. *But why?* What would be the end to these strange means? The *Curios* was owned by the twins' parents, yes, but how did the crows—the perpetrators of the raid—fit into the mosaic?

"It's redundant to *us*," continued Cesare, "but evidence to unaware folk."

Lissandri simpered. "Would make a brilliant show-and-tell piece."

"Precisely my intention." Cesare perched an elbow on Lissandri's shoulder. "De Tullia's upcoming assembly is in two days. Díem zenítis. If we hadn't already been scheming to attend, this convenience would've been the spontaneous push."

I eyed him. "You intend to barge in on an enormous governmental event garrisoned at every fissure by the Minister's elite Imperiálum?"

Eligio crossed his arms, muttering, "And that's not even half of it."

Cesare touched elegant fingers between the sharp protrusions of his collarbones. "Perhaps, if I ask the crows nicely, they'll *let* me through to the Governor's office."

A frown claimed my brow. "How could you possibly hope to succeed?"

"Come along and see for yourself."

"*What*? Absolutely not! What could you want with me?"

"An extra set of eyes is valuable; we need all the help at hand."

"What is this *really* about?" I shot to my feet. "Why were you at *The Arum*?"

Eligio sucked the corner of his upper lip, eyeing Cesare expectantly. *Expecting what?*

With a resonant *click* of his tongue, Cesare wended for the stairs.

Rage lashed me to pursue. "What do you *know*?"

Snickering like a schoolboy, Cesare ascended to the balcony, slipping down the right wing of the two-way capillary. "What *do* I know?" He veered into an offshooting bedchamber.

Frustration flared in my gut like an ulcer as I tracked him. "Don't play dumb with me!"

Candlelit alchemy ignited the cluttered space as I caught up to him in a bedchamber.

Dust and sugary frankincense of old church altars anointed the air, a bedside desk riotously littered with sundries abutting the map-adorned back wall. Innumerable daggers stacked a small table at its left.

I nailed Cesare with an iron glare. "If there's mayhem, you're *bound* to be there."

He removed his bell-adorned earring. "Where there's smoke, there's fire." Sheet music paved the scratched cedar surface of the desk he leaned against.

"You trusted me with your identity. A tad *familiar* of you, no?"

A cipher of a character. Mysterious as the mist. And mists got coachmen killed.

"I don't believe you desperate or pitiful enough to hand me over to the authorities to save your own hide," said Cesare plainly. "I'm sure you've grown a tad too smart to believe De Tullia wouldn't execute you with me. Two birds with one stone: you violated *Sa Nóba Giustíca* too. Of all people, believe *me* when I say such a fortune doesn't make you the Governor's most trusted messenger."

"But… your home, your name, your *face*. The Court deals in secrets just as much as De Tullia. Is it not safer to kill me and preserve yourself…?" I drew guard, conscious of giving him ideas.

Cesare cocked his head. "You really do think I'm evil and it shows."

"You make it easy to wonder."

He leaned intentionally close as he stepped around me. "I'm grateful you keep me in your thoughts and prayers, vólto." His cherry sillage whirled through my head like vertigo, cloying, counterfeit as that maraschino red. Yet beneath the glamour, his cotton shirt smelled of matches and gunsmoke and sugar-steeped tobacco paper, of a night unslept and wounds untended.

My cheeks flushed as I recoiled. "Fiend!"

"Every waking minute I grapple with my curse." Picking up a stilétto, Cesare aimed for a target rendered in chalk upon the far wall, swinging his sinewy arm in a smooth arc. The blade spun through the air, impaling a papercut's width off-centre.

I flinched at the splintering impact of steel breaching wood. "You're insufferable."

"Such *spite* this dark hour." A theatrical hand fell at his heart. "How shall I recover from my emotional distress?"

"Your distress is about to turn *physical*," I hissed.

He made for the dagger wedged in the wall. "Same old, same old."

I loured at his barbed tone. *I traded Basilio for an equally gargantuan pest!*

Overtaking Cesare, I gripped the dagger's hilt before he could, grazing his fingertips. His hand flinched away; his, face flickered with disgust. "Why are you so intent on elusion?" He was keeping a stranglehold on my answers, and I was *going* to wrench them out of him!

"Always be wary of the upper ossíi."

"Well, I am no longer so!"

A muscle flickered in his sharp jaw. "I was at *The Arum* on a contact's request."

"What's this about 'contacts'? Cashing in favours to whom?" *Cue his excuse of an answer:*

"I'm afraid you cannot do what I do *completely* alone."

"Are you involved with The Morettae?"

"There's *some* method to my madness."

"Explain said *method*."

"The acquisition of information." Cesare yanked the dagger out, walking it along with its twin to the weapons table and assuming his position against his desk again. "Tyranny flourishes when watered with ignorance. A blade cuts at the root, but the right scandal's ignition scorches the earth barren. De Tullia wrested power by sullying the reputation of his strongest opponents: a drunkard, a hysteric, a deadman. Thus, he eliminated them on the most fundamental level. What's left in the soil can always sprout." As livid as it made me, I found him mesmerising to listen to. Like gazing off a precipice upon the suicidal drop into the ocean's atramental maw, like your lungs and veins filling, blackening, capitulating, your body an inkwell for a mad philosopher's razor quill—scarring.

I set my teeth. "And the *means* of this acquisition?"

"Come along on díem zenítis." Cesare plucked his hoop earring and made towards the bookcase sweeping the wall severing his room from the hallway, its shelves crowded with crumbling tomes and miscellaneous flotsam and jetsam.

"*Why?*" I catechised. "I *know* you're hiding something."

My stomach coiled up.

Facing head-on the prospect of satiating my knowledge-hunger ripped away my resolve, forcing me to confront my mortality's bare visage. My weakness. *You will always be too afraid.*

Cesare *tsk'd*, brushing aside the thick darkness of his waves. "I suppose you ought to be content to live in ignorance, then." He took to shedding its piercings—a delicate band in his lobe, a row of studs tucked into the conch—a haphazard assortment of gold and silver. *Of course he's that sort.*

My body trembled like chordophone strings ready to snap. "Be damned then!"

I stormed for the exit.

"Why did you let me go?" Cesare's question halted me at the threshold. "To-night."

Resentfully, I pirouetted, resting my hands on the doorframe. "You are *The Bauta*," I scorned. "I…" my brows wilted, "didn't want the Guards to get you."

How ironic—wishing to kill him myself at that moment, yet not wanting the crows to do it because, even to *me*, he was some symbol of revolution. Of a liberation I did not have.

Cesare stepped into view, brow hard. "Guards?"

I pressed my lips into a strained line. "Three."

"They made it so deep into The Court?"

"They pursued a woman." And killed her, dumping her starved body in a canal. I couldn't save *her*, either.

Cesare's eyes widened. "And you let me walk away?"

"I *said* I knew how to deal—"

"Did they hurt—?"

"Don't feign concern!" I snapped. "I don't want your pity." Spinning on my heel, I departed.

None of this ruin was without his complicity.

# SCENE XVI

## FUGUE

*Cesare | Lucrezia*

BLOOD STAINS THE BOY'S FINGERS. *Natural for a defiant child of six years, released to the wilderness of the bustling capital like a young calf with legs barely sturdy. And how much there is to see in grand Du Rrât a du Errèina! How many high roofs to climb and store-lined streets filled with dance and song to race through with local kids, their oppidan accents crisp as the Boy's. Yet his Otherness they perceive distinctly: his darkness of features, the two languages he speaks well as the first.*

*The Boy falls, skins his knee on the setts, and takes it with hearty humour, brushing dust from the thicket of his dark hair, though forced to turntail to the theatre's House of Dance when the window he and his playfellows carouse beneath flings with a nursemaid bellowing,* "Away with you, hooligans!"

*The Woman wipes the blood staining the boy's fingers and knee, her hands darker than his by a couple kisses of sun, her eyes ochre-bright when she laughs at her son's temerity, pinching his cheek. She'd gotten her many clinking bangles from her old dance teacher, a glitter of a Marubhūtri woman from Mojatīya's northwest who'd taught the Woman her diasporic people's ancient roots, the saperā dance with its rope-adorned bracelets especially striking, all serpentine grace.*

*The Woman is the finest performer this side of Errèina, renowned for her vibrant skirts, the coin-adorned ribbons of dorî galbênsa braided into her hair, that mellifluent voice lilting in ballads of her mother tongue. The second language the Boy speaks. The language Errèina's puerile rich clutch their purses at. The Boy finds that ilk dreadfully grim, and likes whispering to his mother as much.*

*Gold-bestrewn purple curtains swathing the doorway flounce as a Man of healthy complexion sweeps into the dressing room where the Woman tends to the Boy. On the sofa plops the Man's guitar and off goes his fedora. Hair hazelnut-brown like his trousers hides under the brims, suspenders and rolled-up sleeves stressing the sculpted leanness of the Man's tall physique. Peridot eyes bouncing across the gaudy chamber like a puppyish king surveying his dominion, he, in orgulous flippancy, exclaims "Hellish vagabond imp!" at his son's skinless knee, jocularly knocking the Boy's head.*

*The Woman tucks hair, lush and black, behind her ear, watching the Man. Understanding something beyond words. The Boy is yet to gain such vigilance.*

*The Man finds no sour verses to recite of the puerile rich—that dutiful ilk raised him, even if soon banished him overseas for daring to seek a life of music over politics. He speaks the third language, a theatrical, poetic sort. Foreign. He'll play his guitar for the Woman when she dances and sings to-night. It kindled their love, years ago.*

*The Woman returns to her Boy, the sun glowing in her smile. "Chi cherî nîchi orajâi zhanô,[75]" she says. 'Neither skies nor priests know.' She means the future is uncertain; she says so to invoke fortune notwithstanding.*

---

[75] Zargòsian 'j' is pronounced as 'hh'/'ḥ'.

*The Man crosses the chamber, humming, fingers clicking. Parquet creaks beneath his brogues.*

*A black pall leaks between the floorboards, tears down the curtains.*

*A tiny house nestles between a raspberry spinney and a dirt track cleaving a southern village. Long ago, the house was a caravan, now broadened, its wheels lost to the moors.*

*Grandmother stands upon the porch, a dry and hardy weaver, a floral scarf knotted at her neck's nape. Crotal bells dangle off her massive silver hoops, singing to the wind as it swirls the frowning autumn sky. She holds a squeaky paraffin lantern against the gloom.*

*The Woman brings water and fresh paprika up the path. They'll need them for the goulash. Her vibrant skirt is dull with wear, her fingers busy with a cigarillo she'd known since her nineteenth year.*

*The Boy plays with the Girl, only a year into life, on yard grass. There are no more setts to skin knees on, but the rascal finds a way.*

*A woodcutting axe replaces the Man's guitar, his palms now callused and cracked. His mother said he'd fail, degraded the Man. Now, he seethes, teetering silently upon a ravine's edge with only the Grandmother—the Woman's mother—to talk into him the sense to step away.*

Neither skies nor priests knew.

*And neither did they know of the bed Grandmother would soon lay on. A festered wound; infected blood. Rigours took her in the night and the pall crawled over the threshold.*

*The scent of paprika always fills the timber-dressed halls.*

*The Man's hum is now a sneer, the click of his fingers a battering fist.*

*Walls crack the first time his fist strikes the Woman. The darkness spills in.*

*The tiny Girl clings to the Boy's bruised arms.*

*The Man roars when the Woman looks to her children, so she looks to them no more.*

*The Boy lies on the bed, joints swollen, skin contused as if the blackness of the house swallows him into its shadow. Perhaps the rigours would take him too—a boy of only nine.*

*Axe to wood.*

*Axe to flesh.*

*Axe to bone.*

Crack!

*The scent of paprika flows warmer, redder.*

*The squeaky lantern shatters. Paraffin spills. Fire rages, demanding freedom.*

*The Boy slumps on his back to see the ceiling. His rended gut disgorges entrails like ropes across unfamiliar sheets. Burns eat his skin. A dreadful fever shakes him.*

*Above him looms the dusky-cheeked Girl.*

*Her head hangs limp off its half-severed neck, a white membrane drawn against the bright ochre of her eyes, yet they peer into the shame shrivelled inside the Boy's crucible. The hazelnut strands of her hair drip blood upon the Boy's face, and it is* she *fallen to chunks of a mutilated doll on the bed, instead.*

Panic thrashed Cesare awake.

He shoved himself off the sheets. Feet grappling for the floor, he reeled backwards in tottering steps, shoulder blades stabbing the bookshelf, muscles aching with torsion.

*I'mgoingtodieI'mgoingtodie—*

He had barely dozed—still dressed—but that's all it took for those foul black memories to tear back his ribs and grip into a cold throttle the nithing of a heart raw and bating within.

It had been fourteen years, *fourteen fucking years*, yet that awful night, that tiny body—strewn across a flimsy mattress soaked so deep blood dripped through to the weathered floorboards, haunted him with the sharpness of a prior day. The stench of death forever marred the recollections of his childhood's timeworn house upon those moors.

And it was meant to be *him*. Should've been *his* damned body lying dead and ruined on that forsaken old bed. It was a cosmic cruelty that he continued to live when two unsullied stars were ripped from the heavens and snuffed out so ruthlessly. The curse to never rest was such a measly tithe for the souls laid heavy as mountains on his back.

Cesare's lungs fought to efflate.

He would force himself to stay awake through two continuous days just to be so exhausted he'd black out into a dreamless sleep. He couldn't listen to screams every night no matter how many unearned years he'd weathered alone with them. But this time around, it seemed the day's distress rendered his efforts obsolete, and demons of a bleak past tore from their oubliettes.

Cesare snatched his waist-cut leather blazer, unhooked the door—always kept it shut on account of the nightmares—and resolved for the streets, sigarétta already in trembling hand. The rush of closely-avoided doom could be the only fuel to keep his light burning against the darkness, and if he didn't smoke after ephialtes, he felt like he would die.

The sight of the corridor halted him.

At the distal end, where desaturated moonlight puddled on the timber, a figure huddled against the foot of a sleeping chamber's door, scratching its shoulders in half-madness before springing upright and throwing itself to the near window in a bedevilled tempest of limbs and curls. Hinges scarcely withstood as the lattice burst open. "*What must I do?*" Giorgianna's shout echoed along the moon's curvature. "How must I weather? Let me *feel*! Even tears! I don't know what you want of me—I do not *know*! It's eating me alive. Let it *OUT*!" Giorgianna thwacked the window frame. "*Gods*, whom did I wrong in what iteration of my Self that you should punish me so?" Her voice broke. "Why did you take her? You let *me* live—look what *wretch* you squandered it on! I don't want it and I *shan't* keep it if I'm made to bleed more! Take it *back*!"

Giorgianna gasped and sprung away, hands clutched at her heaving chest as if something clawed her insides but couldn't be purged. Though her eyes scintillated, her face was dry.

She shut herself inside her bedchamber with a clatter.

Knowing every floorboard by heart, Cesare slunk silently to her door and knelt beside it.

She seemed to sit on the other side, breaths frantic, shuddering, though not with tears. Between gasps, she whispered "*I hate you*" in a fevered invocation.

She had hollowed out. Not physically, but in spirit. Her copper eyes burned red-hot the last occasion he chanced upon her. Now, they cut. Cold. Wishing only to watch blood pour, even better her own.

The reflection of himself upon her countenance did nothing to soothe Cesare as he sank against the doorframe, angling his head to glimpse through the window, its hinges creaking in the zephyr. The moon and her stellar confrère Nereida paled in the forsaken empty sky.

His amôna[76] had been a religious woman, his âma[77] equally so, and Cesare had tried so, *so* earnestly, yet he couldn't keep the faith. How many nights had he prayed to God to be rid of his soul, to not endure the pain of living with the guilt of all he lost, only for his prayers to fall on deaf ears? And it hurt most of all to know that neither his amôna nor his âma nor his phèn[78] sang upon the wind, that they weren't enskied amidst the stars their souls were wrought of. That they simply *weren't*. Embers devoured by the coals.

The nightmare sufficed—Cesare refused to muse further upon fourteen years ago. The scars left behind already reminded him every single day just how much whatever cruel celestial entity reigned had cared for him and the people he loved. If God were real, He wouldn't have squandered life on a wretch like *him*.

Cesare's brows bunched as he flicked the unlit sigarétta through his nimble fingers, still tremulous. Blame and loathing of Self, the wish to end his life to repay a debt, ran so deep within him. Until to-night, he'd never once heard a matching sentiment spoken aloud.

"*Leave me...*" Giorgianna's whisper wuthered from beneath the door.

---

[76] '*Grandmother*' in all Zargòsian dialects.

[77] '*Mother*' in all Zargòsian dialects.

[78] *FEHN*; Marlâre for '*sister*'.

Though reasoning that the imploration couldn't be for him, Cesare abandoned his unintended post and descended into the veins of the theatre, lighting the sigarétta at last. There were still contacts to visit and a violin to retrieve.

"Can *any* ends justify these means?" a mellow voice addressed Cesare.

Eligio stood in the shadows, somnolent and sour, not yet retired from his nightly artist's vigil.

Cesare tutted as he leaned against a wall. "Speak with ease, phrâl.[79]"

Eligio's fingers twiddled with the embroidery circling his kamiz's neckline. "Why did you do that? You signed your life away to a murderous predator—you *know* he won't play fair."

Cesare's heart clenched.

He acted rashly, he owned. He should have killed the pale fucker and damned the consequences but, in doing so, he would have killed his cherished famìlia. "I'd rather take chances with a knife in my throat or a bullet through the back of my head around any wrong bend." He'd rather kill *himself*.

Eligio's gaze dropped.

The older twin kept his seams together like always, but with the *Curios* raid and Davide's intrusion stacked afresh, he frayed. All of it circled back to Cesare and his precarious cause. *Death-bringer.*

He dragged deep into his lungs—something he fain avoided, drawing only into his mouth when he'd rather not gnaw away his own cheek, but the shear on his nerves besought abatement. How his dear mother would both sigh and darkly chuckle at the sight of a coffin nail in her firstborn's hand were she still there. She'd smoked everything from kretek to her ginseng tisane if it meant lenifying the frigid scorch of bloodsucking limelight. And how Paolo would reprimand Cesare for his touching a coffin nail had he known, as if the old impresario didn't himself smell of woodsmoke and sandalwood; as if the old impresario didn't himself burn the midnight oil with cheap back-alley tobacco. But he was a tough geezer. And Cesare was only a boy.

---

[79] *f-RAHL*; Marlâre for '*brother*'.

"She cannot remain in the dark," contended Eligio solemnly.

Cesare exhaled smoke. "It's not my place to run my mouth."

Eligio's forehead corrugated. "You make *those* your loyalties?"

"It's no less daft to me than it is to you, but—"

"We're *lying* to her, Ces," pleaded Eligio.

"Not of our own choice."

"We *choose* to affirm it. *Imagine* the weight of this revelation!"

"Necessary evil." Cesare proceeded to walk off.

"You know you don't mean that."

"For once, the mastermind is *not* I."

"Where are you even going? You're in *danger* outside."

"You speak as if I, at times, am *not*!" Cesare mused like a poet on a whimsical spiel. "Merely a step beyond the threshold—the wind calls me away!"

"You *are* a fiend, you know!" threw Eligio.

"Etch it on my grave!" Cesare passed back and took his leave into the early morning.

THE CLOCK ANNOUNCED díem auróra's three hundredth hour, and the awaited permission to leave.

Lucrezia threw on her colombína inlaid with prescription glass, fumbling to smooth the endless ribbons of her dress before dropping the effort and quitting her maquillage studio. She preferred the utilitarianism of jodhpurs, or the swish of a xhubleta[80] worn by the women of her mother's maternal people, but the illusion a frilled dress cast held the value of gold.

In the blackened auditorium, beyond soaring far windows lancet-shaped as austere spires, the moon burgeoned like a gravid belly, colossal enough to obscure the sky. Lucrezia recalled such scenes from her

---

[80] *khoo-BLEH-tah*; a wavy, bell-shaped skirt iconic to northern Albanian folk attire.

childhood and adolescence, in the midnight hours following those divine liturgies her father and uncle insisted she attend. Godliness was obedience was purity was righteousness, after all, and the High Priest was in their ear. But she never had faith in the Order, not even on its operating table. Not even with her flesh consecrated into its truth beneath its blade. The Order sought more than faith.

Headaches harassed Lucrezia, chasing her from the auditorium and her lunar ruminations.

Basilio's leash on the theatre tightened steadily following his banishment of Giorgianna. He'd taken on all playwright work, *no* prospect of pushback, and steamrollered his vìtae into twenty-hour shifts on threat of expulsion—a death sentence in Vencenza's current theatrical climate.

*Hallway to the right.*

Wide, paved in polished pear parquet and swathed in curtains carmine as freshly-cut game. At its terminus stood a peripheral exit not unlike the one Lucrezia opened for Giorgianna all those months ago. *She's still without a trace.* Lucrezia had *felt* something—*knew* she had to be there in secret the díem lunéra after '*A Bedlamite's Ballad*'; after the outburst of apoplexy Basilio had driven Giorgianna to. Lucrezia had hardly expected what came to pass. Therefore, happening by the impresario's office called for silence. Who knew what whispers one could catch behind the closed doors of aristocracy?

Levering down her saddle shoes to hush the floorboards, Lucrezia inched by.

Male voices mumbled inside. *Lucky strike.*

Lucrezia nestled among the velvet swathes across the hall.

'…*monitor her, signór.*' Smoke roughened the first speaker's voice. Familiar. *Monitor whom?*

'*I only strive to serve dónno De Tullia.*' A smarmy, toffee-nosed quality to the second voice. *Basilio.* Lucrezia cringed at 'dónno'. Basilio's reverence for De Tullia's law rivalled the most ascetic priest's devotion: *more* than enough inclination for a man to taint another's name to uphold himself as treason's virtuous victim.

'*Chronicle and report suspicious conduct,*' the first ordered.

Heavy footfalls neared, the door opening.

Lucrezia snuck a peek.

Pewter cloth dressed the gruff-voiced pylon of a man, the beaked mask fitted across his nose fashioned of dark feathers. *City Guard?* His cape blazoned a silver swallow—De Tullia's bastardised sigil— signifying him as a Liaison between the senate and Vencenza's nobility. *What could he want?* Liaisons rarely left the loop between the ministerial acropolis and aristocrats' residency in the city's north, for that was their sole purview.

'*...circle you've amassed yourself, Basilio.*'

Voices persisted inside. *There's a third!* Fruity and slick as candied apples.

'*I'm sure âto's*[81] *pride sings at* yours *awaking nightly beside gaggles of whores, tsîpi irmân.*[82]'

Lucrezia squinched up her face. *Basilio's brother?* Lucrezia couldn't rack her brain quite enough for the wisps of memory which may reveal his name.

The pair switched to Zâro.

Lucrezia had taught herself the basics for eavesdropping sake, but the pair spoke fast, seemingly turned away, so her endeavour proved fruitless, prompting her towards exeat.

A shuffle nearby startled her.

She doused the darkness in observation, hoping to light upon her perturbation's tinder, but nothing kindled. *Grim lemures!*[83] Unlike Illutèri followers, and much to the antithesis of her attendance of Vencenzani liturgies, Lucrezia believed in ghosts, in demonic invocations, so she fingered her ring embedded with a glassy nazar moncuk,[84] azurine and polished as an eyeball, and considered the discoveries of the night.

*The impresario is purging his vìtus.*

---

[81] Zargòsian for '*father*'.

[82] '*Little brother*' in non-Marlâre Zargòsian ('*tsîpi*' is cross-dialectical).

[83] *LEH-moo-rehs*; restless souls of the vengeful dead in Roman mythology.

[84] *nah-ZAHR mohn-JOOK*; 'Evil Eye bead'; an amulet of protection consisting of a bright blue glass bead painted with an eye.

With Abramo hanging around Basilio like some gremlin henchman, Lucrezia knew she ought to watch her back more closely than ever. She'd grown accustomed to vigilance, what with her sacrilegious childhood and slated convictions, but she felt the eyes of the state creeping ever closer, surveilling her for any hint of dissidence. And Lucrezia had many to conceal.

Past the porch of the peripheral exit, a thin figure bodied her.

She swerved on her heel, almost shoving a man into the canal if it hadn't been for the lustre of his mechanical eye.

"*Ah!*" he squawked. "My *dar*ling Lucrezia!"

"Twat!" she snapped. "Did you stalk me inside?"

"In*s*ide?" He bridled, face practically gurning with appalment. "*Luce*,[85] who d'you think I *am*? Come!" He wrapped her arm around his own and escorted her over the bridge. "Right on the *money, I* was."

---

[85] *LOO-cheh*

# SCENE XVII

## LIMINALITY

*Giorgianna*

LIGHT FLICKED BY THE SUN through the septentrional window dappled the ceiling as if with mirror shards, but I didn't recall when it had risen, or whether I'd slept at all—my wrung-out mind rendered the previous night in no detail.

Incessant thuds beat like a distant heart through the theatre, my sore eyes somersaulting. *It's like he's* vying *to be the utmost insufferable.*

I sat up, plain sheets unmussed beneath me. Sylvan walls dressed the homely chamber, an armoire and empty closet standing sinistral to the ancient four-poster bed, a pointed-arch window to its right. Half hidden behind tawny curtains, an antique table displayed my satchel like a still-life arrangement. A wall-mounted iron timepiece pronounced *ten hundred.*

Falco was bound to have thrown *more* than a tantrum apropos of my absence by now. But even with my gnarling guilt, I couldn't look back. Only ahead. Only at my justice.

Hauling myself out of bed, I freed from my satchel the skirt I'd forced inside months back, shaking it.

Out came flying two small objects.

The first landed within reach: the hiltless, rhomboid blade which gifted my right biceps its second scar in grim reminder of '*A Bedlamite's Ballad*'. Of Davide—now a bodach haunting us all.

Pawing under the bed, I snatched up the second item. *Basilio's tanzanite cufflink*. I wiped it of dust, its violet-indigo gem glimmering, and squeezed the dastardly thing until it hurt.

I wanted no relic of the man who ripped my life from me. Yet, my grip released, jaw unclenching, and I dropped the cufflink into the armoire, slamming it shut to banish the thought.

Casting the skirt to the bed, I grabbed the strange blade and my cards on my way out.

The bedchamber granted to me hid out of sight of the parlour below, an infirmárium a door left. Dimness veiled the hallway beyond the balusters, a boarded window at the distal wall yet-untouched by the sun still illuming the sky's western half. Perpendicular to the infirmárium, around the snaking balcony, ouro faces embossed a solitary door allegedly leading to the rooftop cupola. At the foot of the door to Cesare's chamber, an inexplicable key lay.

I proceeded to the infirmárium.

Dim as a monastic cell, a single clerestory window fed light inside. A seared ash cabinet, tumid with manifold items, flanked the sink by the wall left of the door, whilst a couple paces away stood a solid wood tub, kept company by a nightstand crowned with a lonesome candlestick.

I swilled somnolence from my eyes and dampened my hair, tending to its arduous needs with the little I had at my disposal before redressing my wounds. My withering reflection, its sclerae a-slither with crimson roots of capillaries like a decaying home's porch, watched me from the desilvered mirror. Befitting of my herbarium—dried out and dead.

Knocks thrust me out of my head.

"*Anyo' in?*" Rosalia warbled, voice muffled.

She stood at the threshold when I opened the door, a massive waffle in hand, cheeks puffed. Her knee-length dress sprouted in a frilled heap of vanilla petals, sleeves puffy as magnolias and cream stockings embroidered with white muguets. "D'you wan' footh?" Her tarn-blue eye never rippled with a pupil's dilatory motion. *Unseeing.* "I ma'e vaffel— well, I ma'e mo'e tha' one, bu'."

"No, falemíce.[86]" My brows pinched and wilted. "Are… you well?"

"Room t' ge' wo'se." Rosalia swallowed her mouthful. "Yourself?"

I tried to smile, "Don't worry about *me*," and made to quit the infirmárium.

"Cesare says that a lot."

Rosalia's averment stunned me to a halt.

Rage curled my fingers, knotting them into fists. "I am not *Cesare*." I stormed for the parlour below, following the auditorium-bound route.

Sanguine curtains framed a door at the corridor's terminus, leading me into the auditorium.

A single mezzanine shadowed the stalls unlike *The Crescent*'s two, rose and yellow gold frolicking cheek-by-jowl upon embellished balconies. Where the grand drape remained the alizarin of haem, the peach champagne and rose water aquarelle of daybreak skies washed those flanking them, garlanded in crystalline beads like chips of the sun.

Lissandri fiddled with an antiquated grandfather clock keeping a vigil near the door, gears, bolts, screws scattering the floor. Beside him stood a clay cup of what could be coffee. Among the seats close by nestled Eligio in his sage shalwar kamiz, knees tucked up to his chin as he read a parchment.

"A visit?" Lissandri rolled the sleeves of his blouse as if in greeting. "You shouldn't've." Under his shirt's collar, a striking gold necklace resembling bunches of flattened grapes wreathed his neck, a plaited cinnamon bracelet bracketing his wrist alongside a golden circlet.

Eligio's lips kicked into a beam as he peeked over the parchment. "Bon auróra!"

I endeavoured another failed half-smile. "Salúdi.[87]"

---

[86] 'Thank you' in Salvatrici and Vencenzani. It is '*falehǫfna*' in Mariano, '*falumíce*' in Iutulicano, and '*falastó*' in Ashunati, comparable to Marlâre '*pàri'sastô*'.

[87] '*Hello*' in Faustinian; except Iutulicano wherein it is '*salutámu*'.

"How do you feel?" he questioned, gaze suspiciously inquisitive.

"Liveable." I sat in the stalls, the seats time-worn and soft as red velvet cake. "And you?"

"Better than the alternative all around," huffed Lissandri, the clock emitting a screech as he manoeuvred a gear.

Eligio grimaced at his younger twin, then looked at me with softness. "I'm glad to hear."

"Likewise," my voice came gently.

I nocked my head back and didn't withhold my gasp.

A ceiling adorned with illusionistic frescos wheeled above, a false central oculus circumscribed by a gold parapet of ornamental balusters opening to a rendered chorus of blushing skies echoing with aurated clouds. "Why is this theatre abandoned?" I found my voice. "How is it still standing at *all*?" I met Eligio's gaze. "It's unnervingly close to upper óssium to be *so* thoroughly protected."

Eligio sighed. "*The Sunrise*'s forte was comedic pantomimes. Our impresario, Paolo, refused to accept *Sa Nóba Giustíca*, but understood we were out of business still. *So*, he and the rest packed all they could and left Vencenza. As for how it's still standing…" His mouth tucked at the corner. "You know Cardea and azoth." *But I'm not content.*

Lissandri poked his brother's shin with a wrench. "Where's Ces?"

"The wind called him away." Eligio plucked out one of the paintbrushes sitting in his kamiz's pocket and launched it at Lissandri. "He barely slept, as usual, so when he came home, I locked him in his quarters."

I squeezed my lips, shielding my face as an incursion of clandestine laughter almost conquered me.

Lissandri stared at his brother.

"It's *fine*, I put the key under his door." *Ohhh…* "All he needs to do is coax it to him."

"He has lock-picks."

"I've hidden them."

"He can still *pick locks*."

"Not as well as you and me!"

"Do you *also* know something?" I interrogated with all the grace of an officére, arms crossed.

Lissandri frowned. "Also?" He pelted the brush back at his eldest.

"Much how Cesare does despite claiming contrary."

Eligio's brown cheeks reddled. "Look, *it*... it's hard to explain."

"Why?" My retort jolted him. "What's his deal with *inveigling* me to attend the assembly?"

"That's..." he sucked his upper lip, "also hard to explain."

A heinous shriek of metal rattled my teeth before I could demand more.

"Quit it, Sar!" admonished Eligio.

Lissandri's face wore derision. *"You're* the one who barely helped with stage repairs this morning."

Eligio stuck out his tongue; Lissandri brandished a vulgar gesticulation.

Getting answers out of these people and wringing water from a dry cloth proved equally fruitful, so I let loose the reins on my trivial curiosity with disregard for my aggravation: "Sar?"

"Short for my middle name—Sardûk," explained Lissandri. "Our mạt, Lậlẹn, is Âbạdil."

"Where from?" I questioned eagerly.

"A town called Gwạtishep in the northeast. Devastating floods unfortunately wrack Dayậrabạd: the reason mạti fled home. She spent years attempting to assimilate, but luckily had a change of heart. Meeting our ạbậ and opening *Commegnos' Curios* was a turning point." His disposition dampened. "So much of what's sold there is culturally Âbạdil." He perked up a tad: "Like this!" He gestured to his necklace. "It's called a chamkạli, and *this*," he jangled the bracelets, "the stitched one, is a ragậm."

"We both have Âbạdil middle names!" Eligio joined. "Mine is 'Liwạr', so I'm Eli *or* Li for short."

My heart ached in that warm way of tender muscles at their joy, the love between all of these people I hardly knew. It reminded me all too well of Ema, her love for Lerrkir and its mountains. It reminded me all too well of how little my father knew of his own heritage.

"Speaking of Dayârabạd: *this*," Lissandri pointed to his cup, "is elạichi chạ—cardamom tea. It's a staple in Mojatīya, too. Here," he extended the cup to me, "try it. I have mine with extra cardamom which *this* dolt—" he side-eyed Eligio "—doesn't appreciate."

"I don't like spices much," Eligio defended himself.

"You're a pill."

I took the cup. Liquid the colour of butterscotch rippled inside. "No alcohol?" I clarified.

"Not a drop," assured Lissandri.

I sipped. The tea spilled thick and creamy, coating my tongue with a spiced sweetness. A curve tested my lips. "It's nice."

"She's smiling!" Lissandri kicked Eligio's ankle. "*See*? Told you I make good chạ."

"D'you want food?" Eligio sprung the question Rosalia had. "You must be starving! Mạti brought some kạk—a kind of hard bread—recently, and Rosa's made brunede kartofler and waffles."

I passed the chạ back to Lissandri. "Would I be able to get a chemise, possibly?"

The twins blinked at me.

"Falco demanded all *Arum* lavìri wear *this*." A gesture at self. "Trouble is, we weren't permitted chemises under our corsets, so it chafes."

Eligio's brow creased. "Would you like entirely different clothes?"

I shrugged. "Oddly enough, I don't mind it." And now, the garment was like reclamation.

Lissandri stood, tucking screwdrivers and spanners under his belt from which dangled his pocket watch, and cracked his shoulders, my chest jolting. "No issue—we've plenty of spare clothes."

Eligio elbowed me with a grin. "You *must* eat afterwards, though." My lips curled as he snatched my wrist and pulled me along.

But, as we made our joint way, my gut knotted.

Reasons to not smile were long gone, yet I remained aware of my every quiver, indelibly fixated on the memories of Arturo Dioli's gut-wrenching arrest; that red-haired woman's brutal assault in upper óssium and the murders of the downtrodden I witnessed in the slums; my mother's cold hands as she forced me to look upon the cages.

It was not the *smile* that mattered, but its *symbolism*.

I could have laughed at the thought had I the nerve.

We ascended to the third floor—above the vìtus quarters (the key remained on the floor and I almost pinched it).

Rounded double doors guarded the first two rooms, frosted glass suns with rays like flowing waves crowning their domes. A pair of panel doors, unadorned by windows, stood opposite each other at the terminus. Sun-shaped skylights peered from the ceiling, daylight's luminary draping its diaphanous tresses to the floor.

I dug my heels against the urge to peek inside the remaining rooms as the twins made for the sinistral doors.

Manifold racks, chests, shelves of costumes and accoutrements decked the chamber in shimmering colour. Gem-encrusted scissors and darts, necklaces hung from them, skewered timeworn pantomime posters into foliate walls; jewels strew every sill; sashes of chiffon and batiste dangled from dark chandeliers. Ripening sunlight dripped its nectar through slender windows at the back, the air chiming with whispers of glitter and drenched in the thickening perfumes of dust and fabric as if a giant moth had fluttered through on its powdery wings.

Rosalia scuttled bent-double around the floor.

A rodent's silhouette scurried into a hole.

Lissandri rushed behind his brother. "That's a rat."

Rosalia puffed her cheeks. "It didn't wish to be my friend, I suppose."

Lissandri stepped out from behind Eligio, clearing his throat. "*Any*how." He stuck his thumb towards—"That semi-circular bit at the back's where our clothes are, everything else's basically untouched. The peach curtains obscure the changing booths."

Rosalia squished her freckled face between her palms. "I forgot to prepare lunch for the strays!" She bolted out.

"Call us when you endeavour to go!" Eligio yelled out.

*'Will do!'*

I couldn't shake the knowledge that Rosalia was only a child. Was her aplomb a mask concealing despair? In fairness (and *oh* how little there was of it in this world), I understood too well the necessity of crutches in a world so debilitating.

"She feeds the street cats," informed Eligio. "Though we cannot keep any on account of Andri's allergies."

"Listen," Lissandri raised his hands, "*I* like cats; *cats* don't like *me*."

Eligio laughed. "You're free to come here whenever," he addressed me.

Their keen willingness to welcome my presence pricked my ears, set me on edge.

"You didn't take over the *Curios* from your parents," I noted as we proceeded through the shelves as if a boutique.

"Had to put all those acrobatics skills to theatrical use," quipped Lissandri.

"Not just that," said Eligio. "There is soul in every performance, thousands of dazzling pictures in every word. Storytelling is a force of life—its own magic." His tone brimmed with wonderment. "The hearts of this city have always pumped life into its bones and it's an honour to be a part of it."

Sorrow wedged into my own heart. I knew what was reaped from him. From all of them. From *me*. I didn't even recall the last time spilling the inkwell of my mind into prose upon paper brought me joy. The last time *anything* illumed my tone. "I'm sorry." But no words could be remedy.

"Well, that's what we're working to repair." Eligio unfolded the parchment he'd been poring over like my father with his star charts, revealing blueprints of some nature. "We endeavour to get this place up and running again when this nightmare ends. And it will." *Ema said that*… "Davide left us with more disrepair, but Paolo would want us to; *we* want to." He sounded so sure, so steady in his conviction. *Just like*

*Ema was.* "This city deserves all its beating hearts, not a slow reduction to bone from a spider bite."

I chanced upon a white chemise, wide in the straps. "Why did you stay?" I asked tentatively, sealing myself within a changing booth. "Once everyone left."

"Andri and I *wanted* to stay, but our parents wouldn't hear of it."

"We *were* thirteen when De Tullia came into power," added Lissandri. *A year older than me.*

"Mati and ąbạ urged Cesare to live at the *Curios* with us," Eligio continued. "Predictably, he refused. Our parents didn't understand why he'd *choose* to stay in an abandoned building alone, why he'd allow complete strangers to squat here when they had nowhere to go, why they'd hear the voice of an adolescent speaking to them the words of an adult. They said it terrified them. Not that—I don't mean *he* terrified them, just... the thought of why he'd become like that." I laced up my corset over the soft cotton. "When he first arrived at the theatre, though a year older than us—ten, at the time—" *Cesare is only twenty-four?* "—we were already there." A dither. "He was... cold. Hostile, almost? He worked backstage, unlike us, and, for a long time, the only warmth he'd express would be to Paolo. It seemed... *men* particularly dismayed him, ironic as it seemed. There *was* a girl he'd grown seemingly close to."

"A real piece of work," Lissandri barged in. "A blonde."

"She always had a venomous thing to say to him or us," admitted Eligio. "But she had her own pain and it's unfair to vilify her wholly. And neither is her story mine to retell. As for Ces..." *Is his story yours to retell?* "For the longest of ages, he could only stand Paolo. But Andri and I won him over!" Eligio's voice lightened, though his undertone of gloom didn't elude me. "At seventeen, we moved into *The Sunrise* too, and that was *that.*"

Dressed once more, I stepped out.

The chemise puckered from my corset, its taenioid sleeves slipping down my shoulders unless pinned beneath the corset's straps, but the comfort of cotton mollified my raw skin.

"*Hello!*" Rosalia shouted through the doorway before I could resume speaking. A deep scivedda of minced fish sat in her palms. "Lunchtime for the kitties! Let's *go*!"

"Were we not advised to stay inside on account of Davide?" I questioned.

"Cesare chatted up some of his lot this morning so we're *supposedly* safe within the immediate vicinity," explained Lissandri.

I squashed my curiosity and followed the trio.

A limestone courtyard cut athwart by a narrow street fanned out in front of *The Sunrise*, its distal edge circumscribed by a tall stone partition overlooking a branch of river Vena, carved with sun-shaped windows crested by a row of intricate balusters from which overhung a velarium painted with rousing skies worn by age and weather.

Eligio and I settled on the ground beside the barrier where Rosalia handed the fishbowl to a mottled mother cat and her scrappy litter of three. A particularly tiny black furball found fascination in my unharmed hand and wouldn't stop nibbling my fingertips.

Keeping away, Lissandri sat by the grand entrance, distracted by the clockwork inside his pocket watch. Overhead rose an embossed sun rimmed in tarnishing gold. A smiling face at each undulated ray cried gold tears, smiles wide and mad.

The soul of vague recognition lingered beyond my memory, as if I had once seen the theatre.

Through the partition's sun-windows, oldtown's ancient streets wove at the water's behest. Rotund roofs of theatres, chapels, governmental precincts, imposed like colossal planets among the square edifices, gondoas floating atop resplendent haüyne.

Warm wind played flute through susurrating hollows smelling of brine and late-summer citrus, doves warbling as if a murmur between lovers. A spectral fantasy realm.

In that eyeblink, even within the darkness of this world I saw something beautiful.

"How did you learn sleight of hand?" asked Eligio.

"Papa." I smirked at his awe when I spirited away my cards. "He never told me how *he* learned it." My eyes found Eligio's. "But how did you get by? You were still so little when you moved."

"Eli and I worked at the *Curios*," Lissandri called out, "Ces got acquainted with dockhands at the nearby berth." *Could those be* 'his lot'?

"Sometimes, petty robbery was called-for."

"Tribulations aside, it worked." Eligio shrugged. "As far as I'm concerned, we're triplets."

My chest hurt no matter how much I didn't want it to. Emanuela was the sister I never had, after all.

I set the kitten near its mother and stood, wending along the sunbeam etchings on the sandstone. "Does it bother you that he throws himself at blades?"

"Yes," Eligio blurted.

"Not *particularly*," countered Lissandri. "He knows what he's doing." I didn't believe his tone—still as a lake to Eligio's turbulent river.

"Do *you* know what he's doing?" I queried.

"Doesn't remedy," Eligio said sombrely. "Every day he dissents against a system which will stop at nothing to see him executed. They know he's dangerous. They wouldn't fuss over a single person otherwise. It makes you hold your breath when it's your family."

I let his molten words flow in, mould into understanding. "Do you believe he'll succeed?"

"I have faith." Eligio palmed his chest, tone rich with surety.

"Like I said:" Lissandri rose, "he knows what he's doing."

"*Utterly side-splitting!*" The four of us jumped at the resonant voice.

Cesare leaned out of a second-storey window at the frontal end of the thespian quarters corridor embowered by verdant climbing vines. With the sleeves of his mussed poet shirt rolled to the elbow, small patches of scar tissue glinted along his right forearm like smears of oil, hair framing his sculptural cheeks in unbrushed swathes. He dangled a key off his bandaged fingers, expression wry. "*I'll* be holding onto *this*, going forward."

Eligio lifted his chin with a simper. "Joke's on you—I've made impressions of it."

"You know, I *have* worked diligently to avoid jail time."

"Then go to Etenesh for that hand of yours."

Cesare's pendent earring, shaped into a cart's wheel, effulged in the sun at the tilt of his head. "Is that it, mother? Ought I eat my greens and grain, too?"

"Would do you some good."

"Here." Lissandri took my shoulders. "Take her with you if you're scared to go alone."

My face ignited. "*What?*"

Cesare clicked his tongue, "Excellent," and slipped back into the theatre.

I tore from Lissandri. "What are you trying with me?"

"Etenesh is an apothecary; we trust her with our lives," assured Eligio. "Medicine would do *you* some good, too." He winked. "*Then* you'll have food!"

Etenesh Asmeret's apothecárium tucked itself like a honeycomb-coloured box into the shelves of a complex a couple blocks from the Solar Square. Innumerable vials occupied each nook within, faded illustrations and dried herbage adorning walls elaborately embellished with cruciate motifs.

A shemma ḳemis dressed the Sam'säb[88] apothecary's tall frame, radiant against her dark skin patched with paleness around the joints and

---

[88] One of the four main ethnic groups of Ṣh'ovvā: *Däsrabi* from the South, *Sam'säb* from the north, *Adarēbi* from the West (lowlands), and *Kidhobi* from the East (river). The letter '*ä*' is pronounced as an elongated '*aw*'.

mouth. Her near-black hair wove into intricate albaso braids along the frontal crown, the back left unbound in a fluffy cloud.

Immediately upon our arrival, Etenesh reprimanded Cesare for his perpetual run-ins with the law and the string of unpaid visits to her apothecárium, the latter of which he rectified with a generous pouch of coins—tumid enough to beg the question of just how often he ended up here. When he attempted to pay for my share, I handed over the remainder of my *Arum* yield, instead. The last person I'd owe a debt to would be The Bauta.

I sat shielded from Cesare behind the desk whilst Etenesh inspected my bruises and gashes, respectfully not noting my self-mutilation or stigma. "Nicely sewn up!" she remarked of my *Bedlamite* scars.

"I *did* say my needlework is impeccable," Cesare piped up from where he sat at a stained glass bay window, his hand freshly treated. *Faces, it's like he'll die if he shuts his mouth.*

Etenesh opened my slit left palm, my teeth barricading a hiss. "*Holy Three!*[89]" She started at the fresh cut writhing like a worm through my flesh, then whisked away to retrieve a small crate of glass bottles, half amethyst, half viridian. "I'll use ano-apozem on your hand—"

"Thank you, but…" I stopped her gently. "Katō, please."

Etenesh's brows drew together, deepening her delicate tracery of facial lines. "It will scar, ḥafti.[90]"

"A grim reminder I wish to keep." For Ema. For me.

"*O*—kay…" Etenesh drawled, dark eyes squinted at Cesare. "You sure keep odd company."

Cesare aimed with a humourless smile. "Abyss calls unto abyss, seems."

I recoiled as his remark pried into me—a skinning knife peeling bare my bones. And when, for an ephemeral instant, his glass-shard eyes

---

[89] The three chief deities of Ṣh'ovvā: *Beher*, earth god; *Ästär*, sky goddess; *Maḥrem*, war god. The letter '*ḥ*' is pronounced like '*hh*'.

[90] *HHAHF-tee*; 'sister' in Sam'säban. Used both literally, and as a term of endearment among non-blood-related, femme-aligning individuals. By comparison, '*ḥaftē*', '*my sister*', denoted by the possessive suffix '*-ē*', is used exclusively in reference to siblings.

crossed mine, they looked upon the darkness inside my marrow because, somewhere beneath his consciousness, he *recognised*.

And, for that, I hated him.

# Scene XVIII

## Paradiso Perduto

*Cesare*

A BRIEF 'STOPOVER' AT A GUARD STATION equipped Cesare with contraband: two gladii[91] and a monstrosity of a spadone.[92] Along with his stilétti and six throwing knives, the swords had Cesare armed to the teeth. He wasn't fond of heavy blades, favouring the deftness of a dagger, a swift, clean dispatch. But so few things were better currency than steel.

He lent a circumspect glance and stole down a black Court alleyway, slinking through a derelict tavèrna a-crawl with patrons. At its terminus, he rounded a concealed corner and dipped into a vertical drop, clutching a metal rail running underneath the ledge. Two storeys below, a canal cleaved the ancient stonework, no beginning or end to the watery darkness.

---

[91] Plural of '*gladius*'; a shortsword used by Ancient Roman foot soldiers.

[92] *spah-DOH-neh*; a type of longsword.

Cesare reached across the fissure to a rail at the opposing wall, swinging through the lancet window underneath and landing in a vaulted vestibule.

The door to his right led to Vencenza's subterranean tunnels.

Cesare took the exit to his *left* where dust-cloaked stairs descended into lightless oblivion. Groping his way down, he blindly unlatched the tiny door at the end and ducked through.

His eyelids squeezed against kerosene light.

Colossal buildings burgeoned like an antediluvian forest of weathered masonry and wood, the 'sky' a perennial ceiling upheld by stone pillars like arms of an ossified colossus, severing the city above from the city below. The bones and the entrails. The óssium and the Antrum.

Cesare traversed the thrawn maze of the underworld, its thin alleyways and concrete stairs, worn cobbles from millennia gone by basted in the greasy xanthic light of alchemy.

Denizens dwelling in the Antrum's plutonian pits—dubbed the 'carnesíi', '*of the innards*'—lived in spite of the opulent conurbation of the surface realm, protected by Cardea's sorcery binding The Court and governed by the autonomous edicts issued by the Domíne[93] of whichever cadre held sway over a given Antrum region.

Unknown, and thus free.

The ossíi, Vencenzanii who were the marrow of the city's skeleton, ought never to know the world thumping beneath their limen. Not for *their* sake, but for the *carnesíi's*.

Cesare ducked down an underpass, every step a notch to mark the ticking seconds.

The eve of the Governor's assembly approached.

For months, Cesare had plotted, organised intelligence, collected any loose scrap of information he could get his hands on.

Pieces always evaded him.

But to-night, people needed to be made aware of the fragment uncovered at the *Curios*, as inconsequential as the note sitting securely

---

[93] Gender neutral title of a cadre leader (Dóminus *m.*, Domína *f.*, Dominíi *pl.*)

within the inner pocket of Cesare's jacket might be. Ammunition all the same. To-night, too, people needed to be made aware of *Davide*.

Cesare journeyed deeper into the Antrum's valves.

Many solar cycles ago, a pair of ruffians cornered him by a canal inlet near the Antrum's northeast and left him drenched to the skin with a shattered wrist and two fractured ribs, all because a sixteen-year-old lugged around a head too big for his scrawny shoulders. He nursed himself back to health alone, and, in retrospect, the whole ordeal had been almost in good humour—incentive to perfect swordplay with both hands, at least.

Now, Cesare had acclimated to it all. The twisted shadows. The blood currency. The secrecy and declension. As long as the pyre within his crucible burned, he staved off the darkness.

He ascended a nondescript stone porch and breached the doorway.

A bedimmed vestibule greeted him, stairs spearing a steep ascent towards an internal cortile laved in aurous glow.

Geometric muqarnaş rolled like zastrugi along its ceilings, carob and celeste rawāshīn projecting from circling walls perforated with cusped arches.

When Cesare made to pass, a slender woman in black sentinel leathers blocked the mouth of the entrance hall. Thousands of dark freckles peppered her lily-white skin, near-black hair cut short at the chin and a straight fringe resting on a brow hardened by customary bitterness.

"*You* again," snarled Chiara.[94]

Condottiéri of every stock lingered beneath the archways, skins inked with tattoos: the head of a vicious boar or the figure of a graceful hound.

Something about being more wanted than all of them together gratified Cesare's ego.

He *tsk'd*. "Been getting that a lot."

---

[94] *kee-AH-rah*

"State your business," hissed Chiara.

"A palm reading, mayhap? I *am* merely the useful accomplice to your supreme leader's elaborate plans, after all."

Chiara's grey eyes flashed lightning. "I'll have you thrown out—!"

The door at the hall's opposite end opened, hinging all attention on itself.

A woman towered in the archway—taller than Cesare, dark eyes lined with gold and kohl.

Dóminus Ygạl Najm.

A crushed-beets farwa[95] and loose azure thawb[96] embroidered with nacre and faïence around the yoke cloaked her sturdy limbs, dark tresses perched on their[97] wide shoulders and skin a gilden olive. "Are you riling up my people?" Ygạl's smile stretched the scar running through his lips. "Remember whose house you're in."

Cesare nocked a smirk. "Should I bow?"

A game. A twisted dance he took such gleeful pleasure in.

Ygạl threw her head back and laughed until the vaults echoed with nothing but the maqāmāt of their singsong voice. "Let the good man through, Chiara." She gestured Cesare to the door.

He clicked his tongue and raised an impish brow at the sentinel who growled a curse under her breath, storming off.

Cesare followed Ygạl to her office through a lambent corridor assembled from ceramics and coral running alongside a turquoise natatorium, the orange blossom air humid and balmy.

"Warm welcome *indeed*, nirô javêl.[98]"

"You'll forgive the absence of meze, won't you?"

"Third time in a row? You'll have me thinking I'm an unworthy guest."

---

[95] A traditional coat in Saudi Arabia and the Persian Gulf.

[96] A lengthy, long-sleeved robe worn in the Arabian Peninsula and neighbouring SWANA countries. Here are referenced the Ḥarb tribe female dresses of al-Madīnah al-Munawwarah, al-Ḥijāz.

[97] Not a mistake—any pronoun for Ygạl.

[98] *nee-ROH hhah-VEHL*; 'my lord' or 'my lady' in Marlâre; '*jaûn*' is '*lord*' in other dialects, modified to '*jaûna*' to mean '*mister*'. '*Lady*' in non-Marlâre dialects is '*andêre*', modified to '*andreñôa*' for '*missis*' and '*andreâ*' for '*miss*'.

Ygal opened the door to his quarters.

Mā'il calligraphy adorned ecru walls nailed with tekke rugs and embellished by girih tiles, the air dense with the orchidean perfume of salep. So far from her ancestral homes, the Dóminus of The Boars and Hounds hoarded artefacts of both her bloodlines—Sa'āhi and Koşatlen.

Crossed axes mounted the wall above the desk, a shudder scuttling like insects under Cesare's skin at their hideous visage. He discarded the three swords onto the short intarsia table parting a pair of rubellite sofas at the room's centre.

"The lengths I go to." He sat on a sofa, perching a foot on the table's edge and doffing his tricorn.

Ygal sighed. "You've won me over, Agostini." She approached the oak liquor cupboard where stood a fine gold dallah. "Gahwa,[99] mayhap? *Oh!*" She plucked a crystal bottle with delight, drumming her manicured nails on it. "Amaretto!" He poured two snifters of liqueur, one damn well near brimming, handing over the half-filled glass.

Cesare acquiesced. "I note absent your inamorata." He took a sip, cloying sugarcane and almond delighting his sweet tooth. But alcohol all the same. Cesare rarely touched it, needing control over his own faculties. Always. Most importantly, he couldn't allow himself to be touched, and alcohol, such a normalised killer, was anathema to anyone's inhibition.

"Something about a stick up the boss' arse." The Dóminus brought to the table a glittering glass tray shaped into a grape leaf and piled with semolina halwa, finally sitting. "Heard tell the Court cooperated."

Cesare plucked a slice of crumbly confection and stuffed it into his mouth.

Ygal snorted. "A rarity should *you* be speechless! Keeping her in the dark?"

Cesare set aside his snifter and thumbed clean the corner of his lips. "Not my place to run my mouth," he reiterated.

---

[99] '*Coffee*' in Sa'āhi.

"Either way," Ygạl waved a hand, "the show must go on, as your kind says."

*Your* kind.

Ygạl had never associated with theatre. An unfortunate position for Vencenza's citizen—living in a city built on theatres and water yet bearing no affection for either. Ygạl's deepest love lay in the saxaul forests and rolling plains of Kıcunın,[100] the sunburned mountain welkin and volcanic sands of Sa'āhḍa, the arms of their beloved.

Cesare bitterly recalled his enchantment with Vencenzani theatre, those spellbinding childhood visits to the playhouses of Du Rrât a du Errèina when the sojourning troupes from The City of Masks staged their renowned pantomimes with a flamboyance and glittery showmanship the leagues-more-conservative Zargòsa seldom permitted of its own ensembles. Vencenza's embracing of unconventional, radical looks and comportments had always meant the world to Cesare.

And the recollections of what was taken made the knife of resolve in his side just that bit sharper.

"I bring tidings," he broached the subject.

Ygạl drained her alcohol. "Mine hold precedent." The Dóminus dipped into the drawers and splayed out a scroll atop the gleaming intarsia.

Black ink delicately traced labyrinths of corridors, tunnels, parapets across the parchment, the unmistakable simulacrum of a courtyard spanning the map's centre-south. *The government building.* Sketched in all its terrible magnificence. A vast, elevated moat, circumscribed by aqueducts like chainmail, raised the acropolis skyward, severing it from River Vena which bifurcated and flowed around the colossal complex as if a corpuscle before converging once more at its rear.

Ygạl tapped a finger armoured by rings on the eastern edge of the schematic, proximal to the main cortile: the liminal zone between citadel proper and its old wing. "Isaia and I discovered an impediment."

Cesare raised a brow. "Humour me."

---

[100] *KYY-joo-nyyn*

"Garrisons at the subterranean mouth of the old wing are scheduled to change on account of that Moretta incident. Some extra thirty Imperialíi on patrol."

"*What?*" Cesare shot to his feet, reeling back from the table.

Their plan of entry had been so meticulously assembled. Cesare considered each footfall, every hurdle and snare in the grass. He *never* made oversights. He *never* let himself lose.

Ygal toyed with her pendulous nazar earring. "The order was issued no earlier than this afternoon—Isaia's allegations." *So short notice...*

Cesare ran his hands through the back of his hair, dragging the panic into a dark recess of his mind where he killed it. This could be worse—*had* been worse. Slight adjustments to strategy were never a malady, only a temporary injury. "And Isaia is *where?*"

Ygal flung him a sheepish grin. "Should've waited."

Cesare touched his fingers to his heart and dipped into a mocking bow. "Only the *highest* calibre of organisation from *thee.*"

Ygal poured himself another generous glass. "Don't disregard the effort *I* expend on *your* madcap machinations."

"*You* expend?" came a low voice, quiet as smoke with a flicker of Mariano.

Isaia lurked by the doorway, unnoticed as the eavesdropper he was.

He slunk towards the table, clad head to toe in a sleek regalia dark as night, tugging the cloth mask from his aquiline nose and pulling the hood back from obsidian hair cropped short. He stood at Giorgianna's height, shoulders a sturdy square, all bulky compact muscle. Ebony eyes held Ygal with a flinty regard. "Efforts of *your* Boars without *my* Hounds would herald disaster."

"Quite the catastrophe," concurred Cesare.

The Boars had absorbed The Hounds and their northwestern territory seven years ago, when Ygal had been twenty-three—then a year younger than Cesare now and equal age to the twins—when the previous Boar Dóminus, a ruthless man by the name Sabinus Venator, murdered the last Dóminus of The Hounds, fellow Salvatricii Ambroeus Pitino Carcan, being subsequently mutinied in favour of the fairer, diplomatically-minded strategist Ygal Najm who *herself* had been an apprentice of

Venator. Educated in all his brutality despite the condottiéri's misprizing of her outward femininity. How dreadfully mistaken they were.

"Lower your revolvers, cenapler![101] A drink?" Ygal offered Isaia.

The eavesdropper's stony features yielded nothing. "Not on the job." He removed his gloves, pinning the corner of the map with them.

Symbols of Sancta Maria's Saints—the ones Cesare facetiously bothered on occasion—tattooed Isaia's fingers. Gxerqucca,[102] it was dubbed, all inked on himself, a milder manifestation of the authentic custom practised by Mariano cenobites: branding. Cesare knew too that ink spanned nearly every inch of the eavesdropper's bronze-dark skin. That across Isaia's shoulder blades, over a boar's gashful head, leapt the nimble figure of a hound, seadrakes climbing up his calves and thighs, the map of Sancta Maria unfurling over his navel, daggers and thorns twisting across his chest among coils and coils of bramble. Knew it from ephemeral times gone by and not a spark of them left behind in his soul. Another rare person whose touch didn't repulse him.

"Nonsense, Caruana!" insisted Ygal. "That way you'll never drink."

"I want him sober to explain what the Hell's going on," Cesare intruded.

Isaia produced a letter, handing it to him.

"De Tullia's penmanship." Cesare appraised the neat cursive with disgust.

> '...*tighten the area and leave no fissure*
> *so great as to permit incursion*...'

He reached for the note in his pocket. "I have a matching sample on hand, but in due course."

Ygal splashed gahwa into her alcohol. "No chance we'll make it inside solely through the tunnels or that munted old aqueduct with the subterranea clogged."

Besides the operational aqueducts, its two-thousand-year-old predecessor persisted like a lesion across Vencenza. Though a

---

[101] *jeh-nahp-LEHR*; 'gentlemen' in Kıcunınese.

[102] *g-khehr-QOO'ch-chah*; literally '*Sacred Roots*'.

treacherous route, its hollow insides granted passage directly into the government building's southwest.

Cesare chewed his cheek, bouncing propositions and outcomes between the gyri and sulci of his brain. "We might need to flirt with death a little to do it."

Ygal peered sideways. "You want to sneak past *Imperialii*? The Governor's *elites*?"

Cesare tilted his head. "You sound like someone." Calculation braced his tone fast. "Obviously, not all at once. Reduce the groups to five at most and widen the intervals between their transits."

"Some'll be snuck in Libitina's hearse," added Isaia. Undertakers were required to appear at assemblies. "Others'll take the old aqueducts or tunnels."

"We cannot risk losing Hounds if they get intercepted," warned Ygal. "Split up the ranks: few Boars here, some Hounds there."

"And adjust our timing." appended Cesare. "Make it earlier. The assembly is at six hundred. Make the first party arrive at one; feel out the area for vulnerable spots." His scrutiny tethered to a violin-shaped slot on the old wing's fourth floor, shaded with graphite. The point of *their* assembly.

"I and Caruana'll lead the way," Ygal rolled up the map, flinging the gloves at Isaia's face.

"We'll be close behind," confirmed Cesare. "Come what may, your people retreat the *second* something looks amiss, understand?" He glowered at the Dóminus, treating Isaia alike.

"This oughta be wonderful." Ygal swigged the remainder of her glass.

The eavesdropper turned to Cesare. "Your matching sample?"

Cesare fished out the note from the *Curios*, tossing it onto the intarsia. "How much do you know about a man named Davide Mancini?"

Cesare laid everything out. From the raid to Davide to the note Isaia sat rereading.

He hadn't brought any of it to them the previous night on account of his fellow vitae; there was no fibre of Cesare so cruel as to leave his família in distress. Even now, guilt weighed him like a ball and chain fastened to a sinking man. If he could, he'd remain in *The Sunrise* evermore to protect his loved ones, but the assembly swiftly approached, and he made himself into an instrument of a deadly ploy—forced into compromises for his propaganda of the deed. A duality he could never reconcile.

Ygal paced the lounge, a tumult of tension in her step. "If this 'Davide' *is* connected to bandits like you conjecture, it can *only* be here… Which means *he* is!" Her voice flared. "If Manuele Dioli's legionaries pour into the Antrum because of him, the ruination brought upon our innocents will be apocalyptic. This is the *only* place, the Cove excluded, where The Bone King holds no authority. None of the cadres are strong allies and disconnected we are scarce."

Cesare stepped back from the sofas, needing the movement to oil his brain's cogs.

Crescenzo De Tullia was a soul reaper, ruthless and inexorable. For his tenure to be everlasting, his people needed to be done by fairly, or crushed in his fangs like the insects they were to him. If malcontents lived vengeance, their wrath would grow into an unquenchable firestorm to engulf his rotting empire. This, De Tullia knew and feared, without a doubt's shadow, and so, with the commanding cadence of an imperator, he force-fed his subjects canards and black pedagogy.

He didn't just want your body. He wanted your mind.

And, in *that*, Cesare caught the Minister's furtive confession to vulnerability.

"Davide ought to be dealt with," he stated. "He knows something deeper is at play, I'm sure of it, what with his bizarre postil about Cardea. *I* may be his primary target, but he won't hesitate to sell out the carnesíi. If he *must* be so unfair as to lead the entire legion to me like dogs to a foxhole, two can play that game." He pivoted, all sinewy limbs and sleek, whetted motion as his arm swung in perfect keeping with his body's passage through space. A glistening knife slid from his deft grip, cleaving the furious air to snatch the letter from Isaia's fingers and impale it upon the intarsia. "And better."

Isaia glared at Cesare.

Ygal sighed. "We are overwhelmed with intercadre unrest and don't have many arms to spare."

"I don't need arms. I need ears and eyes within the innards while I keep mine on the bones."

"I can be a pair watching *The Sunrise*," offered Isaia. "Chiara'll pick up some of my duties."

"You're already doing enough."

"It'd be a peace of mind," Isaia insisted.

Cesare opened his mouth to reject.

"Reasonable," Ygal intercepted. "Have your eavesdroppers deployed at all points of interest around our district—tavèrnae, inns, bordellos. See if you can sneak a Hound or two into surrounding territories. I'll send word to Leone to keep his Serpents waiting in the grass. This is *our* home; no sleazy parasite is purging us from this body."

The Dóminus of The Boars and Hounds was never invested in liberating Vencenza. His main and only concern lay with protecting the Antrum.

"There's a reason we get along." Cesare dislodged his blade, hiding it and the note in his blazer.

Ceramic shattered in the antechamber, spattered with bouts of profanity. Cesare silently queried Ygal.

"Itxaro[103] took a finger off Vito after a game of cards the other day and he's been pissy ever since," she grumbled. "That *better* not be my pottery! Authentic Tokuzayan is a beast to come by!"

Cesare donned his tricorn and snatched another halwa slice. "Cue of exeunt."

Isaia tugged on his hood and cloth mask, following Cesare out to the sound of Ygal's appalled but unanswered '*you barely drank!*'

---

[103] *eet-SHAH-roh*; in Zargòsian, '*x*' is pronounced as '*sh*'.

The pair dodged Vito and Itxaro's heated squabbles in the antechamber (lucky for them, the ceramic had *not* been Ygạl's pottery) and exited the granite-grey estate, its windows like rectangular white portholes and walls ridged as a washboard.

"Watch your backs," Cesare reiterated, callus-tipped fingers brushing his mouth of saccharine flakes. "You're already knee-deep in this quagmire without me shoving your heads under, and now around any corner could be knives pointed at your jugular."

Isaia folded his arms, coal-chip eyes gleaming with more than an ember of scepticism. "Will *you* be taking your sage advice?"

A half-smile darkened Cesare's lips. "Relay to Aengus my salutations." With a one-two click of his tongue and a quirk of an arched brow, he stole down the alley.

The cool silence of díem sóle's star-speckled morning met Cesare when he stepped out of the tavèrna.

Merely a block down, his attentive eye caught a man's figure beneath a ginnel's tenebrous draperies. His blood cooled when he sighted the beaked mask. *Crow.*

He flitted into the adjacent building.

Cesare pursued.

# SCENE XIX

## HAUNT ME, THEN!

*Cesare | Giorgianna*

THE WALLS BREATHED, black as a coal miner's lungs, straining against the thick wheeze of shadows spewing through ribs of window frames and tracheae of streets. As if asphyxiated by the fresh blood perfuming Cesare's blade.

He took the liberty of hunting down the Guard, luring him from a nearby hole-in-the-wall and slitting his throat. A man he knew—the soldier he dosed with Basilisk Weep[104] the night of '*A Bedlamite's Ballad*'. A Liaison, judging by the hideous swallow sigil scrawled onto his cape.

Cesare peered into the starscape, its nictating eyes weeping albous opalescence.

---

[104] A soporific powder made from basilisk bile.

Basilisks are a large snake, often up to 20 metres (65.6 feet) long and endemic to Isatōnia. Said to be one of the several reptilian species evolved from legendary dragons. Speaking of which, '*isatōn*' is Ancient Rhalese for '*dragon*'; the continent of Isatōnia (literally meaning '*of the dragon*') is in the shape of a dragon's head. Faustina is located on its lower jaw.

He was glad to kill the soldier—there could be neither remorse nor sympathy for oppressors—but how many more would find their way so deep into oldtown? How soon until The Court was no longer a secret? No longer alive?

Cesare's gaze dropped to the scar grafted onto his palm. Blood signed away to Davide.

Each step he danced around the executioner's blade drained him a little more, yet the road back was too long, paved with bones and ruin. He couldn't stomach retreating when innocents were sent to the gallows and guillotine, confined to flower-spun cages to rot, locked in chains for simply being.

So much stood at stake. So much of himself Cesare was willing to tear to shreds. But with those pieces he could stitch the canvas of a better world for those he loved, for those dwelling within the veins and arteries of the city's deepest entrails and most brittle bones. A canvas to paint Life in all its grotesque splendour with no irons to weigh down the hands, for corruption existed solely upon the inherent goodness of the foundation.

Was that not worth sacrificing a Self already burning?

Cesare's feet gnawed by the time he made it to *The Sunrise*. Home.

He glimpsed the auditorium's fresco on his route by, its golden oculus opening to a painted auróra sky as if a window to the Heaven he was never destined to attain. A Heaven which never *was*.

Cesare climbed a ladder backstage and vanished through a passageway in the fly loft, stepping light-footed onto the balcony circling the parlour.

A tongue of candlelight lapped the walls.

Giorgianna sat at the lonesome table below, furiously writing beneath the candelabrum's rutilance, her revolver and the cards she always flourished resting near.

Cesare slunk into the infirmárium to wash his hands of blood, to rid himself of his jacket and tricorn. He realised he'd chewed into his cheek on his way home when crimson bathed the sink.

When he re-emerged outside, Giorgianna's frustration demanded his heed, so he perched his forearms on the balcony, watching her crush the paper and hurl it towards the kitchen. The candent flame guttered as she snarled, ink-tipped fingers imprinting swirls of her bloodline upon the curls she raked her hands through.

"Writing correspondence?" mused Cesare.

Giorgianna sprang up, revolver gripped.

Her cupreous eyes aimed at Cesare like she might slice him open throat to navel right there, and perhaps that reckless way about him would let her. That *reckless way* made him willing to be the cliff face against which she broke in all her tempestuous wrath, after all. He had his own ends to meet; hers fracturing untimely served no good. But Cesare couldn't deny that he stood wanting of breath in her sphere. Or that the two had been silently sizing up one another for no less than a minute.

Giorgianna moved to dispel the tension first, lowering her weapon, yet scrutinised Cesare with a cautious judgement without fail. "Were *you* behind that ruckus this morning?"

Cesare descended to the parlour. "Must keep the eye sharp for the revolution."

"What were you even doing?"

He made it to the table, drawing a stilétto from his thigh just to flourish mid-air. "Knife tricks serve us all, princess."

A bone-like crunch clicked between Giorgianna's fingers as they crushed her quill.

Cesare sheathed his blade. "Listen—"

"I shan't." She reached for her papers.

Cesare filched them from under her fingertips. "The assembly to-morrow."

"Childish fiend!" She lunged to snatch back her possessions.

Cesare tittered, arm angled back and aloft, her grasp falling barely short. "Yet here *you* are."

"Fall face-first into the Null!" She dealt a smite to his chest and jumped back in a huff, tidying the straps of her chemise, the attar aroma of her skin already clinging to his shirt like thorns. "What do you *want* from me?"

"Join us at the government building to-morrow," Cesare stood resolute.

"I endeavour to find my father and asked for no part in your quarrels!"

Cesare bridled. *Quarrels!* As if it were some trivial disagreement!

"Let me put it this way:" he returned fire, still withholding the papers, "you can live out the rest of your life as a fugitive in an empire you *won't* be able to escape. Fugitive or not, you will be a servant to a man who holds no regard for humanity and would massacre all that goes against his vision of absolute rightness. If you pick that path: pity, but that choice is yours also."

"I *know* tha—"

"*Or,*" he ploughed through, "you can play a *different* role. You can help bring his dominion crashing into the earth." Cesare's callused heart burned, a hand grenade. "One way or another, we *will* be forced to fight. There is no avoiding it, only postponing for our benefit. And I don't believe for a damn minute that you're remotely content with living on your knees at a man's feet." Cesare held the papers still for Giorgianna, a stray corner skimming her cheek.

She seized them back. Her visage hardened to porcelain at once. "What's it to *you*?"

"Every person matters."

"I don't believe you," she asserted.

Cesare felt for a tender spot beneath her mask. "But aren't you curious?" His blade found its mark, plunging. "About what The Bone King has to say to his devoted subjects?"

Her jaw flickered. "I don't need to hear what I've heard since my twelfth year."

"But *this* time, you won't be in the throngs. You want that key to the kingdom, right? That knowledge you're owed?"

Her lashes sank like lush canopies as she gazed slantwise, slim fingers treading in contemplation along the caramel hair coiling by her jaw—candle-touched and byssine. *Her knuckles are scarred...*

Giorgianna beheld Cesare, striking him stupefied. "I assume flaunting a note isn't the sole purpose of díem zenítis."

"Scouting the area and document-gathering are the usual extracurricular activities."

Her hessonite eyes widened, each facet glimmering with intrigue. "Document-gathering?"

Cesare staved off a smirk. "Correspondence, criminal files, legislation, et cetera."

Giorgianna pressed her cherry-red lips into a firm line. "Fine." She grabbed the swealing candle. "I'll join to-morrow if it pleases *his majesty*," her scowl cut, "but know that, should I perish, I swear to the Gods, I'll haunt you into your grave." She barged his shoulder and fled upstairs, the rageful ghost of her rose-honey sillage left to dance with his shadow in the dark.

The moon spied through the sun-shaped lattice at Cesare's bluff, her pallid yarn spindling across the canal's atramentous ridges.

Cesare found the lonely cufflink he always held onto, the gift from Paolo, its other half lost to history months ago, and a hollow pit opened in his chest. What would the impresario think of this mire? The man who took Cesare in, gave him a chance to live again after he was maimed within an inch of his life. The man who taught him all he could—by age nine, attending school in Canronê proved an impossibility when Cesare could no longer hide his bruises, no longer rise from bed from the swelling of his joints, and an undocumented migrant's caste barred Cesare from Vencenzani education. The man who was more his father than the one who begot him.

Would the old impresario understand De Tullia's twisted mind?

Would he commit the violence Cesare did?

Would things be different if he'd stayed?

Cesare had wished he would have.

So many nights he'd suffered alone, a child afflicted by terrors of a past he couldn't escape no matter the miles he laid between himself and those moors. He'd never once thought he might long for a father's fondness, and yet he'd found in Paolo precisely that. A sturdy hand and donnish demeanour. Not one disparagement of Cesare's adolescent snaps and wounded hostility. All the same, when the impresario implored Cesare come away with him and the other thespians following *The Sunrise*'s closure, Cesare refused, for he couldn't bring himself to flee another home. He'd burn with it, this time.

The paper Giorgianna hurled aside beckoned.

Cesare banished his dark reflections and picked up the crumpled globe, folding and pocketing it along with his cufflink, too dark to be read. Per routine, he checked on Lissandri and Rosalia's sleep, then Eligio's nightly painting séance in the back room beside the wardrobe, returning to the infirmárium once his worries palliated.

Emptying his pockets, he lit a candle, filled the bath with steaming water and, fully clothed, submerged, perching his elbows and feet on the railings.

Water was sacred. 'Panîn' in Marlâre, from the Marubhūl 'pāṇi'. Symbolic of ritual cleanliness. Nothing could purify Cesare, De Tullia would surely agree, but the scorch brought incongruous comfort— grounding as the touch of a flame.

He unfolded the paper.

Wrathful hands had scrawled cursive across the page with violent intent, words smeared until losing sanity. Better than *his* penmanship, by alleged accounts.

> *'Find hidden words spat by the blest to this*
> *plane from the celestial lazulum, sentenced to*
> *quietus beneath the soffits of a suzerain's keep.*
> *The overlord shall be defied—impart succour.*
> *Forget not the that which you would rather so.'*

Following lines repeated ad infinitum, paper torn through beneath their brutality:

'...*blood does not wash off blood does not wash off blood does not* **wash off blood does not wash off blood** *does not wash off blood does* NOT WASH OFF BLOOD DOES *NOT WASH OFF* **BLOOD DOES NOT WASH OFF...**'

The ink trickled off the page into Cesare's psyche, perturbing and sirenic.

He admitted to bearing, the night prior, an affection for Giorgianna's pain, one he felt deeper than any cut. But as his ephialtes dispelled, senses returned to him, and he saw an opportunity worth seizing:

In his quest to uproot the hegemony, every tool held use, and rage, even if notoriously unwieldy, was a simplistic sort. All Giorgianna needed was an incentive to pledge her sword.

Affections came second to ideology when the end was liberation.

Cesare slipped the note to the bottom of a sigarétta box, then singed a coffin nail with the candle and tipped his head back, smoke dragging into his lungs to abate his nerves.

Deafening silence consumed until the timepiece ticked over to three hundred, until water ran tepid and wax wept for mercy at candlefire's feet.

Cesare's feet yearned to scale rooftops, fingers flicking insistently at the wheel of his lighter.

But not yet. He knew it, even if begrudgingly.

Revolution tasted sweetest in due time.

DAYS WORTH OF SLEEPLESSNESS sank the face glaring back at me from the wardrobe mirror, every straggling second a fight to keep myself above water.

A pleated cerise skirt, girdled by the translucent white lace of an apron, swished around my calves, my underbust corset panelled with rose-pink ribbons and the chest of my white blouse festooned with a mighty gold necklace pinned with brooches into an 'M' shape, sleeves sheathed by a puce bolero. Though Mother once proudly arrayed herself in the provincial dress of western Vencenza, eventually, she demanded I opt for Vencenzani proper—none of that 'yokel' garb!

Five hundred was the hour summertime sun tore its lances through night's dark armour. Beyond the window, blackness of three hundred garrisoned the horizon, fog obscuring the skyline.

Amidst the vìtae's candy-coloured clothes at the wardrobe's rear, a mask cabinet stood like a centrepiece where, at my eye level, rested the all-too-familiar bàuta. Its porcelain and papier-mâché surface lay bare and bleached, mouthless visage formidable, jarring, cryptic as an eidolon of a primaeval age.

My fingers tingled.

Seeking out my father had been my intention to-day, yet I acceded to Cesare's pharisaic wiles of '...*document-gathering are the usual extracurricular activities.*'

Documents the likes of which could detail Emanuela's murder.

There was not a moon gone by nor a turn of sunlight lived that I didn't miss Ema, wished I could drag her back from the Null myself. But she would never return, her life an unpaid debt.

The bàuta's eyes cradled an abyss, peering into me. Into *mine*.

Perhaps I knew I was robbed of choice.

"I detest it far more than you ever could."

I flinched at the voice, pirouetting.

Cesare materialised like a wraith, clad in his macabre costume bar the headpiece.

"Ces!" Eligio popped into the doorway. His shirt was ruffle on ruffle on ruffle, turquoise and powder-pink, a blushing pannier sitting dainty over aquamarine pantaloons and thulian boots. A befitting hat overhung a pale rose colombína like a bouquet. "I'm taking Rosa to the *Curios*; meet the three of you at The Rib, yeah?"

"The *Rib*?" I gawked.

Vencenza's main bridge—a resplendent monument depicting sprawling mosaics of sea voyages and maskers, a lustrous ruby heart, vessels emanating gold sunbeams, at its centre. How such a peopled landmark was *any* place for clandestine conclaves was beyond me.

Eligio's features melted into a smile. "It'll make sense, trust."

"Don't stoke her expectations," quipped Cesare.

Eligio chuckled and left.

I beheld Cesare coldly. "Here to gloat?"

His brow ticked up, long nails tapping the bàuta. "To retrieve my quasi-visage."

I studied the mask's antiquity. *Why does he detest it?* He must surely relish in the bedlam he ignites. "You know," I pilfered the mask, "some claim 'bàuta' comes from the folkloric exclamation 'báu-bào' used to frighten children." My eyes slitted when they returned to Cesare. "*Báu-bào!*" I shoved the mask into his chest, winding him momentarily.

The click of his tongue plucked my nerves. "High spirits this morn, I glean." He handed me a holster belt, rich as varnished wood. "You'll need this."

Hesitation furrowed my brow. "For?"

Cesare pulled a pair of trim push knives from his jacket and held them for me. "Bullets are costly." He simpered. "And dreadfully uncouth."

I levelled a withering behold but swiped the knives, spinning towards the mirror.

With their polished steel and balanced hilts, the weapons' scant weight sank like revelations to my bone. *A lawbreaker's blade.* Now befitting of me too.

Every breath I drew taught me there was only *one* means to my end; *one* thing which could repay the debt I was owed. *Blood.* Through violence. Filthy yet sacrosanct. But was I ready to draw it, this time? Could I requite myself?

Graceful footsteps echoed closer.

My eyes rose like orange-red suns; the hate in my own gaze had never before singed me.

Hands in pockets, Cesare hovered close behind me, tall and lithe and cloaked in near-perfect darkness. Mirth danced like starlight in his eyes. "Regrets?"

A scowl twisted my heated face. "You're a suicidal maniac."

His haunting laugh contoured my bones. "I'm more partial to irises." He grabbed his headpiece, the sunless cold enveloping my rigid form at his departure.

The blade of the knife in my scarred hand centred my eye's reflection. *To repay a debt...*

Trailed by the foxfire of alchemical lights sprung up like mushrooms along oldtown's dark vasculature, Cesare, Lissandri and I walked west of *The Sunrise* to no logic *I* could discern.

We veered sharply into a crumbling fortress from pre-Empire days, once serving as a protective fortification, coming upon a misplaced well, its innards drowned in stygian blackness like cuttlefish ink.

Cesare, as The Bauta, hopped onto the well's brim.

My stomach dropped. "*Inside?*"

"Be a dear and point out an alternative." He disappeared into the well.

Lissandri waved a hand. "It's not what it seems."

Gulping, I fell for a second cloven in half, landing with a stumble and grunt atop metal instead of water, cramped in with the other two. Cesare's body pumped with blood; emanated heat like a lava lake hidden vulnerable as a wound beneath cracked scabs of rock. He flicked open his lighter to illuminate the slimed brickwork and an iron lattice on which we stood. Water pured beyond it.

He pushed on the bricks.

The structure gave way to a portal.

The lighter barely brought into focus a cobwebbed staircase snaking around an enormous pillar into oblivion.

Lissandri readjusted his high-necked blazer of brass damask, casting a half-smile my way. "Right behind you."

I counted thirty-seven flights to reach the stairs' root: a narrow crypt dim with the cold breath of alchemy.

The passageway forked. We turned right.

The crypt dilated to a colossal catacomb.

I clutched a gasp in my palm. *"Faces…"* Literally. Hordes and legions of them. Carved from sombre stone, they stared from the ceilings, the walls. Darkness shed viscous as ichor into the clefts between the visages, eldritch and grotesque, decayed as the skeleton of this ancient city. "What is this…?"

Etchings of grandiose celestial skies unfurled beneath my echoing feet into a cosmos rendered in stone older than language. Father's astronomer heart would have thought these floors magnificent.

"Gallery of Faces." Lissandri's words bounced off every gaunt cheek and stony brow. "Tunnels from the Empire days. Some say it's real people. Prisoners, slaves, the works."

My attention wandered into the swarm of faces, like corpses petrified in centurial passage, long-dead wails of their tormented souls haunting the acheronian corridor. Tinnitus rended my skull.

*The Empire will never cease to plague us.*

The gallery meandered and the hordes trailed. I never forgot our inevitable destination.

Around a corner appeared Eligio. "Here I am."

I frowned. "You said you'll meet us at The Rib."

My eyes followed Eligio's forefinger as it pointed ceilingward, and realisation struck like a pelted rock.

The Rib was half a city away from The Court of Secrets. How extensive were these tunnels if we now stood below it? *Below water…*

Lissandri snickered. "You don't know the half of it."

I handed him a vexed glare in response.

"Reports?" Cesare asked Eligio.

"Imperialíi up ahead. Ten in this next area alone."

*Imperialíi.* 'The griffins', apropos of their emblem—the child of a valiant lion and noble eagle. Gold and steel, dazzling and deadly. Trained for decades to protect. More pertinently: to kill.

Dying in the cold innards of Vencenza was the last thing I looked forward to in all my days.

Whether by luck or divine intervention, we stole through unseen, in perpetuity shadowed by the hiss of capes like basilisks, and ascended through a long-abandoned guard station into the citadel's oldest hallways —the buffer between the museum and Ministerial house proper.

"Shame," mused Cesare. "I'd been holding out for apéritifs of mortal peril."

"Such a *let*-down," said Lissandri mordantly, dusting off his brown rhinegraves.

Stepping down a short staircase to a sheltered door, Cesare plucked from the cinch of his jabot a lockpick, manoeuvring it until the deadbolt clicked.

We entered a vaulted chamber chiselled into unadorned limestone, aerated by empty lancet windows and peopled by four. *Condottiéri.* The twins had at least forewarned me.

By the distal wall, a man of about my height stood upright as a soldier, black leathers head to toe and features bar his coal-dark eyes obscured by a hood and cloth mask. With him chatted a titian-haired man in tartan trousers and grey shirt, freckles dusting a bearded face and body slung easefully against the wall.

A shadow-cloaked Gazaari woman hunkered in a nook beneath the ceiling. Long hair shone radiant as freshly-fallen snow against her warm tan.

At the navel paced a woman surpassing Cesare in height. A loose şalbar and waist-cropped çapan[105] the hues of sunset dressed her, a peşkabz[106] and curved saif belted to her solid waist, shoulder-sweeping chestnut hair restrained by a tie.

A scarred grin stretched her stately features. Brown eyes narrowed on Cesare. "Look what the vultures dropped at my door." A burr I couldn't quite place barely echoed in her canorous voice.

"So long no see, Ygal," said Cesare, audible smirk and all.

---

[105] *chah-PAHN*; a Central Asian coat or cloak.
[106] A type of Indo-Persian knife.

# SCENE XX

## EPINOIA

*Giorgianna | Cesare | Giorgianna*

OF ALL I EXPECTED from the odd company, alacritous comradery was not remotely the first.

The hooded Mariano man was Isaia. The Tír Línmharne[107] redhead eagerly introduced himself as Aengus. Ygạl, a Koşatlen-Sa'āhi woman who went by any reference, was the Dóminus of The Boars and Hounds, a condottiére cadre. I didn't catch the white-haired woman's name before she flitted through the door opposite our entrance.

I hovered by my lonesome near a high lancet window, my eyes creaky with sleeplessness and head full of needles.

Below, eburnean flagstone paved the vast courtyard, a mezzanine soaring at its distant end like an enormous throne projected from an edifice risen dignified into the milky sky. A narrow balcony circled the mezzanine's rear a step below, followed by a second, elevated, all

---

[107] *teer LEEN-muhr-neh*; the people of Tír Línmhar.

elaborate stucco and cartouches. No extraneous colour marked its skeletal pallor bar the guillotine's carcass at the mezzanine's feet and the black ropes upon the gallows, the citadel a stark patch of bleached bone within the city's soma.

"A proposition of armistice." I heard Cesare.

When I faced him—his mask—he offered me sigaréttae.

"There's something to be said about novelty." I plucked a dart, slipping him one more snipe—"if you'll cease talking"—before holding the sigarétta to my mouth to test the sugary wrapping with my tongue's tip.

Cesare opened his lighter with a half-laugh. Sheltered its flame in a gloved palm to char the pale paper. Tobacco shrivelled, succumbed, an acrid scent dizzying me as mist gathered on my tongue like a fleshy ashtray.

He hid his lighter, rapt gaze deserting my lips in search of my eyes which, in turn, snubbed his.

A door opened with a restrained creak.

"Pleasant morn." A woman's voice chimed silver as coins.

My gut keeled, feet pivoting in place at their own volition.

"…couldn't tell *if*—" the woman halted, Ygal's long arm securely around her.

A collared white blouse, sleeves flaring to elbow-skimming triangles, clad her rubenesque form under a nephrite satin vest, plain jodhpurs and boots sheathing her legs. Glossy black waves tumbling down her soft shoulders wove loosely into paired plaits. Protuberant eyes, grey as storms, stirred behind a pince-nez.

"Lucrezia…?" I breathed, and the sigarétta came plummeting from my fingers to the stone.

"O—*oh*…" Petite palms folded over her mouth. "Giorgianna." She ran towards me, arms outstretched like a mother to a child she'd thought perished. "Dear *Gods*—"

"Don't touch me." I stumbled back, voice bumpy as a rubble road. "What is this?"

The chamber fell silent.

"It's all right!" Lucrezia clutched her chest. "Let me explain, I *promise* I can."

I looked at Cesare. "Did you…?" His eyes were impassive, and comprehension bore down on me with the weight of an ocean. "I will kill you."

"*Nonono!*" Lucrezia grabbed my forearms. "Step aside with me, Giorgianna, *please*." She pulled me into an offshooting vestibule, shutting the door.

"*You* are why he was so intent on dragging me here." I spat. "Was the night of '*A Bedlamite's Ballad*' because of you?"

"*Listen*, look—" She breathed tightly. "*All* I do is eavesdrop at *The Crescent* to keep watch of Basilio and deduce the movements of the state however possible. I am *not* there for Cesare; I had no say in his schemes."

"The day after, you let me out of the theatre." My eyes thinned. "Did *you* know something?"

"I had an awful premonition. I believe in demonic spirits—*that*-that's not the point, *I*—I tried to find you." Her words squeezed my chest. "All those months… Then Donatello told me that *perhaps* he'd seen—"

"*Donatello?*"

Lucrezia blinked. "*Y*…yes?"

"Your *friend* from lower óssium you spoke of?" I sneered. "A *dollmaker?*"

*Donatello tittered…*
'*…shall be* thrill*ed to know.*'
'*A season's passage was all it took.*'

The scattered shreds began to sew into a grotesque picture.

'*Lucrezia* shall be thrilled to know'… *Lucrezia* had been the 'contact' upon whose request Cesare was at *The Arum*. And what she'd told me: '*This is not the world we should wish to live in.*' How eerily it aligned with Cesare's '*Is that a world you want to live in?*' As if an omen.

"Giorgi—"

"How long did you know my whereabouts?"

Her cheeks drained of colour. "Early morning of díem auróra."

My jaw slacked. "Díem auróra…" *It's díem zenítis…* "And you didn't think to come to me? You didn't think to *tell* me? About this? About *anything*? To at least give *some* indication I wasn't forsaken? Do you fucking know how *excruciating* my loneliness was?" The words I spoke were pathetic and forlorn, so I anchored my tone in rage—the only solid force I still knew.

"I *couldn't!*" pleaded Lucrezia. "Venturing out of upper Vencenza's bounds could be *suicide*, hence mine asking Cesare to accompany Tello in my stead."

"So, he *knew*." I'd said so! "They *all* knew…" Betrayal boiled my blood. "And he said nothing?" *Lowlife fucking bastard!* "He was at *The Arum* specifically to confirm if I was me, he *spoke* with me—I'd *questioned* him, yet he *still* withheld the truth?"

"I told him to," admitted Lucrezia.

"*Why?*"

"*I* wanted to tell you about all of this—me. Myself."

"That's foolish!"

"I know." The mercury of Lucrezia's eyes rippled, a piteous expression smeared across her face like cosmetics. "I should've done this better." She reached for me.

My trembling fist gripped a push dagger in a heartbeat. "Stay away from me." And I fled down a dark hallway, ears shut against Lucrezia's pleas.

In The Court's slums, every tender word could mask venomous turpitude; every kind gesture owed a due. Yet I allowed myself to cease glancing over my shoulder. Just like the governing body, these people—*strangers!*—thwarted my every step, steering me off my path towards justice. Every one of them a crook. A *liar*.

Shadows cocooned me as I disappeared someplace I did not know.

FIRST OSSÍI TRICKLED ACROSS THE UNADORNED CANVAS of the square like much-needed paint.

"What do we do if there are people on death row?" asked Lissandri, peeking through a spy window in an oriel. Below, the undertaker, a white-skinned iridite with dollish corkscrews pink as fairyfloss, dragged her black hearse: an enclosed granite cart smuggling condottiéri, ornate and gothic as her frilly dress.

"You'd need to be closer to them than the Guards," noted Cesare. "The only way to do *that* is to quite literally *be* them."

He'd tried stopping executions before, but the authorities' determination to kill their convicts ensured that the guillotine *or* gallows being thwarted made no difference. Spathae, pugiones, crossbows, the executioner with his hideous scythe, were never at a shortage. And if all else failed, a beating from a seasoned soldier could do it.

By the far mezzanine circled Illutoríi in ouro-plated armour and helms, capes the cascade of arterial blood. Ruby eyes encrusted eight-pointed stars at the hearts of their breastplates, lips of their gold vólti black as scripture ink.

Cesare scrutinised their clustering around The Bone King's throne like flies to a corpse pile, their parasitic numbers. Scores of Illutoríi normally accompanied the Minister of Churches, but the High Priest was nowhere in sight. As all else, Cesare chronicled the details with a mathematician's precision.

"Never taken on an Illutóre," mused Ygal.

*Best case scenario, you won't to-day.*

Cesare lent an unseen smirk. "There's something to be said about novelty."

THE FIRMAMENT ENGORGED with sore shades of lividity, on the verge of rupturing into a haemorrhage of harrowing daybreak in the likeness of a heart aneurysm.

I'd descended a storey, fleeting along a balcony pinched against the flank of the edifice. Colossal peristyles shot heavenward from the foundation to bolster the jutting terraces above. Up ahead, the balcony protruded into a loggia, bulbous and small.

"Whatcha doin', girl?"

A recoil electrified my limbs.

The white-haired condottiére perched on moulded ornamentations under the loggia's dome. Orange-rose clouds embroidered the squared neckline of her gridelin blouse, seemingly hand-sewn to resemble a dəəl,[108] cuffs knitted with an endless knot ulzii khee.

Onyx eyes sparkled beneath monolids. "Have your own plans?"

"Legends tell of scouting the area and document-gathering." The quotation cut like a mouthful of rusty nails.

"Nobody of ours is in the building."

*Another lie.*

Something in my visage must have shifted, blackened, because the woman's tan blanched as if a ghoul had conjured itself up before her. "You're practically trepidating!" She hopped down, petite and light-footed. "I'm Sarnai." A smile perked up her round cheeks. "Apologies, I reported for duty at Isaia the Eternal Snore's request and hadn't the opportunity for introductions." Glossy suyh[109] dangled from her ears and a harness strapped three daggers to her leather-sheathed thigh.

My shoulders loosened as I stepped to the railing. "Giorgianna."

---

[108] *Deel*; traditional Mongolian attire akin to a folded robe, a square-shaped flap on the outside of the garment sporting hasps also present below the armpit and over the shoulder.

[109] Mongolian earrings, long and often adorned with colourful enamel.

The square droned with mutters like a hive, order reigning the crowd. An artificial symmetry I once pretended to fit, at the behest of my mother's strike contorting myself into the double-consciousness of adolescent comprehension that to be 'Othered' under despotism was to die. So, I killed myself first so I may survive. *Yet here I am.*

"I like your hair." I heard Sarnai say, her features beaming when I beheld them.

A meek smile hurt to attempt. "And I yours."

"In truth," Sarnai brandished a white tress, "charcoal brown, these locks are."

I met her with intrigue.

Her laugh flurried, glittering and cool. "I tailored it!"

My brows sprung up. "You're a flesh tailor?" A magus.

"Learned it in Vencenza. Only hair, though—tailoring living matter is agonising." She chuckled. "I know. Why would I leave peaceful Örgön Gazaar? Well, believe it or not: not *so* peaceful. War with Gĕikùx̄hésh[110] loomed, so conscription officers came to my settlement in Jegün Kəgər[111]—recruited *me* at sixteen. I made a runner off the army wagon and…" Sarnai gestured between us, "now you and I're chatting."

My heart sank. "That must have been dreadful."

She shrugged. "Little skin off my back, ultimately. I love my family, of course, they were all wonderful, but I knew to return to my settlement was to bring death unto them at the hands of the military, and I'd long-desired worldly adventure."

"Scars in the flesh are half of the wound."

"What wounds one might only scratch another."

Words abandoned me when silence reaped from the square every voice, rustle, clink.

Even the rush of wind died.

---

[110] *geh-ee-koo-KHEH-sh*

[111] *jeh-GOON keh-GEHR*; 'East Steppe' in northeastern Örgön Gazaar; also known as the '*Örgön Gazaar-Gĕikùx̄hésh Grassland*'.

# Scene XXI

## Demiurge

*Giorgianna*

FIVE MINISTERS FILED ONTO THE MEZZANINE.

The General led, armoured in hammered gold, the Adviser following in bronze-trimmed umbrinous robes and a biretta, salt-and-pepper hair laced into a waist-brushing braid. The Grand Judge I detested with everything in my soul shadowed him, robes and bourrelet black as the death-dealer he was. In his tow strutted the Magister in a zone-front gown and escoffion of fuchsia brocade. Finally trailed the bejewelled Minister of Coin in fur-lined garb: a grim emanation of his 'Treasurer' title.

Breath withheld for another spell before out swept The Minister of Churches—High Priest Benetto Abelli.

Their[112] dalmatic thrummed bright as haem, a triangular chest piece projecting far past their shoulders beset with the drizzled ichor of rubies.

---

[112] The pronoun 'they' is adapted by the High Priest of the Order of Illutère regardless of own gender identity not only for honorary purposes, but because it is utilised as a

The two diagonal peaks of their papal headpiece, disconcertingly tall, dipped into a central concavity, sanguine painting the lips of their burnished gold aperúcca.[113] Gripped in Abelli's red-gloved hand, a ceremonial sceptre stood heads above their height, apex mounted with a triple face haloed by sharp rays.

Two Illuteríi clad in flowing realgar accompanied them. Translucent veils draped their heads, skimming their hips to hide them from the eyes of the world.

"The Divine Invocation ought to be intoned prior the proceedings forthcoming commence." Honey-voiced and silver-tongued, their archaic words hummed a choir's hymn as they lifted their hands, palms opened Godsward to cup the trickling dawn. "In this material form, we subjugate ourselves to our high deities, the Triple Face, their sacral light. Watcher, cleanse our eyes so we may see no evil. Speaker, cleanse our tongues so we shall utter no vice. Thinker, cleanse our minds for we ought not think transgression. Purify this flesh, purify this blood, purify our tarnished nous so we may be worthy of thy totality. All were one and will be again. The fragmented shall coalesce." The orison, once reserved strictly for the intimate communions of votaries within the basilica's walls, played the keys of silence, its echo forever dimming in the cosmos.

*'Turn a blind eye; dwell evermore within thy ignorance.'*

Pre-Imperial Illuteríi considered personal revelation in the divine to be the basal stratum to salvation, not faith in ecclesiastical authority, nor man-scripted doctrine. *How far we've strayed…*

Then, upon his skeletal kingseat, arose the Minister of Dominion.

Sepulchral darkness scuttled across the courtyard like spiders at Crescenzo Zuane De Tullia's pace—susurrant with the pewter silk swathing his slim frame, obsidian tendrils of hair, waved and long, spinning around sharp shoulders fitted with an impearled ribbed doublet. His black hat's brim cast a shadow over raddled flesh, his jaw gaunt,

---

*plural* in this specific context as an homage to the Illutèri pantheon—the High Priest is regarded as a sort of 'medium' of the Triple Face.

[113] *ah-pehr-ROOCH-chah*; literally 'sacred'. A full-face mask worn by the Vencenzani High Priest.

mouth dour, nose thin. A swallow pin perched upon his breast. An ashen cadaver.

I shuddered, skin filthy with webs as his shadow crawled up my spine. A darkness of injustice. Of a corrupt order.

"Mèi ossíi.[114]" De Tullia's voice resonated deeper than surely possible, plangent, rich as venom dripping into my blood. "The dissension over bypast turns has assuredly plagued you with doubt. Rebel hosts vying to break us asunder, infect us with fear, accost our bones. Yet, through the insubordination, the treason and heresy within our veins, we persevere. Few words can mollify, for when a pestilence rots this body, empty verses deal little remedy against the true ailment. We must excise it at its genesis, piece by piece if demanded. And piece by piece it shall be done. To-day, and beneath the blessed eyes of our Gods, our blood shall be rid of filth."

Half a dozen crows escorted three figures to the gallows.

Maskless faces, shackled wrists, pressed clothes, pristine persons: just as Vencenzani death row inmates always were. To see killed someone you might, shallowly, deem reputable, *confronted*. It could be *you*. Grimy scraps and bloody noses granted the populace detachment. But if the highest paragon of virtue wasn't safe, where did that leave the rest of us?

I studied the convicts.

A red-haired woman in geometric emerald.

A statuesque blonde in sangria satin, tottering and babbling inanities.

A young man in turquoise, black-white striped waspie cinching a slight waist, auburn hair adorned by a beret.

Recognition struck me. *No…*

"Zilia Meneghel," *the woman assaulted by soldiers the morning of 'A Bedlamite's Ballad'*, "and Calliupa Soriano." *The lavìre from someplace better who frequented* The Arum's *tavèrna…* "You are sentenced to death for suspicion of conspiracy and treason against Vencenza's state and people." My throat dried to powdered glass. "Arturo Dioli." *My old*

---

[114] In Faustinian linguistics, the possessive noun '*my*' corresponds to the gender of the *speaker* unless in plural. Faustinian has three grammatical genders: male, female, neuter.

*neighbour, arrested that final time I saw papa...* "You are sentenced to death for suspicion of conspiracy, treason against Vencenza's state and people, and murder."

My breath amplified in the hollowness of silence, pulse pounding at my temples.

"Yet, to-day is not without glad tidings. A prolific criminal, long-evading justice, has been caged. A conspirator and traitor." It seemed as if De Tullia could have smiled if it were within him. "No blood can be absolved no matter how old it grows, for with time it only grows harder to clean."

*Blood does not wash off...*

Seven crows walked a singular man towards the gallows.

I peered at him.

Tall, limber, diamantés sewn into the cosmic black of his swallowtail coat like asterisms, hair dark as leather-bound ancient tomes.

A harrowing realisation corseted my ribs.

*Father.*

# SCENE XXII

## ACATALESSIA

*Giorgianna*

"LUDOVICO DAMIANI." *Don't!* "You are sentenced to death for conspiracy, treason against Vencenza's state and people, for repeated debased and underhanded acts, for espousal of insurgency, and for harbouring literary documents long forbidden."

I couldn't breathe. Couldn't breathe. *Let me breathe!*

"Maggots are worthy of no final words." De Tullia's voice thundered —a dreadful demiurge.

The euclidean plane dissipated into nothing but the gallows, my father, a blameless man, unmoving at its centre. *Nonono please I cannot lose him—not him! I have no one!*

The condemned stood upon the soaring gibbet, Guards delicately wreathing their throats with ropes as if mere jewellery.

A crow held the jerking Calliupa so she wouldn't fall untimely, Arturo's shoulders shivering with tears, whilst Zilia shrieked a banshee's condemnation: *"No Godly light upon your transgressions—*

*you shall* pay *for your inhuman vice, both you cacodemons*! *The mind is* uncontainable! *The mind is* impregnable! *The mind is not to be* des—!" A baton's smite snapped her sentence asunder, her cheekbone cracking and oozing like an eggshell.

The High Priest and their Illuteríi hummed a prayer, cherubic voices unified beneath a bleeding miscarriage of a sun and Gods' remorseless beholds.

De Tullia's pale hand touched the sky. And came down.

The executioner yanked the lever.

Gibbet floors gaped: a maw into the Everlasting Null.

The snap of necks, the choking, laboured gargle of futile struggle made the welkin ring. *pop! pop! pop!* And the callous will of high justice played out in a bloody pantomime.

Horror squeezed me until I burned with the coarse abrasion of ropes above empty gravity. Helpless pleas clogged my throat.

*Oh Gods.*

> *Gods.*

>> Gods!

>>> *Nonononono please Gods* WHY?

*How many times must I relive this?*

The sick dance of the strangled stilled, Death releasing their muscles, liberating them of pain, and I remained to feel *all* of it.

"Giorgianna?" Sarnai's voice sounded far away, but I saw nothing.

Did Cesare know?

Did the twins know?

Did Lucrezia know?

Is that *too* why they insisted I come today? Why Eligio couldn't bring himself to speak the truth of Cesare's intentions?

*It must be.*

*It must be…*

*It must be!*

"Let this stand as warning to every rebel, each traitor and wayward crook and lowly tramp seeking to incite sedition," pronounced the Governor, and I wanted him to die. "Your blood shall be upon you."

De Tullia's chin tilted where the sun bled and bled and bled. "One more fire snuffed out—"

*"And one more fire lit!"*

# Scene XXIII

## Heresiarch

*Cesare*

MORNING WIND SMELLED OF SUMMER. Beneath it, the tang of foreshadowed upheaval crackled through Cesare's veins.

Feet perched on a high parapet's edge, he gripped the railing, his dark visage suspended over the murmurs and exclaims sweeping the square. "You never spoke my name." Mimicry of woe clipped Cesare's voice.

"*LEGIONS*!" Steel burned bright as soldiers drew weapons at the General's command, closing around the Ministers like shields.

"Look alive," mocked Cesare. "I've always wondered if a griffin really bleeds gold." He swung over the balusters onto sheltered stone as crossbow bolts cleaved the raging air.

Three soldiers, two griffins and a crow, dropped with black-fletched arrows in their necks, a third griffin tumbling from a far balcony and smashing open inside their armour against stone. Red.

Gasps swelled.

The General shouted for a halt. Ministers and their minions huddled like a flock of puffed pigeons upon their miserable mezzanine.

In the umbra of high windows prowled sharpshooter Hounds.

"Growing rusty at this game, De Tullia," tutted Cesare, stepping onto a balcony's rail with feline balance. "You denounced those people as criminals, *traitors*, accused them of lawless collusions, yet *you* send love letters to bandits and condottiéri, recruiting them for your dirty work." Cesare extricated that faithful note, pinching it between two fingers above ensnared eyes. "In your handwriting, *mèus dónno*."

"Your words ring hollow," declared De Tullia. "A babbling hangdog with not a modicum of integrity or virtue who feeds on upheaval like a tick to blood and serves nothing but his own wretched ends to cripple us."

"If *virtue* is what *you* have, I'll gladly burn in Hell." Cesare walked along the slender bannister, open air shrieking an unanswered invocation for his fall. "I'm fond of irony, that old playwright's trick. You wish to speak of self-servitude? Of *integrity*? Tell your subjects why you command the General to pardon bandit crimes in lower óssium so long as they retain utility for you." Cesare displayed the note he acquired in the immolated gondoa. "Far be it from me to lament one rolling head fewer, but if your loyalty is with the people as you claim, why do you exonerate those who commit violence against them? What was that dónna Meneghel spoke of you?"

"Men who seek to mislead shall always find those callow and soft-headed enough to follow their false teachings," De Tullia put simply. "You and your lies shall never achieve anything but."

"*There's* that irony," sniped Cesare. "Would you like another set of eyes to ascertain your words?"

"*Poisonous vermin!*" bayed Manuele Dioli.

Three Imperialíi knocked their bolts.

A dark arrow tore from the eaves.

A griffin fell.

One dead.

Cesare drew a revolver.

***Boom!***

A swing around a caryatid to the perpendicular railing.

Crossbow quarrels whistled a hair's breadth by him, unbloodied.

**Boom!**

*Clatters.*

   *Clangs.*

      Three dead.

The Imperiáli trio lay massacred.

"You didn't answer my questions, Ministers," hissed Cesare.

"Your calumny deserves no such charity." The Governor's dour face never flinched. "Mark my word, terrorist: your next time in this courtyard shall be upon the guillotine."

"How assuring that my damned soul shall be granted a next time."

"You are a cancer," spat De Tullia.

"Bloodborne," Cesare fired back.

"And metastasising," a voice called below—a man loitering among the distant colonnades.

Confused murmurs reverberated through the square.

Cesare squinched at the man he'd never seen nor heard speak.

The stranger seemed to grin, then donned a morètta black as death.

# SCENE XXIV

## ALEXITHYMIA

*Cesare | Lucrezia | Cesare | Giorgianna | Cesare*

MORETTAE SWARMED THE COURTYARD. A furore erupted as hordes of the populace crashed over each other in frenzied desperation to escape slaughter.

The General spat choler, his Blades thrusting into the fray to rip it asunder. Murders of crows descended. Honed steel clashed against crooked daggers. Morettae fell by the dozens, no fewer soldiers and ossíi joining their gruesome demise as blood and innards drained across bleached stonework. In the hidden halls of the old wing, Ygạl bellowed over the din.

Cesare turned on his heel.

A bolt hurtled towards him, crested with gold and aimed for his chest.

THE TWINS SCREAMED from the window as Cesare hurled his shoulders out of a bolt's path and stepped back, stumbling over the edge of the rail towards the pit of pandemonium.

Lucrezia yelped and shut her eyes.

Glancing back, she found Cesare gripping the balcony for dear life before swinging himself two balusters over to dodge another shot which tore his cape.

"Pull back as negotiated!" Isaia shouted.

"Damn negotiations!" proclaimed Ygal. "I'll not let The Bauta bask in *all* the glory!"

Lucrezia's gut somersaulted. "Don't be ridiculous!" She clutched Ygal's wrist to the muscle, gripping her lover's scintillating gaze. "This isn't *glory*—it's a fucking bloodbath!"

"We won't leave Ces behind!" retorted Lissandri, he and Eligio with knives in their hands and fire in their eyes.

"We promised," Isaia hissed.

Ygal gnashed at his eavesdropper. "And I *ordered*." She kissed Lucrezia's cheek as if it could bring respite, and advanced with the twins and Isaia for the doors into the government house—the same direction Giorgianna fled in.

A snow-haired condottiére ducked under Ygal's arm on her hasty return to the vestibule.

"*Sarnai!*" Lucrezia all but threw herself at the flustered woman. "Have you seen Giorgianna? Tall, curly-haired."

"She ran into the square."

Lucrezia's heart dropped. "What?"

"She seemed… distressed."

Terrible realisation dawned on Lucrezia. "Ludovico was her father…"

Through a dextral door, Chiara burst in a huff. "We're attempting to syphon us out notwithstanding Ygal's imbecility." She advanced for the door into the house proper.

"Giorgianna is in the courtyard!" exclaimed Lucrezia.

Chiara let out an unsmiling scoff. "She's not making it."

Lucrezia's hands clammed up, tears flooding her lashes as she clasped

Sarnai's elbows. *"Oh,* I messed up *I messed up I messed up,* I should've come to her earlier, Sarnai—!"

Fingers rapped Lucrezia's cheek. *"Luce!"* Sarnai grabbed her collar. "Not now! We gotta *leave."*

Lucrezia burst into tears, but relented.

CESARE SWUNG HIMSELF FORWARD, tumbling onto a balconet.

Humiliation wracked his body with tremors. *Thwarted!*

The implications of the bedlam spelled a disastrous unmaking.

A Moretta was what he needed. To understand *why.*

He bashed the glass from the window with his revolver's grip, exchanging the firearm for stilétti and slipping between the jagged fangs.

Three crows swooped in.

Steel screamed against steel as Cesare parried, shoved, slashed, narrowly dodged a sword to the throat and a pugio to the back.

*Quickest first.* He bobbed and sidestepped, kicking a crow's legs from under them. Swung. Deadly lòthmir ripped their throat, arteries spraying like geysers.

Cesare revolved with the momentum of the slash, hoisting himself upright to bury his second knife into a soldier's sternum with a *crunch* of hard bone.

*One more.* He rent his stilétto free, blades dripping blood in an orbit around him as if his body was a pivoting fulcrum before meeting with a spatha's whetted edge. The soldier exploited their rare height advantage to kick Cesare in the abdomen. He reeled back, winded. The spatha came down. Faltered mid-air. Clanged to the marble.

The soldier convulsed.

A karambit's tip protruded from their neck. Blood rushed down gaping lips, and the soldier slumped lifelessly to their knees.

Isaia stood behind.

Cesare hauled breaths. "I told you to retreat!"

"Boss' orders."

Ygal rounded the corner on cue.

"What is *wrong* with you?" Cesare bristled. "We're all *dead* if one of your people gets caught!"

"Worse comes to worst, they know the drill. Be*sides...*" Ygal's sentence faded when Cesare saw the twins.

"Why did you come down here?" His question shook.

"We're not abandoning you," avouched Eligio.

"Neither are you getting yourselves fucking killed on my behalf!"

Lissandri half-grinned. "Looks like we all see eye to eye for once in our lives."

"*HALT!*" Imperialíi streamed into the hallway.

Cesare pulled the twins behind him. *Each footfall, every hurdle.* "Everyone get back!" Fishing the saltpetre pouch from his blazer, he launched a cascade of spagyric gunpowder at the legionaries, flinging his opened lighter like a fulgent comet tail after it.

Saltpetre erupted into a grandiose firestorm, frenzied screams a chorus to accompany the chaos litany outside.

Cesare doubled back, eyes shielded from the inferno.

Transient in its fiery birth, the powder burned through within seconds, leaving capes, eyes, flesh of the fallen and choking to smoulder, sarcoid and offal-sweet, stomach-turning. Yet powerless to tear down empires, and that's where Cesare's fondness for saltpetre ran cold.

He'd burn to the ground the entire rotting kingdom.

FRENZIED COMPULSION CHASED ME down the longbones of the citadel's hallways.

My vision barreled in my push against currents of legionaries and citizenry, hair writhing like snakes as I launched down a stone staircase and under a hypostyle cloister. The white-toothed orifice of the roaring courtyard gaped ahead.

Sunlight had torn open the aneurysmal sky, clementine blood and icterine sanies pouring into the cyanotic noontime blueness of death. *Father…*

I plunged into the maelstrom of Morettae and soldiers, of condottiéri and ossíi and brutal fury.

CESARE DESCENDED TO THE COURTYARD, flames and lost souls in his wake. Corpses and Morettae clogged every passage. Few condottiéri proved so stupid as to run into suicide, but some favoured Dóminus Najm's whimsy.

Their party dispatched a flock of crows at the court's mouth, grizzled, nine-fingered Vito and his Abeslâri nemesis Itxaro joining their ranks.

The seven Ministers long-since fled the site of battle, their gold griffins, silver peacocks, rubious Illutoríi likewise, leaving pewter crows to mitigate the havoc. *Cowards.*

Cesare drove a stilétto between the neck and shoulder of a crow grappling with a Moretta, swinging its twin at the bug-eyed fucker's throat and slitting it wide with a bloody spritz.

The corner of his eye caught a flash of poppy-and-rose darting through the swarms. *Giorgianna?*

"We need to clean these Morettae up!" called Ygal through the clamour.

"What *you* need to do is get *out* like you were *told*!" Cesare demanded with a voice to destroy legions. "Do you *want* to die?"

"He's right," insisted Isaia.

Someone cried a warning.

The sun blotched black as iron bolts tore down.

Cesare lunged sharply to cover Eligio with himself.

Cries soared, Cesare biting down his own as his shoulder blades took a shot.

The incursion ceased.

Cesare searched frantically for Lissandri through pain-swamped vision.

The tinker huddled behind a column. Unharmed.

"*Move out!*" Ygal finally conceded, limping from a quarrel impaling her shin.

Cesare tore the quarrel from his back, vision black momentarily. "Eligio, Lissandri!" He gripped the twins' shoulders. "Morettae are worn thin. Get vólto and *leave*."

Eligio paled. "But you—"

"Don't worry about me," Cesare said curtly and slipped into the choking throng.

# SCENE XXV

## DRUNKEN WITH THE
## BLOOD OF THE SAINTS

*Giorgianna*

I HALTED AT THE GALLOWS WHERE CORPSES SWAYED in the sanguine summer breeze.

My eyes soldered to the man dressed in velvety midnight, those asterisk-shaped iron stars along his lapels, five on each side, dim as his eyes. And his face was *mine*: the indented lip, the heart-shaped cheeks, the vulpine facets.

Tremors lay claim to me. *I lost my father…* The man I'd yearned to find again. The only person I had left. *They stole him from me!* Just as those faceless men stole Emanuela.

My bones snapped like the necks of the hanged, *pop! pop! pop!* as that rage festering inside me clawed out. Starved, vengeful. *A Shadow.*

A step ahead, ignorant of the massacre surrounding, the executioner studied the dead as if admiring his work.

*All of you are SCUM!*

I lunged, stabbing a knife into his shoulder, yanking him down as he shrieked, and driving the second into his throat. Flesh squelched as I wrenched the blade to rip through the thick column of his neck. Blood sprayed my cheek like a trickle of tears down my maskless face.

The push daggers followed the executioner and his scythe down. His nose smashed with a wet, bony *crunch* against pallid flagstone.

My eyes locked upon the murder, upon my hands—a butcher's instruments—where blood, heady and scalding, pooled in the orphic crevices of my palms, seeped under my nails, bejewelled my fingers in the scarlet of garnets.

One slash, one vengeful caress, and the degenerate choked. *So easy to kill.*

All my life I had Run.

Now, I wanted to drown the wretched world for everything it reaped from me. *Blood does not wash off.* And no justice could ever be imparted under this vile authority.

Shouts clangoured. *"Murderer!"* Three crows swooped, swords gleaming.

Darkness blotted my vision. "Like *you!*"

My fists choked the snath of the executioner's scythe, hate turning it paper-light as I swung, blade the blinding flicker of a newborn star, and rived open a soldier chest to pelvis.

His entrails sloshed in clumps from the spewing orifice of his gut.

His eyes hooked into mine, pin-picks for pupils, the blood surging from his lips his only scream.

A gladius sliced my waist, hip; my lungs cast a scream into the death-imbued firmament.

Wrenching the scythe lengthwise, I decapitated a soldier. His head sailed the wind and *thunked* across the stone, blood scattering the air and running through my flicking curls.

The final crow swung his sword.

A death knell rang, quaking the sphere at the meeting of our steel.

I thrust the soldier away, burying the scythe in his head with viscid squelches of brain like a cloven coconut. His worthless life extinguished.

It was with strain that I endeavoured to free the scythe.

Fingers clasped my wrist, my legs stumbling into a forced sprint.

I braced a red-sheathed fist to punch but halted myself barely in time.

"Are you out of your *mind?*" wheezed Lissandri. "Why are you out here?"

"*This way!*" shouted Eligio.

We vaulted over eviscerated bodies—southwest of the courtyard where the ancient aqueduct's black gullet swallowed us.

# SCENE XXVI

## QUOD ME NUTRIT,
## ME DESTRUIT

*Cesare*

CESARE CROSSED THE DISCORD, slinking into labyrinths built atop the mouth of the old aqueduct, its pristine ivory smeared alizarin.

A circular cortile spat him out like blasphemous words, a City Guard at its omphalos preoccupied with a beaten-half-unconscious Moretta.

**Boom!** The Guard dropped with Cesare's bullet halving his spine.

The Moretta rolled onto their belly, flailing to clamber upright.

Cesare slashed their tendon, grabbed their scruff, and hauled them onto their back, fisting their collar. "I'll ask *once*," he hissed. "What did you idiots think you were doing?"

Their larynx bobbled. Broken teeth sprung up along gums as cracking lips peeled back. "We ma… 'is choice. I *thou*—we thou… we 'ad it figu… ou… but we didn' coun… on slaugh… of us… like 'is…"

"Are you daft?" Openly attacking the most guarded place in all of Vencenza and not expecting massacre!

The Moretta's lashes fluttered. Muscles slacked. "*...we were lied to...*"

"Lied by whom? About what?" Cesare thrashed the Moretta. "*Talk—*" A bolt found its bullseye in the Moretta's neck. Cesare dropped them, narrowly evading the ruption of gore.

"*Halt!*" Into the cortile poured legionaries. One griffin. Four crows, two of them sharpshooters.

"How malapert, officéri," jibed Cesare. "We were conversing."

"Surrender!" the Imperiálus barked. His spadone glistened as much as his armour—untouched by carnage. "You are surrounded."

Cesare shifted his weight, surveying the pavement's flatness, grip. If fast enough, he could clear the biggest threats no issue. "Don't take me for a fool." He shot one marksman.

Veering, he dodged a bolt, two, his movements sharp to preserve energy as Isaia taught.

**Boom!** The second sharpshooter went down.

The Imperiálus mirrored Cesare's steps—a soldier knowing every trick in the book—the rogue never out of his sight. "Make this easier on yourself, criminal: drop the tiresome game."

Cesare touched bloody fingers to his jabot. "Exhausting *indeed* it must be to chase without end, clinging to the hope that one day I too might tire." A thick muscle in the griffin's jaw flared, delighting Cesare. "Such a *burden*." He spun the revolver in his hand, finger to the trigger, and pressed the barrel to his own forehead, hammer clinking melodically. "Yet takes so little to relieve it." His forefinger flexed.

"Lower your weapon!" the Imperiálus cried.

Cesare's brow wilted in mock penitence. "You're right. Our Lord of Bless'ed Dominion likes them alive for the slaughter. I wouldn't wish to pilfer the wind from his sail."

Legionaries descended.

*Three on one.*

Whirling from a falchion's path, Cesare flung two knives.

Steel wedged in the neck and jaw of a crow.

*Two more.*

The celestial circle rattled, metal singing merciless battle songs as Cesare clashed with the Imperiálus, a divine wight and a shadow wraith, two powers evenly matched.

"Hope you enjoyed your laugh to-day, clown," grunted the Imperiálus, spadone screeching against Cesare's stilétti. "It shall be your *last.*"

Cesare's muscles trembled. *Too strong to shove back.*

A remaining crow closed in.

Cesare freed a stilétto, his arm buckling beneath the griffin's force. Skidding along the stone, he pivoted towards the City Guard, his blade's edge prone as it slashed cloth and meat with a *shuurng*. The crow wailed, scrambling to scoop intestines back into himself.

Cesare rolled as the griffin's spadone struck stone, barely missing his veil.

He swung his legs across, flipping onto a crouch stance in tandem with the passage of the spadone, then sliced the griffin's shin to stun him, sprung up, and thrust his stilétto through the griffin's eye. "They say he who laughs last, laughs best." He slit the soldier's throat to end his pitiable anguish, the heap of muscle and metal that he was crumpling.

Imperialíi knew every trick in *the book*—taught the art of murder through recitals of combat theory within the cushioned confines of their golden cage. *Clueless.*

Bedlam waned in the square, the world jarringly quiet.

Where the floor had been ivorine, blood and fleshy wads of leftover human now bathed it crimson, the ferric stench of butchery in the air coating the airways with smothering sludge.

Cesare retrieved his knives and stole into the rete feeding the cortile, stumbling against a wall. His vision blotched. A stab carved his thigh, dozens of cuts littering him like corpses upon a battlefield. Now, nothing remained to draw his mind from the consuming pain. From the shame.

Morettae decimated his stratagem, sleepless nights squandered just to grant the Governor all the more ammunition to propagandise The Bauta as his scapegoat—the very demon the citizens ought to revile.

Cesare's head throbbed as he replayed the recent occurrences: Davide, the *Curios*, the underhanded government correspondences, The Morettae. *It must connect.* The bigger picture lay shattered and it was Cesare's to piece together.

They would not quell him. The regime held no power to break him. He was only as relentless as his hand was forced to be, and it was forced more and more each ticking second.

He needed a stronger advantage. A key to the kingdom of his own. But his heart bated—a desperate creature.

*Not now.*

It hurt…

*…too much.*

# SCENE XXVII

## GNOSIS

*Giorgianna*

BELLS. BELLS. BELLS.

Belfries denounced unrest at the citadel as we crawled from the aqueduct's intestines.

The cityscape realigned into recognisable detail. *Aegidius Boulevard.* The street where lived—

"*Mother*!" I bolted with no explanation.

Vencenza clangoured, daylight glaring down like the Gods.

Bloodlust ebbed, wrath stepped away, and with no rage to be my raft, I couldn't breathe as despair drowned me.

Mother's apartments reached six storeys into the welkin, ornately carved of golden sandstone beneath *The Zenith*.

I vaulted to its apex.

The door to my mother's home yawned—opened as a funereal omen, and mere steps before it, a skylight shone the effigy of a xanthous sun onto the floor.

My lungs fumbled breath, sinew sewing, but I forced myself to enter even as my legs dissolved to seafoam beneath me.

Not a tendril of aroma marred the air, every maple shelf fastidiously arranged with hand-blown lattimo glass and feather-dusted books.

I slewed into Mother's office.

Schematics of buildings wrapped the walls in place of wallpaper, houses, patios, cathedral apses illustrated by a meticulous hand. Mother had sought work in Vencenza proper as an architect, wishing to strengthen the homes of Ferréli, her family's village, the disrepair of which had begun taking lives. Now, with its inhabitants gone or dead, a labour camp replaced Ferréli, and Mother sought a different perfection.

The woman sitting at the drawing board shot to her feet, statuesque, clad wholly but the face and hair in the darkness of raven wings. *She didn't attend the assembly.*

Our eyes, equally amber, clutched one another.

Elenedda Murgia's silk over-skirt had been raised in the back to be slung over her head into a veil,[115] her wide shoulders laid with the same caramel coils I had.

"Giorgianna." The coldness of her tone lanced me.

I feared her, just as *she* feared *her* mother. But a pitiful splinter of me wanted to be held by the woman who begot me into this slaughterhouse of a world.

"Why papa?" I choked out. "I don't understand, he—"

"Was a crook," she accused.

My head shook. "Of *all* people?"

"You are clueless, Giorgianna," mother sneered, pacing towards the window overlooking a wide canal.

Dried blood tugged at my skin as my hands balled. "*Explain* then!" My tongue bled against the words—I developed a taste for it, that sapid suicide. "He *never* gave me the answers he promised! I *know* you know, so *tell me!*"

Mother waited out the clock's torturous ticks with steel-spined dignity until a heavy sigh sank her shoulders, poised enough to seem rehearsed.

---

[115] An element of north Sardinian attire called '*faldetta cupaltata*'.

A tamed pupil of a tyrant's pedagogy. "He was a card dealer in The Court of Secrets."

I frowned. "What?"

Dealers oversaw card games, *dealing* cards to players each turn. Vencenzani practice. They were known to accept bribery—to deal cards rigged in the highest bidder's favour.

"Where do you think he learned sleight of hand?" My mother's tongue flogged. "Why do you think he was always so evasive about his youth?"

> '...the sheer magnitude
> of what I must say daunts
> me; I must ensure I handle
> everything with proper
> grace and caution.'

The terrifying image gained detail.

"How long…" I swallowed, "have you known?"

Mother throttled the temper I knew she detested. "Before he and I first spoke."

My lips pulled from my teeth. "But you are disgusted *now*?"

She turned like a prodded asp, beholding me with eyes that were mine, and I wondered if—*how much*—she hated it. Hated *me*. "I was mistaken, thinking him anything but a reprobate."

My torn-up heart fell hard as a body from a balcony. "Dealers aren't punished with death." *Something else, then…*

From the bottom-most slot of a bookshelf at the room's opposing end, Mother shovelled chunky tomes, reaching into the gloom and pulling out a dagger holstered in dark leather. A baselard with a golden hilt. A garnet eye encrusted its pommel, upon the crossguard embedded a matching teardrop.

"This was his." Mother grimaced. "Of better use to you than to me, no doubt." She handed it over like a cursed grimoire.

The dagger sank in my tremoring grasp, its eye gazing back at me, red as the blood on my hands. I pulled the hilt. The luminescence of distant planets iridesced within the blade's pale steel.

I stepped into the gelid waters of my mother's gaze. "Did he kill?"

"No." Her jaw fluttered. "It made him no less a criminal."

"But what did he *do*?"

"Stuck his nose in things he oughtn't, Giorgianna!" snapped Mother. "And after all these years, it finally caught up to him."

De Tullia's sonorous voice shuddered my memories:

> '...*sentenced to death for conspiracy and treason... underhanded acts... harbouring literary documents long forbidden.*'

My father was a dissident.

*And he endeavoured to tell me.*

My teeth clenched. "De Tullia kills because he likes to and has nobody to restrain his tyranny. He knows fear is the strongest sedative."

Mother stuck a finger at me. "You *shan't* blaspheme the Governor's name before me!"

I tensed as if expecting an acquainted strike but squared my shoulders defiantly. "I don't believe you revere this regime, mama—"

"Elenedda." The brusque word struck like her palm.

"...What?"

"You shall refer to me by my name, if you refer to me at all. You are your wayward father's daughter—*not* mine."

"But I didn't do anyth—"

"Look at your hands," she spat. "Look at you!" Witch pyres rutilated in her eyes. "Like calls to like." *Abyss unto abyss...*

She marched from the office.

I followed frantically. "How can you be so heartless? No compassion yet you wear mourning garb?" My voice splintered. "How did you grow to hate him so much? You had a *child* with him. You *loved* him—!"

I lurched at the lash of her hand across my cheek, the spike of pain and the algid surge of terror. "*GET OUT!*" Her fingers locked in my curls, pulling out of me a yelp. "I do not wish to hear from you; I do not wish to see you; I wish *nobody* to utter your name in my presence. Be *grateful* I do not turn you in like you deserve, you misbegotten harlot!"

She all but hurled me.

Words backed up in my throat, arms curving around myself like a small girl again.

Donning her aura of propriety, Elenedda Murgia pinned straight her spine and lifted her chin. Her steel-cold gaze drove into my chest—a scissor-blade. "Get out of my sight."

And I had no one at all.

Terracotta light spilled into the àtrium when I made it to *The Sunrise*; I ached all over as if beaten senseless.

"Giorgianna!" Eligio's fretting tones, his figure a smear at the summit of the stairs. "We were…"

My legs swept from beneath me, joints locked and muscles wound tight as springs ready to rip me apart as I clung to my father's dagger like a child to their dead parent—the only piece of him left. A grim reminder, again and again, that I had no one. *Everyone I love leaves me…*

Tears spilled down my face for the first time in almost a decade. Sobs ripped from my chest as I asphyxiated on the agonising, helpless desperation to do *anything* to cease my pain. But there was nothing.

*I couldn't save you either…*

I screamed a banshee's call into the pitiless cosmos, and everything drowned.

# ACT II

*...and that became*

*shadow matter*

"I want to dig up your body still clothed in heaven and give you back to the world, give you back as lightning, as the electric volt that rides through a man, through the chair he's strapped to, his last words transcribed for the record, known, remembered, unrightfully saved."

—*Crime and Punishment*, Traci Brimhall

The following chapter contains a scene of *graphic self-harm*. The text up until the first chapter divider can be *skipped* if necessary.

# SCENE XXVIII

## TRANSGRESSOR

*Giorgianna | Lucrezia | Cesare*

*HOW MANY TIMES HAVE YOU MET DEATH?*

*Poppy tears in your áti's pipe to opiate the knee fractured by her helpmeet's truculence. The way she and your mother shouted.*

*Your mother's hand fan dripping in the blood of your knuckles. The tally marks of scars on your father's arms. On your hands.*

Steel dug through my thigh, deep into my quivering muscle.

*Falco's whip riving your back.*

Putrid blood pulsed with unearned life down my legs, into the gullet of the rough and empty bathtub's drain.

*Those men who broke your fingers, who killed your dearest friend.*

Its hungry gurgle laughed at me.

*Those men who stole your life.*

Jeered.

*End it. Flay your flesh. Peel it back with your teeth and leave your half-eaten husk to fester with your past.*

I buried my face in my folded knees, father's dagger clutched to my shallow heart, and wept and wept and wept until my tears surely ran bloody as my skin, my form a shivering crumple.

*Death always floated near you, its scythe splitting you in twain—that cursed diptych. Your one face: Love unto Grief. Your second face: Rage unto Vengeance. And it was Fear hinging them, a barrier, a link.*

Whatever wretch of a soul remained within me, I would forsake a thousand times over to be a flower bud again—innocent and small. To be *flesh.* Human. To feel the touch of love, to have my life, my father, my beloved friend with me again. Even the strike of my mother's fan with my every imperfect cello recital, her hissing *'nothing is worth it'* in my ear beneath those creaking cages. To be a girl.

*But when you held that scythe, did Death* become *you? Was the scythe a reaper in* your *grasp? Did you break that barrier, or did you shatter into one unrecognisable heap? Shadow devouring itself. Ruination unto yourself.*

Agony tore out as I slashed my thigh.

*Ruination unto the only person who ever loved you.*

I deserved to be hurt by my father's blade for the death I cursed him with—a blameless man; a precious spark of kindness extinguished from the awful world.

*Maybe you were Death all along.*

My blighted ichor became the walls, a carpet slathering the floor, the tiny room a bloody womb ripped from a mother's mangled corpse. *Misbegotten.*

Hinges creaked like the squeals of butchered pigs.

*You are alone now.*

And I deserved to be.

LUCREZIA STILLED in the infirmárium doorway.

"Giorgianna?" She raced to the tub.

"All those stars are dead—glowing corpses hanging from the sky like gallows millennia away," Giorgianna raved in a thin voice clotted with tears. "I cannot look at them. I cannot think of papa. He is a ghost glowing among the planets—" A sob broke her open. "I won't know peace so long as the cosmos unspools each night *and I cannot look upon myself without seeing him, I cannot endure this pain, it will never leave me, my veins will never be cleansed unless I rip open my wrists and let the putrescent past pour from my deepest well until nothing is left within me and you* knew, *you all knew they'd kill him yet you dragged me to* see *it!*" She blocked her ears, fisting her hair, gasping as if drowning.

A garnet-encrusted baselard clanged from her hand, its blade blood-sheathed.

"*Grim lemures…*" Horror seized Lucrezia when she beheld the slits across Giorgianna's thighs, gaping and fresh beneath her skirt's ruffles. "Give me that!" Lucrezia groped for the dagger.

"*Leave me!*" she shrieked as she huddled away.

"You are *hurting*—"

"*Why am I* hurting, *Lucrezia?*"

The deadbolt clicked.

"What's going on?" Cesare peeked into the infirmárium.

Lucrezia's heart jumped. "*Ah*—" she sprung up, "could you please go?"

"*Cesare,*" hissed Giorgianna like a snake coiled in the tub. Her eyelids split open, sclerae drenched with blood. "*Let mine be the last face you see on your deathbed.*"

The gravity of her words tilted the ether, spacetime lurching against her condemnation. Her *hate*.

Cesare's gaze soldered to the magma of Giorgianna's eyes for several breaths too long, his teeth clenching, unclenching, strain abating only when her glare slit cold as obsidian for Lucrezia. "I see venturing into oldtown is no longer *suicide*."

Tears threatened Lucrezia. "I only ever wanted to help."

Giorgianna embraced her emaciated knees as if she had nobody at all. "Leave me." All she had left to give was a brittle whisper.

*I'm so sorry…*

Lucrezia dashed across the infirmárium and dragged Cesare out with her, whirling to face him once they stood on the dim balcony outside. "We messed up, Ces." He recoiled from her touch. "And she *hates* us for it." She clasped her fingers under her chin. "I thought I was doing *good*."

"But was it *right*?" questioned Cesare.

She frowned. "Is good not also right?"

"Then *was* it?"

Lucrezia continued fighting tears. "She's spent over a month in anguish. She's barely eaten or slept, and—" She caught herself before she could blurt what Giorgianna was doing to herself. "And she's right, you know? I'm such a fool for being here now yet not when she needed me. *Should* I've let you and the twins tell her the truth?"

Cesare held her under firm scrutiny. "Go home, Lucrezia."

She eyed his tricorn, his jacket. "And *you're* en route to…?"

"Consult your miranrô[116] on the Moretta ordeal."

"How are you faring?" She held back the urge to tack on a '*hypocrite*'.

"Leads on Davide are scarce if at all to be availed of." Cesare's jaw fluttered as he nibbled his cheek. "I might be forced to resort to grasping at straws." *Does he ever stop to breathe?*

Lucrezia studied the geometric face gilding the infirmárium door, hollow coldness occupying her chest. "There is something immensely wrong with the world, and she is its sickness reflected. Yet she won't let anyone console her." When Lucrezia's life fell apart, she wouldn't give Donatello a second of peace from her wails, awful as that man was at *anything* by way of comfort.

Cesare's features blunted. "Meet to-morrow at the gallery." He descended to the parlour.

"Did you know?" demanded Lucrezia.

Cesare halted at the bottom of the stairs, half-turned. "Know?"

---

[116] Masculine form of '*lover*' in Marlâre. Feminine is '*miranrî*'.

Lucrezia embarked on her own descent. "Giorgianna believes we knew her father would be executed, that *that's* one of the reasons you insisted she come along to the assembly. You snoop around government precincts plenty. So, I'm asking you: *did* you know?"

Cesare stood squarely facing the dainty woman, jaw hanging unhinged, eyes struck wide. "Who the fuck do you think I am, Lucrezia?" She flinched at the utter affront in his tone, made all more jarring by its quiet, its stern serenity. "*I* who watched my own mother, whom I *loved*, be murdered in *front* of me—you think I would *do* that to somebody? Willingly? *With premeditated callousness*? You think I didn't see how she loved her father? You think I didn't care?"

Shame inflamed Lucrezia's face and chased her eyes away from the pyre of Cesare's. She'd thought it good to ask, but hadn't considered deeply enough the tone she employed, the subject she broached. Intricacies of familial ties had long since receded from the forefront of Lucrezia's consciousness, she owned. *Is good always right?*

Cesare's expression cooled, eyes descending once Lucrezia braved a glance. "Just go home," he urged almost gently, and fleeted off.

*But where* is *home?*

Lucrezia donned a colombína, pocketed her arms in her virid pelisse, and made her abashed departure.

The night's cimmerian organdy swathed oldtown as Lucrezia stalked its warrens.

She gazed longingly down a south-bound turn, thumbing her nazar ring for comfort, and wished with all her might to run into Ygal's arms where she couldn't be harmed, where she was no longer an unloved wastrel in this rotten Hell of a world. Where she had a life. Was *someone*. Maybe that's why it struck so sharply to witness Giorgianna's sorrow. She comprehended her loss, to a degree.

Notwithstanding the ache in her heart, Lucrezia cleared oldtown, the Solar Square, and re-emerged in upper óssium, capillary-bursting blood pressure induced by the veil of ancient azoth abating.

She dipped her masked face as she passed a cawing squadron of City Guards herding a line of convicts chained by the throats and ankles into a black gondoa. A metal blindfold was welded to the prisoners' heads: one strip across the eyes, one bowed over the skull, a simulacrum of a fox's snout embossed upon the front as if to mock.

Lucrezia's pulse quickened anew with her pace, her feet carrying her against a current of vermilion-clad votaries of the Order, yet halting when her eye snared upon a civetta owl—perched atop the pinnacle spearing for the black heavens above a chapel's frontispiece. Its orbs glowed an etheric yellow, dimming all the stars beside them, and Lucrezia's throat bound to a choke.

When Lucrezia had been eleven, her uncle persuaded her father to bring her along to a Defacement, a ritual performed by the High Priest of the Order of Illutère which had once been reserved only for private religious congregations, much like the Divine Invocation intoned at the assembly.

Illutèri eschatology professed that an individual's pnèuma could not reintegrate with the trimorphic godhead of the pantheon if their material form died without a physical face, or if their face was flayed from their body within The Eleven Days of Liminality—the first eleven days following death during which the pnèuma purportedly hovers in a liminal state between materialism and the spirit realm.

Thus, Vencenzani criminals who died in prison or stood on death row were subjected postmortem to the 'Defacement' rite wherein skin was cut and peeled from their face, then cast into a fire, their body finally confined to the dirt with no immolation as otherwise customary in Vencenza. This supposedly rendered the mutilated individual 'faceless', in a spiritual sense, damning them to never transcend hylicism.

*That* had been the final nail in the coffin within which perished the hope of Lucrezia finding faith in the Order. Seeing the Domínie[117] in crimson gloves, their sacrificial dagger fouled with blood—the same blade that had been put to her body, the church floor a pulsing placenta and all those gilded curlicues becoming mattery decay, the unnamed

---

[117] An address of utmost reverence for the High Priest.

prisoner flayed of a face in a grotesque display of 'purification' whilst everyone looked on unmoved, Lucrezia understood for the first time that she lived not in a home, but a cage. A dagger may only be worked by a High Priest, after all. In anyone else's hands, it was sacrilege. *A Malefactor's Mark.* And blood was filthy. Yet sacrosanct to the flesh.

And now, talks of curfews and military checkpoints floated among the populace, votaries of the Order flocked to the streets, the Governor spoke of a 'purification' in reference to the slums and the oldtown—that the lower castes of society were blood-sucking parasites. Lucrezia knew the fourth step of genocide was dehumanisation.

Yet, somehow, Lucrezia feared the worst was yet to begin.

*THE SALACIA* HAD ALWAYS READ like some unfortunate joke. A hole-in-the-wall tavèrna, little more than one big, empty barnacle, yet named after the heavens' grandest constellation.

The salted air twirled with accordion and alcohol flowed bitter, guffaws and ribaldry and wooden clunks rippling out of the porthole windows and across the waters beyond. Patterns emerged among the motley of eccentric and dastardly characters—tattoos of harpies, wyverns, seagoats, monstrous masks with many mouths. And beneath the virescent glow and revelry: a deadly gleam of blades, a leering iron grin, eyes glinting and high on a night's sybaritism. The undertow of violence waiting to surge through the sphere at any wrong stumble.

Shaded by the far booths, Cesare sat with Isaia and Ygal, the eavesdropper's cloth mask drawn up and the Dóminus scanning the scene from behind acoin-decked baṭṭūlah.[118]

"The riot." Cesare stabbed his stilétto into the beaten wood table, speaking Calvessi. "I wager a guess that it's traceable to Davide. There's

---

[118] Gulf burqa; a stylistically diverse half-mask-like fashion garment from the Arabian Peninsula and Persian Gulf.

little loyalty in this world and I don't foresee *him* proving to be its embodiment regarding the Bone King."

Isaia folded his arms on the table. "You think he's a turncoat for The Morettae." The pair of condottiéri wielded a slower, more broken alloy of the mercantile cant, given their separation from the surface world and seldom crossing of paths with mariners, but the little encryption they could impart upon their verses sufficed to dispel some paranoia.

Cesare nipped his cheek. "When I broke off during the riot, I got hold of a Moretta." And hadn't yet told anyone despite well over a moon's cycle passing. *This habit of mine is getting out of hand.* "He claimed they were 'lied to'." Cesare leaned against the bench's high back, planting a foot up onto a stool at the table's head. "Davide isn't stupid—the unfortunate nature of our predicament."

Ygal sipped her third wobble glass of cognac. "That's peachy keen fantastic, Agostini," a hefty helping of agitation soured their breezy tone, "but our strategy's stale as pirate piss. *Your* strategy, frankly."

"We need our own key to the kingdom." Cesare plucked at the ruffles of his black blouse. "I propose we look to the people surrounding De Tullia: his Adviser, his pet griffin. We've given it over a month; the city no longer whispers so shrilly of the assembly and the legionaries' senses dull once more."

Ultimately, the ruling class cared for nothing but the retention of their governance, *themselves* enacting cruelty beyond anything availed to the proletariat. *Violence is fated fruit.* The Morettae acted misguidedly, killing the wrong target, but it was the officére's club that bred criminals to begin with. After all, neither The Bauta nor The Morettae existed before De Tullia.

"In the coming days," continued Cesare, "I intend to inspect the northeastern periphery of the government building: a neck of the woods I haven't given much thought to previously. It backs into the building's old wing, sentinels stationed en masse all around, more so now." He pushed past the sting to his pride, the shame of failure. "The fourth floor holds the Adviser's office; the one below's reserved for the treasury." His tongue clicked. "I'm sure the former keeps a treasure trove of information himself."

"I'll remind you that I've got few fucks to give about the ossíi and their overlord's political games," Ygal bit. "My concerns are *only* with carnesíi, you are *well* aware of that. I will not endanger *my* people for *your* sake."

"What will you do when the ossíi overlord tears down your carnesíi's home?" Cesare fired. "As long as Davide walks, that risk looms." He leaned closer. "We've established that if we get to Davide, we knock out one of the Governor's strongest tactical advantages *and* one of the biggest threats to *you*. Not only that, but we get to The Morettae, I'm *sure*."

"And if you're wrong?"

Cesare stood, pulling his dagger from the table with a *crunch* of timber, gaze not breaking from Ygal. "I'll prove it. *To-night*. Dare me." He sheathed the blade. "I *always* win."

The Dóminus scoffed into her near-drained glass. "Maniac."

"You *really* sound like someone," mused Cesare. '*Let mine be the last face you see on your deathbed*'. "Sparring to-morrow?" He banished the uninvited voice.

Ygal flashed a grin. "I'd never pass up an occasion to take a swing at your smug face."

Isaia nodded in concurrence.

"Then *I* dare *you*." Cesare levelled a narrow-eyed smile and, with a tip of his tricorn, quitted *Salacia*'s carcass for the backstreets.

# SCENE XXIX

## TROVERÒ UNA STRADA,
## O NE FARÒ UNA

*Cesare | Giorgianna*

AUTUMN CLOUDS SPLOTCHED THE SKY like water on wet ink, smearing the luminaries above Smugglers' Cove into a grey sombre as the moors of Cesare's grimmer childhood.

The confession that he was stumped lodged in his throat like a fish bone. Even *with* that elusive key, Cesare knew *he* could never infiltrate Vencenza's highest circle, and to continue fighting from the outside alone waned in efficacy by the day. But to burden another with his cause was to admit defeat, to leave a flank unguarded, and Cesare could *never* lose.

A slim figure lunged from an offshoot, knife posed for a killing thrust.

Cesare volted, unsheathed stilétti. The assailant's blade placed a tear in his sleeve. They stepped across, blink-quick, blade swinging inches from Cesare's throat as he dodged and blocked the succeeding strike. Their weapons bound. *Black mask: round eyes, no mouth.* Moretta.

Cesare's veins crackled. *Fortuitous.* He swung his second dagger, pushing with the first against the Moretta's. They sidestepped nimbly and slashed for Cesare's abdomen.

He dashed to block—*false attack!* The Moretta spun, hacking their knife onto Cesare's shoulder, at the base of the neck. Blood spilled down his chest. Searing pain faltered him.

They turned sharply to land a hit.

Cesare deflected just in time, kicked The Moretta in the abdomen, sent them reeling back and falling. He kicked their knife away, crushing their wrist under his boot's heel, and flung his stilétti at their chelidons, blood spurting as he crucified his opponent to the ground. A fighter, a dangerous one, but he needed them alive.

"Look at *you*, Moretta," panted Cesare, leaning a knee onto their sternum, "falling into my hands *just* when needed." He yanked free a dagger to sever the sash of the Moretta's mask.

Rasps broke from their throat, gold teeth glinting. "Were ya 'xpec'in' me, Bauta?"

Cesare squinted. "What gave it away?"

The Moretta wheezed a laugh. "Ya'd love to know, wouldn' ya?"

"Oh, I *would*." Cesare's voice dropped, lulling. "And I don't like it when they don't *talk*." His fingers locked around the Moretta's jaw, pressed hard into a skin-deep nodule behind their ear to stun them with vicious pain.

He eased his grip, waiting out the Moretta's attempts to collect themselves.

"Over my dead body," they slurred.

Cesare smiled with no amusement. "If it pleases thee."

He gripped his stilétto by its quillons, and, holding the Moretta's face prone, sliced the perimeter of their jaw.

The Moretta flailed like a hooked worm, shrieking as blood poured from their chin and down their neck in a scarlet sheet.

"S'op it! *S'op!*" Torn-pupil eyes bulged from their skull. "I'll tell ya wha' I know, fuckin' *s'op!*"

Cesare kept the dagger close to their throat. "But I thought you'd only talk over your dead body."

The Moretta gaped. "I don' know the man's name," they sputtered, "but he says he can ge' us to the Governor. He pushed us to go through wi' the rio', and sen' me afte' ya to-nigh'. Tha's all I know, swear!"

Cesare's lips quirked. *Never off the mark.* "What exactly *are* your intentions?"

"Kill the Governor," they choked out.

"And *then*?" The Morettae couldn't hope simply killing one man would change a system which could never be reformed.

The Moretta gawked, speechless as if bestowed with a divine revelation.

*Well then.* Flicking his arm, Cesare slashed their throat. A gag and gargle spewed forth before dying along with them. *Halfwits.*

He went to rise, halting when his attention caught a symbol peek from beneath the Moretta's sleeve. He tugged the cloth, revealing a bluish tattoo. A three-headed wyvern. Cesare had seen the sigil on occasion— one of the smuggler bands he didn't know the name of. *Saints…*

How likely were The Morettae to be of the smuggler grain? It would explain why even Isaia's Hounds couldn't suss them—Smugglers' District was barred territory; the smugglers answered to no cadre or ossíi above their respective band's captain. So easy for Morettae's activity to fly unnoticed, and for Davide to cover his tracks.

And *there* was that bigger picture, its pieces falling into place.

I SCRAMBLED OUT OF THE BLOODY TUB, knees slamming into the hardwood floor.

My stomach tossed, rough as a sea. I wanted to empty myself again if only to relieve my agony by a sliver, but my body already consumed itself to nothing.

I screwed my eyes shut, my nails scraping the timber like a demon, my Shadow now me, my flesh hateful and thrawn as skin shed and bloodletting began.

A whimper knotted my throat, tore out in a strained half-snarl as I crawled backwards, shoulder blades striking the far wall. With vignetted vision, I followed the tattered paths of scars across the hills and valleys of knuckles, trodden by my mother and the nameless men. My chest heaved as if invoking rage. Rage at the snake Basilio and the demiurge De Tullia and the harridan Falco and every one of those vile beings who tore and drained this body confining us.

I retched, slamming a hand over my mouth as my spine bowed, and held my father's baselard in a tremulous grip. Its bloody eye gazed into me, its weight worth an ocean. And I stepped into my senses, into the calamitous throb in my skull and the salty fingertips of dark morning breeze skimming my bare shoulders, and *forced* myself to rise to my trembling legs. To open the window. To breathe in the chill and behold the architecture of the moon—a thin, waning lune like a sectioned trachea mounted on the glassy slide of the sky. *A crescent.*

Nausea scraped my throat.

My father loved the moon, Omika, but every time he beheld it, his eyes would dim as if its silvery glow cut into him. I never knew why, but I never knew anything.

*A dealer…* A dissident.

I looked at my palm where my blood promise to Ema, to *myself,* marked my flesh indelibly.

'*Forget not the that which you would rather so.*'

Father, Ema, me… I didn't believe *any* of it stood on its own. If I learned of my father's past, I may finally grasp my key to the kingdom, and with it break open the locks barring me from the truth of Emanuela's murder.

> '*No blood can be absolved no matter how old*
> *it grows, for it only grows harder to clean.*'

Is that not what Our Lord of Bless'ed Dominion proclaimed?

SFARDA L. GÜL | 223

My reflection found me in the dagger's effulgent blade, dressed in blood, no longer a frightened girl clutching books of forbidden philosophy to her chest, but an outcast. A fugitive. A scapegoat. *'You are your wayward father's daughter'*. I wouldn't be his blood without scripturient compulsions and reckless abandon. And if I folded my hands, I would be betraying the subjugated I had lived among. *Survived* among. I would be betraying everyone I loved and lost.

In the luminance of the night's celestial watcher, the eye and teardrop encrusting Father's baselard glittered like crystallised blood, a herald of death worthy of a soulless tyranny. Grand Judge Giordano Veronesi, Governor Crescenzo De Tullia. No doubt the other five ministers weren't exonerated. *Blood does not wash off.*

They would rue the day Their debt grew too great for Their bloated coffers, the day the wounds They maimed me with healed wrong, for they *healed*, nevertheless. *And you will pay your dues in blood.* The regime killed with no mercy. Let's see how They liked that scythe turned on *Them.*

The blade dug into my palm. Flesh succumbed to steel easily as fine silk, crimson haem and vengeful black ichor weeping an anointment down my wrist.

Perhaps Death became me.

# SCENE XXX

## METANOIA

*Cesare | Giorgianna*

"*AGH!*" Eligio yelled as Lissandri narrowly avoided stepping on him. "Watch it, clod!" He grabbed a paintbrush from the box of old art supplies before him and smacked his brother in the ankle with it.

"Don't sit in the doorway, how 'bout?" Lissandri mocked Eligio's tone, threatening to knock onto him a book off the dust-dulled pile he hefted—retrieved from the garret they'd been cleaning out.

Beside the rosewood desk flushed against the balcony of the deep loge from which chairs had been uprooted long ago, Cesare tuned his violin, its strings replaced after Anukka slashed the previous (punishment for forgetting his instrument at *Three Suns*). This time, he'd made the same blunder with his bàuta at Etenesh's apothecárium. He could only *hope* she'd break the evil thing.

Across the auditorium below, the sorry state of the stage pierced Cesare's eyes like splinters. He and the twins spent over a month attempting to salvage it after Davide and No Tongue's encroachment, but their coin was meagre and afforded no panacea for the ruin, and neither one of them could bring themselves to beg for pittance from Lâlẹn and Micheletto. They already gave too much whilst receiving a serious compromise to their safety in return. But they *needed* to fix the theatre. For Paolo's sake at least—the old impresario would wish it.

Cesare shelved the despondent thoughts when Lissandri shooed him out of the way. "The attic's brimming!" He piled the desk high with books. "I've been low on reading material."

Footsteps thumped up the narrow stairs and through the entrance walked Rosalia, box in hand and cheeks puffed like a hamster around the last of her crumbly sfogliatella. "Dash wha' 'appensh whe' you ge'—" she gulped, "through a book per day." She sucked her teeth, handing her load to Eligio and twirling for the balcony. Her voice rimed the auditorium's walls as she sang a flurry of impeccable notes learned from an early childhood of classical opera and harp-playing.

"Imagine getting through a book at all." Lissandri tapped the girl's head with a tome.

"Is that '*Apognosis*'?" a startling voice questioned.

At the threshold stood Giorgianna in her hitched claret skirt, the straps of her corset and chemise loose on shoulders frighteningly shrunken within her massive hair.

"Gualtiero Savona's work," she remarked apropos of the cyanic cloth cover stamped with a title and author initials in Lissandri's hands. "'*A willing abandonment of knowledge*'."

"…Is that not my copy?" Cesare slipped in a query.

"Well, it's got your ugly scrawl in it." Lissandri flung the book at Cesare.

He caught it and cracked the spine.

"*Huh.*" Eligio rested his chin on Cesare's shoulder. "One of De Tullia's outlawed titles."

Giorgianna snatched it. "Hence I hid my copy in the ancient crypts of the necropolis when legionaries made their book-burning rounds." She squinched at the tight penmanship graffitiing the twenty-fifth page, more hideous than any doctor's.

Cesare perched his wrist on Giorgianna's head. "The allure of delinquency calls to us all."

"Perhaps *one* day," her red-webbed eyes flung him a hateful glare, "the allure of *silence* will call to *you*." She pulled his hand off by the frilly cuff and placed '*Apognosis*' onto the book pile (now a dump).

Eligio eyed Giorgianna. "How… are you?"

She laughed a bleak, haunting threnody from deep within her lungs. "It's *almost* liveable." Her abyssal gaze aligned with the velvet floor. "Why is this loge gutted of chairs?"

"Cesare likes being a sword-spinning nuisance in here," jibed Eligio, pointing out the chips scarring the walls—dealt by Cesare's one-too-many mishandlings of a sabre.

"*Careful*—" Lissandri scrambled to catch a book slipping over the balcony, "he's *wistful* to-day." He hooked an arm around Cesare's neck, dramatically laying his head against his.

"Because he enjoys misery." Eligio flicked a paintbrush under Rosa's ear to tickle her.

The twins' banter, their *truth*, weighed Cesare's heart. He couldn't reconcile touching the people he loved—people he'd rip his own heart out for—with the same hands which, mere hours prior, took a man's life in cold blood. Even if the end justified the means, and the sacrifice of one ensured the survival of thousands, Cesare harboured more mercy than he wished to admit.

The incongruence of his dismal existence clashed with the world—like he was never meant to be incarnated. Like his body was never supposed to be his. "There's a certain romance to misery." He jabbed Lissandri's stomach with his bow. "Ygal expects us for sparring, and *I*…" he drew the opening notes to '*Elegy of Spring*' on his violin, "bring tidings."

His eyeline stumbled on Giorgianna's—fastened to him like a mooring rope. Her inanition-sunken face bleached, nostrils flared, lips parted. He could hear his own blood pumping through his ears when he beheld her eyes—burning anew, ravening as crimson sunlight. Cesare expected a reaction, but hadn't anticipated which sort.

"Lucrezia will be there," Eligio spoke gingerly, stealing Giorgianna's behold, "so you needn't go. Rosa'll be at the *Curios* if you'd—"

"No." Giorgianna wreathed too-thin arms around herself, pallor not leaving her cheeks. "*I*—I'll go. I'll speak…" she swallowed dryly, "to her. It's time I took things upon myself."

Cesare frowned, watching her famished form sway a phantom's dance—a walking cadaver devoured from within. He was far more than acquainted with the visage of grief.

"Well, you're *eating* first," insisted Lissandri. "Mạt and ạbậ'll do away with us if they hear we've been starving somebody."

Giorgianna tried on a smile wilted as herself. "Powers of persuasion beyond words."

Lissandri cracked his knuckles, slinging his arms around Cesare and Eligio. "Off we go then!" Giorgianna seemed to have greened at the pop of joints.

"Can't risk Ygạl's disapproval," mused Cesare.

"We've got kạk and sajji still?" chirped Eligio. "I too am peckish."

Rosalia latched onto Giorgianna's arm; the woman immediately steadied herself against the girl as if to stave off a collapse. "We can feed the strays on our way!" the girl chirruped.

Giorgianna's shoulder barged Cesare's on her route past.

I TRAILED SEVERAL PACES BEHIND CESARE, huddled from the roscid morning within a bolero, trousers loose over my legs and my blue fingernails warming themselves against the slice of the hard flatbread I nibbled.

"See?" Lissandri nudged me, smiling. "Food does you good."

*Indeed.* It was like a different pit opened up inside me.

I had barely slept the night, and now, trepidation shook me, mounting with every step closer to Lucrezia, but I would *force* myself to walk. To crawl, if that's what it took.

"Why the bandage?" Eligio asked about the muslin over my palm.

"A reminder." My eyes flickered to Cesare before I murmured, "I'll tell you later."

"It's all right," Eligio said. "We've all got them. Well…" a half-shrug, "me and Andri less so."

"Luckier than most," concurred Lissandri.

"I'm grateful to God, but our mạti and ạbậ above all. They're the only semblance of normality we have." Eligio's gaze stalled on Cesare, crestfallen. '*As far as I'm concerned, we're triplets.*' I wondered what Cesare thought of our discussion if he was listening in, and surely he was.

Eligio's head bobbed side-to-side. "Unless rejection by countless men counts as a tragedy."

I rolled my eyes. "Men *are* the tragedy."

"You're telling *me*! Andri doesn't get it—attracted to nobody at all in any sense of the word." Eligio pouted as Lissandri brandished a middle finger larkishly. "Wish I had at least an alternative."

I voiced a smug '*hm*'. "Glad I do." In truth, I hadn't realised I could fancy men at all until age sixteen. And what an unfortunate revelation *that* was! Even still, my markedly sapphic predilection persisted, though it took *far* more than arbitrary and reductive biologic attributes to enkindle my desire.

"Rub it in, why don't you," grumbled Eligio.

A tentative giggle gusted from my chest, the twins joining in, and warmth spread beneath my ribs like water of tropical seas.

Eligio's brow drooped. "We're sorry, you know."

I stiffened, face swiftly dropping.

"Seconded," said Lissandri. "We withheld from you our correspondence with Lucrezia. But I will say wholeheartedly that we had *no* knowledge of…" he dithered, "what happened." He needn't say it aloud, and I was glad he didn't.

"Even though we *did* endeavour our hardest to ensure your comfort," Eligio carried on, "we ultimately failed to do the most important thing of being honest."

I crossed my arms, eyes downturned. But anger at the twins was pointless when they'd been nothing but kind to me, when they hadn't known of my father's sentencing and were compelled to dance to another's fiddle, so I waited out a breath and said, "I forgive you," my voice coming out an octave louder than a whisper. Fault lay elsewhere.

Cesare led us through a door tucked at the base of an ostentatious old building, all its curves as if wrought to distract a passing glance from the furtive ingress.

My step stuttered past the threshold.

Dust and evanescent memory tarnished the terrazzo floors once veined with gilt, selenite-white and pale pink paint peeling from a dark superstructure of scagliola-inlaid walls like desiccated flesh flensing off a carcass, sweeping windows blinded by membranes of rosolite-and-heliodor curtains. Gloom folded its ancient hands around the edifice, only deepened by the grisly artworks set into ornate gold frames. A bathing pool of severed heads. A deer hacked to pieces and stitched together. A fleshed, toothless skull. Vultures pecking out a woman's intestines like worms.

Cesare sauntered for the curling staircase, footfalls an echo. "I fit right in."

"With the eldritch horror?" I jibed. "Certainly."

His curt laugh bounced off the edges of the hollowed hall, tracing my spine.

The lineart of an anatomical heart tethered with aurated vessels ornamented the rococo ceiling. *How could all this go forgotten?*

We ascended a floor, the subject matter shifting from grotesque to daliesque, and entered a room at the terminus. Paintings of gardens and sprawling landscapes adorned oaken walls sprouting with alchemical bulbs like blooming craspedia, black tulle swathing windows glaring at a too-close building across a water duct. A melee weapons rack unfurled in the corner where Isaia inspected an estoc with apparent disapproval.

"*Ākh*!" Ygạl's exclamation came from the high table by the far wall. She cut Cesare a gleeful grin. Amaranth şalbar and a gold-hemmed köynek adorned her imposing height. "I've been holding out for your arrival."

Beside her stood Lucrezia, clad in taupe pantaloons and a tailcoat of verdelite velour.

When our eyes met, my heart kicked into a sprint.

"Charmed," Cesare hung his jacket and tricorn on the clothing frame by the door, "but not even a 'bon auróra'?"

Ygạl glimpsed the ceiling, catching me unaware when his eyeline steered to me. "Bon auróra, Damiani hanym." Their deep voice flowed toffee-sweet, yet I flinched at my surname. My father's. "To what do we owe your gracious appearance?"

I removed my mask. "There's something to be said about novelty."

"In *that* case—" Ygạl unsheathed her saif, "first we fight, then we talk," she paced the room's centre, "then we fight again."

My eyes kept flickering to and from Lucrezia. Hers mirrored.

"*Do* leave me in a sound-enough condition to speak," Cesare told Ygạl facetiously, tying his hair.

"Oh, but could you *not*?" I implored—only a half-jest. "He'd deserve it."

"She's got a point," chuntered Isaia, sitting on the bench by the door to polish his falchion.

"Not a beloved, recently," quipped Cesare; Ygạl's scoffed when he pulled from the rack a curved backsword.

"A Sa'āhḍi saif against a Zargòsian sabre, Agostini?"

Cesare spun the blade through his wrist as the pair circled. "You against me, Najm."

"Smug little *shit*!" She lunged, saif glowing.

Cesare whirled from its path with the fluid swiftness of an unbound flame and swung to land a strike. Ygạl pivoted, caught Cesare's blade on hers with a *clash*.

He clicked his tongue, "Don't grant me more incentive, now," and shoved against her weapon, ducking from a slash, and their blade-dance resumed. Mere entertainment for them, flecked with colourful obscenities, not a blood drop spilled, yet my enrapt attention fastened to every glint of steel, each flicker of bone-white ruffle and sun-gold hem.

Cesare narrowly voided Ygạl's strike, swinging his blade with a flourish to parry two more hits in quick succession. Their swords bound. Cesare gyrated his sabre. Spun Ygạl's saif from her grasp and caught it. *Damn you!* He pointed the saif at Ygạl, sabre held out askew, his smirk easy as ever. "A saif *and* sabre against *nothing*, then."

The woman huffed, palms held up. "Cannot argue."

Cesare twirled the blades and flung me back an infuriating look. "You'll survive your disappointment."

I scowled. "*You'd* know your way about disappointment well."

His eyes narrowed. "Contraire." He faced Ygạl, returning the saif and ushering us all into a circle. "Our chat last night? A Moretta waylaid me a few blocks from *The Salacia*." I frowned at the title. *The Mermaid constellation holding the noctilucous Nereida?* "With a little coaxing, I got them to talk." Cesare *tsk'd*. "Davide isn't stupid…"

Ygạl crossed their arms. "So, he's in cahoots with Morettae?"

"Pardon?" I must have misheard. "Davide '*I have a duty to my Governor*'?"

"He's confused, then," contemplated aloud Isaia.

"As am I," Lissandri cut in. "What in the world?"

"Davide was the catalyst behind the riot, playing both sides for Saints know why. Bizarrely, the Moretta didn't know his name." Cesare chewed his cheek. "Something else: a tattoo inside their forearm. A three-headed wyvern."

Isaia gawked from Cesare to Ygạl. "A location like that…"

"Precisely," Cesare confirmed whatever Isaia thought. "In view of the defect of our current state of affairs, I've begun assembling details regarding the government building's northeastern wing."

"You want to go in *again*?" asked Lucrezia.

"Yes," Cesare replied plainly.

The twins exchanged pale-cheeked gawks.

Consternation polished the obsidian of Isaia's eyes. "*How* many Imperiáli outposts surround it?"

"Ten at the best of times. *Realistically*, we only need to bypass three or four."

Lucrezia squinted. "By what logic?"

"What do you do when the tactics of the ruling party elude you?" Cesare commenced a spiel. "You look to the folk they keep in their company, for *that's* where they tend to leave their flanks open. De Tullia doesn't keep anything of true import in his quarters. The next best bet is Clario Barsotti, and the northeastern wing of government house proper is where the Adviser's apartment is located."

"And the *plan*?" drawled Isaia.

Cesare beheld Ygal's scepticism. "When are you free?"

She rolled her eyes. "I *was* intending to put forth an invitation for a liquor-and-sweets night at the Antrum to-morrow, but I didn't know *you'd* barge in with your politics." *There's that 'antrum' again.*

"The bed we made." Cesare shrugged. "But count me in. Hear me out before shooting me on sight and... preferably be sober enough *to* hear."

"Watch it, Agostini," bit Ygal.

"Giorgianna?" The voice I heard drained my blood to my feet.

Wide eyes, platinum-pale behind a pince-nez, met me.

I grit my teeth, drew a stilted breath, and nodded in assent.

As I followed Lucrezia out, past the beat of blood on my eardrums, I caught Isaia and Cesare's exchange:

'...*Saints, if you*—'

'*Yes, yes. Promise I won't endanger your hide. And I'll bring a votive for your esteemed Dóminus.*' A tongue-click. '*Haven't terrorised the crows in a while.*'

'*You'll kill yourself like that...*'

# SCENE XXXI

## OH, DRUNKEN GODS OF SLAUGHTER, YOU KNOW I'VE ALWAYS BEEN YOUR FAVOURITE DAUGHTER

*Giorgianna*

ONLY THE EBB OF MY BREATH and the falls of our feet bruised the silence between us.

Lucrezia turned to me. "I can explain—"

"You better hope you can." I cut her a sneer, our voices reverberating through the high vaults of the rococo chamber. "It's why I'm here at all."

"I know I did this poorly," Lucrezia began. "I thought it would be wrong to have information about my dissent come from an indirect source, so I wanted to make sure it was *me*. And *yes*, mine showing up yesterday *was* hypocritical. I *was* a coward, and I *didn't* think this through, and I'm so, *so* sorry, Giorgianna. But I promise, I *promise* you I did *not* know about your father's sentencing, *at* all. I would *never* cosign something as cruel as making you stand witness." Her expression grew inscrutable. "*Y*—you don't care, probably, but…" She inhaled jaggedly, squaring her shoulders. "My father was a politician. He ran for office ten years ago but he, like every other opponent of De Tullia's, bar Veronesi, was killed. Sword to the chest. Right before my eyes."

My ribs clenched. *Father killed by the state just like mine…*

"Mother died years ago—a half-Shpokëze servant. I was taken in by my father out of guilt. Mother…" Lucrezia trailed off, "wasn't… *supposed* to bear children… After killing my father, De Tullia shoved me into a barrel and threw me into the canals, but the barrel broke and I washed up in lower óssium. Montefiore is my maternal grandfather's surname." She hesitated, deserting my gaze. "My father's name was Constantino Asile De Tullia." She looked up. "My father was Crescenzo De Tullia's biological brother."

My stomach twisted. And I *saw* him in that onyx hair tumbling in waves to her elbows. *She is of* his *flank.* But where his eyes were oak-brown, hers swirled with grey storms, and where his cheeks were gaunt, wan, hers were plump and rosen.

"You know something about my father." Words found me.

Lucrezia gnawed on her upper lip. "I know there *is* something. I recall Crescenzo speaking of him, calling him 'Damiani', but never heard the reason. Damiani is a very rare surname in Vencenza, so when you came to *The Crescent*, it immediately rang bells. And when circumstances grew uneasy with Basilio, an aristocrat I know to be close to the senate, I felt that history was coming to knock on the door." Her eyes welded resolutely with mine. "But I didn't foresee *any* of this. Not your father, *nothing*. Yes, I knew about '*A Bedlamite's Ballad*', but I didn't suggest it, I can *promise* you that."

The threads of this tenure spun around us all.

"I believe you," I conceded. "And…" My lips pressed together painfully. "I'm sorry for my words. My accusations."

"No, don't. Even if the outcome bespoke otherwise, I intended nothing nefarious, but you…" Lucrezia shook her head. "I cannot imagine what you endured." My eyes stung, hands wringing. "I just want to keep Ygạl and their people unknown to De Tullia. They don't want *anything* to do with the óssium. They just want their little corner of the world." *The fabled antrum?* Lucrezia outstretched her arms alongside a sheepish grin. "Friends?"

My smile broke through like snowdrops from sleet, brows slipping as if to fight it. "Friends." I took Lucrezia's soft hands.

She chuckled and pulled me in for a hug, her citrus-perfumed being, zesty as petitgrain and saccharous as lemon meringue, so warm against my famished coldness. I frowned. "*Um…* so, how did *that* come to pass?" I pulled back. "A cadre leader?"

Lucrezia sat down cross-legged, patting the terrazzo in front of her.

Alarm jolted me when the bony cradle of my pelvis rammed into the hard floor. *I'm so unwell…*

Lucrezia swatted the air. "*Quite* the story." I was all ears. "So, *Donatello.*" She sighed. "I know… He's been my friend since my fifteenth year—the one who found me washed up in oldtown. I still live with him. He's also a *competent* gossip. Four years back, at his dollmaking parlour, on a couple occasions I spotted *Ygal!*" Her eyes kindled, fingers curling as she threw her head back. "I love a behemoth of a woman." I tittered. "'Competent gossip' isn't just a generous compliment. See, I didn't know Cesare at the time, but *Tello* did, which ties into why Ygal came by his parlour, unheard of as it is for carnesíi to ascend to the bones. I knew my position at *The Crescent* could be useful to them—the Lanuza family conducts surveillance for the senate: informants, essentially, hence I gleaned your danger. So… I offered my sword. It took… a lot. Ygal, the stubborn dunce, was *vehemently* bent on keeping her distance." She led a triumphant beam. "But I succeeded, in the end." Our eyes realigned, and her expression turned troubled. "What about *you,* Giorgi?"

I rose abruptly, approaching the painting of a pool of severed heads, so vast it spanned the wall. "They've always withheld knowledge from me." My gaze trailed the oil-painted blood, crests rough and gleaming. "I don't believe Emanuela's murder and my father's execution are separate; with what you've said of the Lanuzas, neither do I believe my banishment stands on its own. De Tullia's oration portrayed Father as far more dangerous than a mere objector. I think he knew something more. If I learn about him, learn what *he* learned, I may have my key to the kingdom. And, with that, the knowledge of Emanuela's murder."

"And then?" asked Lucrezia.

My fingertips touched the old painting. "I am owed my dues. With *blood*."

A gasp. "You want revenge…"

A sneer hooked my lips. "I want *retribution*. For Their deceit. For my father and Emanuela's lives. For *mine*." I rotated to face Lucrezia. "I'll drain Them of every drop if that's what it takes to settle Their debts." And whatever Sarnai had seen upon my visage that wretched díem zenítis of my father's murder must have conjured up once more, draining all colour from Lucrezia's cheek.

I stepped away from the painting, and I could've sworn she flinched. "What is 'antrum'?"

She blinked, clearing her throat. Then, her eyes suddenly fulgurated, her lips tilting up. "It's not safe for any of us to take you or speak of it— anyone *any*where could be watching—but you know whom you *should* talk to?" Her smile widened as she wrapped my arm through hers. "Donatello. At the *Barge*."

My heart kicked. "Barge?"

We walked back to the sparring chamber. "Short for *Stalker's Barge* —a tavèrna not far from the Solar Square."

"One of *The Arum*'s lavìri was permitted by The Court to venture only to a place she called '*the barge*'…"

"Most folks keep it anonymous. The culture." We ascended the stairs. "Donatello practically *lives* there off-work."

Donatello was one of Nara's clients, so if *Stalker's Barge* was what she spoke of, and if *he*—a 'competent gossip'—was a known patron of it… *that* must have been how that waif of a woman so proficiently caught whispers!

A thrill rushed through me. "How do I find it?"

Lucrezia giggled. "Fifth beam of the Solar Square, past the glassmaking parlour. Walk until the seventh right turn. *Stalker's Barge* is in that busted-up capillary. Go during early daylight—the place crawls with charlatans. But you'll always find whom you're looking for." She winked. "The *Barge* lives just as much as anything in Vencenza's oldtown."

We returned to the sparring room. Lissandri sat on the floor beside a talwar, glowering at Cesare who palmed his face in an exceeding effort to stifle a guffaw. Eligio helped his brother up notwithstanding his own snickering, receiving a light elbow in return.

"Reinforce our district," Ygal ordered Isaia as she brought Lucrezia her coat. "I'll contact Leone—hopefully get his Serpents organised if the wanker can put his cock away."

Lucrezia smacked their shoulder. "Don't be vulgar."

Ygal chuckled, running his fingers through her dark waves, and I flinched at the unexpected ache in my heart for a lover's touch.

"If abolition is what we seek," Cesare spoke, and I wanted to claw his throat open, "Davide is merely *one* concern. Infiltrating the acropolis will grant us documents which could incriminate the regime *and* lead us to Davide. The assembly's fallout proves that fighting from the outside alone no longer suffices. *This* is our first move upon this new chessboard."

Isaia frowned, hood and cloth mask pulled up. "I know they say, 'two birds with one stone', but not when *this* dire."

"To Hell with two birds!" exclaimed Cesare. "Strike down the entire flock; choke the shiny fucker in the sky with feathers."

"And our course of action should we get *Morettae*?" voiced Ygal.

"How are your skills of persuasion?"

The woman stared as if Cesare had libelled her bloodline. "The mouthless wankers?"

"They *supposedly* crave revolution. How fortuitous that *I* don't merely claim to." He tossed a stilétto in the air, letting it spin once, twice, before catching it. "*I'll* deal—"

"You'll '*deal with this little predicament*', we know." Lissandri pivoted his torso, vertebrae *pop! pop! popping!* like an old man's skeleton.

Like necks.

Panicked heat flushed my body, my breaths choking, vision tunnelling. Lucrezia's fingers found my hand and gently squeezed. I clenched my fist where muslin wrapped my tender blood promise wound to anchor myself to the pain. The grim reminder.

"...*morrow better* be worth my time, Agostini." The world returned to my awareness, as shaken as my heart.

Cesare dropped a mocking bow. "If it pleases nirô javêl."

"Prick," Ygal scorned him.

I exchanged farewells with Lucrezia before the women departed, Isaia stating he'd be outside, and I didn't understand why until Eligio aimed for Cesare with a glare so scolding I tensed up on his behalf.

"Are you dead from the neck up?" snapped Eligio.

"Let's not get ahead of ourselves."

"It's the fucking house proper, Ces!" Lissandri blustered. "You didn't think to tell us? In there, it's *one* falter and you're dead."

Cesare's lean jaw flickered. "This is what I do—you *know* this. I don't need either of you losing sleep over me."

Eligio's brows sloped. "Yet you *know* we will."

The twins and Cesare fell silent, gloom drawn over their faces.

A pang in my heart urged me to soothe Lissandri's tight shoulder. Regardless of what I thought of Cesare, of how sharply my conversation with Lucrezia reminded me of all his lies, the twins loved him like a brother, and the pain of seeing the madman throw himself at blades cut them just as deeply.

Lissandri cleared his throat. "Eli and I're heading back while it's still light. Isaia's on us." He patted my hand and the pair departed solemnly.

My teeth set, baring in a glower at Cesare. "You *spoke* to me that night! You could've *told* me why you were at *The Arum*. How fucking *dare* you withhold such information, then *lie* just to rope me into attending the assembly where my father would be *murdered*?"

"I had my *quarrels* to serve," he sneered. "You want an admission of guilt, is that it? For *Lucrezia's* ridiculous ploy? *I* never lied."

"Is omittance of the truth not a lie, if it makes you believe exactly what a lie would? And you *did* lie! Apropos of *The Arum*. And you *willingly* partook, *admitting* her ploy's ridiculousness, so *curse* you into the Null, Cesare!"

He neared. "Believe me, I don't need *your* help."

I shoved his chest with fisted hands. "Lowlife fiend."

"Look at yourself." Cesare's blasé tone reddened my vision. "You *aren't* an autocrat's prim little citizen any longer, you're right. But do you know that that makes you a low-born vagabond *rat* like *me*?"

I lurched back. "Do not compare me to you!"

"Because *you* have *such* the moral high ground?" he threw my own words at me. "You stumbled back to *The Sunrise* drenched with blood." Nausea thrust against my throat. "If you are to be vermin to this city," his voice lowered, glim-soft, "then you ought to be just as deadly. Knife tricks serve us all, princess."

"Stop calling me that!"

"Pick up swordplay, a gun to boot, given your awful aim, and you can *make* me, *princess*. Now: your dagger." He opened his scarred palm. "If I may."

I clutched the weapon to my chest. "Pry it from my cold, dead hands!"

"Saints! Just *show* it to me."

I squinted, but conceded hesitantly, holding the baselard for Cesare to study.

"Lòthmir—Ithilweni steel," he noted breathily. "Smelted with masonry,[119] an iridite technique. Heals fractures and notches in the blade." He held his gleaming stilétto beside it. "As are mine. Stronger alloy makes stronger radiance." At its pommel, the sapphire shifted indigo, violet, purpureal. *Sapphire...?* A thorn of recognition pricked me. *Have I seen—?*

Cesare sheathed his dagger, resuming his inspection of my baselard, brows ducked close to his narrowed eyes and cheek slipped between his teeth in earnest fascination. *Do I look so peculiar staring at roses?*

I glimpsed his eclectic assortment of gold and silver earrings. Hoops in his rook and lobe. A double ring hugging his conch. Studs through his tragus and flat. Delicate and clinquant like embers of burnt-out stars strewing his skin. And that instant struck me as if I saw him for the first time.

---

[119] The most well-documented form of corporeal magic, involving incorporation of azoth into the manufacture of any given item, particularly weapons.

"Are you done?" I sniped, needing to withdraw my trembling hands.

Cesare looked at me, those andalusite eyes mirroring flames as if he always gazed upon a pyre, and never once had I felt such gnawing, carnate pain at the beauty of another.

He flung me a switchblade smile, stunning features ever-silvered with a dare. "Better learn footwork before you put me in the ground."

# SCENE XXXII

## CORRUPTISSIMA REPUBLICA
## PLURIMAE LEGES

*Giorgianna | Cesare | Lucrezia*

"YOU TRICKED ME!" I hissed at the blunt pain radiating through my bony hip, knowing a bruise would soon blacken it. I'd gone to block Cesare's strike, only for him to change lines last second and knock me to the ground: a 'feint'.

"Foul play is how you stay alive." Cesare passed a stilétto between his hands whilst striding lazy circles. "Predictability is anathema to your victory."

My head pounded as I rose, heart weak. "Say *why*."

He met me with perplexity.

I reined back any incensed remarks. "Why did you choose to go along with Lucrezia? *You* of all people don't simply comply; you could've spurned her request. I'm not asking if you *cared* about me—you wouldn't. I'm asking if you *thought*. At *all*."

He chewed his cheek for a few lulls of silence before drawing a breath. "One could say... I was content with Lucrezia's plan blowing up in her face."

"You *know* who would have been at that blast's heart."

Cesare's brows gathered, but he did well to keep his big mouth shut for once.

My jaw clenched. "Look at my hands." I held out a palm, fingers kinked a smidge. "Your fingertips have the same calluses, right? I'm a cellist. I know '*Elegy of Spring*' by heart. There was no reason for you to *appraise* your violin strings by playing such an adagio piece except for the fact that it's the opening of '*A Bedlamite's Ballad*' and you wished to spite me."

Cesare flicked between my eyes as if reading verses scrawled upon them. Then, I knew I'd discerned the truth. Then, he stalled because he saw inside me what Lucrezia had, what Sarnai had. *My Shadow*. But, instead of paling, he gestured to the space between us. "Would *this* have changed had I played it differently?"

My chest groaned from the force of my heartbeat. "Maybe for *you*." I sheathed my baselard, storming for my bolero. "But be proud!" I whirled to face Cesare with the mocking histrionics of a cabaret proprietor. "Hope I was a worthy pawn."

CROSSING VENCENZA'S MAIN WATERWAY to reach the aqueduct presented the first intricacy to untangle if Cesare wanted to infiltrate the acropolis.

He staked out near a sheltered City Guard station in the oldtown's north, the thing little more than a small booth floating atop water just below the wharf. A patrol gondoa was moored near.

Cesare slunk shadow to shadow towards the station.

Knives sang cold as wind, a crow cut down, swift and clean. Rehearsal for the grand show.

He perused the desk tucked against a wall. Among the disarray of paperwork, Cesare happened upon a schedule detailing the patrol hours for the upcoming month. While he knew anything could throw a wrench into such programmes—the flocks were cautious, to Cesare's eternal frustration—no piece of information was wholly without consequence, so he folded the schedule into his jacket, swiping keys off the felled crow and venturing to inspect the gondoa.

Opening the trunk, he halted dead in his tracks.

Two women huddled in a cramped corner, bruised wrists shackled to the wall, frilled gowns bloodstained. One looked eighteen. The other couldn't be older than Rosalia.

"*Please*—" the woman blurted and coughed, blood-streaked saliva dripping from her split lip. Her forehead oozed claret, the girl's right eye livid and swollen shut.

Swallowing his horror, Cesare kneeled near. "What happened?" He took to unlocking the shackles.

"A mistake." The woman gulped hard, lashes beaded with tears. "*I*-I voiced my disdain for seeing people hang, I *d*—didn't think anyone was listening but Guards came to our home to-night with accusations of insubordination when we did no such *thing*!" Her ruined lip wobbled, sobs tearing from her throat in gusts of panic at her entire world falling away beneath her. Cesare's gut churned.

A singular misspoken word: a falsely perceived instigation of dissent.

The slightest transgression: a death sentence.

These women, *girls*: just two of the bodies the machine grinded to mince for its sustenance.

The moment the chains fell from the girl's tiny wrists, she latched onto the woman, and Cesare spotted their stark resemblance. Same black eyes and hair, same warm skin and high nose. *Sisters.*

Cuffs let go of the woman, her arms immediately enveloping the girl.

"Amíta[120] ordered never to speak in upper óssium," the girl murmured.

*There's a warrant out on them...* Cesare racked his brain, paging through names of his few óssium contacts. "Can you walk?" The woman nodded to his question, wiping her face with a carroty taffeta sleeve as Cesare helped the pair up. "Do you know the nearest merchant docks? Oldtown outskirts near *Three Suns*, southeastward?" The woman's chin lowered half-hesitantly. "Go there and ask either for dockmaster Iyad Amāl Maram al-Uwwād or innkeeper Anukka Mişşi. Explain to them what happened. They'll help you."

"*But*—" The woman gripped Cesare's forearm. He recoiled, stomach flipped. She didn't seem to register, staring at him with bulging eyes. "That Guard..." Her whisper fumbled amidst half-sobs. "He wasn't human—*I mean*, not... *I*-I don't mean like *that*, I just..." Her head shook slowly. "There was nothing inside..."

Cesare beheld the depth of her fear, its mirror upon the girl's ceruse cheeks, and dread opened a pit in his gut—an inexplicable horror he could not grasp the way the human mind cannot comprehend an immaterial astral entity.

He composed himself. "Move fast, dodge crows."

The woman clasped her hands over her heart. "Falemíce, signór! Dél'ì lùtius e vísus benedétti."

Fingers laced, the sisters headed southeast.

Cesare returned to the station, the glorified box stinking of crimson salt and boneyard silence.

He unfastened the soldier's helm, brushing aside blond oakums of hair. In the flesh amidst the roots, a dark cavity emerged.

A healed aperture.

Recollections of Iyad's intel struck Cesare—gathered from a couple dock urchins' gossip with servants from The Bone Palace: '*...some Guards ... walk around like unblinking ghouls ... one claims she found a hole drilled into the skull of a soldier...*'

Cesare doubled back as if pushed, skin crawling.

---

[120] One's father's sister.

Iyad and Anukka had dismissed the cryptic detail, yet there it was, corroboration and all. *But what does it mean…?* Could this somehow be connected to the condemnations Zilia Meneghel threw at the senators upon the gallows?

Consolidating the revelations as much as he could, Cesare found his matches and saltpetre, sprinkling the station, the gondoa, igniting a flame, and setting the entire wharf ablaze to cleanse it, the fire's beat against the air guttural as a hungering beast's growl.

He tore off a wooden plank like a limb, its end charred, and, upon the wide concrete curb severing the pyre from the city, scribed the words 'VÍTAM DI RIVOLUZIÓNE', spitting a hex upon the empire as a parting gesture.

LUCREZIA RUSHED off the porch of *The Crescent*, haphazardly tossing on a habutai veil glittering with snake scales. Starlight liquefied upon the briny expanse of the Vault of Faces where thousands of vessels floated. Their sails rolled cloud-like against the night.

Lucrezia knew her deliberate pleas with Basilio to grant her a lengthier recess would mean that to-morrow she'd be a prisoner at the theatre, unable to attend Ygal's eminent liquor-and-sweets night. The sacrifice was necessary, but no less dispiriting when Ygal was just about Lucrezia's only unconditional comfort. Even Donatello, the man who got Lucrezia back onto her feet and granted her lodging, maintained transactional alliances, hence her reports and eavesdropping.

Lucrezia's breath halted with her train of thought.[121]

---

[121] Trains *do* exist in Gethlem. Manufactured by the *Besuzaqalar Railway Company*, their sole function is to transport passengers via 'Qarıstıqır' ('*Watchful Crossing*' in Gǝnil) across Empty Faith, the desert covering central Isatōnia, habitable only by belluine creatures like the giant olgoi-khorkhoi sandworms and the lion-snake-bird hybrids mušmaḫḫāt. The *Company* was established by the Gǝnùyshi nomads of Besuzaqalar who frequently traverse the desert on foot or horseback.

Phantasmal shadows twitched by *The Crescent*, flickering and dissolving into the darkness of its córpus.

A shudder rolled down Lucrezia's limbs, her tread down *Vicari's Lane* hastening.

She'd uncovered that Basilio's brother was Marcián Lanuza, aged thirty-seven to Basilio's forty-one, the middle child of nobles Salbador Lanuza-Corbalán and Simonetta Marini, the youngest sibling being thirty-one-year-old Ofelia Marini-Lanuza. Forbye that, Lucrezia knew little. Not what Salbador's enterprise besides *The Crescent* could be, not whom Basilio maintained contact with, not even a clue as to why Vencenza's citizens were vanishing.

Even living among aristocracy, Lucrezia had never come across the Lanuzas in earnest. Her father's reputation for hosting unruly bacchanalias put him at disaccord with not only his puritanical brother, but Crescenzo's close allies, of which Salbador was one—a known bigot when it came to anything opposing his *beloved* nonsensical notions of 'traditional wedlock' or 'a male and female's dutiful roles', at that.

Lucrezia could never pin Basilio down, and it was growing more dangerous to try. She understood that the time to lay low and retire from dubious conduct fast-approached. So, perhaps it *was* better she forewent attending Ygal's home, no matter how deeply it tormented.

*Better safe than your bones picked by the crows…*

# SCENE XXXIII

## HEURISTIC

*Cesare | Giorgianna*

THE AIR INSIDE *COMMEGNOS' CURIOS* BUBBLED with soapy zest and agave.

"Finally," puffed Lâlęn, bringing stools out from the back room. "I'd begun losing hope that we'd ever get the place clean."

"Thank you, all," croaked Micheletto as he hauled upright the last chiffonier with Cesare's aid. "We appreciate all your help, always."

"It's the least we can repay you with," said Cesare.

The parlour gleamed once more, but echoes of demolition rang in the walls still. In the missing furniture, gutted gables, sparsely-tenanted vitrines.

Guilt crushed Cesare's chest. How unpained all their lives could be if not for him.

The twins had assumed a spot near the front desk, Lissandri chatting with Giorgianna about his recent read whilst she took care of Eligio's bleeding brow, dealt by a fallen vase. She'd reacted near-instantly, as if at her own pain, despite Eligio laughing it off as barely a scratch, which *was* true, but didn't mollify Giorgianna who demanded to patch him up.

At least she had eaten that morning. Lâlęn practically gasped at the sight of her, and fed a good three-meals-worth of food to all of them before ten hundred. Cesare hadn't dared to accept when burdening the Commegnos would only weigh heavier on them all.

"*So!*" Lâlęn fixed her silver-hemmed cornflower veil, beholding Cesare and Giorgianna with a beam. "Where are *you* two off looking so soigné?"

Cesare tapped his tricorn. "Public enemy number one of the De Tullia administration duty calls."

Lissandri's eyes turned. Eligio's gaze averted.

They'd barely spoken to Cesare that morning besides the inescapable communication throughout cleaning, and their every glare carved into him. But revolution was his raison d'être, the fire that forged all he was. Sustained him. *Became* him. Consumed and destroyed him. The least he could do was keep his only familia from the spitting embers. He couldn't be the reason he lost them too.

Giorgianna tidied away the aid kit. Single caramel spirals draped over her shoulders, the rest gathered into a wide updo adorned by a feathered bicorn. "Taking measures into my own hands," she declared, neatening the vertically-striped outer skirt furled over the boot-sweeping taupe layers of her long-sleeved dress, her torso cinched by a black-and-white corset of a matching striated pattern, replicated likewise on the thick stockings bared by a slit up the skirt's side. A vólto white as kaolin hid her face, stamped with the simulacrum of a tarnished gold colombína traced in calligraphic whorls, its lips a gleaming ebon.

"Be careful," Eligio urged no one in particular. "If things look in *any* manner ill-omened: run. It's not worth your life."

Giorgianna squeezed his hand and walked for the peripheral door without an acknowledgement of Cesare. Perhaps deserved, for his prodding.

"I'll take a brief detour to Iyad before the Antrum to-day," informed Cesare to the chime of the shopkeeper's bell. "It's díem stelláre and I generally play at *Three Suns*," in his peripheral vision, he registered that

Giorgianna stood yet to breach the threshold, "so I'd better inform Anukka of my non-attendance to-night." When his words concluded, so did Giorgianna's standstill, the door smashing shut behind her.

CESARE WAS THE VIOLINIST AT *THREE SUNS*. The one I listened to each week on the nights bridging díem stelláre and auróra. The most lucent glimmer through the darkness of my misery.

The stained glass mosaics embellishing *Commengnos' Curios* sparkled in the sun like hard candy. My step faltered at the mouth of the twitchel, my breathing strained. I didn't know what compelled tears to urge me so impassionedly. Not joy—*far* from it. Despair, yes, but not the woeful kind. *Damn you!* My nails hooked. *Why won't you* leave *me?*

Knowing by the strappado and crows that I no longer stood in the concealed depths of the city, I pushed away the thoughts and briskly advanced down the fifth beam of the Square's central mosaic as Lucrezia advised.

Touched by the ascending sun, the glassmaker glittered as if crystal teeth at the dark capillary's maw, wind shepherding cotton-white clouds across the celeste vault drizzled with the rosaceous honey of ebbing dawn.

The street constricted. My trachea followed.

I once more saw myself through the omnivident eyes in the walls, tinnitus rattling my skull, skin writhing with horripilation. If I stopped, the walls might recognise me, so I flitted by, counting five streets, soon six, one more. *Quickly.*

I turned right.

Oxblood light gashed ajar a solitary door at the alley's terminus like a laceration. With it flowed forth the discordant ripples of chordophones. Above the archway, a fragment of an obsidian helm gleamed, curlicues below inscribing '*Stalker's Barge*'.

Drawing a breath, I stepped inside.

The matter of space recoiled against me, my presence a pebble into a millpond, its purl shifting the flesh of the edifice, worming into my marrow. *The Barge lives.*

Not one masked face paid me heed as I traversed deeper into the red rutilance, stifling air, saccharine and hazy with mu'assel smoke, nipping at my sclerae, bodies a glittering black undulation of liquid tar. Yet those watchful eyes never shut.

"NOTHING FOR YOU HERE," sotto voce tones frightened me.

In the archway of an obfuscated chamber curtained by red beads, The Rams loomed like paralysis ghosts.

"DEEP IN THE ROT, FOXFIRE GLOWS," the woman spoke, black eyes draining all light. "AS YOU HAVE BEFORE, SO TOO AGAIN YOU MUST TRAIL: THIRTY-SEVEN; LEFT—CHEEK TURNED TO THE HORDES— BURROW UNDER THE BELLY OF THIS BLASTED FLESH."

Black pall slithered from the floor—snakes to its charmer. To the man. "CAÈGUM NEL ECCÁTO LÙTIUS." *Blindness in pure light.* "CALÍGINI FABEDDÍ VERITÀ." *Shadows speak truth.* "BOUNDARIES BROKEN; LIMITLESSNESS ATTAINED."

Faces emerged in legions from the shadows as if a catacomb's walls, shivers leaking down my skin like cold blood from a dead body.

"*Well*," a voice ripped up the dark, "would you *look* at th*is*?"

I whirled, sickly illumination once more drenching the chamber.

Before me stood a reedy man with notched brows, a mechanical gold sphere for a right eye, knee-length magenta jacket sewn with buttons and long legs wrapped in fishnets.

When I glanced over my shoulder, The Rams were nowhere in sight. Just like our last encounter.

Donatello tittered. "Our be*lov*ed strangelings, those are." His fingers clinked with armour rings. "One with Cardea-Dearest's *a*zoth, word *ha*s it. They implant their name into your *mi*nd."

"Thirty-seven…" I murmured.

He blinked. "*Par*don?"

"Foxfire glows deep in the rot—as mushrooms feed off decay." Those alchemical lights we followed a month ago to the well, to the stairs winding into Vencenza's entrails. "'Cheek turned to the hordes...'" The right turn at the foundation took us through the Gallery of Faces to the government building's old wing. *But there was a left!* One through which I may '*burrow under the belly of this blasted flesh*'? An 'antrum' was a stomach cavity, and De Tullia's regime was an accursed resurrection of the Empire.

And, for a pitiful second, things made some backward sense.

I dashed to bolt, halted, returned to the perplexed Donatello. "Tell Nara I haven't forgotten our bargain." My lips pressed into a smile he couldn't see. "I haven't forgotten *her*."

Along The Court's vasculature, I chanced upon those foxfire lights, chasing.

Donatello's assertion of The Rams' oneness with Cardea's curse intrigued me. And it *was* true! I had no grounds to call them 'The Rams', yet the title came to me all the same. If only I knew more of goëtic arts. I'd dwelled long enough in this city's netherworld to glance inside a closet and pick an ivory coat from a skeleton. But when facing The Rams, *whose* closet did I peer into?

I divined upon the well, submerging into its stygian bowels. My feet struck the metal lattice, and I damned myself for not thinking to bring a light. *Too late.* I palmed the bricks until a wall gave way to the winding stairwell. Uttering a silent prayer, I descended blindly, counting each flight. *Thirty-seven* in sum.

At the base, a passage blanketed in alchemical hoarfrost forked.

The Gallery of Faces was to my right.

A lump stiffened my throat as I turned left.

I could gauge a sloping ascent to the labyrinth, a lone alchemical light flickering every few turns, yet not a soul nor rush of wind dwelled near, only a damp, brackish coldness sneaking beside me.

Across the gloom around the next corner, I spotted a door, heartbeat quickening with my paces. Bolts screeched as the stiff door yielded.

Light poured over my eyes, the watery blur shuddering and aligning into a vaulted vestibule, its age-roughened limestone painted with chipped palmettes in berylline and watchet hues. A tall lancet window perforated the wall to my left. Past its sill yawned a steep drop into an athwart canal. Across the atrous water, a bare stone wall, carved with a scalloped archway up high, reached for the sun. Hubbub seeped from within.

Clearing the vestibule, I opened the opposing door.

Another staircase disappeared into lightlessness.

Frustration tugged my nerves, but circumstances grew more curious with every step, so I pawed the spiderwebbed brickwork down.

My fingers tripped on a latch, discerning that it came with a door. Undoing the mechanism, I ducked through.

A city towered for lightyears overhead, battered stone packed tight as it wended around daedalian vennels, colonnades propping up a wood-paved ceiling like a titan's arms holding the sky. *Holding the óssium above…* And I realised that I had found that elusive Antrum.

Over the cobbles streamed a sheen, the oleaginous hue of midday, but sickly as bile, not quite real—too potent to be merely from the kerosene lamps yet impossible to be an emanation of the celestial sun.

Uncontained azothian energy thrummed and spiralled through the ether in a rush of hot blood: an aphrodisiac pulling me into the dark shimmer of the arcane realm.

I let myself be beguiled.

A nearby nameless tavèrna summoned my spirit of inquiry with its peculiar scene of broken literature draped in wispy candleglow, dandelion liquor tingeing the balmy air.

Minutes ticked into hours as I spectated from the back of the timbered chamber, chronicling the ebb of characters, the flow of dialogue.

'*...s'pposed to tell him?*' My senses submerged in a conversation between newcomers behind me. '*That we're loiterin' on Domíni turf?*' Jaunty male tones whistled with a Zâro twang.

'*Game 'round 'ere's weak.*' A Damtani[122] accent rumbled through the responding voice like an echo between mountains. '*None of 'em carnesíi know a three o' stars from a moon goddess!*'

Breath caught in my chest. *Cardsharps!* I swung around in my seat, "Deal me in," propping my elbows onto the card-crowded table.

Gawks of three smugglers greeted me. A scraggly man with a black eyepatch to my left, a rust bandana around his blue rattail. To my right— a willowy individual I couldn't ascertain, platinum hair cut short around high cheekbones bar the long braid hanging from the back of their head, translucent membranes of irises portraying their eyes a pale ruddy. An iron blade replaced the left hand of the bearded man across from me, black hair brushing shoulders clad in a chokha[123] and broad as a doorway. I went cold at the third man, his thewy build and prodigious height, the thickness of his hand.

Eyepatch peered at me. "What's an ossíi doin' down 'ere?"

I sought to compose my trepidations. "Catching whispers."

"Gossip, ey?" Beard chuckled, gathering up the cards. "What're we playing on, kalbaṭoni?[124]"

"Information," I asserted. "If I win, I get to ask you a question for a truthful answer."

Beard smirked. "And if *I* win?"

Fear be damned, I smirked right back, fingers steepled. "*If.*"

---

[122] The language and primary ethnic group of Usaz'khili.

[123] *CHOH-khah*; a woollen coat sporting bullet holders diagonally across both sides of the chest. Commonly worn by Georgian men, as well as other ethnic groups across the Caucasus.

[124] *kahl-baht-OH-nee*; Damtani enay for '*madam*'.

The smugglers passed around a snicker, Beard running a thumb along his blade-arm. "Rookie confidence." My awareness trained on the baselard strapped to my thigh. "But so be it." He handed the deck to the fair-haired individual who dealt out the cards, five each, face down.

Along the table's centre, Dealer placed the house deities: moon goddess, sun goddess, god of stars, god of faces. The objective was to be the first player with all four houses full, deity to eremite. Emanation from the godhead as the theology books and chapel liturgies inculcated.

I turned over my hand.

*Three of faces, five of suns, seven of suns, two of stars, moon eremite.*

Dealer brandished a pètra.[125] "Priest or sovereign?"

"Priest," I called.

"Sovereign it be," mumbled Beard.

Dealer tossed the coin.

Beard made the first move.

The clock hands *tsk'd* in a steady thump like paces of a professor through an examination hall, the slip of cards, their lacquered weight and scrollwork surface, more my fingertips than their own bloodline prints as I placed down a star eremite, completing my houses.

I threaded my fingers into a cradle for my masked chin. "As bargained, signór."

Beard reclined and flung his remaining cards on the table. "Get asking, 'en."

"Ludovico Damiani." The name crushed my heart. "Ring familiar?"

"Never 'eard of a *Ludovico* Damiani."

*Oh?* "Then you've heard of a *Damiani*?"

His grin bared pearly teeth. "'No'er question?"

I flourished three cards through my fingers. "Another round of your humiliation?"

Eyepatch tittered with glee. "Can't trust ossíi further than I could toss an 'arpoon."

---

[125] Faustinian coin.

Beard propped his elbows on the table, the others huddling in like we were about to exchange scandalous gossip. "Any two blokes can share a surname, but '*Damiani*'? Doozy—don't gotta tell *me*, an *Ujmajuridze*! All I know's 'ere was a dealer by *Marcello* Damiani several years back. *I* wasn't 'ere—ain't '*at* old! Only 'irty-eight. 'Damiani' wasn't what 'e went by—just some'ing folks worked out later." A thrill fluttered through my belly. It was papa without a doubt's shadow! The surname was a smoking gun. "Man 'ad friends. 'Bout four? All disappeared. Well… 'cept one." I noted the throwaway line. "Mostly ran in oldtown, but a bit in 'e Antrum."

"What is 'the Antrum'?" I seized my chance.

Eyepatch opened his skinny arms. "You're lookin' at it!"

"But what *is* it?"

Beard motioned with a six of moons. "'No'er round of my 'umiliation."

We played again.

When he put down a faced eremite, my stomach sank. *No!* He *had* to have cheated!

"Lucked out!" Eyepatch hopped from his seat, kissing Beard on the cheek and *shooing* him like a bothersome bird before nestling into the seat across from me. "What's the name, girly?"

"Bianca." The surety of my response startled even myself. How simple it was to be a nobody behind a vólto. Faceless. Anonymous.

"A'righty, Bianca, what's with the curiosity?"

"I'm sure you know of the assembly riot over a month ago." Marred memories flooded my ears with that wet *pop* of necks. I cleared my knotted throat, gripping to reality. "The people on death row interested me." I placed my cards onto the idle deck. "Again. I wish to know about the friends—"

"*I'LL MAKE JEWELLERY OF YOUR TEETH, TOSSER!*" A thunderous *crash* thrust the tavèrna into bedlam as a brawl erupted at its nave, furniture and dishes already aflight.

"Wassat?" Eyepatch exclaimed, face beaming with a gap-toothed grin. "'ound and Cyclops quarrellin'?"

A stalwart man, fur pelts draping his back, raged at the storm's eye, bald head shiny as a polished marble and mammoth fists swinging at a brunet half his size. Amid the fray, a small woman in black fighting leathers weaved in a clear attempt to escape, her hair waist-length and white. *Sarnai!*

Dealer snorted. "Doggie caught up in a Cyclops tiff."

I darted to the walls as a pair of drunks hurtled towards our table, demolishing it to splinters, the smuggler trio yelling obscenities as they scrambled.

"*Sarnai, watch it!*" I shouted.

She swivelled from a cutlass and tore in my direction. "I have an impressive no-kill streak to maintain so *run!*"

Fingers entwined, we ducked from a flying stool, my bicorn almost a casualty.

From behind the bar sprung the vivacious blonde innkeeper, a scar down her face and a musket in hand, and we took such developments as our cue to bolt before she opened fire. Wooden crunches and glassy shrieks hot on our tail, we slunk out and booked it a couple blocks down into a quiet side street.

"Found your way to the Antrum, *huh?*" panted Sarnai, hands resting on her bent knees.

I untied my mask, haling air, my side stitched with pain and legs feeble from weeks of languishing. "How is this possible?" I gestured to the architecture now dripping in a dimmer shade of lamp oil. "I lived in the slums yet never heard even a *suggestion* of this!"

Sarnai threw back her hair and stood upright. "Apparently, as early as four thousand years ago, it used to be a temple of Vencenzani pagans, built into the ground under the surface shrines as a symbolic connection of the worshippers to their revered earth. In the early Empire days, a massacre took place here—imperial Salvatrici forces slaughtered the pagans and destroyed their monuments." She gestured to the ancient pillars upholding the ceiling. "These are the only remnants, supposedly once etched with sigils that were sanded away, but they didn't want to deal with the possible fallout of the earth caving in if they were demolished. They wanted to keep this place from consciousness, too."

Sarnai scoffed. "Didn't work. During the Empire, impoverished folks began to people this place, especially when word got back that Evangelio wanted to '*cleanse*' the slums—somebody got tipped off. Eventually, the Antrum's discovery came to be prevented by Cardea's enchantment on The Court."

I sealed my parted lips, blinking the mystified haze from my eyes to observe the facets of reality I'd never once lucidly beheld. "And... what has the Antrum *become*?"

Sarnai gave a sheepish smile. "Guess nobody explained, huh?"

I folded my arms. "Imagine that."

A shrug. "Folks are paranoid over their property."

In the distance, gunshots rang out.

Sarnai looped her arm through mine, a pretty smile plumping her tanned cheeks. "I'll show you something."

In the eaves of a lofty edifice skirting the Antrum's central square, we perched like strange birds.

The ceiling, dozens of storeys high, unfurled into a tapestry of alchemical constellations, an enormous mechanical orb encased in dual metal shells, free to gyrate around a core lucific as the celestial luminary, suspended from it—constructed through the magic of masonry. Angled mirrors erected at the heart of the square projected the sun's serous luminescence throughout the realm.

"The folk here go by 'carnesíi'," Sarnai explained as we watched the people in question go about their lives, so serene with no crows circling, free to laugh and revel. "'Of the innards'."

"Fitting."

"The Antrum's about the size of a city quarter up on the surface, split into a few districts governed by what we call 'cadres': minor political groups the leaders of which are Domiríi. Ygal runs the north. She likes the masculine 'Dóminus'—says it sounds better with her surname. The northwestern sector *used* to belong to The Hounds before Ygąl's Boars absorbed them. We're now a subsidiary, mostly spies, sentinels, *assassins*, the like. The southwest is second-largest, governed by Leone Caivano's Serpents. The leftover's split between Lucanus Arnza's Cyclopes in the southeast, Vitture Muscarà's Stags to the south, with The Hyacinths' tiny district at the centre of it all, run by Valentina Nin-kalla: little more than a bordello and the surrounding blocks. Territorial divisions are dictated by our cadre laws—Condótta."

An entire sovereign society hidden beneath the skeleton of Vencenza. A stowaway world. *A secret.* Such a grandiose creation in all its gnarled splendour.

But I knew its idyllic façade couldn't be the whole truth.

When there was no shortage of corruption in the world, nothing remained unmarred.

"*So.*" Sarnai's voice chimed like I'd imagine snowflakes might. "Whatcha doin' here, girl?"

Sighing, I repeated everything I had told Lucrezia and then some until the shells of the not-sun drew shut like eyelids, the constellations, misty as white-gold chyle, alighting in its icteric glow's stead. I didn't dwell on the sight lest it rouse my father's ghost.

"Time off duty is scarce on my end," chirruped Sarnai, "but I'm partial to some retribution! Not that I'd kill anybody—impressive clean streak and all that. These bad boys?" She brandished a black karambit, running it along her palm to draw no blood. "Keep them blunted for stunning. Doesn't mean I'm unhappy to be an accomplice."

I smirked. "Your enthusiasm inspirits." But my mood swiftly darkled. "I need information regarding my father. What I uncovered to-day is intriguing; these tavèrnae could serve me well. Gambling houses, too." Marcello *was* my father, I knew it in my bones, but *that* wasn't the crux of it. I needed information regarding his *exploits.* And *then* I needed that bastard kingdom's key. Withal, in the Antrum, *Davide* became my bane. One lonesome run-in with him was one too many, and one more could spell death.

"Your hair…" I began hesitantly, Sarnai meeting my gaze. "Could you teach me tailoring?"

Her onyx eyes twinkled as she beamed. "Really?"

I nodded with a demure smile. "Yes, please."

Sarnai hooked her arm around my neck, her leather-and-lingonberries perfume enveloping me. "You tumbled into good hands, girl." She bumped my collarbone. "It's getting late, you should come to Ygal's liquor-and-sweets night! Signór Revolution's gonna be there for his political science lecture, but nevermind that! Ygal can *cook.*"

I let out a sceptical '*hm*'. "Perhaps not…"

Sarnai made a dull face. "You'd skip on *food* just because you'd rather not face *one* person?"

My lips squeezed. Stubbornness only kept me at a torturous standstill, I owned. "Then you've convinced me." I could endeavour to ignore Cesare.

She cheered, leading the way down to the street and into the dusking twists and turns of the Antrum, demanding I explain my playwright work and old life in Vencenza and its provinces along our route.

# SCENE XXXIV

## APOCATASTASIS

*Giorgianna*

SOONER THAN MY MASK CAME OFF, Ygąl pulled me through the condottiére abode, chipperly describing the Sa'āhḍi rawāshīn in the foyer, pausing to explain the Kıcunınese teke rugs in her quarters and her own pink çyrpy[126] with its silver tsçapraz coat fasteners before plopping with a piyāla of amaretto onto one of the central sofas, magenta like rhodolite, parted by an intarsia table glossy as a mosaic of caramel and chocolate. Beside them, Sarnai nibbled on a crock-full of pistachio nougat and dates, tapping her feet on the floor in a peppy beat.

The candlelit chamber smelled of dulceous almonds and agalloch, air warm, heavy as salep, the oak desk crammed with more alcohol than a brewery: cognac, summerwine, oghi, sūbiyā, araq. Maiolica pottery cradled nabat, glacé cherries, rāḥat al-ḥulqūm, cremino, trays sparkling with ma'mūl and lugaimat and pişme. All prepared by Ygąl. Learning I

---

[126] *Chyrpy*, a lavishly-embroidered Turkmen ceremonial dress/overcoat.

didn't drink, she'd poured for me sugared rose water she called '*gahwa baydā*', white coffee, much to my delight.

Isaia shadowed the desk, wordlessly topping up Aengus's snifter of poitín, a once-in-a-blue-moon smile cracking the cold statue of a man when Aengus kissed his cheek.

"You ink all your own tattoos?" I asked Isaia. Little of his supposedly full-body tattoos was visible—only the Gxerqucca on his hands and the sun and hawk feather on his neck—but their intricacy alone sparked admiration.

Isaia nodded, generously diluting his tablespoon of vodka with lemon-and-orange-blossom water. "I ink other condottiéri." He spoke serenely as night, almost monotone. "Sigils, art, covering scars." His eyes met mine—perfectly level in height. "Ask, if ever you'd like."

The offer caught me off guard. "I... don't have such money."

"No charge."

"Surely! For such mastery."

He shrugged, imbibing.

The spirit of inquiry compelled me further: "How did you come to be here?"

He cleared his throat. "Twenty-two years back, my father was running from Sancta Maria, murder charges—my mother's family who had honour-killed her, and wound up in the Antrum, somehow. Trick of The Court. He—*we*—inadvertently trespassed on Hound territory. Serious deal back then. I was five and got taken in by the condottiéri."

I blinked. "And... your father?"

"Three shots to the back."

My throat closed up.

"Ambroeus Pitino Carcan—" Isaia continued in a mutter "—was the last Dóminus of The Hounds before The Boars absorbed us. He was eleven to my five when we met, and became my mentor. A decent man, he grew to be. That's why the Boar coup happened. Sabinus Venator's murder of Carcan wasn't taken well." Isaia glanced at—"Ygal knew him—same age. She's a diplomat."

"More or less when I wish," Ygal called out.

Above the desk, *the Dóminus' desk*, a pair of axes gleamed in a gem-encrusted cross, and I wondered to what extent Isaia resented The Boars. Or did he see them as liberation from The Hounds? As retribution?

My breath hitched when to my side swept Cesare, ever-blazing eyes framed in messy hair and lined with flicks of liquid kohl along the inner and outer canthi. "Descended into the abyss, vólto?" He hoarded candied cherries into his palm like there was no tomorrow.

I scowled at his customary taunt but turned my cheek only for a lone platter to grip my attention, the thick rind of a candied citrus gleaming like an orange gemstone upon it.

"Sa pompia intrea?" I gasped at Ygąl.

"Ākh yes!" She splashed coffee from a juzwa into her alcohol—cardamom-spiced and roasted Sa'āhḍi-style instead of raw and sour as the Lerrḳirakan soorj Emanuela would share with me.

Arpineh called the brewing pot '*srjep*', and so I couldn't think of it any other way.

"A merchant from the western provinces taught me the recipe," added Ygąl

"My maternal family is western!" Giddiness rolled through my chest as I cut a slice onto a lattimo plate, the fruit's innards bursting with honey syrup. "Áti and ápa's home was embowered in the trees, so in winter we'd make sa pompia intrea and s'aranzata." Few of those rare instances when mother and áti saw eye-to-eye without áti's opium, and the *only* time áti smiled after ápa's death, even if that very opium served as her medicine for his violence. Mother never understood how she could love him still: one of the many geneses of her rage.

"Please," Ygąl raised her piyāla to me, "enjoy."

My beam demurred, but I brought it forth all the same, unable to deny the comfort in my chest, that I warmed to these strange people's company.

Feeling a gaze on myself, I tossed a querying glance at Cesare.

His focus flickered up from my dessert. "Like your eyes."

I started, then scoffed. "What, empty and glazed?"

His head tipped, vagabond bangs brushing his full lips. "Amber."

Heat pricked my cheeks. "What would *you* know?" I poked my fork at his face.

Cesare passed back with boyish laughter, eating three cherries at once as he made for the empty sofa.

Whatever Sarnai implied with her cheeky smirk, I spurned by pulling down my lower eyelid and mouthing '*òcio!*'

Ygąl went to pour themselves another round of amaretto.

"*Hold* the fucking gun." Cesare pulled the glass away, Ygąl stopping herself just in time with a curse. "I need you *mildly* sober for this." Cesare darted to an escritoire, all sharp, lissom elegance.

I turned to my sa pompia intrea. Zesty bitterness edged its honeyed lushness, rind tough and chewy between my molars. Bittersweet and toothsome as a candied treat ought to be, yet not the way it was in my childhood, and I realised it could never again be so. A labour camp stood in Ferréli's stead, áti and ápa passed long ago, and mother was now Elenedda to me.

"Better be worth it, Agostini," warned Ygąl.

Cesare flattened a scroll atop the intarsia, a schematic rendered upon it. "The Bone Palace's northeast," he commenced. "Ten Imperiálum outposts guard it at the best of times; three routes feed into it. The eastern requires a circumnavigation via upper óssium; the western can be accessed from *lower*; the subterranean's self-explanatory. Each option excludes a good four to five to six outposts, but each comes with its own pitfalls."

Ygąl tapped her temple with a long, filigreed zhǐjiǎtào fingernail guard of Gěikùx̄héshi crafting. "Define 'outpost'."

"Contubèrnium." *Eight legionaries.* "Subterranean is out, given last month and Davide considered. The issue with the *eastern* route is rampant City Guards—a continuous legion cycle. Upper óssium cannot be avoided, and neither can the crows. It's further complicated by the rock outcrops bordering the river. *So*, our best bet is the *western* route. However, there's the issue of *getting* there. The government building is an elevated acropolis making intruders vulnerable to spotting."

"And the moat?" queried Isaia. "It's circumscribed by a rampart: the first fortification."

"The operating aqueducts are built against that rampart. *That's* where our first contubèrnium is stationed. The only reliable means across the moat and into the citadel are via the drawbridge, or by a gondoa through the reticulária[127] at North Eye, the former being out of the question on obvious grounds."

*He worked out* all *of this?* Envy thorned me anew.

"Asinine architecture," Aengus expressed. "Why's an aqueduct also a defensive wall?"

"The moat is filtered by masons and water speakers operating within the aqueducts," I informed.

"Why?" Aengus made a face. "Let moats be disgustin' as they ought to!"

"Irrelevant," interjected Cesare. "The rampart's west abuts Vencenza's main waterway: River Vena. I've sussed a crow station near the northeastern end of The Court, not far off *Three Suns*. It's out of the way, but utilised by legionaries nevertheless to cross the river to the aqueduct. I propose we seize a patrol gondoa there and disguise ourselves as Guards. All cards played right, Imperialíi should grant us passage through North Eye's reticulárium." I couldn't fathom the incongruity of Cesare dressed in crow feathers. "We'll need to make it to the fourth floor of the northeast," he continued. "Then… we're more or less in blind. But the plan is simple notwithstanding: go in, retrieve some documents, get out. Barsotti's archives are *bound* to have something—such heavy guarding isn't coincidental, and I *don't* believe it's merely for the treasury."

Sarnai peered. "*How* do you get out?"

"Better to infiltrate close to our mark but escape by a well-travelled route: the *ancient* aqueducts."

Isaia shut his eyes. "Madness."

"Plan's 'bout as stea'y as a stack o' boulders," concurred Aengus, Sarnai nodding along.

---

[127] Gates within Vencenzani fortifications, barring watercraft from passage along canals.

"Volatile machinations yield lucrative outcomes." Cesare leaned his elbows onto his knees, regarding the Dóminus earnestly. "I don't need all your condottiéri, Ygal. I need one to watch my back, and I need *you* to have faith that I know what I'm doing."

I polished off my sa pompia intrea, sipping honey off the fork as I affixed Cesare with a ponderous gaze, wondering how much it bruised his pride, how deeply it twisted the knife into his gut to beg for aid. To bribe the Dóminus with steel. To know his own objective was too immense for him alone. He'd tackle it anyway.

"Which way does a house of cards fall?" My words came forth before I could vet them.

All eyes snapped to me.

A shallow dent blemished the centre of Cesare's brow, his lips parted in befuddlement.

I wanted into De Tullia's kingdom too, for Ema and for my father. Cesare's endeavour could give me my key. If not, I'd know the pitfalls for my own good.

My jaw clenched, chin tilting aloft a smidge as I jilted his scrutiny and levelled my attention to Ygal's verdict.

She voided the bottle's burden of amaretto. "Very well…" A drawl. "Take Isaia."

Cesare crossed an ankle on his knee, elbows perched on the sofa's back. "Magnanimous, nirô javêl."

Ygal's eyes flashed. "Don't push it."

Isaia punched Cesare's shoulder. "'*Promise I won't endanger your hide*'!"

"You're welcome to keep your hide *well* away from the fleshing knives; watch from afar. This shall take a month or longer to organise, anyway."

Cesare *did* know what he was doing, Lissandri was right to trust him, but did he not care for the means if they led him to the end? Did he not care for his own life?

The door slammed open.

A slender woman stood at the threshold, black-brown hair cut at the chin, a straight fringe resting on her frowning brow and lily-pale skin peppered with a million dark freckles.

"Howya, Cheera?" Aengus chirped.

"*Chiara*," she hurled icy contempt. "We have *work*—district unrest to quell. You should *know* since you're so cosy with Top Dog."

"Careful, Chiara." Isaia prowled closer, a lour denting his countenance.

"She's just a sour one." Aengus kissed Isaia's lips, grabbing his flat cap and following Chiara out.

Ygạl massaged her eyes. "*Waja'*... all I wanted was to get drunk." They threw back the last of the amaretto. "Clear out! *All* of you!"

Isaia dissolved into the darkness, the rest of us flitting off close behind.

The mechanical sun had sealed its orb by the time Sarnai, Cesare, and I emerged in the street, buildings adrip in the milky lymph of artificial stars scintillating across the sky-ceiling.

Just before exeunt, Ygạl handed me the remaining sa pompia intrea in a miniature basket with the demand to return it clean, whilst Cesare robbed her table of its cherries alongside a couple chunks of nabat and hazelnut chocolate, his hands undoubtedly sordid with sugar.

"The nearest exit is a yellow door a few blocks west," explained Sarnai. "You'll emerge deep in the oldtown through an ancient gondoa terminal." She glanced at Cesare. "Though it's a fair way, from what I hear?"

I pressed a clasped palm to my heart. "Thank you, Sarnai. For everything."

She tucked snowy locks behind her ear and sprung to her toes, launching my heart into a balter as her lips pressed a soft kiss to my cheek, sparks igniting my skin. She grinned, "*I* think you and I're gonna get along splendidly," and dogtrotted up the porch into the estate.

Warmth poured through my cheeks, a giggle simmering in my chest. My eyes flinched from Cesare's as if from fire and launched for the not-sky.

I missed the roses I'd press between pages of old philosophy books scrawled by slated madmen, anthocyanins staining the faded beige insomnia like lipstick prints, Death preserved. I missed *The Crescent*'s pantomimes—carved from eyelids never baptised by tears of anything but pain, never permitted to. Perhaps I missed the old thespians, those faces rendered upon my memory's canvas in distorted oil paint like tongues held by scissor-blade silence.

I did not miss that theatre—that frozen, hollow skull. I did not miss an upper world baying for my blood. My mind.

Once, I misshaped myself to fit the mould of a realm I held no place in out of fear, knowing Otherness meant Death.

Now, finally, I saw the universe tending towards entropy, unfurling both without and within like tempestuous waters, rebirthing my Shadow.

*Blindness in pure light…*

This lucifugous world, the heartbeat of caliginous darkness inside its flesh, was… totality. My duality beginning to seal shut.

*Shadows speak truth.*

Justice was due to me, but there was no justice in this world.

Only violence. Only blood.

*So I shall avenge.*

# SCENE XXXV

## BABEL

*Lucrezia*

OVER TWO MONTHS HAD LAPSED since that Moretta riot rattled both the Vencenza-wide assembly and The Bauta's schemes.

Lucrezia had spent six weeks retiring from that dubious conduct of hers at *The Crescent*: not contacting condottiéri, restraining her instilled inclination to eavesdrop, embarking on no bypaths to and from home, even offering to take on lengthier shifts at the theatre.

Her skin itched with sleeplessness each day, eyes dry and stomach gnawed by hunger, but the fruits of her labour revealed themselves in Basilio's eased comportment in her presence, in the way his eyes no longer analysed her every movement and ears didn't listen in to each off-beat breath.

That díem tramòne night, two precarious months endured, Lucrezia stood before *The Sunrise*, intent on speaking with Giorgianna. She'd ached to see Ygal again after a month of separation, but Giorgianna stood two steps from the grave the last time they'd spoken, and Basilio granted

Lucrezia a mere four-hour respite—a timeframe within which she hoped to also sleep.

A shower had rushed through, leaving the stone baptised and the halo of smiling faces above the front door a-glisten as Lucrezia stepped into the theatre's darkness, routing for the vìtus quarters. Lissandri and Rosalia slept at such hours while Eligio kept vigil until the deep morning, painting masks and vegetation. The surly pair, however, were a mystery.

Music vibrated through the wood-laden hallways. *Chordophone.* Yet too sonorous to be that violin of Cesare's.

Lucrezia advanced for the room across from the wardrobe.

Moonglow crept across its interior, curtains dipped in sunrise, typically sundering the chamber in twain, drawn to reveal a small stage bedecked by a motley of instruments left behind along with the forgotten theatre: stately contrabass, ethereal harp, dainty organetto. A snapshot into a past life.

By the far wall stood a dust-cloaked piano. On its duet bench, occupied with a maple cello, sat Giorgianna, her skirt spilling like dark blood around her. She looked up, brows high.

Lucrezia smiled sheepishly. "Long time no see."

"Indeed!" Giorgianna set aside her instrument, tucking the strap of her chemise beneath that of her corset. "How have you been faring?"

"Basilio ploughs us into the ground but…" Lucrezia kneaded her pounding temple, "I'm abiding."

Giorgianna clicked her fingers. Kohled eyes ignited with a simper. "Victuals?"

"An entire horse, if you please."

Giorgianna laughed, hauntingly dark, and led Lucrezia with her to the kitchen two floors down—a cosy chamber lamplit feebly as an anchorite cell, its singular window, fitted with a sun-shaped black lattice, opening to a narrow duct trickling between the buildings. A kitchenette stretched along the terminal wall and a sturdy cypress table stood centrally.

Giorgianna went about preparing Lucrezia carasau flatbread with sarde in saor and a glass of flat chinotto. Meanwhile, the pair discussed recent developments, from the Lanuza brothers, to Giorgianna's scouring of every Antrum and oldtown tavérna and gambling house for information regarding Ludovico, to Cesare's painfully-crawling endeavour to infiltrate the ministerial house.

The second she sat at the table and took her first bite of sipid sardines and crispy bread, a black hole opened in Lucrezia's insomniac gut, demanding to be nourished. Giorgianna lit a sigarétta, smoking into her mouth like a cigar the way Cesare did. Her olive skin shone gold as candlefire, hip-length coils a lush tangle of autumn canopies, svelte frame fleshy and junoesque once more, yet her vulpine eyes harboured gloom, her shadow dark enough for two.

None of them deserved the pain of tearing to shreds, or the arduous fight to sew themselves back together so crookedly, but none of them had a choice. Mending oneself was an impossibility. Skin to callus: only change ensured life.

"Why do you not seek retribution?" asked Giorgianna. "Against De Tullia." And though her question came gingerly, curiously, her undertone gored like thorns.

Lucrezia gulped a mouthful of myrtle-orange tonic and wiped her mouth, giving up a sigh. "My father, Constantino, didn't care for politics or strategy, though *was* rather smart with both. He preferred parties, women, he was cocky and commanding without authority." She picked at her nails. "He felt himself... immune, even *with* his parents reprimanding him. They didn't raise him or Crescenzo like *parents*, but more *tutors*, cold and distant, demanding to be called by their surname and title: Generals Asunzsion Liona Varese and Larentu Seneca De Tullia. I'm not even sure they considered me family at *all*.

"Crescenzo was nothing like Constantino, but observant, cunning, a favourite of Asunzsion and Larentu. He never... struck me as someone *wanting* power—he *had* power. He wanted to be *right*. And I think it's through both his observation of the world and his parents' teaching that he... came to the conclusion? that emotion is human folly." Lucrezia shook her head. "Besides the point." She propped her elbows on the table. "Father, very much *un*like Crescenzo, *resented* his parents. And while he was leagues more 'liberal' than Crescenzo, it wasn't enough. It never is. He was wealthy, entitled, and *that's* where my mother comes in." Her head bobbled. "I mean, I don't know if 'mother' is quite correct."

An exasperated breath broke from Lucrezia. "Remember how I said she wasn't *supposed* to bear children? She was Shpokëze maternally—hence her name: 'Ardita'—and what's called a 'sworn virgin', taking a vow of chastity to live as a man." Giorgianna stared pale-faced, as if sensing where the story headed. "She was a servant at the citadel and…" Lucrezia's gut rolled. "That entitlement of my father's? Well… he… hurt my mother. Hence…" she gestured to herself, "*me*. When I was thirteen, I learned from the other servants that he… killed her: sent a poisoned dessert to her dorm with *whatever* story had been made up, I don't know. And because she *was* a sworn virgin, it could be pawned off on suicide as a result of what he did to her. Several poisoning deaths of this likeness occurred close together, including Asunzsion and Larentu—my grandparents. Servants at the time speculated *Crescenzo* may've sussed Constantino and either redirected portions of the dessert to other people, or poisoned others in a similar manner? No one *knows*, so they cannot bring this forward as incrimination.

"It was clear that, whilst Crescenzo held no familial sentimentality towards them, Constantino *didn't* want his parents dead, despite everything." Lucrezia snorted blackly. "It was *guilt* that made him take ownership of me in the first place, *guilt* which convinced him to allow me to come into the rightful female body I wasn't born in. Not because he wished to be a good parent or even a good person who'd care for another's wellness, he *never* did, but because he wanted to soothe that shame within himself for the crime he'd committed, and yet he went on to commit another the *moment* he cottoned on that I could be on his trail." All those words had always gotten in the way of the tongue, wedging in the teeth; Lucrezia wanted to spit them out. Now that she had, tension began to abate. "Ten years ago, days after my fifteenth birthday, I watched as the last snow of winter melted, and Crescenzo came into our old family home. He had everyone massacred, killing Constantino—his brother and my father—with a sword to the heart."

Lucrezia held Giorgianna's unbroken gaze. "He may have cast me into a barrel and thrown me in the canals to die, but the way *he* didn't resent his parents for treating him coldly, *I* don't resent Crescenzo for killing my father." She soothed her drying throat with chinotto. "He refused to send me to educated professionals save for the direst surgeries, my father—yet more evidence for just how little he cared. You know where he sent me instead? High Priest Benetto Abelli. *They* oversaw most of my procedures, supposedly with audience of Magister Ilenia Farnese given the 'scholarly' nature of those operations. Sometimes I wonder if an even darker motive existed—Father never sufficiently justified his decision. And it was all exploitation of my pain, my body, despite Benetto looking down upon me for 'revering the flesh'." Abelli considered all but the soul to be filthy afterbirth of creation, and while Lucrezia never internalised such teachings, she dreaded to think of all the poor children like her who did. "They turned something imperative to my *survival* into some exotic spectacle for themselves: ignorant little voyeurs who could *never* understand the intricacies of my positionality and had no right to any of it." Lucrezia finished off her tonic and palmed her eyes with cool fingertips. "I thought I could *finally* attain normalcy at *The Crescent*, but got nothing of the sort. I guess I'm also to blame, what with my meddling." A frown strained her brow. "Legionary visits to *The Crescent* grow frequent. Basilio always whispers with them, becoming neurotic. Violent. There've been reports of him yelling at and striking thespians."

"Lucrezia." Alarm punctured Giorgianna's tone. "You must get out."

"I've been displaced so many times, Giorgi." Tears pressed against Lucrezia's eyes, insistent. "I just want to *stay*, for *once* in my life, but *life* doesn't fucking want me to." Her voice broke.

In her first years at *The Crescent*, things seemed different. Hopeful. But she learned hope only deceived.

Giorgianna sidled onto Lucrezia's bench, wrapping the petite woman in her long arms and attar perfume. "I'm so sorry, Luce. There's so pitifully little to say, but just know that you have people who care more than anything."

Lucrezia knew Giorgianna understood pain, but she hadn't expected to become a recipient of her compassion. It brought a comfort she hadn't felt in aeons. "Thank you, Giorgi."

The night's silence distilled to perfect purity, and maybe, Lucrezia thought, they could scrape out some wayward way.

Giorgianna walked Lucrezia to the back exit, the pair chatting along the way.

Idly swinging open the door, Lucrezia ran into Cesare.

He staggered back a half-step. Eerily dilated pupils blackened his eyes where sclerae ran bumpy with florid twigs of capillaries.

Lucrezia frowned. "Are you—?"

"Don't touch me." He flounced past.

Lucrezia noted his thigh harnesses, his hip baldric for revolvers and swords, yet no daggers to go along. The incongruence unsettled her. Cesare and weapons went together like canals and water. He didn't drink, and had abandoned needles years ago, but what else could be responsible for his state?

Giorgianna watched the darkness into which Cesare vanished for a second longer before whirling to Lucrezia, jaw momentarily hard.

The women exchanged their farewells. Before ushering her off the porch, Giorgianna fetched for Lucrezia a mighty tome titled '*Spagyrism and Spellwerk*' by some Nashĭgostu Kurilit Gostiata. When Lucrezia questioned the offering, Giorgianna assured it might prove enlightening before slipping into Lucrezia's hand a tiny pouch of buranelli butter cookies alongside a shiny-wrapped gianduia chocolate, and wishing her goodwill and safety on her way.


The moon throbbed like a snaggletooth in the bruised sky, pouring nacreous light like sanies across the streets to fester the shadows into blighted apparitions.

A block of narrow buildings approached, black sockets of windows overlooking the canal. Dog barks echoed somewhere in the distance as if to frighten Lucrezia specifically.

Passing a narrow offshoot, she halted and doubled back, convinced she'd seen something at the other end. But she sighted nothing.

A shudder crawled through her as she quickened her pace, fleeting past another offshoot.

Light blinked out of existence in the corner of her eye.

Lucrezia's breathing shallowed. *Grim lemures…*

Her turn-off towards the Solar Square approached.

A trot impelled her past the final alley.

Blackness flashed by again. This time, she swore she heard footfalls.

The frore hand of terror gripped Lucrezia's heart and juddered it. Walls blurred as she whirled down a tenebrous snicket between high stone fences, shoving through persimmon branches and tearing in zigzags through the warrens.

Footfalls pursued like pelted rocks.

Lucrezia sprinted wildly, half-panting-half-sobbing, body a rag doll bashing around corners. Breaths amplified in her ears when the tiny alley squeezed between *Commegnos' Curios* and the adjacent watchmaker sucked her inside. She shuffled through in a tempest of panic, knuckles and arms scraping on the brickwork, head tossing back every step to check for the stalker.

She threw herself out of the tiny crack and into the Square, pulse battering as she trailed the courtyard's perimeter and slipped down the third beam.

Azoth eased its oppression over Lucrezia with her exit from oldtown; blood pressure dropped like a boulder off a precipice.

She barged into the building directly outside the outskirts of the Square, dropping the book, pulling off her mask, and dumping herself to the floor of the gloomy foyer. A squall of fatigue rushed through her head with her occiput striking a wall. Her burning lungs inflated around still, musty air.

"*Ah!*" a man squawked.

Lucrezia looked ceilingward with a start.

Donatello leaned over a railing, mechanical orb whirling. "My *dar*ling Lucrezia!"

She rose shakily, picking up '*Spagyrism and Spellwerk*' before ascending the stairs to the loft. A corridor snaked around it like a tumbledown street, leading to Donatello's dollmaking parlour overlooking the Solar Square. The loft itself doubled as a lounge, decked only with a tea table, a kitchenette, a chesterfield, and Donatello's secretaire cluttered with dismembered doll parts, his behemoth gold scissors reclining against its edge. Three tightly-spaced doors dotted the far wall: a washroom and two bedrooms, all timeworn and sombre, paint flaking like a boarded-up chamber in a haunted château. Underneath the loft wedged the tiny home of an elderly Temistochlisi woman they knew only by 'Sincimmeno'.

Lucrezia discarded her colombína and the tome on the table and slung herself across the chesterfield. "Somebody chased me in the streets," she slurred into the leathery roughness.

"*That*'s nice, love," Donatello mused in his wonted flippancy. "Let the Doggies and *Pi*ggies know."

Lucrezia stared blankly into the back of his head. The man tinkered with the mechanisms inside a wide-grinning rubber head, a pair of seven-toed feet its only body. The noise tingled Lucrezia's teeth. "Could you… take that to your quarters? I'd like to sleep."

Donatello turned, practically gurning. "You *ha*ve a *be*droom…"

"You know how I get with small spaces when stressed." Ever since that barrel, Lucrezia couldn't even wear a vólto lest panic overcome her.

The dollmaker stood with a huff, flicking his russet curls. "*Ill*-bred company." He swept that 'doll' monstrosity into his arms like a babe and strutted to his room.

Lucrezia turned off the flickering lights, only a slippery glow seeping from beneath Donatello's bedroom door, and plopped back on the beat-up chesterfield, unwrapping the gianduia.

Vencenza never slept, but Lucrezia welcomed the hum of the city—like worker bees, a scurrying ant colony busy in the night. Her heart still hammered, blood alight.

From the politics she'd been born into, to the incongruous male body she was almost forsaken to inhabit, to her fall from grace and deadly two-ness now, she felt she'd been on tenterhooks her entire life—never a moment to breathe. For all her luck in the grand scheme of the world's tragedies, Lucrezia understood that, one way or another, scraping a way out would be like digging oneself from a grave.

# SCENE XXXVI

## THE WITCHING HOUR

*Cesare*

FRESH.

The body's livid limbs, frail as snapped twigs, twisted around black rivets crucifying it to the wall above the Antrum's yellow door, its riven throat dripping long, viscous strings of clots like limp chameleon tongues. Wadded flesh puckered in place of fingernails and teeth, scalp peeled away from the purulent pallor of a skull. *A child.*

Within the slick cavity of their gutted stomach glinted a silver pin, a scrap of blood-softened paper skewered onto it.

Cesare tugged it free, the scrawl across the note turning his stomach worse than the ripeness of flesh untaken by rot:

*'Walk carefully, Bauta.'*

Ygal stirred at his rigid shoulder. "What was your job, Vito?" She sauntered towards the nine-fingered Boar sentry petrified nearby, the silver gonjik and gülyaka talismans draped down her sternum glinting like executioner swords in the artificial starlight. "What was your *sole—*" the Dóminus cooed "—*job*? Vito."

The grizzled man rippled with a tremor. "Sentinel duty, Dóminus."

Zhǐjiǎtào *clinked* as Ygal's fingers furled, unfurled. "And what is *this*?"

"Negligence." Vito paused to swallow. "Dómin—"

"Otiose *slug*!" Ygal grabbed the sentry by the collar and slammed him into the guts-slick wall.

Vito crumpled to the ground, bleeding head clutched. "I beg—"

Ygal brought their boot onto his face. The watchman's nose flattened with a bloody crunch and spilled down his face in ragged hunks of meat and gristle.

Cesare's lip twitched. Isaia watched on unmoving.

"You endangered my district." Wrath boiled Ygal's tone. "You endangered my *people*!" They crushed underfoot Vito's four-fingered hand to gangrene.

"*Please…*" He crawled onto all fours, gawping up at the towering woman. "It was an oversight…"

Ygal stilled, features grave-cold. Colour drained from Vito's face. Isaia muttered a quiet prayer to his Saints.

"These are defective, I gather." Ygal's hands thrust forward, thumbs crushing the swivelling balls of the watchman's eyes like squelching gourds. Pulpy blood sloshed out. Vito shrieked. Ygal swung out their revolver and silenced him in one shot, his head exploding in sarcoline sponge and dead husk flying backwards.

Gut in knots, Cesare beheld the note through vignetted vision. "We may have ourselves a dilemma…" *Davide is here.*

"*You* may!" Ygal shouted. "The Morettae are *your* dilemma!" Their forefinger aimed for Cesare's face—a blood-dipped blade. "That two-faced freak is *your* dilemma! *He's* the reason the Antrum's vulnerable to the Bone King's greedy fucking corpse hands, and now *you* are making the lives of innocent people *my* dilemma!"

"Ygal," warned Isaia.

"Wanna go eyeless too?" The Dóminus held him at gunpoint.

The eavesdropper fell silent.

"I didn't *choose* this!" Frustration accosted Cesare. "Don't redirect the blame onto me—*you're* not absolved. Your halfwit watchman *missed* this? And *you* put him on a task so vital, *knowing* him? This is *our* dilemma, and we'll get nowhere with bickering like children."

"We'll get *nowhere*," Ygal's voice dropped, the coldness of her revolver's barrel biting between Cesare's collarbones, "with *your* ineptitude, Agostini." Cesare's blood chilled. "You enter the government house to-morrow night. You've had a month of devising, a *month* of my and *all* of the Antrum's citizens in danger. Return with that *key* of yours," the hammer clinked, "or return to the pit you crawled out of. Days are numbered for us all, but for *you* I'll make sure they are." Ygal shot a glimpse at the wall. "I've never considered crucifixion."

The Dóminus pulled back with a flick of glossy waves, barking some order Cesare could no longer hear, and the condottiéri departed, Isaia sparing Cesare an unreadable backward glance.

Cesare looked up at the child's mangled corpse, down at blind Vito with his sopping chunks of brain matter dribbling down the fuscous brickwork. *A memento mori.* Ygal was a diplomat, sure and true, but she took no prisoners and enacted no light punishment. And it was *Cesare's* throat on the line, this time.

He'd scoured the citadel's northeastern wing top-down, no stone left unturned, strategically selecting the upcoming díem crepúsca night to infiltrate, and yet *weeks* after the attack on him in Smugglers' District, *almost three months* following the assembly riot, Cesare had no leads on Davide or The Morettae. The sole intel he got his hands on completely negated his efforts—there *was* no smuggler band with a wyvern for a sigil—dumping Cesare back at square one.

He rubbed his face, breath quickening as prickly heat sprung up beneath his skin. *He* had *never* made oversights. Nothing *ever* stumped him. So what changed?

What darkness impended?

False stars leaked light like pale mucus down the weathered walls of the Antrum as Cesare made his way through the deserted capillaries, not wishing to exit by those yellow doors.

"Oh *my*," a man crooned behind him, not close enough to strike, but certainly looking to. "*Quite* the predicament you've found yourself in, Bauta."

Cesare drew his stilétti. "Quite the *nerve* for someone so spineless— threatening the Domínii." He turned. Davide lingered in obscurity, a bodach. Cesare couldn't let himself believe that he'd been followed all this time. "Bored of two-timing The Morettae and your imperator?"

Davide's foul smile stretched, eyes the lacquered celadon of beetle elytra. "Perceptive." He stepped forward. "Do you know why your twins' precious parents are still breathing?"

Cesare's chest clenched. "Humour me."

"They weren't legionaries," said Davide, "the attack on *Commegnos' Curios*. I handed some crow uniforms to a Moretta troupe to trash the parlour. That note you flaunted at the citadel was for me—*I* left it for you to find." Davide tutted. "It's my *freedom* I want, regardless of my means towards it. With The Morettae set up like I wanted, I needed *you* to attend the assembly, and I knew that something so... *peculiar*, would seal the deal if you weren't already intending."

Cesare's eyes narrowed. "You miserable nonce. You'd go *so* far just to catch little old me?" He paced, guarded, watchful. "You think your Lord of Bless'ed Dominion will grant you what you want? You *genuinely* believe you're not just another fly in his web? That he won't crush you just as eagerly?"

"You *know*..." Davide sibilated, "you *are* still so young to me."

Revulsion shoved Cesare backwards. "Sicko!"

"*Though*, sadly, I never much liked boys... but *Vivinna* was no boy."

Cesare jolted. "What—?"

"How *deeply* it must've cut to see her disgust when she beheld you, when she neared you."

"We were children—"

"She despised those violent pictures etched into you, didn't she?" taunted Davide. "Yet the venomous nymphet was such a *sweet* thing.

Lovely blonde locks and youthful face. Such a *pretty* specimen for my collection, she could've been. Her insides and soft limbs colour my dreams."

Cesare's stomach heaved. "You are vile."

Davide snickered. "All have their pastimes. *You* start fires and hunt crows; *I* enjoy taxidermy. And we aren't wholly *un*like each other. Equally clever, equally conniving, equally damaged. Some might call *you* vile."

Cesare's throat burned with acid. "Either side of a coin." He lunged, stilétti poised to kill.

Davide sidestepped. "We shan't fight to-night." He swung his fisted hand.

Bluish-white powder blinded Cesare's field, bringing up from him tight coughs. A mephitic odour smothered him as weakness seized his limbs. *Basilisk Weep.*

"My *Lord of Bless'ed Dominion* wouldn't approve." Davide's voice blurred in Cesare's panic. His vision skewed, blackened. His legs weakened. *NO!*

Cesare *needed* to keep hold of his faculties, *needed* to be in control of himself.

He couldn't…

let himself…

…*lose.*

*Axe to wood.*
   *Axe to flesh.*
   *Axe to bone.*
Crack!
   *Red sky. Black pall. Blood rain. White flame.*
   *Hearts torn from chests. Entrails falling from the red sky.*

*Sere grass of the moors burns beneath the Boy's feet—a demon treading hallowed ground. The hideous sun burns peridot as the Man's eyes in the red sky.*

*He'd fallen so many times, scraped his knees on the cobblestones of Du Rrât a du Errèina, the dirt tracks trailing through Canronê like scars, yet never once had the Boy seen so much blood.*

*He tastes it first, anointing the air. Once paprika-sweet, now iron.* Now death.

*Crimson branches down the Woman's face as if roots of a forsaken bloodline sprouting from her cracked skull, the moors awash in the Girl's dismembered chunks, the Grandmother a maggot-eaten grey corpse. Three chthonic matriarchs hanging on umbilical nooses from the red sky above burning moors.*

Blood on your hands.

*Iron rips the Boy's flesh like wood, three hacks, blood-sap, termite guts spilling into twig-thin fingers.*

'They weren't supposed to get in the way!' *bellows the Man.*

'It was only meant to be *you*!'

*Only the Boy.*

Only me.

*The Boy's senses drown in screams.*

*In death.*

Because of you, Boy.

*Cesare?*

Let me rest!

*Cesare.*

Their blood will never wash off you.

*The axe comes down.*

*To wood.*

*To flesh.*

*To bone.*

Crack!

'Cesare!'

Cesare's lungs inflated.

He pushed himself off his stomach—the arrangement he slept in to mollify his perturbation. A torrent engulfed his body, muscles stiff and quivering as tightropes, face numb. *I'm going to die—*

"*Cesare!*" A woman's voice spilled cold as oceans into his veins. "You are *back*." The pressure of hands against his shoulders wrung Cesare's innards. "Listen to me and breathe—"

"Don't touch me." He recoiled from Giorgianna and made for the infirmárium, rushing past the dark mirror and lighting the solitary candelabrum with trembling fingers. He couldn't look into the hideous eyes that would reflect back at him—half that man's just as his putrid blood.

Turning the tap, Cesare let it haemorrhage, candlelit vapours rising from the water.  .

Calid heat surpassed his clothes, bit his flesh as he sank into the filled tub and crossed his ankles on its distal rim. Pain pierced his skull as if a pincushion.

Hinges squeaked and into the chamber peeked Giorgianna.

"Is… everything all right?" She slunk inside, holding a slender water glass. Confusion held her face, no doubt at the sight of Cesare sitting fully-clothed in a filled tub.

He released his cheek from his teeth. "Far from my first." He pulled from the nightstand a sigarétta box, taking the final one. A folded paper ensconced at the bottom.

Giorgianna placed the glass beside the candelabrum. "Water, if you need."

Wry amusement tugged Cesare's lips in spite of himself. "Poisoning me yourself, at long last?"

She rolled her eyes. "Don't be a fiend."

He let candlefire singe the tobacco, fingers gruing, and tugged up his sleeve over the lantern oil burns splashed across his right forearm when he noted Giorgianna regarding them with that inquisitiveness of hers. "How did you get inside?"

Giorgianna's slim hand lingered on the glass for a moment longer. "Your door was ajar." She sat against the tub like a nymph by the waterside.

Cesare stared silently at her. He always kept his door shut precisely on account of his nightmares. *Another oversight…* The screech of teeth deafened his ears, the nausea in his gut bubbling at the barbed heat wracking his body.

Fingertips brushed his sleeve. "Are you sure—?"

"Don't *touch* me!" Cesare recoiled.

Giorgianna jolted as if he'd burned her. "You won't tell me why."

Cesare drew the sigarétta to smoke out his panic. "I like to think of myself as something of an enigma."

A shake of the head. "What is *this*?" Giorgianna gestured to the tub.

"Grounding."

Her gaze firmed. "What happened?"

Cesare recognised the true meaning of her query, and didn't intend on answering the way she wished. "We found a crucified carnesíi with a note inside their emptied stomach at one of the Antrum's entrance points: a threat from Davide." A tongue-click. "Appears Ygal means to make a matching display of *me*."

Giorgianna frowned. "Why?"

"I'm making too-slow progress. And it's clearly on *my* account that Davide's gotten so deep into the Antrum. Friendship isn't an adequate transaction when, to Ygal, ensuring his cadre and territory's safety eclipses my pertinence of retaining allies." He flicked his sigarétta. "She'll drop me if to-morrow night proves fruitless—'drop' meaning my dead body into the ocean." Cesare's panicked tongue thrust forth words before he could contain them. Only the twins had seen him in such states, Isaia once. Not even Vivinna, his first… not *love*—Cesare had certainly never been in love—but '*tenderness*'… for lack of a better word? And he wasn't prepared to let anyone else stand witness. Especially not

Giorgianna. It was as good as exposing his weakest spot to an assassin. "An opportune run-in with Davide to-night confirms his puppeteering of The Morettae, at least," he rejoined.

Giorgianna's brows rose. "Elaborate?"

Cesare recounted his tête-à-tête.

"He is no ally of Morettae," said Giorgianna once his narration concluded, flourishing cards she'd drawn from her hiked skirt. "Their incursion on the assembly decimated their ranks."

"*And* succeeded to tarnish The Bauta's reputation through conflation with Morettae, all precisely as Davide intended."

"A deceiver leading the blind around."

"Directly into the spiderweb." Cesare exhaled the last of his smoke. "Precisely *what* Davide wants in the Antrum eludes me. What *doesn't* is that *I* need to get *him* first, no matter by how roundabout a way. He knows something. And my stilétti are an added incentive."

Giorgianna hid her cards. "By which you mean…?"

"He stole them."

Her jaw slacked, doing *oh* so well to take some edge off the humiliation! "That's… not possible."

"Basilisk Weep."

"Sedative…"

Cesare perched his chin onto the back of his palm. "That which I used on the crows the '*Bedlamite's Ballad*' night so they'd let me wreak my havoc."

Ire glittered along the aventurescence flecking Giorgianna's sunstone eyes, yet Cesare's amusement snuffed out awfully fast. "None of this should've blind-sided me." He crushed his sigarétta's filter tip, too-long nails piercing crescents into his skin. "They are *not* going to win. Even if it kills me off, they *will* not fucking win." His veins burned. *Rage.* He despised it, his father's vice, but in that moment, it felt good—better than pity, yet a drug he vowed to never develop a taste for.

"Of anybody in this world," Giorgianna's voice overcame Cesare's heed like crepuscule, "I doubt *you* could allow yourself to lose to anyone." Gossamer candlelight draped her skin, her lissom figure illuminated like a chiaroscuro painting within the shadows she wore for a halo. "It matters most." Her head tipped, weeping-willow curls skimming the water, and Cesare's urge to touch them, *her*, almost conquered him.

He dropped the crushed filter tip onto the nightstand. "Go to bed, vólto."

Her lips pressed together. "You… seem quite shaken still."

Cesare conjured a smirk, leaning his temple onto his knuckles. "How thy façade lies."

She treated him to the dirtiest glare—such cherished familiarity. "Infuriating through and through." She towered beside the tub, a deiform sculpture dressed in the colour of wrath. Of blood. Of love.

Cesare inhaled, eyes averting from her.

He couldn't admit to himself that he noticed Giorgianna in that way, that he spotted the moles under her eye and on her cheek, the shape of her lips, the first time he looked at her maskless face. Cesare had never fancied seafaring—such an immense exertion of control over himself he could never permit—but standing in Giorgianna's field made him a sailor buckling to a siren's song, besotted, a madness. *Purposeless.* She detested him, and he was a death-bringer already claimed by the other side.

Giorgianna dawdled a little longer before walking off, shoulders squared and spine steeled. Alert. Vigilant. Prepared to defend herself at the drop of a hat. Saints only knew the true darkness of her reasons.

She paused one last time at the threshold, not turning. "I'm off to the Antrum."

Cesare frowned, teeth salted with haem. "Did we not *just* discuss Davide?"

A mirthless half-laugh. "Don't feign concern." Giorgianna's jibe took him aback, then the door shut, and Cesare drew a deeper breath as footsteps retreated.

He eyed the glass of water on the nightstand. *Why* your *concern?*

The refraction through the water distorted strangely.

Cesare frowned, moving the glass aside.

Behind it lay a gianduia chocolate wrapped in tawny aluminium.

A huff broke from Cesare's tangled chest, his head knocking back as he laughed at the girlish gesture before catching himself, pressing the pads of his clammy palms against his screwed-shut eyes. *Saints, I'm an idiot.* He lured the aimless musings into the alcoves of his mind where he walled them in to die.

From the confines of the empty sigarétta box, Cesare retrieved the note to read.

> '...*hidden words* spat by the blest *to*
> *this plane from the celestial lazulum,*
> *sentenced to quietus* beneath the
> soffits of a suzerain's keep...'

Cogs ticked in his brain, constricting the aperture of his mind's eye. *Clario Barsotti.* Cesare couldn't explain *how* without sounding mad even to himself, but every detail substantiated more and more that the Minister of Emissaries *must* hide something of great consequence in his archives.

He knew the surrounding layout of the northeast top-down. All that mattered now was getting inside, finding that proverbial key, whatever it may be, and making it out with intact guts.

Only time would tell, and *Cesare's* time grew overdue.

# SCENE XXXVII

## E IL NAUFRAGAR M'È
## DOLCE IN QUESTO MARE

*Giorgianna*

"THESE PEOPLE KNOW MORE than they let on." I lit a sigarétta. "But they're impossible to wring information out of."

Sarnai shut the door of the inn bedchamber after herself and kicked off her boots, plopping onto the creaky bed and stretching across me like a cat. "That's the Antrum for ya."

With a scoff, I tapped ashes into the tray perched on the wrought iron headboard behind me.

Sarnai frowned at the stranger asleep beside me, slithering over to lift a vermilion-dyed lock obscuring their ruddy face. She gawked at me. '*Is that* Mair?' she mouthed.

I swathed my bare chest with hair, shrugging coolly. *The Arum* had stolen my flesh, now came my turn to reclaim it. I would never be owned again. I was mine.

"Coincidence!" chirped Sarnai. "They're my duty buddy to-day." She climbed over my legs. "Tailoring?"

"Say less." I dropped my unfinished sigarétta into the ashtray and sat knees-to-knees with her.

Treading my fingers through my hair, I attuned to the cold thrum of azoth in my blood, frost veiling my skin from the inside. Vessels in my skull engorged with a vulnerable ache as curls coiled around my fingertips loosened to flaxen waves. One could always *feel* tailoring. Like a tug of crusted blood or a poorly-healed scar.

Azoth concentrated at several points throughout the body: its core reserve in the pericardium; the secondary in the frontal lobe; the residual in the liver and wrists. Transmutation of core azoth to functional magic essentially equated to another humour pouring into one's circulation, drastically elevating blood pressure. Splitting headaches, nosebleeds, myasthenia accosted the lucky few. Some suffered heart attacks, strokes, aneurysms from magic use. Others ripped open from the inside. Anyone could learn magic, but it became glaringly obvious why most did not.

"You're getting good!" gasped Sarnai.

Along with masonry and mind scourging,[128] flesh tailoring was a corporeal magic.

Principal magics were the arts of speaking to fire and the earth, the waters and the wind; of weaving shadows, bending light, bringing storms and winter chills.[129]

Sorcery was more arcane. Enchanting could be learned, whilst dream walking,[130] along with hindsight and clairvoyance, were the only inborn

---

[128] Includes mind reading and manipulation, but is broader. Its negative side effects can include permanent schizophrenia and psychosis, as well as physical brain damage. An individual under a scourge's influence can feel them burrowing through their brain.

[129] These magics are as follows, corresponding to the essential cosmic constituents: Shadow weaving; light bending; fire, earth, water, wind speaking (base magics); storm and winter bringing (*chimerical* magics: derive and amalgamate from base speaking magics); blood singing (a subtype of water speaking—blood singers always start as water speakers).

[130] The ability to leave one's corporeal form and enter peoples' dreams via submerging into a sleep-like catatonia wherein one's consciousness exits its material

magics, though texts spoke of peculiar cases wherein certain forms of cerebral damage seemed to puncture the occlusion in the frontal lobe which impeded illimitable capacity for transmutation of azoth.

Most of my knowledge I obtained from '*Spagyrism and Spellwerk*' by Ilinka occultist Nashĭgostu Kurilit Gostiata, the book I had lent to Lucrezia on account of what she spoke of the High Priest, and one which I *may* have stolen from *The Encephalon*—Vencenza's great athenaeum—into which I snuck three weeks ago.

Gostiata was one such peculiar case himself. He dubbed the direct transfer of pure azoth into the bloodstream a 'transfusion' rather than a transmutation. He was known to wield his blood like blades, infusing it with transfused azoth and voiding his body entirely of its vital supply through slashed wrists. In the end, a bloodborne infection took him, but he'd begun to grow mad with azoth blight long before.

I dropped the tresses, willing them to coil and darken, already swooning with fatigue. I couldn't bring myself to tailor living matter yet. Skin and flesh, bone. The pain frightened me; I'd felt too much of it already. "Why did you choose white?" I gestured to Sarnai's hair.

"It reminds me of Jegün Kəgər." She stroked her locks, then the embroidery of rosen-apricot clouds unfurling across the murky gridelin sky of her shirt's dəəl-esque collar—all sewn by her deft hand. "In the winter, snow carpets the steppe in the purest white you'll ever see." She smiled, easy as ever, yet my heart panged all the same. "Magic in Örgön Gazaar is so different. Most of our magi are speakers. Something as bizarre and mystical as sorcery is practically unheard of. It's different here—always a *mystery* about. You can't tell if you're looking at someone's *face*, you know? A mask over a mask." She snorted. "Don't know *what* you people have against your own visages!"

---

form which is still sensate. Like hindseers and clairvoyants, walkers often require IV drips during their submersion.

If a walker's physical body dies while their consciousness (technically azoth) is in a target's dream, they continue to live for as long as the target remains asleep. Once the target awakes, the walker's azoth disperses as it does in death. Dream walking is the rarest form of magic.

"Perhaps you mightn't wish to have your private dealings pried upon," I mused. "Centuries ago, masks were a weapon against the northern oppressors. Anonymity is a cosmic power." A smile scythed my lips as I met Sarnai's ink-blot eyes. "Not that there's irrefutable fault in masquerades." It was the face that yearned freedom; the face the despot sought to rip away.

Sarnai giggled. "A balladeer you are, Giorgi."

I laughed along, eternally grateful for her comfort and company. When, years ago, Emanuela spent eight months at the infamous *L'Académie de Danse* in Auréli on a ballet exchange programme with *Su Palázzo del Canzóni*, we sent letters to one another, the endeavour swiftly devolving into a contest of which one of us could write the most pretentiously dramatic poetry. I won without fail, and Ema always said the same thing.

Mair stirred, languorously raising their head.

They peered at me and Sarnai through half-lidded eyes, going to roll out of bed before shoving themselves back and scrutinising us with alarm. "Hold on," they wheezed hoarsely, Yrnmyg[131] accent breathy.

I pursed my lips. "No."

Mair's shoulders loosened. "Righ'." They pointed at Sarnai. "So wha' you doing here?"

"Isaia the Eternal Snore expects me and you for sentinel duty."

Mair slid off of bed in a whirlwind of coughs, searching the floor for their strewn-about clothes. "So long as i's not Smugglers' Distric' or fucking bu'cher Lucanus' territ'ry, I'm golden."

My ears pricked up. "Smugglers' District?"

Mair peered at me. "...Iah? The s're'ch of coas'line pas' old'own and An'rum."

I jolted. "There's *another* region?"

"*Ooo*, you don' know!" realised Mair. "Figures."

Sarnai squinched my way. "Haven't you been hanging around smugglers for a month?"

---

[131] *EERN-meeg*; people of Yrdagwlat (*eer-dah-goo-LAHT*).

"*Seldom*," barely once a week, "and I *said* wringing information from them yields nought."

"Well, I know nothing of Smugglers' District—never stepped foot there."

"A'righ'." Mair threw on their lovat clothes and leaned their bony elbows onto the bed. "No' even sligh'ly surprised you've no' heard a peep. If you though' *Dominii* were secre'ive… '*Wringing*' may be too gen'le to ge' corsairs talking. Risky exploi', smuggling." They drew a whistling breath into their barrel chest. "*Basically*, i's this par' of Vencenza's southern coas'line where all the smugglers live—a seaside township. You can ge' there by the An'rum *or* old'own. Never followed the la'er bu' I *be'* i's safer. If Glàvca's manning the bar, ask her for a map."

I blinked, gaping for a moment before asking, "*Realistically*, how did I never hear of this place?"

Sarnai chuckled. "There *is* no 'realistic' down here, girl." She planted a kiss on my nose bridge, hopping off the bed. The most intimacy we'd ever shared were kisses—I couldn't stomach the idea of fearing Sarnai if *The Arum*'s demons reared their heads.

Mair eyed me with a smirk. "One for the road?" They reached for me without my assent.

I swung my baselard in a reverse grip from under a pillow. "I'll empty you."

They raised their palms. "A'righ', a'righ'."

I realised, too, that I found little bona fide pleasure in the touch of transitory lovers. As much as I wanted to be mine, and I *was*, I wanted to be *flesh* again. Not cold meat for tearing by predators, not the rabid wretch of thorns and needles I'd transmogrified into, but warm and shivering and *human*. Because my lovers were still a bitter pill I downed for my pain, and they still cut themselves on me for a narcotic rapture.

In Faustinian, 'love' was '*ataínè*': 'eater'. 'Gnawer'.

I'd reclaimed my husk of a body, but I couldn't earnestly enjoy it without blood in my teeth and fingertips on my insides. Without lovebites blooming to a garden of lilac flowers in the troughs of my collarbones. Without love.

Sarnai flicked my curls into my face. "Don't run off on suicide missions without direction, okay?"

"I won't, I won't." I shovelled hair off my eyes, drawing an 'X' on my chest. "Cross my heart."

Sarnai scoffed. "Yeah right." And the condottiéri slunk out, singing their farewells like drunken barflies.

I fell back on the creaky bed with a huff. *Pirate bastards.*

The gnarled ceiling suspended an oil lamp, its festucine flicker luring spellbound moths. Rusting nails wedged themselves crookedly in the withered walls, yet the nameless tavérna I'd divined upon a month ago stood fast.

My cello-callused fingers idly tread my thighs and violin hips, endowed with flesh once more, yet far from soft. *Wayward.* Perhaps my mother had been right, but her condemnations hardly wounded me now—little more than scrapes. Her demands for perfection, for silence, no longer my burden, for I knew I could no longer shoulder it.

I *wanted* to be filth. I wanted to be wrong and twisted. Deprived and ugly. *Misbegotten.* Tears, scratches, bruises, scars, brutish ferality and pitiful rage. Humanity.

Freedom would *always* be worth it.

I shimmied into my boots and black pants, tight around my curves once more, slipping on the whispering fluted tulle of an incarnadine blouse before lacing my faithful overbust corset over-top. Strapping my dagger to my thigh and holstering my revolver, I slung on that trusty satchel of mine and descended into the subdued hum of the dimly-glowing taproom, air aromatic with dandelion and mead.

The ever-vivacious Glàvca tended to the bar, a pudgy woman with thick blonde corkscrews and an enormous scar traversing her face. Two years back, she'd supposedly attempted to retrieve a spice crate from a high shelf, knocking down a stack of knives.

"*Yours*," I placed four pètrae onto the counter—my share of the night, "and *mine*." I held out my palm. With my need for coin, I performed on the aerial silks for the femmes at her inn. Another reclamation. Back in the dark, but the *too* dark was mine.

Glàvca wiped her hand on her wine-stained apron and placed into my palm a small pouch. All the money I didn't expend, I either gave to the twins for *Sunrise* repairs, or to beggars as I would in the slums. Escaping that purgatory meant I held an even greater obligation to care for and stand with those still trapped.

"You ain't half bad on 'em shilksh," Glàvca remarked, her breezy provincial accent starkly northern.

I simpered, hiding the coins. "Even *you* wouldn't let me touch them if I were."

"Oy, lishen in." Glàvca leaned on the bar. "Namesh've been floatin', but one'sh bogglin' my noggin." She lowered her voice. "Ilenia Farneshe."

My eyebrows entwined. "The Magister?" Lucrezia's recount of her adolescence among the spider nest that was the senate overcame my mind like black clouds.

"Dunno why, but intereshin', innit?" Glàvca effervesced. "Minish'er namesh don't fly over 'eshe waysh unlesh it' that raper Dioli." *The Minister of Scholars, Irene Farnese, no less...*

"Whom *did* you hear this from?"

"Up 'e shupply chain—shmugglersh an' 'em."

I glimpsed my opportunity. "Legend has it you've a map of Smugglers' District on hand."

"If 'at ain't goshpel!" Glàvca eagerly *bracked* her way through the cupboards, pulling out a folded sheet of parchment. I sat up on the bar as she unfolded a map embellished with curlicued text and illustrations of sailor mythology, the depicted territory unfamiliar to me. "Shmugglersh've got 'eir own lawsh like Dominíi, but *'eir* 'territoriesh' are 'eir shipsh, and 'eir 'cadresh' are '*bandsh*'. Dishtrict itshelf'sh more a 'no-man'sh-land'. Dominíi aren't to touch it."

"How is it that you know so much yet most folks don't?"

"I run an inn. Where'd you think I get my shuppliesh? Shmugglersh're a keyshtone shpeciesh."

I decoded the geography of Smugglers' District: West Fin to the left; East Fin to the right; a narrow stretch called Buccaneer's Landing to the southwest, illustrated with wharfs reaching into a cove. Bloodink marked the spot where the Antrum's southeast met East Fin. A dangerous route, if Mair was anything to go by.

Inspecting closer, a fine slit of bloodink underscored a tavérna—northeast of Buccaneer's Landing, West Fin. '*The Salacia*'. Where Cesare said a Moretta had attacked him a month ago.

Excitement thrilled through me as I pointed to the mark. "Can I get there via the oldtown?"

Glàvca took to polishing all the wine glasses—a habit. "Hard, *but…*" She wagged a finger before slipping a book from under the bar. Inside it sat a map of The Court of Secrets, dainty as a postcard. "Shmugglersh' Dishtrict ain't on it, but on 'e bottom you'll shee '*to the Cove*'. 'At'sh what '*at* meansh. It'sh far out of 'e way, expectedly, but you shouldn't shtray wi' a map."

I hopped off the bar. "Thank you so, *so* kindly!" Perhaps I could find more leads on Marcello Damiani at Smugglers' District! So much time had already slipped through my fingers like sand, so I sought anything solid to mollify my spirit of inquiry. *I have direction now, Sarnai!* That being said, if Smugglers' District *did* yield me answers, I'd rip those pirate bastards' faces off.

"Gladly!" Glàvca grinned heartily. "An'in' elshe?"

"That." I pointed to the small yellow rose in a treen vase on the bar.

Her unscarred eyebrow clipped up. "My tavèrna decor?"

"*Rosa luteus*," I mused. "I sort of lost my over-a-decade-old herbarium to the government and feel some degree of spite over it."

"Take 'e damn plant, 'en!" She waved. "I don't want none of your shpite!"

"You're a treat, Glàvca." I plucked the rose, tucking it carefully behind my ear. "Your salubrious establishment retains its charm," I added over my shoulders. The woman rolled her eyes with a smile as I breached the threshold.

Beyond the tar-thick umbra of overhanging eaves, light barely touched the cobbles. *The sun is not yet on the rise, above.* Aware of my weapons and back, I advanced through the choroid streets.

Shadows writhed serpentine and black at my feet, within my skull, slithering through my brain and behind my aching eyes.

"SHE SHALL WEAR MANY FACES." A drone sluiced my skin like gelid water, jerking me to a halt.

Darkness veiled the world, and in the living caliginosity swayed The Rams. Their irises drank from my soul as if esurient cosmogyral entities, birling within milky sclerae devoid of vessels.

"Shadows indeed speak truth," I found my voice amidst the sickness fraying my mind.

"BOUNDARIES BROKE;" their whispers unified, "LIMITLESSNESS ATTAINED. SHEDDING OF THE CHRYSALIS BEGINS."

"Was it the Antrum you spoke of?" I questioned, heart pounding with understanding—a measly, frangible morsel of comprehension.

Blackness grasped for my eyes and plucked them out.

My feet squelched against blood-streaked flesh, the air warm, cloying, dense. Pink tissue sprawled into walls, ceilings. Light streamed through the lustrous cusps of sinew yawning overhead. *Am I inside a right heart ventricle…?*

My arms split, twisted, stretched into optic nerves, the nails of my every finger bloating and ripening into eyeballs a-swivel with carnelian irises. *My* irises. "THE THIRD EYE BLINKS AS THE MIND BREAKS BENEATH THE NEEDLE OF THE GODS' BRAT."

Panic thrashed—imprisoned in my ribs.

Ahead arose a throne twisted of seven skinless arms, a sodden crimson feast of new-culled flesh, bulging orbs cradled within the centre of their palms. "WHAT KIND OF LIGHT KEEPS YOU IN THE DARK?"

A shriek ruptured from me, dagger in my hands—my fingers mine again—gashing the flesh, the shadow cocoon bleeding darkness in pulsating tidal waves. Mortality's reek drowned my lungs as I swung my blade like a sinking man fighting madly for the surface.

A solid force knocked me breathless.

I toppled, swinging defensively on all fours.

The darkness slashed away.

My blade stilled a hair's breadth from a man's neck.

The man was Cesare.

He gawked up at me, hands hot as a metalsmith's pincers gripping my forearms back from plunging the baselard. "We ought to stop meeting this way, vólto." His larynx bobbled as he spoke, tendons and veins flushed tight and waiting to the silken flesh sheathing the slender column of his throat, his voice claret-dulcet. And I hungered for it—to carve a gateway to his core and crawl inside.

I tore myself from his hold. Stumbled upright. The last tendrils of shadow retreated into their nooks and left my breaths to heave and tremble as I doubled back, back further, cheeks hot with a rush of blood. *What is wrong with me?*

Cesare arose, dusting off his jacket and recovering his tricorn. "Pleasant morn to *you*, too." He clicked his tongue, eyes slitted. "What say you join me for sparring this fair day? Seeing you missed the last two occasions."

I tidied my curls and composed myself, flower-sweet venom on my tongue and lips as I warbled, "If it pleases his majesty."

Cesare rolled his eyes and walked briskly into the city's rete.

I caught up. "What were you here for?" I knew nothing worthwhile could come of enquiring about his state of mind. He'd never divulge, not to me. Maybe not to anyone.

"Final consolidations with Isaia."

"Regarding to-night's infiltration?"

"The one and only."

I made a brief pass of his nonchalant countenance. "You know you'll get heinously butchered if the house of cards falls *your* way, right?"

He smiled darkly. "*Try* to contain yourself." Insouciant as ever, yet I couldn't believe his hard-bitten mask when I'd seen it slip.

But he didn't care, so neither should I.

# Scene XXXVIII

## You Love Blood Too Much,
## But Not Like I Do

*Giorgianna*

CESARE AND I ARRIVED AT THE ART GALLERY by dawn—when sunlight dispelled at last the haze veiling the autumnal horizon.

We circled to the swell of silent overtures, holding each other at long point. The rapier came to be my favoured sword, ornate and elegant in its construction. Cesare's choice remained the neat sabre.

"How do you know all that about the government building?" I struck. He deflected. "Too many nights spent staking out around its walls." His blade thrust.

I voided per Sarnai's counsel, sword guarding my body as I pivoted to keep Cesare in my direct line of sight. Despite shirking sciamachy and shooting practice with *him*, not a day went by that I didn't train. I wouldn't be exploited again, so I honed myself with magic and steel and bullets. "Alone?" I switched lines and slashed.

Cesare blocked, enviably effortless. "For all intents and purposes."

Starting out had been awful, my wrists creaking and sore, deep blisters eating my flesh, but as days flickered by, I grew stronger, assured. "Could you not ask the twins to help?"

Cesare shed my blade, flourished his sabre through his wrist and across his torso to guard. "Theoretically."

"Why don't you?"

He struck hard. "Because I *need* them to *live*."

I parried and passed back. Steel rang in strident glissandi. "*They* need *you* to live."

"They know better than to demand from me such promises." His blade met mine again, the two of us face-to-face. "I am an instrument, and my purpose is set."

Cesare enveloped my blade before I could ask what he meant, trapping it beneath his guard, and thrust towards my low line.

I volted with a yelp, beating my blade against his.

"Keep at attention, feet planted. Your balance is off. If an opponent catches on, they'll nudge you right off your feet. What you should've done is passed back and let my lunge fall into a void, or parried, preferably a septième. If parrying, immediately riposte." Cesare lifted his sabre. "In guardia."

We waltzed circles. Andante e stringendo.

*Feint, disengage, thrust, volt, reprise.*

"You hope for a quick stop-over?" I panted as we danced apart for a heartbeat.

"Ideally." He reprised, all the fluid grace of flames whilst my muscles fatigued with each twisted step of our dance.

"*Knowing* what befell The Morettae?"

"We—" his blade shoved against mine "—*know* what we're walking in on."

Amidst deepening breaths, I strung together the words—"You're dead meat, Agostini."

Cesare angled his sabre and pinned my rapier, tip to the floorboards, beneath it. He stepped across with catlike legerity swifter than I, in my weariness, could register, his arm locking around my waist and elbows to restrain me against him. "Didn't know we were on a surname basis, vólto." His breath skimmed my ear, voice glinting with a white-fanged smile.

I pushed against his solid frame, unable to lever my arms and free my sword. "Nor on such a close-proximity basis, *bàuta*." I dug my elbow into his rib, stunning him just long enough to pivot.

He tripped me. A scream deserted my throat as I tumbled backwards. I extended my foot and rammed his ankle, sealing my fate but knocking him down with me.

Pain drummed my bones when I struck the floor.

Cesare's sabre met my rapier, the flat edge of my blade almost at my neck and the foible of his hovering above my nose. "Throw me off." His legs pinned me down. His blade inclined forward.

Panic rose my gorge as I pushed my left palm into the flat edge of the blade to hold the rapier stable, both elbows planted into the floor. "At least let me use my arms," I gritted out. I'd forgotten how strong Cesare was. So limber and trim yet he was all muscle.

He hardly simpered, sly and sour. "Look at *you*, admitting your shortcomings."

"Hypocrite!" I hissed. "All you *ever* do is deny weakness and refuse aid as if you won't *kill* yourself this way!"

Hubris—he couldn't dodge its bullets forever.

"Then I supplicate absolution for robbing *you* of that pleasure."

I pushed my rapier. "I *hate* you."

"Say *why*, then." He drove his sabre against me, voice a wildfire, humourless. "Do you despise that everything I told you the night of '*A Bedlamite's Ballad*' rings true? Does it frighten you that you've begun to see *you* when you look at me? Do I *gnaw* at you, vólto?"

My arms trembled with rage. "You're a *bastard*."

Cesare angled his chin. Loose bangs skimmed my cheek. "Incorrect, legally speaking."

"You have a comeback for everything, don't you?"

"And all *you* have to retaliate with are insults."

My lips hang parted, unable to shape into speech, and it made me shake all the more.

Cesare clicked his tongue, then stood to his feet and set his sword upon the high table. Beside the golden rose.

He held out his hand as I sat up.

I swiped my blade at him, only barely missing.

He *tsk'd*. "You wound me." I clumsily stood whilst he went about pacing. "*I'm* the one who reserves the right to hostility, you know. Considering yours poisoning *and* shooting me."

"If only I *had* better aim!" I spat all the bile I could bring up.

"That's *IT*!" Cesare shouted.

I flinched as his voice rattled the gallery.

Never once had heard him speak so.

His eyes blazed when they met mine. A solar flare. Like empires burst into flames. Like the first time we stood face-to-face. "Why are you constantly being so fucking awful?"

My lips curled from my teeth, senses alert as a shark to blood. "Where ought I *start*?" I clasped my rapier by its ricasso. "Everything happened to me because of *you*! Your *stupid* fucking machinations turned my life on its head in a day! *Your* hand set this bedlam in motion the night of '*A Bedlamite's Ballad*' you so love to rub into my wounds!"

"I'm *sorry*?" exclaimed Cesare. "Everything happened because of *me*?"

"You were *always* around the corner! '*A Bedlamite's Ballad*' and *The Arum* and Davide and his flunkeys cornering me! Where there's smoke, there's fire, right?"

"You *know* Lucrezia told me not to disclose anything. And you think you'd've made it out alive the night of '*A Bedlamite's Ballad*'? You don't think *you*'d've been heinously fucking butchered? I wasn't 'always around the corner'—I couldn't give two fucks about you! I went to scout an area suspiciously void of Guards, that was my *only* reason for bumping into you and I'd be grateful to *every* deity if I were in your place. *I* didn't make you talk back to your impresario! *I* didn't sway your mind towards beliefs you *already* held deep down! You've forgiven everyone else yet keep at *my* throat because you cannot accept the part *you* played in your own fate. You *chose* to give Basilio a piece of your mind and you fucking should have, but don't blame me."

"You *lied* and mocked me again and again without remorse and you dragged me to that forsaken assembly *knowing* what you were doing!" I bit back. "I lost *everything. Every single thing* I *ever* knew was reaped from me—I had *less than nothing* in the *worst* place I could fathom where I was tortured *every fucking day* and couldn't escape!" It took everything to keep my voice intact. "And *still* you went out of your way to not tell me crucial information until the *very last second* or not at all!"

"You *know* none of this would've changed had I played it differently," said Cesare. "Truth can be as explosive as deception—you broke in the worst way."

"Yet what did you do the day of the assembly?"

"*Vólto, I didn't know what would* happen—!"

"*I have a fucking* name, *Cesare!*" My screams all but clawed my throat raw. "And *you* needed me sane just a *smidge* longer to suit your little schemes."

"Little schemes?" he snapped. "These '*schemes*' you dub so 'little' are demolition of a tyranny and liberation from oppression—how fucking *dare* you belittle me when everything that motivates *you* is self-serving!"

I swung my rapier to him, vision red red red! "*TAKE IT BACK!*"

"Do it, princess." Cesare pinched my blade between his slender fingers and pressed it to his chest. Just shy of where I'd shot him. Over his heart just *so*. "Paint the floor scarlet with my insides like you wish you could." The point breached his skin, a tiny red flower blooming upon his shirt's white cotton. "Your favourite colour, right? Like blood and rage and roses."

My eyes locked wide open. My body rebelled as pulse beat within me.

"If you hate me so much," Cesare's voice dropped, "say *why*." His head tilted, resentment obnubilating the burn in his eyes. "Or did you forget?"

My fingers clamped around the hilt, twitching.

And I plunged the blade.

A gasp broke from Cesare as he jerked back. Scarlet ran down the length of his torso—spilt paint staining his ruffles to petals; the steel sank a finger nail's depth into his flesh.

"Take. It. *Back*." I trembled with wrath on behalf of my father and Ema and all my anguish and grief Cesare spat on. The brass neck of him to speak of mine 'breaking in the worst way'—feigned concern through and through!

Cesare's jaw set tight, pupils miniscule. "You first." He grabbed his tricorn and jacket, sabre left behind as I let him walk away.

My bloodied rapier clanged to the floor and I followed it, crouching into myself, chest so tight I asphyxiated on my own distress.

Thoughts in my head began to writhe and whisper like the groans of a dwelling entwined with souls, my nails sunken into my scalp.

And what if he was right? What if I'd led my life blinded by nostalgia for a time gone by? A time I could no longer recall in all its truth? Blinded by a crusade to avenge not whom I judged to be my most beloved friend, but *myself*?

*No. No. No!*

My lungs heaved air as I hauled myself upright and grasped the table, gripping onto my fraying threads to darn myself together inch by inch until I breathed again, saw again, reasoned again. Until my blade lay in my hands again.

*I need to find The Salacia.*

The music died when I slammed the door behind myself, and the coda never came.

Dewdrops blistered the sills reaching into oldtown's streets, windows swaddled in moisture like lanugo. Though sunlight climbed to vanquish autumn's chill, Vencenza's nautical winds burned the way only salt could, christening the air with purity.

Following Glàvca's map to The Court of Secrets' southwestern extremities, head a-spin with magic and unending turns, I skulked through an underpass embossed with stone constellations before crossing a narrow canal.

The altitude elevated, water splashing dark and crisp two stories below the rootbound stone bridge.

I shouldered through a tight alley onto a cocciopesto-laid cortile garrisoned by buttercream buildings lacunose with ogee arches. Its distal end dropped into a defile. A cliff-face loomed across the oblivion, its hide ulcerated by a ledge-fringed cavity. Between the two verges swayed a threadbare rope bridge.

Water lapped at the cliff's feet when I gazed over the edge. *Ocean!* I was close.

Footsteps sealed with surety, I stepped onto the bridge. Timber winced but persevered, tottering with each stride. Rarefied air, salt-kissed and fierce, thrilled giddily through my ears as vertigo sang me a berceuse. To gaze from a theatre's mezzanines was merely a gateway narcotic. Here, waltzing with the sky, walking on air, even the wind feared, screaming out poetries of madness. *I* never feared.

On the other side, the cavern turned illimitably on itself, jagged stone cold as graves.

I alighted upon a circular hatch in a concealed nook.

My stiff fingers prised open its hinges.

A cramped chamber revealed itself.

At the dilapidated floor's centre, stairs spiralled into blackness, sandblasted windows betraying nothing of the landscape beyond. *A lighthouse watch room?* With no service room overhead, the heavens gazed down, freezing winds filtering in ghostly soughs.

Nothing bespoke life as I descended the tower. No artefact of a lightkeeper. No cooled gaslamps or old wallpaper. How deep did loneliness run on a bona fide lighthouse, with only the crash of waves and a gull's shrill call for companionship? Or the occasional storm—an unwelcome visitor?

Coldness gnawed my skin beneath the tulle by the time I stepped onto the lowest floor.

It took my whole body to open the door, the tower spitting me out into blessed warmth.

Water of the shallow inlet lacquered ebony rock in aquamarine sheets, sunblinks a-bounce along its serene crests. Afield, seas deepened, swelled, rolled, curled, plunged in rhythmic motion. Cliffs socketed the bay—an eye gazing at the sprawling ocean where skerries and stilts like black lashes cleaved the waves. Onshore breeze scaled the craggy fortifications and spilled across a township to my left where wharfs overhung the coastline, dotted by dainty gondoas and grand ships with rippling sails. *Buccaneer's Landing?*

My belly fluttered with nervous glee.

*I made it, it* must *be true!*

Not far from the rock-encased lighthouse lay its smashed dome, housing the ocean's bestiary in its munted carcass.

I hopped boulder to boulder across the water and landed on the settlement's doorstep.

*Right, best get to work.*

By ten hundred, I arrived at *The Moonshine*, a dingy little tavèrna north of *Corsair's Promenade*.

Inside, the innkeeper chased a young thief off her premises to the cheers of sailors too drunk to know where to look.

Dodging a rum bottle, I snuck to the back tables where two people caught my attention: a blue-haired man with an eyepatch and bandana, and a rose-eyed androgyne, pale hair cut into a bob save for a long braid. Danilo, or Eyepatch Dan, and Ren, short for Risten, two of the smuggler cardsharps I met on my first day in the Antrum.

"Lucky coincidence, signóri.[132]" I sidled onto the bench beside Danilo.

"¡Ayyy!" His gap-toothed grin glinted. "'ow's it goin', Bianca?"

"Where's Korneli?" I enquired of the black-bearded giant, uninterested in the question.

---

[132] This plural is both masculine *and* gender-neutral.

"Ship duties," Ren responded dully, ver Vilgëkki[133] accent faint enough to be nought.

"What brings ya to our 'umble District, girly?"

Ren peered past ver pale lashes. "And *how*?"

"Not by help from *you*," I sniped at Risten before addressing Danilo, "I endeavoured to visit *The Salacia* but have been steered off-course."

The mariners swapped looks, eyebrows high on their foreheads.

"D'you want directions?" asked Ren. "It's not far."

The eagerness stunned me. "You've been chary of divulging much until now."

Dan held out his scraggly arms. "Safety first, they say. But chary no more!"

I perked up. "Then tell me about the District. It's a 'no-man's-land', I hear?"

"A'righty! *So*," Eyepatch Dan clapped and rubbed his hands vigorously, "it's a bit fiddlier. Ain't it all? 'No-man's-land' in *theory*. Trouble's that some bands establish monopolies in tavèrnae in precincts they supply, makin' them their ''ubs', meanin' some o' them can be *reeeally* unfriendly to rival bands."

"How many bands are there?"

"Twelve," Ren said. "Lucky you walked in here and not a door over, the *Dancing Worm*. The Blood Dahlias run there, and *Hangman's Dowry* pulled into harbour last night. Blood Dahlia's their captain's sobriquet— a ruthless old fishwife."

"Strung up the guts of an 'andsy bloke on 'er bowsprit, one time," Danilo chimed in. "My kinda woman if I fancied 'em."

We chuckled together, Ren's eyes spinning.

"Them *aside*," Danilo took the helm, "Steer clear of The Black Tongues, White Lotus, and Unsung Brotherhood. '*Specially* that last one seein' ya're a woman and all—apologies if judged wron'. Chances are, ya've already attracted attention with that mask and bein' a newbie. Ya *did* decide well on wearin' them weapons loud and proud. Anywhoses,

---

[133] Indigenous people of Vilges Island in northern Pohjaaperä. The country's majority group is Laaksö Ihme.

them bands gather at *Dead Glories*, *Grand 'ost*, and *The Old Toad* respectively."

I winced inwardly. *Dead Glories* was the first tavèrna I visited. "And *your* band?"

"The Salt 'ydras, girly," Danilo declared proudly. "Us got not one problem with nobody."

Ren snorted.

Dan smacked ver forehead. "O'course, District's not just *a smuggler's district*. Folks live here like over *there*," he gestured oldtownward, "and down *whatsit*," then to the Antrum. "Our supply runs're necessary, but District 'olds good all *'cause* of ye fishermen and dockyard workers and shipwrights."

Ecosystems within ecosystems. A fantastical macrocosm oscillating with life.

"Do you want those directions?" Ren pressed.

I nodded.

"Out onto *Corsair's Promenade*; walk 'til *Siren's Wynd*; left turn; follow 'til the armoury; sharp right; the signage guides you to *The Salacia*."

"Thank you, signóri. Truly." I went to stand.

Danilo tugged my chiffon sleeve, beckoning me to lean in. "Korneli won't like us blabbin', but chat up our cap'ain at *The Salacia*—Fabio Amadi-Spýros."

My wariness soared. "What's Korneli's concern?"

"Lover mine's the quartermaster." Danilo shrugged. "Cap'ain don't like bein' bothered."

My narrow eyes flickered to Ren's donnish face, then back to Dan's grin. "I see." And I left the bootleggers to their gin and shanties.

# SCENE XXXIX

## IL TUO RICORDO PER
## SEMPRE ETERNO IN NOI

*Giorgianna*

EMBRACED BY CANALS LIKE TENTACLES, *The Salacia* pulsed with accordion, packed to the gills and virescent with the eerie thalassic glow of algae.

I asked the keeper for Fabio Amadi-Spýros; he pointed me in the direction of a tenebrous corner where a man sat alone.

My feet halted mid-passage; astonishment snapped my eyes wide upon him. Greying hair curled around his chin, his long greatcoat the colour of south seas dulled by wear and salty squalls, necklaces wreathing his neck abundantly.

A man I'd met once, in another life.

Gloom weighed his shoulders, his head low as he tapped an eight of suns on the card-littered table. The tumbler of watery absinthe at his elbow completedthe sombre picture.

Hesitant, I sat across from him. "Deal me in?"

Lines of age underscored his sable eyes, clouded as a welkin threatening storms. "What're we playing on?" Hoarse and glum: a voice I recalled.

"Information."

A disgruntled sigh. "So be it."

We arranged the deck; tossed a coin; commenced.

"I see you fetched no hefty sentence, captain Amadi-Spýros," I broke our silence.

His bushy eyebrows drew together. "Do I know you?"

"Without Cardea, you and I'd be pushing up daisies no question," I quoted in Themistoklísika.

He gawked. "The madwoman whom I sailed to the Misersi Quarter?"

I half-smiled. "Slums and cajoling."

"Can't believe a loose screw like you lived."

"I won't frighten you with the recent goings-on." My stomach sank. "But… I *am* sorry for putting you in Death's way."

"Water under the bridge," said bleakly Fabio, continuing in Themistoklísika.

"Your gloom is tangible," I yielded easily to my inquisitiveness.

"Heartbreak and woe, if you're so agog."

"Would it help to speak of it to a stranger?"

"Why the curiosity?"

"Commiseration."

He scoffed, mirthless. "From *you*, girl?"

"Still so hasty to assume." My tone bleakened.

Fabio trawled a deep breath. "I had… a friend…" His eyes glazed and I went to retract my request, but he continued, "Spent our youth together, but drifted apart. A month back… I learned of his death." His jaw clenched. "The spider De Tullia got his fangs in him too."

The words punched me.

"I'm so sorry." Lachrymosity twanged my voice. "I lost someone in a kindred way." I cleared my throat to drown the nightmarish echo of *pops!*, of gargles. "*W*-what…" my lips pressed, fingers fidgeting with my idle cards, "was… your friend's name? *If*—if you've the spirit to share, of course."

"Marcello."

Everything ceased.

"Damiani…?" The syllables squeezed my throat.

Fabio's eyes welded to mine. "How do you know that name?"

My head shook slowly. "That's not his name…"

He tossed his cards and leaned in. "What do you know?"

Thunder beat my eardrums. "De Tullia executed Ludovico Damiani almost three months ago. That was Marcello, wasn't it? *Ludovico* was his real name."

"What's it to *you*?"

"So, it's true." My eyes burned.

"*Y*… yes, but…" Fabio lost his words to bewilderment.

I tugged loose the ribbon holding my mask in place, bearing to him the truth of my face.

Ludovico's face.

"Do you see it?"

Realisation tumbled behind his eyes, burying him beneath its infinite force and draining his aged face of colour, his mouth opened in silence. He gulped, almost wincing. "You're uncanny…" Fabio breathed, and I nearly broke all over again. "What's your name, girl?"

"Giorgianna," I choked out.

"You have Elenedda's hair."

My trembling hands unsheathed my dagger. "I also have *this*."

Fabio studied the weapon as if an artefact of a lost time. "Haven't seen it in years…" He unclasped one of his necklaces. "The motif." The gold chain suspended a pendant shaped into a weeping eye, garnet-encrusted —a circle for the iris and a teardrop for its namesake. Just like the baselard's hilt. "Ludovico's. Made on a whim in The Court. Supposedly symbolic of one's existential sorrow upon perceiving the truth of hegemony." He huffed. "Loved his meaningful nonsense no less than I."

I watched the gems, like droplets of almandine ichor, coruscate beneath the tavèrna's verdigris light. "Always a flair for the dramatic."

The universe paused for a breath, waiting for Fabio's eyes to cease roving my face. "How did this star-scribed circumstance come to pass?"

My head shook with no rhyme or reason. "I've been trying to find answers for so long," I fumbled for my brittle voice. This man—a bootlegger I met one fateful, awful night amid suicidal hopelessness—was a fragment of my father's past. Of my *father*. Of what had been robbed from me. "He was a dissident."

"He—" A breath stumbled Fabio's tongue. "Eight years ago, Ludovico left the District. We parted on a fight." His rheumy eyes trained aloft. "And I'll regret nothing in my life more than letting him walk away without resolution." A crack splintered his verses. "Now he's gone, and we will *never* put those words to rest." His fingers shook as he cradled the pendant, gazing into its ensanguined eye. "There were six of us. After *that*, the other four vanished one by one. One died at sea. One was... far from what we'd thought. One moved on to a life in The Court. One drifted away."

Sorrow cradled my heart. "And you were the remaining..."

Alone, that dispute a shipwreck leaving him marooned, his comrades mere ghosts to haunt his bitter and ageing memory, melancholy too deep to wade through so he floated amidst it. And those ghosts—now gone. Lost. Or dead.

"Aye." Fabio fastened the pendant around his neck. "Ministerial letters, courtroom transcripts: everything Ludovico could get his hands on, he would. Kept it all in his apartment here in the District. He... claimed he discovered something too grim to disclose even to us, and he took it to his grave, I wager." My ears pricked up all the more. "He hated De Tullia—wanted him out." Fabio's eyes dropped to the card-laden table. "And *I* wanted out of twisted political games."

I looked to my palm, its glistening scar. An indissoluble promise. "I want *justice*," I asserted. "I want the people who took him to pay." My gaze fettered to Fabio's. "I need the documents he accrued—"

"Forgive me, Giorgianna," he shook his head, "but I cannot tell you that."

I jumped from my seat. "He was my *father*!"

"And I don't want you dead like him."

"His death must be *requited*!"

"Let him *rest*! He left because he too wanted out of the trench that was politics, the trench that was *killing* him. Let him, at least in death, be free of it."

"Is he *free*?" I fired. "It was killing him, and killing him, and killed him anyway. To wash your hands clean of politics is to side with the oppressor. He died *because* of politics and now it hangs over his grave, for he died at the hands of the *very* people he fought, and *They* got to go on living in Their castles of gilded bone and rotten flesh. What kind of 'rest' is that?"

Fabio's heavy gaze scoped the tavèrna.

I could see his mind at work. Brooding. Mulling. *Please...*

"Fine."

Breath rushed into my lungs as I sat and held his cold hands, head bowed to the table. "Thank you."

"But I won't aid you unless you come forward with *how* you intend to 'requite' him," he added.

My stomach cooled. "*I*—I will. I promise."

"Precisely what scares me."

I grinned. "No debts."

Noon sun hung high at zenith when I stepped out of *The Salacia*, the sea a glistening larimar mirror.

I unfurled Glàvca's map. The map which brought me closer to my justice. To Ema's justice. To father's.

At the northeastern corner of East Fin, a bloodink loop marked the point of descent from Smugglers' District to the Antrum. To The Cyclopes' district. '*Butcher Lucanus*', Mair had dubbed their Dóminus. Yet, against reason, I ventured northeast.

A lift bored through the coastal cliffs in the northeast, pulleys hoisted by an operator deep beneath the surface. *Last chance to turn back.*

I stepped into the iron cage.

The screech of rivets sent me shuddering side to side down the shaft, light draining with the descent before the bilious glow of that mechanical not-sun lacquered the peeling floor. Below, the Antrum's unfamiliar end oscillated into view like mud and wood adrift atop dark water.

The lift rattled to a halt.

My eyes locked with the operator's; their green-dyed brows pinched close. "Sure you wanna go that way?"

I stepped off the platform, checking each weapon, touching a hand to my heart in thanks, "*Want*, sure and true," and proceeding into the subterranean city's plexus.

There was never quite enough light in the Antrum's day, too much in its night, and in that skewed arrangement, everything in The Cyclopes' territory took on sinister proportions. The smashed cobblestones, the foetid aroma rising off the ducts, the yowling alleys a-crawl with rogues and oozing shadows like pus.

"Hello, little shrew," a sibilant voice whistled through half-decayed teeth.

And the alleys fell silent.

# SCENE XL

## CLOSE CALLS

*Giorgianna*

"AWFULLY ODD FOR A LOVELY DÁMA TO TRAIPSE THE SLUMS, no?" the toothy man crooned.

I damned my spirit of inquiry into the Everlasting Null. "Déjà vu." Two sword-lengths separated Davide and me when I turned. "What do you want?"

He stepped forward, umbra-cloaked and beady-eyed. "What *you* want." At his hips, twin stilétti glittered to the counsel of artificial light. "Your father knew things."

My vision juddered. "You'll know better than to speak of—"

"My former comrade?"

The world beneath my feet tilted.

"Ludovico and me," Davide resumed. "Soft-hearted Matìa and dead Durans. Captain Fabio—"

"You are a liar!"

"I've never spoken anything but truth," Davide asserted. "I *told* you the Governor had me at his beck and call; I *held* to my promise of leaving your theatre be; I *even* enlightened your most beloathed of the *Curios* debacle." The epithet jolted me. *Only one person knows it...* "Now, I'll come clean of my little chase with Luce through the oldtown the prior night."

My stomach fell. "What?"

"Fear not. Alas, I didn't catch her. You're an awfully *darling* vixen for giving her sweets and kind words for departure, that little book of mysteries." His titter slithered along my skin like leeches. *He had been watching us.* Had he stalked Cesare from the Antrum? "Ludovico loved to play big brother to us kids at that shithole of an orphanage. That's how we met—when I got dumped there by my whore mother and alky father." Davide's head tilted. "Never much good at stealth, your tender-hearted dad. Got his alias on record. But that's not what did him in, why I chose to serve."

As if epochs-old dust brushed off a telescope's lens, I, at long last, saw the moving pieces. "They traced you from his pseudonym," I thought aloud, "so you divulged his real name to protect yourself... and your assumption about The Bauta was your key to the jail cell." I locked eyes with him. And I understood what it all meant. "The Moretta riot at the *Ettàva*... served also as an assassination attempt on me, didn't it? As did '*A Bedlamite's Ballad*'—your connections to the state allowed your activity to go without interference, hence Cesare cited no patrols along the street. They *wanted* you to murder me." '*A long time coming*,' he'd told me that night...

"Smart little shrew."

"Yet you didn't disclose The Bauta's name. Why?"

"I wasn't certain."

"Right, but now you *are*. And why not kill him? You *had* the upper hand, why squander it? Basilisk Weep last night: cut this throat and be done with it, no?"

"Eager for his death, are we?" Davide snickered. Sauntered closer. "Such hate in that wicked heart of yours."

"Answer my question." My voice flared, muscles rigid.

"The Governor *froths* at the *mouth* fantasising about The Bauta's execution. I didn't feel like losing a hunk of a brain for pilfering from him. I'm *well* aware how frivolous it was on my part, that I should've killed you all." He pressed a hand to his heart. "My one confession to weakness."

"What do you want in the Antrum?" I pushed.

"Not the *Antrum*," he pointed ceilingward, "but up *there*."

My blood cooled. "You knew my pursuits in Smugglers' District." And he wanted my father's documents.

"*Dead Glories* was your first mistake. A Moretta fellow picked up your trail—saw you chatting up some Hydras, then Amadi. I figured you'd come out the other side wiser, and *look!*" Davide toyed with my curls, my stomach demanding to rise. "Vixens are some of my *favourite* study subjects, you know." His piranhic eyes gleamed. "I *too* want your beloved father's documents, confirmation of that grim secret he learned, but my knowledge of *where* in the District they are is imprecise at best. Besides, I'm known up there, not just by Amadi. Dying won't help me, and Morettae can't be trusted with the crucial matter of information retrieval." My throat stiffened as his fingers skimmed my cheek, bone-cold, yet dread fettered me in place. "My motivations require me to play the game De Tullia's way," he went on. "You understand the necessity to pretend for survival, I'm sure. So help me help you; help me get those documents for both of us. I'll be free, *you'll* be safe from the noose. You can satiate your *every* curiosity, avenge dear dad, watch The Bauta's head roll and bleed and bleed and bleed. Just *think*."

Davide's every wile was whetted to cut away my resolve, to dig into the darkness within my bones, hoping to harvest it for himself, promising counterfeit triumph.

Because Davide served a corrupt order. An order which necrosed the body imprisoning Us. Which murdered my father, failed Emanuela, kept thousands of innocent souls subjugated. To reign triumphant was to fight against it with all it couldn't reap from me.

*Freedom is always worth it.*

"You'd sell out your own God." I slashed with my dagger, blade mauling Davide's face.

Blood streamed through my hand as I kneed him in the bollocks and bolted down a street misshapen as a diseased bone.

"*HARLOT*!" Davide shrieked—a crazed demon, giving chase.

**Boom!**

An explosion of splinters forced me to veer.

**Boom!**

My face swung to evade spraying glass as I weaved through webbing streets, gunshots raining in furious pulses.

**Boom!**

**Boom!**

**Boom!**

A turn.

A tapering passage bled of light.

*A dead end.*

Panic bated in my throat.

At the building's foot, a decrepit trapdoor cowered.

*No choice.*

Kicking it in, I crawled inside.

Acrid stench gagged me like a wet cloth. *Formaldehyde?*

I scanned the abandoned warehouse. Staircases led to upper levels, shards of flavescent light falling through the tattered roof and shattering across crate-strewn rubble—barely enough illumination to discern my own feet.

Enough to discern what my occiput bumped into.

Meat hooks suspended a torso, ashen as carrion and rubbery as an anatomical display, skin zipped off its drained muscle. *A child...*

Horror clamped my throat as I saw more.

Shelves and tables arrayed the back wall. Adorning them stood metal spikes skewering human heads, sockets gripping glass orbs. Cotton-stuffed mounts of limbs and organs shrivelled up like mole rats, countless jars holding brains, eyes, kidneys, genitalia. Blood-crusted surgical equipment sat in ironware: scalpels, scissors, trephines, amputation saws and syringes, circumcision knives and cervix dilators.

*Boom!*

*Boom!*

*Boom!*

I scrambled into a wooden crate, dragging boxes with me to block its opening and curling into the corner, clamping a hand over my mouth.

Footsteps *thumped*.

*Thump.*

*Thump.*

*Boom!*

"Little shrew…" A smile oiled Davide's voice. "Didn't anyone teach you not to enter strangers' homes?"

*'Vixens are some of my* favourite *study subjects…'*

*Thump.*

*Thump.*

*Thump.*

A wood object smashed to pieces.

*Curiosity killed the cat, the proverb goes.*

*Thump.*

*Thump.*

Quieter.

I waited, lungs itching with stifled pants.

My hand lowered from my mouth.

Wood exploded as a slender blade ripped the crate.

I screamed and scuttled out. Davide stabbed the stilétto into the crate again, impaling my shoulder and tearing the tulle.

I toppled. Floorboards skinned my palms.

Davide yanked my hair and hurled me. "Your old man and his friends made me an *outcast*." He gripped my neck, pinned me to the wall, and *squeezed*. "It was *his* and that *cunt* Fabio's fault that I was chased out of

Smugglers' Cove." Air leached from my trachea as his grip tightened with every emphasised word. "Your *dad's* the reason I'm in this shit!" He rammed me with his knees to still my thrashing legs. "Without him I'd've *never* bent to De Tullia to keep my head." My draining lungs heaved helplessly between clenching ribs, puckering, burning, collapsing. *I cannot fight…* "Accept my deal, and I'll stop, or I'll skin you alive and make your husk a trophy for my *pleasure*. I fancy my specimen *dead*, but I won't let you leave this world without torment."

I retched, meeting his desperate, pleading gaze. And I understood what truly mattered to *him*. "Your resolve is admirable, but—" My hand snuck into my pocket. "*I will not serve, like you.*"

Iron glistened as I drove that tiny, rhomboid blade from the night of '*A Bedlamite's Ballad*' into the base of Davide's neck.

He unleashed a cry, grip loosening for a moment.

My lungs glutted on air.

I landed a fist onto his mealy face. Kicked his legs from under him.

His arm swung as he went down, revolver cocked and aimed for my head.

Frost shot my flesh.

**Boom!**

*Crunch.*

Davide wailed.

Sharp pain spiked my stomach. My knees drove into the floor as the hot perfume of molten pennies throttled my nares. Blood dripped down my lips. My gullet lurched, hacking dark, stringy grume onto the floor, bloodstream blazing, freezing, stilétto wounds a-buzz. *Azoth…*

I hadn't gotten shot.

Davide's left forearm bent hideously out of shape, snapped bones protruding from gory lacerations in his riven flesh.

*I tailored his arm in half…*

Marrow-deep fatigue swam in my head, blearing my field, yet I careened up the stairs, knowing I'd grasped a lifeline.

**Boom!**

I hobbled over broken furniture with a bullet in my thigh and a whimper caught between clenched teeth.

At the hallway's end, the wall was blown out. Floor dropped into a narrow canal which sundered the warehouse from the next building.

Gunshots hailed.

I jumped.

Pain lanced my legs as I landed on cracked bitumen.

Davide emerged from the warehouse, gripping his wounded neck. His broken arm dangled like offal off ragged muscle.

I flung myself between two buildings and ran—*limped*—trusting the mechanical sun's revolution to guide me north. My footfalls notched the seconds. *Tuh-thump. Tuh-thump. Tuh-thump.*

Veering a bend, I knocked into someone at full pelt.

"You—" Isaia gaped, karambits engaged. "What—?"

"*Hidehidehide!*" I dragged him into a side street.

My heart thrashed against my endeavours to listen out, but the Antrum hummed undisturbed. "I lost him…"

"Whom?"

"Davide chased me from The Cyclopes' district."

Isaia's jaw dropped. "You went—"

"Hush." I waved. "Thinking he'd kill me, his loose jaw spilled his deal." *Stupid man.* And yet, had I been a smidge weaker, slower, poorer a fighter, had it not been for that tailoring fluke, I'd be dead without question, and he'd known it. But he *hadn't* known that I *wasn't*. Not anymore. Never again.

"Yes?" Anticipation bracketed Isaia's tone.

"Do you have time?"

"Seven hours until I meet Ces."

A grin cleaved my blood-slathered lips. "Ink me."

# SCENE XLI

## EPISTEMOLOGIA

*Cesare | Giorgianna*

WITH THE SUN LAID TO REST, clouds heavy as funeral shrouds swathed the nightfall sky. Now and then, the moon reached her pale arms through the chrisom to touch the sleeping city in lackadaisical reassurance.

*Twenty hundred hours*, read the hanging timepiece.

Cesare checked the six throwing knives in his blazer and Paolo's remaining cufflink he kept for luck, lamenting the absence of his prized stilétti. He drew his eyes at the sliver of window glass over the theatre's rear door. Moonlight shuddered, snuffing out.

"Ces!" Up the corridor stood Eligio. Lissandri leaned against the wall beside him.

Cesare tucked unbound hair behind his ear. "Listen—"

Eligio held up a hushing palm and approached Cesare, firmly cupping his face. "Promise me you'll come back."

Cesare saw it in his eyes, then, clear as cut glass. *Fear.*

He didn't stand alone. With him were willing to stand his friends—his only família. And it was both a mercy and a horrible, *horrible* cruelty because with him, too, they were willing to burn.

Cesare half-smirked, "Swear on the Saints and all Inferno's angels, áma," and crossed his fingers at his side.

"*Truly* a fiend," Eligio grumbled, letting up a begrudging smile when Cesare laughed.

The rear door opened and Cesare met honey-red eyes.

Eligio's forehead creased. "Giorgi?"

"I'm all right." She smiled tightly at the twins, rose water and ocean wind trailing her into the theatre. Darkness stained her clothes. *Blood.*

Cesare frowned deeper as he espied cuts on her arms and a charred tear through her thigh. *Gunshot.* His stomach coiled up. *Davide.* It *must*'ve been! *And she lived...*

Lissandri jerked his head to gesture after Giorgianna, Eligio flinging Cesare a parting glance before following the woman.

Lissandri neared. "Cesare." He hooked his palms onto his shoulders. "Leaving your hubris a little battered won't kill you. The hubris *itself* might."

"You *know* I know what I'm doing." Cesare smirked. "I'll be fine."

"Your '*fine*' is three stab wounds and a bolt in your leg at *ab*solute least."

"Precisely," Cesare patted Lissandri's cheek, "so you needn't fret."

"Maybe I'll let Eligio slap you when you return."

"Last laughs and all that."

Lissandri's dry smile dropped the second he turned away, eyes dimming.

Cesare disregarded both by force, even as it tore him inside.

BETWEEN HELPING WITH MY WOUNDS and dealing with his Hounds, Isaia didn't progress beyond the linework of my tattoo—now swaddled in the bandages around my *Bedlamite* scars.

Eligio accosted me with jittery concern, soon joined by Lissandri, and I unloaded everything.

"*Now*," I leaned against the balustrades, "I'm stuck figuring out what to do about Fabio."

We'd relocated to the cupola at the apex of the theatre where clouds rolled like listless waves, never still in the winds wheeling through the firmament. Stars and moon blinked at the city as if unable to understand why such a fragile thing existed in the limitless multiverse.[134]

"I *would* propose speaking to Cesare…" drawled Lissandri.

"We…" I plumped for gentler phrasing, "aren't on the greatest of terms."

"*I'll* say." Lissandri snorted. "He practically ranted and raved about your exchange of pleasantries this morning."

"Oh?" Contempt envenomed my tone. "I've wondered how he speaks of me when doors shut."

"*Stop!*" bit Eligio, my heartbeat catching its step. He never raised his voice. I realised they all barely did. "I've had it up to my neck with both of you!" He pressed his twitchy hands to his eyes. "All you do is get at each other's throats when there's no *reason!*"

"No reason?" I snapped indignantly. "After *all* he's said and done?"

"Dues must be paid, no?" Eligio's words beat the breath from my chest. "*I* don't uphold such eye-for-an-eye philosophy, but *you* do. Ergo, if you were so *vicious* to him, by reasoning of your own, he holds *every* right to retaliate." Lissandri stood at Eligio's side, a firm hand on his brother's stiff shoulder. "*Or*," Eligio pointed at me, eyes frantic, "*neither* of you should've behaved so. But you're hardly different from each other."

"Stop *telling* me that!"

---

[134] Within this world exist three parallel universes which are *theoretically* traversable and inhabited by vastly differing beings, but that is a story far too long and tangential for this tale. Another time, perhaps; in a book where it plays a role of greater import.

"Is it that you wish to mitigate some perceived misery by denying that truth to yourself?" Eligio fired back. "You claim to seek knowledge. If such is the case, be ready to confront the bitter revelations it brings." A sigh left him. "Talk to Cesare—*properly*." He addressed Lissandri with: "Figure I'll take a page out of your book and retire abed early. Lest I worry myself into the grave." He kissed his brother on either cheek. "Bon rèquiem, all." With a tense smile and overcast eyes, he left the cupola.

I sat on the floor and slung my elbows over my knees, head slumped forward.

Yawning, Lissandri plopped beside me. "Discord, huh?"

"Will Eligio be all right?"

"Some valerian and he'll black out." Lissandri cracked his knuckles, the sound no longer startling me quite so viscerally. "He's worried. And I empathise. But Ces promised him he'll come back. I trust him."

My eyes traced the constellations I could see: Amphisbaena, Cocaktrice, Aspidochelone, Crocotta, that haphazard nine-star multiplex I never remembered.

Did stars really arrange themselves so, or did pareidolia impel us to search for patterns all around?

Did we simply seek confirmation that we weren't so achingly alone in this cosmic void?

"He's right," I murmured, but where I thought I'd be choked with shame, I instead saw reality. I'd been breaking against Cesare like waves over cliffs without concern for whether he might crumble beneath my unrelenting force. Cesare hadn't been the one to take my eye, so I had no right to his. "What if..." I faced Lissandri, "a part of me is still programmed by that horrible machine?"

He looked at me dryly. "You spent *God* knows how many years trapped under totalitarianism. With a mother like *that*, to boot. Propaganda works hardest of all stakhanovites and folks are *chillingly* unaware of how deeply in takes root. You can't be expected to heal your bloodline so abruptly, anyway. All that matters is you strive."

*Fresh skin cannot emerge without pain.*

The hegemony was the First Cause of my fall, of Vencenza's calamity, yet, without cognition, I almost played into its puppeteer hands.

I swallowed the lump in my throat like a water-polished rock, its cold weight sinking into my core. "There's so much to tackle at once." Father, Ema, Fabio, Davide, The Morettae, Vencenza… "Am I doomed to stumble?"

Lissandri rubbed his chin scar. "Our impresario, Paolo, oversaw everything. He… cared. And he sure loved his meaningful nonsense. During trapeze rehearsal, the one where I got this scar: toppled face-first onto a stage prop—was sure Paolo'd have a heart attack and Cesare would laugh himself into asphyxiation. But anyhow, something our old impresario told us then forever gripped me: '*We spot because, by doing so, we ensure another person lives. You will never truly fall if you have someone to catch you*'." Lissandri beheld me with earnest eyes. "I hope you know you have people who will catch *you*."

My heart balled, eyes sore as they watered. After losing Ema, I ceased believing verses like those for a long time. Perhaps, it could have turned into forever.

Lissandri loosened a sigh and slipped his arms around my shoulders, resting his chin on my head.

"You don't hug people." My voice cracked.

"But you definitely need it."

I held onto his arm and took in his scent of books and clock oil, unable to deny the easement closeness brought. "Thank you, Andri." Neither Ema not my father would ever again hold me like that but, just maybe, I *wasn't* so achingly alone any longer, after all.

He pulled away after several heartbeats. "I'm off to bed. Get rest, yeah? Your wounds and battered noggin will be beholden. And speak with Ces."

I smiled sadly, tracing an 'X' on my chest. "Cross my heart."

Lissandri grinned and left me by my lonesome on the cupola.

My head knocked back against a balustrade.

Purple tinged my nail beds, my blood still cool with azoth.[135] I recalled the sight of my fingers smeared with blood. My beloved colour—so grotesque. So mortal. That vital nectar. And I was willing to let my hands bathe in it again. Let this whole city drown in it. Forever stained. Unwashable.

*And yet...*

---

[135] Cuts inflicted by masoned blades (*e.g.* lòthmir) trigger a chemical reaction between the azoth in the steel and haemoglobin, resulting in a buzzing sensation at the wound and coldness systemically. As such, this phenomenon does not occur in iridites, owing to hemerythrin replacing haemoglobin.

# SCENE XLII

## TO WHAT ENDS?

*Cesare*

BLOOD WASHED THE GUARD STATION FLOOR, splashing at the *thunk* of lifeless soldiers, and streamed towards the parched lip of the foráminis.[136]

Cesare lathered the back of his palms with the ink which once scripted a crow's life, pulling his leather gloves over top. Isaia matched. Nasty, but necessary for later.

The emblem of he whose ichor anointed him named an *Arón Da Rúa-Soutomaior*. Strange, Cesare thought, to know the name of his kill. Stranger yet to see a C'linèse.

Stripping what they needed off the three Guards, the rogues cut their torsos, opened their lungs so they would flood, and lowered them into the

---

[136] A square aperture through the floor opening to the water under the foundation; a common feature of Vencenzani structures built directly onto waterways, granting easier access to the trestles and supports holding the construction to its larger system. Generally used for repair works.

foráminis. Water blackened, rust drenching the air in the sharp token of a life's price.

How many had Cesare slaughtered like cattle, their hopes and dreams and loves killed alongside them? Perhaps any semblance of their Selves had been excised long ago, occupied instead by reverence for their Lord of Bless'ed Dominion. Perhaps that alone was worth pity. But how could Cesare mourn crows who picked on the bones of their subjects' dead at the Governor's behest? However 'kind' they may be in their private lives, soldiers struck their bloody batons down at the masses, upholding an institution of abuse. And it would never be the duty of the subjugated to be peaceful with oppressors who sewed violence into the fabric of the system.

This would never be a clean fight. This was revolution. Abolition. The old ballad of means and ends, as it were.

And the resistance would live on for epochs after Cesare's passing.

The rogues wiped blood from the floors with a leftover cape before drowning it too, and donned the crow uniforms: a tight-fitted jacket Cesare barely pulled over his own, vambraces stamped with that vile winged sigil, dark cape, feathered mask, helm. His stomach turned at wearing the oppressors' symbolism.

Suddenly, the empty-eyed murder was easier.

Suddenly, he wished to turn it on himself.

Cesare sheathed a gladius and pugio. "Twenty minutes to reach the aqueducts, give or take."

Isaia strapped a spatha to his back as they descended to the docked gondoa. The eavesdropper worked mercilessly with the bodies, near-medically, never sparing a passing thought to carnage. Cesare almost envied him, but he envied De Tullia's caricature of The Bauta above all. If only he *were* so senseless. So much more of this kingdom he could lay waste to. So little he could care for the collateral. So little he would *have* to care for.

But what would that make him?

The citadel's behemoth fortification rose at least twenty storeys into the murky darkness, shot through with spy windows like empty orbits. Flush to its flank, the aqueduct soared all the taller, arches stacked on arches, hollow to conduct filtered water into the lymfática[137] and throughout the city state. A leviathan apotheosis of engineering.

An Imperiáli guardhouse garrisoned the aqueduct's feet, every legionary a dime a dozen in their aurulent filigree: Cesare and Isaia's first hurdle.

The gondoa neared the final stretch of water.

In the fortification's windows, ìgnes fatuíl[138] blazed alight.

The La'esánus[139] barked an order. Five griffins approached the shore as the boat docked, mooring it. Ordinarily, an advancement of legionaries signalled to Cesare a fight or run for his life. Permitting them to stand so dangerously near enkindled his every faulty self-preservation instinct, but he bit back the urge to fall on the defensive, pulling his hands from his weapons and unwinding his stiff shoulders.

The La'esánus bombarded through, demanding from Isaia and Cesare the slated reports. Cesare had taken the liberty of forgery—omitting names and botching addresses. The empire didn't deserve any more blood to oil its serrated gears.

The La'esánus gave a once-over to the intruders. "The third Guard?"

"Hung back at the station," expertly bluffed Isaia.

"On what rationale did he choose to not accompany you?"

---

[137] Literally 'lymphatics', a generalised term for all drainage and water systems of Vencenza.

Approximately eight-hundred years ago, at the dawn of the Faustinian Empire and with many Salvatricii migrating south, construction of the lymfática began to urbanise Vencenza. Around that time, prominent communities of workers from Themistóklis settled near the Vencenzani coast, playing an integral role in erecting the lymfática, the name of which derives from the Themistoklísika 'lýmphos': 'lymph'. Themistoklísi settlers remaining in Vencenza formed its Temistochlisi ethnic population.

[138] EE-ñehs fah-too-EE; signalling fires.

[139] Contubèrnium leader; derived from Faustinian 'la'esán' for 'ninth' as a contubèrnium consists of eight soldiers, making its leader the ninth.

"Public safety concerns." Upper Vencenzani intonation spilled across Cesare's voice to polish away the remaining edges of his Marlâre accent. "Questionable activity in the vicinal óssium."

Silence ate away at the ambience like maggots at rotting carrion as the La'esánus contemplated, gaze roving from Isaia to Cesare, mistrust in every expelled breath.

His scrutiny lingered on Cesare, then snapped to the eavesdropper. "I see," he said, handing over the documents. "Report to Imperiálus Diodato Casca, stationed at North Eye. He'll forward onto General Manuele Dioli." *Casca.* The soldier who stood by as his fellow griffin murdered a parent right before her son's eyes.

The La'esánus directed the trespassers to the elevator shaft running through the fortification.

*One down.*

They stepped onto the apex of the fortification. Aqueducts towered overhead, air rarefied.

The moat lay like a coiled dragon around the acropolis, its water limpid alike lead glass *whilst oldtown's canals rot.*

A gondoa was procured; the sail for North Eye and the second contubèrnium commenced.

*One step closer.*

The half-way point came and went, the government building now clear and detailed: a palace of bone.

Isaia drummed his fingers on the boat's edge. "No guarantee the Adviser'll be abed."

"A guarantee he'll be absent entirely."

"Explain?"

"The Minister of Emissaries and his silver peacocks, accompanied by the Treasurer, are off to the provinces."

"Hence you chose to-day…" Understanding echoed in Isaia's voice. "You could've said earlier!"

"You're not going into the apartment with me," stressed Cesare.

"Like fuck I am!" Isaia snapped. "What'll happen if you don't find a smoking gun?"

"Kiss my intestines goodbye, I guess."

"And if legionaries discover you?"

Cesare scoffed, subfusc and mordant. "Fucker got me."

Arduous documentation checks passed, Cesare and Isaia disembarked near the outpost of the second contubèrnium at North Eye. Imperialíi ensconced in bartizans like birds in eyries, griffins and crows patrolling the crenellated parapets.

Isaia handed the worthless reports to Imperiálus Diodato Casca, a titanic stela of a man—nearly seven feet tall and half as wide—with a head bashed into a tree-bole neck.

He called on another soldier.

Hair spilled in an obsidian waterfall down the newcomer's willowy back, their skin grey as graphite, iris-less sclerae pricked with pupils and pointed ears slit in two. *An iridite.* A cabochon bloodstone encrusted their breastplate to signify their rank as a blood singer of the Imperiálum—a Sánguinus. A manipulator of blood.

Cesare and Isaia gave the dead crows' names.

The singer opened a cabinet housing thousands of tiny blood vials, drawn from every legionary. The perfect vetting system to ensure no intruder made it in or out of The Bone Palace.

The Sánguinus held a vial in one hand and touched the back of Isaia's palm with the other. Just over the crow blood lathered beneath leather: the first blood source for their magic to sense and thus a shield against discovery. Nasty, but necessary.

They nodded an affirmation.

Cesare's turn.

He dragged his consciousness to the background of his mind's stage and allowed the Sánguinus to place widely-set spindly fingers to his hand, dead blood heavy as a guilty conscience on his skin.

The singer bobbed their head.

Casca granted the intruders passage.

*Two down.*

Beneath the cover of wuthering squalls, the rogues, cloaks discarded, scaled the isabelline flank of the citadel's third floor in the northeast. Open to the wind. A single misstep threatening to expose them to a vertical drop, or slaughter—the final outpost patrolling below with gimlet eyes.

Cesare's foot slipped.

He held onto balance by the skin of his teeth.

Moments lapsed.

Imperialíi stirred to investigate, but mercifully did not look up.

Heart in his mouth, Cesare slunk after Isaia through a window into the black-fingered shadows. *Three down.* One more flight until the Adviser's quarters.

Fleet-footed, they slipped by oriels and reverberating corridors, arriving at a marble staircase.

Cesare grabbed Isaia's shoulder. "Stay." He'd go it alone from there.

"I'm *trained* for this!"

"Precisely why we cannot afford your loss." Cesare started up the flight.

Isaia clutched his forearm to the muscle. "I was *supposed* to watch your back—"

"From *afar*. I'll signal if Hell breaks loose." Cesare shed Isaia's grip. "*Stay.*"

"You'll fucking die!" hissed Isaia, but Cesare wasn't stalling any longer. Nor was he arranging his burial beneath this moon.

Sidling into an alcove, he surveyed the wide halls shrouded in alchemy, the citadel opening to grand buttresses and bannisters, multifarious balconies and flyovers hanging high. Down the passage, Imperialíi flanked the door to Clario Barsotti's quarters. *Marvellous.* Cesare couldn't take them out without raising an alarm. Kill and leave no trace, or don't try. No half measures.

Slipping out a throwing knife, Cesare measured by eye the dimensions of the swollen cavitation beyond the balconies. Down an adjoining cloister, above the parapets, he espied clerestory windows nestled deep into lacunae. *Better than nothing.*

He planted a kiss on the tiny blade and flung it.

Glass smashed, shattering against the marble floors. *Sniper's vision.*

The sound drew the griffins.

When they passed, Cesare emerged from his hiding place. Seconds were all he had.

He tried the door. Shut. *Lockpick it is.*

To and fro along the hallway his eyes darted amid cajoling the lock, time closing in, but the latch wouldn't give.

Breaths clung like mucilage to Cesare's lungs.

Footsteps echoed.

*Comeoncomeoncomeon.*

*Click.*

Cesare snuck inside. Locked the door.

Heartbeat bashed his sternum, turning his head light.

The office wound in a labyrinth of packed bookcases, the shelves standing at attention around the carpeted walkway leading to a stately mahogany bureau. In the gables of the groin-vaulted ceiling, bizarre architectural elements settled: cavitary wooden balloons akin to giant alveoli sliced along the sides. Umber curtains drew the window shut, moonlight reaching through a slit to brush the thin mirrors decorating the bookcases' slanted corners—another oddity to chronicle.

Three paintings adorned the far wall: a pomelo and shaddette arboretum; a blood pool stretching like lids around white eyes; Vencenza's grand basilica.

An archive in its own right. To Cesare, this was the *real* treasury, so he set about scouring.

Countless documents, yet a red herring each.

Panic compressed Cesare's diaphragm. None of this made sense! How could the *Adviser* have *nothing* when his chambers brimmed? *I don't believe it...*

Those mirror oddities snared Cesare's eye.

His pupil dilated, focusing on a second mirror behind him in which Cesare saw a third reflected, within which, again, yet another, and one more.

He tilted his head, frame of view shifting.

In a cranny behind a tome marked *'III'*, he noticed the head of a hammered-in nail. And went looking for it.

The nail proved to be an aperture. *A lock...* Cesare dealt with it.

A *snick* and *boing* sounded inside.

A tiny trap door opened in the shelf above.

Cesare removed his gloves and palmed within, grabbing fine, delicate metal. *A key!* A tiny thing, its bow twisted from gold threads into an eye, a ruby like a drop of bright capillary blood suspended at the bow's centre. An idea struck. *Perhaps...*

Cesare dashed for the paintings. The second. Blood and eyes. Equally petite as the key.

Behind it, he discovered a keyhole and demarcation lines almost concealed by the panels. The key turned smoothly.

Inside hid a cupboard of liquors. *A ruse.*

Cesare pushed past the bottles, conscious of the *clanks*, of fleeing time, of soldiers outside.

A ridge at the back of the cabinet barricaded an inward dip. He groped within, tugging on a sash. Something heavier dragged along until, out of the darkness, Cesare pulled a leather-bound notepad.

He glimpsed but a few lines of immaculate cursive.

'*...never spoke, and unsure I should
bring such things to his attention...*'

*A smoking gun...*

Voices murmured outside. Metal and capes shuffled.

Cesare scrambled to lock the cabinet and hang the painting, no time to return the key as the office door *clunked*, so he buttoned the notebook in an inner pocket and climbed a bookcase, nestling inside one of those wooden alveoli just as the door opened.

Six Imperialíi sauntered in, dispersing throughout the chamber.

"Comb," one ordered. "Leave no leaf unturned nor a single damaged or misplaced."

A griffin opened the curtains, gloomy weather a small favour to Cesare. He needed to wait, so he counted—just like he did while hidden within closets and cupboards in his Canronê home—knowing that, with every culminating moment, he grew safer. More likely to stay living longer than he was wanted.

He caught his reflection in a sliver of looking glass, clad in those awful feathers.

An Imperiálus shoved their arm into the nearby shelf's depths to pull out papers.

They turned.

Cesare met their eyes in the mirror.

*Fucker got me.*

# SCENE XLIII

## CEDERE NESCIO

*Cesare*

"*INTRUDERS!*"

Cesare swung from the alveolus and kicked an Imperiálus' face.

He pivoted through the air, switched his grip on his abandoned hiding nook, directing his body toward the top of a bookcase. Unsheathing his purloined gladius, he hopped a gap to the next shelf as bolts *whished* by.

His hand dipped into his jacket.

With a sharp swing of the arm, he sent saltpetre aflight. Black powder rained. An open lighter followed.

A fierce blaze combusted, gorging on capes and papers and wood.

Embers spat into Cesare's eyes, fire biting his hands. He hissed, disoriented momentarily.

Three Imperialíi pushed on the bookshelf.

It lurched, tilted.

Cesare invoked the Saints and jumped, latching onto the top of the door frame. The shelf toppled and broke with an explosion.

A griffin blade tore a gash into the back of Cesare's thigh as he swung himself towards the corridor, stumbling with a pained grunt into the cherished coolness.

Bellows shook the building to its foundation. Footsteps pounded. Drawn steel chanted deathsongs.

Cesare flicked off the flames clinging to him as he veered from a longsword, releasing a pair of throwing knives to maul a griffin's face. Turned. And he would've been gutted had the Imperiálus behind him not fallen to Isaia's karambits.

The eavesdropper wheezed. "What did you do?"

"Irrelevant. Southwest—*go!*" Cesare tore deeper into the government house, every footfall shooting a painful bolt through his leg.

The rogue pair weaved through hallways and down the stairs and balconies and flyovers knitting the grand skeleton like ligaments.

Bells tolled to signify insurrection. Steel and bolts glinted. Gold gold gold plated every turn.

A quarrel grazed Cesare's rib, another lodged in his shoulder.

Hurdling bannisters, he stomped on a griffin's shoulders, driving a gladius through their helmet and brain with the viscid *crush* of a carved cantaloupe.

Isaia ran a crow through, slit another's throat, cleared a path down a new corridor, but legionaries swarmed like lice, separating the eavesdropper from Cesare.

Blood caked Cesare's hands, hardening to rind beneath his overlong nails, a limp knocking his step and lungs stiff as he caught momentary peace in an alcove of a sheltered capillary. He discarded the useless crow jacket. Slumped against decorative stucco. *Click.*

He looked down.

Amid the curlicued embossing, an eye-shaped aperture opened, revealing a keyhole.

Cesare stared mute.

The eye shut.

He inspected the stucco, spying… *a tiny lever?* He wiped his hand and pressed the contraption. The latch gave way, the eye opening once more. *Eye…*

Fumbling for the key he filched from the Adviser's quarters, Cesare tried it. The deadbolt clicked. Unsure what to do, he rammed the wall with his shoulder. It cracked open a smidgen before jamming.

Cesare slipped through. Shut the concealed door. *Click.*

A deserted labyrinth plenished by alchemy sprawled in an endless reticulum, silent as catacombs. *Secret passages…* Just like oldtown!

Beyond, the acropolis howled, bells reverberating in plangent ululations through its hollow skull.

Cesare needed to find Isaia. He couldn't—*wouldn't*—leave without him. If he were caught, Isaia knew the drill, as Ygal put, and Cesare wouldn't allow that either, so he wasted no time navigating the hidden halls.

He took a flight down to ground floor, chronicling his path. *Right. Left, left.* Into the darkness of a pin-thin capillary. He struck a match he always carried, swept its meagre flame across the wall.

Amidst the ornamentation, a familiar lever nestled.

Cesare repeated the methodology, peeking past the wall-door.

The moon came out to spectate the mayhem, what he gleaned to be the citadel's prayer room anointed in its opaline myrrh. *These passages must link various points of the citadel.* Columns hemmed the chamber's perimeter and guarded its archivolted narthex, the presbytery window a sun-shaped mosaic of frosted glass beneath which a triple-faced altar, outfitted with unlit candles, glistered gold-and-ruby. *Ground floor, just north of the southwest.* And blessedly empty.

Across the skeletal expanse stood a peripheral entrance.

Cesare only prayed he found Isaia as he slunk into the shadows.

His head pounded within that cursed helm, feet gnawing. Two sleepless nights' worth of fatigue gained on him.

He cried out in pain—like a shot, tottering but retaining his foothold. A throwing knife buried in his thigh, its hilt a gilded wing.

Leaving it, Cesare darted for the door.

Another knife lodged into his calf.

Cesare tumbled forward, bloody knuckles slipping along the marble. *Snap!* He bit down a scream. A nail on his left hand split down the centre, spouting red like a ruptured aquifer.

Footfalls thumped.

Cesare's eyes flicked to the room.

From the shade of the colonnades stepped the Minister of Blades. A gold-wrought titan. The flanks of his helm fanned into graceful wings, a cape tumbling in dazzling cascades of pure sunlight from his colossal shoulders. Gleaming spikes beset the knuckles of his gauntlets, sharp as talons, his aura every inch a brutal war god.

"Felicitations, General," Cesare croaked through wickedly smiling lips, clambering to his knees.

"Rabble!" Manuele Dioli hurled another blade.

Cesare rolled from its path and sprung clumsily to his feet, throwing knives throbbing like enormous splinters in his leg but he needed all the blood he could keep. "You scorn my geniality."

From behind his shoulders, the General thrust an enormous flamberge. Its flat blade curved in a dozen perfectly-sculpted undulations, fulgid as if starlight lay trapped within the steel. *Lòthmir.*

"I scorn your worthless *life.*" The General moved too fast, his sword a flame surging for Cesare.

He voided.

Manuele gnashed pearlescent teeth. His eyes—a smouldering azure—flickered with massacre as he slashed.

Cesare blocked with his gladius, aiming his pugio for Manuele's side while his flamberge was engaged. The Minister stepped across effortlessly; Cesare's dagger swung nothing.

He parried Manuele's horizontal strike, greatly misjudging as its violent force sent Cesare's pugio flying clean from his grasp.

Their swords clashed in explosions of white like a smith's hammer to steel, its melody bouncing off the walls in hideous vibrations to the dissonance of pealing bells. No revolvers could grant Cesare loathed advantage, the sword he wasn't accustomed to growing unwieldy in his slick fingers, pain overwhelming every movement in a vicious crescendo. And the General was beyond worthy of his title.

He hacked his flamberge diagonally, opening Cesare's forearm. Blood gushed, hot and punitive. His gladius clanged to the scarlet-smirched marble.

Manuele kicked him in the abdomen, sending him staggering breathlessly before hoisting his flamberge to knock Cesare's helm off.

Cesare doubled back from a reprising thrust and attempted for his pugio.

His hand grazed its pommel. Grasped its hilt.

A scream clawed free as the Minister's sword dug with a sopping *snap-snap-snap* of delicate bone through Cesare's hand.

"Runt," snarled Manuele. His steel-toed boot crashed into Cesare's left side.

He rolled, head bashing against a colonnade.

Paraesthesia seized his muscles at the impact. And yet, limbs quivering, nerves electrified, Cesare crawled to his hands and knees. His throat wrung out a bloody retch. And *yet*, he forced himself to rise. Unwilling to give in. Un*able* to.

"So pitiful: you." Manuele brandished his baton and struck hard, smashing Cesare's temple. "Little rogue playing with its little needle." He hurled Cesare across the floor—an offering before that moon-touched altar. "Maggot begetting sin and heresy and *dirt!*" He stomped on Cesare as if an insect.

His ribcage screamed *crack*. Cesare couldn't scream at all.

The General's fingers sank into Cesare's hair, dislodging his mask as he flung him onto his stomach. Ramming a plated knee into his spine, Manuele ripped a knife out of Cesare's thigh.

Cesare attempted to throw the General off but failed, his body drenching the floor every shade of a sacrifice beneath the ogre's untarnished might.

"Sprung forth from a *whore's* womb!" The spikes on Manuele's knuckles tore into Cesare's wounded ribs. The knife carved a gorge along his back, and Cesare realised what Manuele was doing.

*I'll be dead meat for the crows.*

"Look me in the eyes when you kill me, coward."

The Minister growled, enraged as a starved lion by Cesare's jibe, and tossed the rogue onto his back like a blood-soaked rag, pinning his sternum with his knee.

Cesare couldn't breathe as iron flooded his lungs, as the General clasped a powerful hand around his jaw and dashed his head against stone. "Defective *vermin* like you are only good for a needle through the skull." The world wobbled in a frenzy, the moon giggling and hiding behind her cloudy veil. "Or a *dissection*!" Manuele's eyes glittered as he slammed Cesare's head again. Exhilarated. Aroused. A killer who got off on it: a bona fide butcher.

Cesare was faster. More agile. More keen and astute. A dagger precision to Manuele's claymore might. And he'd thought that would be enough. But he had to *make* it enough. He couldn't fall at the sword of a glorified executioner when he'd forced himself to survive so much worse.

"*You will not fucking win.*" Cesare's throat tightened, tongue lashing as he sucked in his cheeks and spat a mouthful of blood into Manuele's eyes. He pried a throwing knife from his jacket and pierced through a slit of skin left bare by the General's gauntlet, thrusting the blade deeper into the sinew with every scarlet spray.

Manuele faltered.

Cesare kicked himself free, drove another knife through the Minister's lips and into the gums and tongue and hard palate.

The Minister of Blades roared.

Through the harrowing pain and dimming vision, Cesare ran from the prayer room.

Arm pressed to his abdomen, Cesare stumbled through the knelling citadel, alizarin handprints marring the pristine ivory. He limped around a bend.

A blade slashed for him.

He sidestepped, kicking his assailant, swaying in desperate efforts to stay conscious.

"Ces!" a deep voice exclaimed.

"Isaia," gasped Cesare. A slowly-oozing gash marked the eavesdropper's abdomen, his shoulders bleeding out through bolt holes. *But alive.* Relief almost buckled Cesare's legs. "Fucker got—" he choked "—my rib. And I think… an organ."

Isaia grasped the collar of Cesare's blazer. "You need to get out. The aqueducts are nearby. I'll lead soldiers away."

"You cannot go it alone!" protested Cesare. *Not for me.*

"Hypocrite!" Isaia snapped. "*Go!*"

Cesare grabbed Isaia's arm before he could leave. "Tell Ygal I got something."

Isaia's eyes widened. "You did?"

"Tell them I did." *And hope it's true.*

As Isaia cast a prayer and ran off, Cesare hobbled for the aqueduct's entrance, blinking hard against the hideous radiance in his skull as the black orifice of the mammoth structure ingested him.

His draining heart bated—a feeble, desperate creature.

*Not now.*

It hurt…

…too much.

But he couldn't…

let himself…

…*lose.*

# Scene XLIV

## Apolutrosis

*Giorgianna | Cesare*

*BLOOD…*

An oil spill of tarry scarlet slathered the parlour, dragging a smear up the stairs to the infirmárium door.

My throat constricted as I fumbled with the door knob, fingers slipping from the viscous gore.

Inside reeked of an abattoir.

Cesare braced himself against the bathtub's edge. Vermilion draining from innumerable wounds spared almost nothing of his unbuttoned shirt, a ghastly purple bruise bleeding across his abdomen and spilling out from the shredded flesh at his left ribs.

My feet moved before I could think. "What did you *do?*" I grasped his arms. A fissure bore through his right hand, his forearm gaping like a snake's slit gut, a nail on his left hand split and spurting.

"Don't touch me." He grimaced, half pain, half disgust, voice box bobbling as he swallowed the blood staining his bleak lips.

"*I'm…*" His voice fizzled and he listed.

I caught him. Clutched his shoulders thoughtlessly. "Oh Gods, oh no, I'm sorry!" I lowered his heavy frame against the tub, ensuring he sat up.

Blood from his abdomen daubed my arm. Gelatinous. Near-black.

My body cooled. "…I think you have a ruptured organ."

Cesare sucked air through bloodied teeth. "And one or two broken ribs." Sweat drenched his skin—deathly-pale beneath the carnage, his breaths heavy and wet.

"We've no more apozem," I muttered, stomach sunken deep. "And sutures won't help that…" *Nonono* he couldn't die! Not like that, not *now!* He—his cause was too important. So many people wanted—*needed*—him to live.

"Cauterise it," he muttered. "Abnu išātu.[140] In these drawers…" a shiver, "*somewhere…*"

Vision a tunnel, I dug up the fire stone, scrambled to strike a match—breaking two before one lit—and passed the flame across the tablet's smooth pane. Fire ignited, waning as the stone swallowed it, and I thrust the scalding surface against Cesare's skin.

Agony wrung him, yet he barely made a sound. *He endures so much…*

When I pulled the abnu išātu away, an inflamed amalgam of curdled pink flesh seethed underneath.

Cesare heaved, occiput thudding against the tub.

In my panic, I hadn't registered his scars. *Faces, those scars…* Three brutal swathes of bundled fibre twisted cross his torso. Old. Relics of wounds he should not have survived.

Flustered, I scrambled to peel the cloven sleeve back from Cesare's slashed forearm. *How did he make it back?*

"I'll get thread." I careened for the cupboards.

"I'll do it," he rasped out.

"Are you daft?"

"I'm left-handed."

---

[140] *AHB-noo ee-SHAAH-too*; 'fire stone' in Ancient Rhalese; a rectangular rock tablet, one side polished smooth and able to absorb heat, the other rough, gritty, and heat-resistant for grip. Mason-crafted for cauterisation.

"You'll be *one*-handed if you keep this up." Threading a needle with trembling fingers, I dashed back to his side. "Don't roll your eyes at me!" He winced at my touch as I took to stitching the gaping gash, blood coating my arms like grisly evening gloves. "Talk to me, Cesare. What happened?"

A groan deserted him as his head lolled.

"*No*," I cupped his face, "don't slip away—stay *with* me!" I fought to catch his eyes, tucking a lock of thick hair behind his ear, his bled cheeks left claret-smeared beneath my touch. "You promised Eligio you'd come back!"

"And I did," he breathed.

"Prideful bastard!" I turned to the sutures. "I told you! I *said* you'll get heinously butchered! You never listen! Why do you *never listen*?" I wiped an angry tear, smudging blood across my cheek like rouge.

Cesare pulled a weary smile I wanted to smack off his face. "My dry heart forbids me."

"Insufferable through and through." I grabbed the bandages.

"Give them to me."

"Stop being difficult!"

"I'm absolving you—"

"You'll be dead come dawn!"

"All the more incentive."

"Quit refusing *help*—"

"Vólto!" Cesare's voice flared. "I hate being touched—it makes me sick! Just give me the bandages if you want to help so bad."

My innards twisted. I wanted to scream and beg him to let me stay, to *help* him, but *his thick skull just won't fucking budge!*

Rising, I handed over the gauze with all the hesitation in the world, already sullied.

"And—" He snatched my wrist, my alarm surging all the higher, for his hands were never cold. "Don't say anything to the twins."

I stared, hearing the supplication in Cesare's too-green eyes. Pulling my arm from his grasp, both our hands red, I obeyed his wish.

But I couldn't let him die.

I burst through the apothecárium doors, bloody as a crime scene.

"*Etenesh!*" I leaned against the front desk. "*Please*, it's—"

"*Slow* down!" The Sam'säb woman placed aside her crate of supplies and rushed to me. "Do you need help?"

"It's Cesare, he's hurt. Broken ribs and stab wounds and I *th*—I think internal bleeding." I gulped, head shaking. "I need healing apozem. *Please*, I-I don't have any money now, but I'll pay you back however much you ask, I *promise*."

Etenesh considered me with stern eyes for too many horrible heartbeats, fingering the sunflower-yellow ṭibébé weave trimming her netela.[141] "We have a custom in our family: every favour granted, you return two-fold. If I give you apozem, you'll owe me more than coin."

"I'm willing to take any bargain."

Etenesh bobbed her head, hefting her crate. "I have a birthing to attend, so my wife Kasumi will fetch you katō-apozem. The Fingers, to speak to her—she's unhearing. Apply the elixir topically, but tell him to drink it too."

"Thank you, Etenesh!" I gasped out, hands clasped over my racing heart. "I cannot hope to express my gratitude."

"Eventually…" muttered the apothecary gravely.


One arduous hour later, I'd scrubbed the theatre clean, but nothing could banish slaughter's putrid perfume.

Throughout, I ceaselessly saw to Cesare's sleep, having ensured he drank at least a little of the apozem lest he died, and growing irater with myself each time I returned to his side to check for a fever or cleanse his cheeks of blood. I saw him then as so vulnerable, his limbs taut even in slumber as if he were a knocked arrow, always readied to strike a threat, always fighting himself. He was so young.

Whilst I swabbed the last of the parlour, a voice rang out: "Giorgianna?"

---

[141] A two-layered shemma (white cotton) headscarf worn by Ethiopian and Eritrean women. 'Ṭibébé' refers to the colourful woven borders of netelas.

Rosalia loomed at the top of the shadowy stairs. A ghost-white nightgown ell to her thin ankles, swallowed her fingers, her orange hair unbound. "Why's there so much blood?" The girl loped down the stairs, face crumpled with repulsion.

"*It's okay*—it's mine!" I scrambled for an excuse no matter how flimsy whilst gesturing to the muslin swaddling my tattoo.

Rosalia rocked from her heel to the balls of her feet. "I don't want anybody to be hurt." She shook her head, tepid eyes frisking mine as if I'd accused otherwise.

I winced. A child didn't deserve a part in this horror.

"Nobody is hurt." I embraced the girl, smoothing her hair and whispering those three words ad infinitum. As if trying to reassure myself that the lie was truth.

EVERYTHING BURNED WHITE.

Cesare's body thrust forward.

Everything blotched black.

He cried out, falling back to the bed. Blood and bitterness filmed his tongue as he dragged laboured breaths. Barbed pain squeezed his thorax with every twitch of his brittle ribcage.

Light scraped away the darkness and he met eyes rich as rosehip.

Giorgianna's shoulders eased. "You're alive." Black boots and trousers sheathed her legs, her broche-adorned white blouse embraced by a vinaceous waspie accented by curlicues of gold leaf and festooned with paired chains of lemon-shaped aureate buttons.

Cesare smiled wryly. "You'll survive your disappointment."

"You know your way about it well." She soaked a cloth with half of an apozem phial. "Apply topically and drink."

Cesare eyed the offerings. "Why the concern?"

Giorgianna was the last person he expected to tend to him, let alone so fiercely. Yet there she was.

"I've no patience for your martyrdom!" she snapped.

Cautious and agonised, Cesare reached for a throwing dagger to cut the sodden gauze from his abdomen, exposing the ancient scars on his stomach alongside the fresh addition to his copious collection. As much as he wished to care, to demand Giorgianna leave or turn away, he knew nothing could take from her the knowledge of the foul things maiming him. He knew, too, that she'd want to question, but hoped she wouldn't.

Cesare's veins pulsed slowly, shallowly, air leaching from his windpipe.

Death, with its lullaby voice, coaxed his heart to still; laid its bony fingers on his eyes to shut them. Such relief it would be to sink into a dreamless slumber. Coveted peace he was cursed to roam the world without.

But he wasn't finished.

Clutching the cloth against his ribs, he swigged bitter apozem and slumped on the bed, hair snagging on the corners of his mouth.

His skin pulled into thread. Cartilage polished to needle. Muscle spun into yarn. Bones welded shut. Fibres knitted his wounds.

His lungs inflated, that bastard heart of his still beating as sullen Death stepped away. *I said you wouldn't win.*

Cesare plonked his pillow over his face and groaned in chagrin. None of this should have transpired as it had.

"Don't tempt me," he heard Giorgianna.

"A little heartless—threatening an almost-goner." Cesare flung the pillow at her.

She caught it. "You're such—"

"A prideful bastard?" Cesare sat up, one sleeve rolled from bloody muslin and his unbuttoned blouse hardened with blood, his whole person dishevelled as a street cat. He rarely wore shirts with buttons, wondering how he contrived to pick his wardrobe so appropriately for just such a grisly occasion.

Giorgianna's arms slacked, fingers still clutching the pillow. *Bloody.* Cesare recalled getting his head bashed into marble and back cut open.

"How do you feel?" she asked. "What happened?"

"Like I've bled out half my body weight." Cesare perched his elbows on his knees, untangling his hair—so tousled it damn near obscured his face. "And the Minister of Blades happened." He didn't doubt for a second the rumours about Dioli's licentious perversions.

Giorgianna tossed the pillow to the foot of the bed and sat down, gaze frisking his eyes. "I'm sorry, Cesare." The gentleness of her tone, her voice soft and vespertine enouncing each syllable of his name, struck him stupefied. "For being so awful," she went on. "You were right. I... and this is a *terrible* explanation, but... it's as if I sought a receptacle for my rage—the only solid force I knew. To project onto a proxy for my misfortune. *So*, anything you said or did, I wanted to be false. I suppose... I almost *wanted* you to have dragged me along to the assembly on account of yours knowing my father would be executed—I *wanted* you to be that cruel. Perhaps, I didn't wish to admit that I *did* empathise with your philosophy all along. I couldn't let go of my antagonism for fear of having nought... Because I'm empty without rage. I don't know how else to live." Giorgianna hugged her knees. "I don't hate you—I never did. I'm sorry for the insults I hurled, about your 'little schemes' or wishing my aim had been better. And..." she heaped thick curls over her ear. "I'm sorry for stabbing you? I don't know what gets into me."

Cesare wanted to hear glibness, to find cracks of insincerity, but couldn't no matter how hard he scrutinised.

He chewed on his cheek.

She suspended her pride and admitted her error with such ease, as if all that mattered to her was honesty. Cesare couldn't help but envy her. "You project anger because it hurts to look at your grief."

"I don't want any more *grief*, Cesare!" Giorgianna argued, eyes chatoyant. "Rage kept me alive when I was trapped in the most awful place I could fathom, when grief and sorrow drowned me and I had nothing."

"You cling to rage like a raft," Cesare posited despite the terrible ache in his chest for her.

"I don't want to be exploited again!"

"You may be ignorant to it, but your pain forged you. Yes, it broke you, but here you are. Grief is a guide to navigate darkness, to know yourself deeper, to *build*, not destroy." Cesare sighed. "I'll never blame you; I *know* the crushing heaviness of loss. But you won't reclaim it by clinging to rage. That's all you feel, hence that's all you *see*, and that's what makes it destructive."

Giorgianna pressed her lips, hair spilling over her shoulders as she lay her head atop her knees.

Minutes ticked softly by, rosy-fingered dawn peeking shyly through the clerestory windows, before Giorgianna's eyes found Cesare again. "I think you're wrong," she put so simply. "Rage is a liberator when one listens to it and understands why it dwells within them. Silencing it brings no peace of mind—certain things need to be destroyed. Yes, the guidance of grief may build, but rage *transforms*. It is the *sharpest* weapon of reclamation."

Cesare leaned his chin against his palm, never breaking Giorgianna's gaze. "Only when you *do* listen, not when you use it to mark shallow cuts in someone."

She frowned. "*You* goaded me relentlessly, Cesare—recall your '*Elegy of Spring*' performance? Seemed you were rather fond of my rage when it amused you."

"Don't start."

"Oh?" Her lips strained sourly. "For thee but not for me?"

"All right, yes, listen…" Cesare exhaled. "You frustrated me—that's not an excuse, it's *my* explanation—and I allowed that frustration to warp my senses because…" Shame clenched his jaw, and he couldn't force his teeth apart without changing course. '*Prideful bastard' isn't even the fucking half of it.* "I… expected you to bring forward your qualms, knowing full well *I*'d've said nothing."

Giorgianna scoffed. "And would dodge every query like bolts."

"I…" Cesare's brows dropped, "know that's what I do."

"That's not *all* you do, Cesare."

"I know that too," he admitted, gritting his teeth against her insistence to repeat his name, the way her pitch plunged and duskened upon its first vowel as if she thought the moniker beguiling. "I didn't enjoy withholding information from you," Cesare rejoined, palming the warmth on his cheek in hopes of masking it with irritation, and he realised she must have cleaned his face when his fingers came away unbloodied. "I'm sorry I chose to be content with Lucrezia's plan blowing up in her face. It was myopic; I *hadn't* thought."

Giorgianna glimpsed sidelong, mouth tense, exhaling a '*hm*' before reconvening with Cesare's gaze. "I suppose we're even?"

"I stitched your wounds, you stitched mine."

"Please! I bathed to the elbows in blood for you. *And* bribed Etenesh for the apozem, so Faces know how much debt *I'm* in."

A laugh caught in Cesare's throat. He clamped his mouth with his arm and coughed, wet and sore. Blood stained the last white patch on his sleeve.

Giorgianna's hands braced like she's gone to reach for him.

Touch repulsed Cesare—a heinous reminder of the violence he once endured every waking moment. But when Giorgianna's careful hands bore no cruelty, when she held his face and brushed hair from his eyes, her scarred skin tender and sun-warm, her touch felt... fine? After everything between them, no part of her should've cared for his life. *And yet...*

Cesare wiped his lips. "There goes thy façade, vólto."

She rose. "You're an idiot."

"Maybe. But you *did* strike a bargain for me."

'*Ces?*' Eligio's alarmed voice echoed through the corridor. '*Are you back?*'

The door cracked ajar. The twins peeked in.

Lissandri began, "The place smells like—"

"*Good Lord!*" Eligio barged his brother aside and darted for Cesare, grabbing his wrist to behold the soaked bandages. "Faces, that's so much blood! Do you need—?"

"I'm fine!" Cesare upheld. "It's not so bad."

"He's lucky he's not septic," sniped Giorgianna, hip cocked.

The twins' eyes flooded with horror. *Damn you.*

Giorgianna's glare aimed at Cesare. "You're welcome. For your life and all."

Cesare touched his fingers to his fluttering heart. "Must you add insult to injury?"

"Another injury, then?"

"*Saints*. Can't help yourself, can you?"

Lissandri threw up his arms. "Someone explain what in the world?"

Cesare stood. The dim world swam but he remained steadfast. "My excursion proved fruitful." From his cluttered desk, he plucked the leather-bound book he pilfered. "I *hope*, or the term 'gutless' shall assume a novel definition."

Giorgianna approached the desk. "What is that?"

"A journal from the Adviser's quarters. Found under lock and key."

"*That's personal*," whispered Eligio.

"Precisely."

"But—"

"This isn't the time to discuss the ethics of stealing an old man's diary."

"Should we take this to the parlour?" Lissandri asked.

Eligio eyed Cesare. "I suggest you *bathe…*"

"Please do," agreed Lissandri. "You reek of fresh roadkill."

"While you wait," Cesare curled a dry smile, "complete some required reading," handing the journal to whoever would have it, "and feedback to me."

"Riveting." Lissandri accepted the offer.

"The pommels of your stilétti aren't sapphires, are they?" Giorgianna asked strangely, pulling away from the desk to meet Cesare's gaze.

He raised a brow. "They're tanzanites."

Her eyes, widened, flickered momentarily to Cesare's right ear. "Of course they are…"

# SCENE XLV

## AURIBUS TENEO LUPUM

*Cesare*

"KISS MY *SPLEEN* GOODBYE, sure and true." Cesare sat with feet perched on the parlour table cluttered by kohl-smirched twigs, begrudgingly clipping his cleaned nails. The one he'd broken snapped off in two chunks.

Lissandri shook his head. "You're gonna get so many colds."

Cesare gestured to Barsotti's journal in Giorgianna's hands. "Yet behold the spoils of war I bring."

She glared at him to match Eligio, then flicked to recent entries. "'*I note odd behaviour among a number of soldiers recently,*" she read. "*Ioana agrees. Stuporous, blank-faced, their voices drone—nothing stirs them. They seem… removed. But I cannot explain it, and my queries are dismissed. Such an Adviser I am—not permitted to advise!*'"

Cesare sprung up, hastily taking the journal. "'*I once called that man my friend—it is by his wish I abandoned my envoy mission in Salvatrice*" *to advise him!—but he accepts nought in dispute with his word. I do not wish to see his tenure carry on, but fear we are too far gone.'"*

"I think we have our key to the kingdom," breathed Giorgianna.

Cesare's heart pounded, fire crackling under his skin.

After all this time, could this really be it?

Lissandri adjusted the veil around his cylindrical headpiece, dun to match his stays. "So he's a silent dissident. *How* do we make use of this?"

"Play this game from the inside," said Cesare. "Infiltrate the ministerial house." His declaration struck silence into the parlour. "In earnest. If we know the inner workings of The Bone King's court, we will find his most vulnerable spot."

Eligio stared wordlessly, face blanched.

Lissandri held out his hands. "Hardly promising chances for a bunch of *picaroons*—one of whom is the most wanted man in the city state, apparently!"

The four caught the rigid strings of silence and held them tight, exchanging glances fairly as their minds raced. He was right, and Cesare, underneath all that crushing pride of his, knew he had no cards of his own to play. With that, shame noosed around his throat.

"I'll go in," Giorgianna's voice snapped the silence.

Cesare beheld her incredulously.

"Are you *mad*?" exclaimed Eligio.

"If *he*—" she referenced Cesare "—cannot infiltrate De Tullia's nest, why not I?"

"They know who you are."

"They don't have to." Taking a generous handful of her hair, she looped it through her hand like a needle's eye and, in its wake, the helices unravelled, blackening to onyx.

Cesare gawked, mystified. "You can tailor..."

"*And*," she dropped her tresses, willed them to coil and bleach once more, "I've made discoveries of my own." She leaned against the table. "I went to *The Salacia*. *There*," she held up a finger to silence Cesare's intrusion, "I met captain Fabio Amadi-Spýros of The Salt Hydras. He..." her lips pressed, "was one of my father's comrades. Father's dissidence wasn't merely through thought: he collected incriminating government documents, supposedly striking something so grim he never shared it with even his friends. But Fabio refused to disclose their location unless I propose how, *pragmatically*, I intend to requite my father's death. *That* is why I put forth the proposal that I go in." Her tone hardened to diamond. "I want retribution for my father. For *myself*. So I *will* go in."

Cesare turned away, cheek gripped between teeth and eyes slitted, wicked mind hard at work. Right then and there, he understood that his key wasn't so much Barsotti's journal, or even Barsotti himself, but *Giorgianna*. She could be *his* instrument—a weapon to be wielded the way he cannot himself. And, right then and there, he saw truth in her every accusation against him.

He locked eyes with her. His tongue pressed the roof of his mouth. *Click.* "Yeah." He paced slow circles, the twins' fretful faces out of his field. "We can toy with the idea."

"But… Cesare…" Giorgianna's gaze bored into him. "One of Father's comrades was *Davide*." Cesare halted. "Not a friend—far from it—but in the circle. He was supposedly from the same orphanage as my father."

"Davide *did* mention being an orphan," Lissandri corroborated.

Cesare pushed through his dismay, asking: "Anything more?"

"Davide wants those documents."

"So we must get them first."

"Meet Fabio at *The Salacia*, then."

"We promised our help at the *Curios*." Eligio wrapped a headscarf—sage silk painted with apple blossoms—before donning a tawny cavalier hat. "Rosa's with us."

"Cesare and I should suffice," assured Giorgianna. "I'll be down in a second." She bolted upstairs.

Eligio neared. "And Ces…"

Light exploded across Cesare's eyesight, a strident *smack* ringing through the theatre followed by the echo of Giorgianna's delighted guffaws in the distance.

"*Agh!*" Cesare doubled back, a cold hand clutched to the sting on his cheek. "The fuck was *that* for?"

Eligio rubbed his palms. "Good measure."

Lissandri grinned like a cat. "*Told* you I'd do it."

"Traitor," hissed Cesare.

"Maniac."

A match struck alight, charring Cesare's sigarétta. He dragged, smoke pale against those dark monstrosities of storm clouds reflected upon the shuddering canal.

Somehow alive. Somehow survived.

Despite it all, he was yet to disclose to anyone his sinister finding of an aperture in a soldier's skull, unable to make sense of it himself and unwilling to bring it forth with nothing substantial to show for it.

"Cesare," Giorgianna called from *The Sunrise*'s rear door. "I think this is yours." In the palm of her hand she cupped a silver cufflink encrusted with an indigo-violet tanzanite.

Cesare couldn't believe his eyes as he held the trinket, tightness pushing between his ribs. "Where did you get that?" He was sure his gift from Paolo was forever lost to history.

"On the stage floor that '*Bedlamite's Ballad*' night. Thought it was Basilio's so you can imagine my temptation to hurl it into a canal."

Cesare dug its pair from his pocket. "You'd be equally tempted if you knew it was mine." He swapped out his ametrine cufflinks.

"I would've gone through with it, in fact." An acescent smile reddened Giorgianna's lush lips. "So be grateful my assumption was wrong." She turned to walk with an off-hand beckoning gesture.

Thunder rumbled like a furious beast over the waters of Smugglers' Cove as Giorgianna placed down a sun eremite to complete her deck.

Cesare slumped back in his seat, pride bleeding from Giorgianna repeatedly pummelling it into the gambling table. *But a fourth time? Really?*

She materialised a card from nothing. "Another round?"

"I swear on the Saints you cheat."

"Your Saints must find you awfully bothersome, and I empathise."

"Not *my* Saints," corrected Cesare. "I picked up the habit from Paolo at *The Sunrise*." The old impresario, like Isaia, was Mariano and a believer of the Saints. Most in Sancta Maria were, and if you weren't, you certainly didn't admit such heterodoxy. "I pray to no deity."

Giorgianna rested her elbows on the worn table. "Were you born in Vencenza?"

"Du Rrât a du Errèina."

"Tell me about that—your life in Zargòsa. Fabio is yet to arrive."

Cesare's ribs clenched in. "It's a long story."

Giorgianna's eyes, vivid as ripe persimmons, sheened with intrigue. "I rather like long stories."

Despite himself, something about her limpid behold and autumn-rain voice pried those ponderous words from Cesare. He dragged rum-tinged briny air, numbing his mind before he could speak. "My father," his gullet lurched on the word, "Raul Agostini, strove to be a musician. His mother reviled him for that, wanted him in politics which he always detested, and he never much liked the theatre. So, he abandoned Vencenza for Errèina. Andelia Daiena Gebara—*my* mother—was a performer in the area Raul settled. Don Kapêli. Just shy of uptown. And, well," Cesare didn't halt his scoff, "Raul and his guitar struck gold. My parents became a duo of sorts."

Giorgianna cupped her face as she observed Cesare. "That's how you know the violin?"

Cesare nodded. "My mother learned from hers: Golipên Elgani. We lived in a playhouse in Errèina[142] until..." his throat tightened, "my sister's birth. Erosabel Lillai." The syllables singed his tongue in an aching reminder of why he so often opted for sobriquets. "My mother had this one dance teacher, Gulabo, a Marubhūtri woman from Mojatīya. She taught her our pre-diaspora roots, and mother taught me in turn. It's our ancestors who grant us permission to practise our customs. In the capital, I was lucky to watch theatre and belove it."

His disposition darkened. "Mother never felt entirely safe as a Marlâre woman in a state like Errèina, but, even as an immigrant, Raul refused to see her qualms for too long. Until it was too *late*. Around my seventh year, the monarch at the time, Fertús Feli of the renowned *Pedrolas*, began stoking wariness of *'Others'* in, specifically, Du Rrât a du Errèina's gentry. That meant *anyone*: minorities, immigrants, refugees, the impoverished, 'unconventional' sorts. The powers that be scarcely cared for the Marlâre unless we entertained them, anyway. And suddenly, when the fire poker touched *him*, Raul cared. *So*, my family fled to live with Golipên in âma's birth village in the southern moors, Canronê." Cesare snorted derisively at the moniker. "'*Merciful*'." He abandoned Giorgianna's rapt scrutiny. "My amôna was a dressmaker, and my mother could weave, so she adjusted quickly enough. Raul... became a woodcutter."

Cesare's head canted; brows lowered. "He wanted nothing more than to prove his mother wrong, to reign triumphant over her condemnations of his shortcomings. And, in his eyes, he failed. Once amôna passed— tetanus—and Raul hadn't anyone to pull him from the edge—he wouldn't hear âma's pleas—circumstances spiralled for three years..." Cesare's tongue clicked, gaze reconvened with Giorgianna's, "and here I am."

Her eyes searched his as if reading verse in a language she vaguely understood, and Cesare hated it. To think she may one day decipher that language terrified him.

---

[142] Unlike in Vencenza where it is optional, in Zargòsa it is mandatory for theatre staff to reside on-premises.

"What…" her question swithered, "were they like?"

Cesare chose his words with caution, "At which point in time?"

"So I take it you figured out the impossible, girl," a too-familiar voice said. Glum. Smoke-hoarse.

"Fabio!" chirped Giorgianna.

Cesare turned to the new arrival.

His chest yanked so unbelievably tight, every sound snuffing out as he stared at the man before him—a smuggler in a faded turquoise greatcoat, tanned face lined with age, dark eyes riddled with bewilderment. "Paolo…?" His breath proved scarcely enough to squeeze the name out.

"*Paolo*?" he heard Giorgianna exclaim.

"Hello, Cesare," the man who was Paolo spoke with a gentle ghost of a smile, and Cesare's heart fractured.

# SCENE XLVI

## SPIRACLE

*Cesare*

CESARE'S MIND REELED.

Paolo left when *The Sunrise* shut—had been the one to instigate it as the impresario. Why was he *here*? Had the man whom Cesare saw as more of a father than his own blood familia been right under his nose this whole time? *Without my knowledge?*

"This…" Paolo—*was he?*—darted his eyes about; dark, familiar eyes Cesare knew too well, "isn't an ideal place for this." He beckoned Cesare and Giorgianna. "Come."

"Where?" Cesare's voice almost ran through with a crack.

"*Antigone*. Salt Hydras' ship."

Cesare's limbs wrung stiff as a deadman's, but he forced himself from his standstill, forced his feet over the threshold into the whiplash of salty squalls.

His sleeve gently tugged where his burn scars hid. "Ces—"

"Don't touch me," he snapped at Giorgianna, teeth already sour with blood.

Though modest, *Antigone* was a spectacular galleon, tethered to the berth with algae-draped chains, its hardwood hull worn by seas and weather. Unending sails flapped like deafening white wings in a sky ruled by dark turmoil. Wrought of faded metal, the vessel's name embossed its bow, the deck clanging with sailor commotion. Webbed wooden flesh haloed the bow figurehead of a gurning seadrake. Two smaller simulacra wrapped their willowy necks around the main beast and settled beneath its jaw. A hydra. *So he is a band leader.*

On the stern deck perched a scraggly man with a black eyepatch and a bandana navy as his rattail, shouting like a parrot at Giorgianna, "*¡Hurra*, she knows!" His skinny fists pumped the wind.

She shook her head. "Cannot believe they let *you* be master gunner."

"Better believe it, girly." He curled each shoulder in a dance. Giorgianna smiled with an eye roll.

A whistling sailor swabbed the deck, promptly receiving a light thump upside the head from his captain. "Siɣí!¹⁴³" Cesare started at the language he didn't understand rolling off Paolo's tongue. "You'll whistle up a storm!" He followed his guests into his quarters, the wailing wind slamming the door shut for him. Salt mingled with the warm aroma of smoke and sandalwood—scents the old impresario always wore at *The Sunrise*. Faded teal curtains half-lidded the eyes of windows, a desk hideously littered with paperwork and trinkets standing near. Cesare halted at the realisation of whom he picked up that anarchic habit from.

He affixed the man who had once been Paolo with a glare.

The captain's breath shook. "Cesare—"

"What is your *real* name?"

---

¹⁴³ *shee-GHEE*; Themistoklísika for '*silence!*'

"Fabio Amadi-Spýros."

Cesare grit his teeth. "You never said you were Themistoklísi."

"For safety. And I am Themistoklísi by my mother only." Sighing, Pao—*Fabio* let go of Cesare's eyeline and doffed his greatcoat, revealing an unruffled beige poet shirt, sleeves barely reaching his wrists. "When De Tullia's office commenced, I knew he'd come looking. That, as some punishment from the Saints, he'd get *me*." He gestured to the awkwardly-loitering Giorgianna. "You've heard of my friendship with Ludovico, I'm sure. So of *course*, I had to go—had no choice!"

"Then why not leave Vencenza altogether like you'd said?" *Lied.*

"I had a *life* here. Didn't you think it odd how often I'd be out by night? Or the lengthiness of my 'visits to Sancta Maria'? I didn't expect you to—would've defeated the purpose—but…"

Betrayal clawed Cesare's eyes. "All this time?" *Did I really know nothing?* The urge to beg Giorgianna's forgiveness brushed his mind.

"I'm so sorry, Cesare," pleaded Fabio. "I couldn't force such a burden onto an adolescent."

"What *burden*, Paolo?"

"Fabio." His voice hardened. Cesare's eyes blew wide; chest seized. The old man's brows drooped. "No, I'm sorry. It…" His breaths strung together like a fragile pearl necklace. "I wouldn't forgive myself if you got in harm's way."

Cesare crossed his arms. "Well do *I* have a tale."

"I figured," said Fabio to no surprise of Cesare's. "I know I went about this poorly. I should not have kept you ignorant. Can… you find it within yourself to forgive me?"

Cesare let his eyes burn, permitting the tears to take hold if they wanted. They didn't, so he loosened a breath and shook his head. "Later."

Fabio nodded gravely and sat at his desk, Giorgianna occupying the armchair across. Cesare opted for the sofa nearby.

"I've been dreading this," the captain grumbled.

"I *said* no debts." Giorgianna produced from inside her satchel the Adviser's diary. "Cesare got his organs stabbed out of his body to get hold of a peculiar ministerial document."

She proceeded to explain.

"You want to move through the Adviser?" the captain finally spoke, brows sitting close.

"I want to move *inside* the government house," replied Giorgianna. "I'm far from unprepared. Neither are we alone. We have Domínii."

Cesare rolled his eyes. "If Ygal doesn't stab *further* organs out of my body."

Fabio made a face. "Cesare, what've you been up to in my absence?"

"And you, *Fabio*?" Cesare's sneer received a narrow-eyed pout. *Is that something* I *do?*

"Quit your childishness!" Giorgianna aimed copper-bullet eyes for Cesare, leaving him to recover his breath when she returned to Fabio. "Something else: Davide Mancini."

Fabio groaned. "*Saints…*"

Giorgianna's brows bobbed in empathy. "He wants my father's documents, but claims he's 'known' here, that you made him an outcast. I don't doubt he was tasked with locating whatever my father collated, especially that elusive secret, should it remain. Davide *is* at the Governor's beck and call."

Cesare chewed his sore cheek, muscles begging for movement.

Throughout his time at *The Sunrise*, Davide's true face had been so well-masked that it took Paolo almost too long to see it. Such glaring proof of just how close people could get. That even in the most guarded places, evil creatures may prowl unnoticed.

The captain rolled up his sleeves, resting his elbows on the table. "The Adviser is the least useful senator to you, besides perhaps the Treasurer. In the same vein, he is the *safest* whilst the Treasurer is certainly not."

Unable to sit still, Cesare roamed the quarters, bound for the window behind Paolo.

"How do you endeavour to convince him?" he questioned Giorgianna.

"Blackmail works wonders, I've gathered."

Cesare turned away from the rough ocean, eyes falling to Fabio's forearm. Upon tanned skin mottled with moles and liver spots was inked a three-headed wyvern in faded blue.

Recognition speared Cesare's memory. *No… never a* wyvern!

"...*enough* to swindle his way out of even the Governor's web, I fear," spoke Giorgianna.

Fabio drummed his fingers on Barsotti's journal. "If the government catches wind of us, the theurgy won't protect—"

Cesare stabbed his dagger into the desk, a whisker from Fabio's forearm. The man jumped.

"Cesare?" Giorgianna's voice tightened.

"A Moretta attacked me the other month." Cesare rested an elbow on the captain's stiff shoulder. "Your tattoo."

He heard Fabio's hitching breath. "...What?"

"Davide is involved with them," hissed Cesare. "Looks mighty suspicious."

"I swear I've no clue about The Morettae." Fabio wagged his head, swallowing. "Let me call on my quartermaster."

A massive Damtani man with a black beard and a blade for a left hand—Korneli—joined them, receiving what Cesare gathered had been a deserved slap from Giorgianna. Cesare wondered how fiercely she wished to treat *him* to the same.

"Giovanni went missing 'round 'at time," Korneli said, rubbing his rufous cheek.

"Gold teeth, slim build, torn pupil?" listed Cesare.

"Aye, 'im."

"I *would* apologise, but I fear my tone might betray me."

Korneli snorted. "Good riddance if 'e was wi' 'em freaks."

"Why would one of the Hydras collude with Morettae?" raised Pao—

*Fabio! Fucking Saints!*

"Hardly the question these circumstances beg," Giorgianna noted. "If there's one, there could easily be more."

"Nothing stopping Davide from leading the legions *after* The Morettae *into* the Cove since he's playing turncoat," added Fabio.

"Precisely the concern of the Antrum's cadres," said Cesare.

Korneli crossed with meaty arms, dark gaze remarking disdain. "We don't like 'em cadres, up 'ere."

"Your choices aren't abundant," fired Cesare. "You are *both* at risk of decimation."

"He's right." Fabio nodded. "We must ensure the safety of our territory." He addressed his quartermaster: "Keep your eyes and ears keen on *Antigone*'s whispers and send word to allied bands. Most of them are asea and will be for the foreseeable time, but The Grey Pearls and Brass Teeth are docked. Their leaders ought to be aware."

*The Grey Pearls*. The band who saved Ygal's life years ago.

Korneli tipped his hat and left the cabin.

Fabio sighed. "Seems this quagmire of yours is overflowing."

"So?" Giorgianna beheld him with hope. "Will you help us?"

"I *don't* want you to do this, girl. These political games killed your father, and I *cannot* have them kill you. But you won't hear of it."

"Certainly not."

Fabio let out a heavy breath. "Then, yes. I will."

"Thank you, Fabio." Giorgianna pressed laced palms to her chest, head bowed, and uttered something else in that language Cesare guessed must be Themistoklísika.

"However," Fabio switched to The Fingers, '*I will write the address and hand it to you on your way off. I want to take every precaution.*'

'*Understood*,' Giorgianna glanced from the captain to Cesare. "I'll let you speak," she added, and Cesare's heart folded into a fist. "Perhaps Danilo wishes to spar." Wisps of rodomel perfume lingered in her wake as she breezed out onto the wind-washed deck.

# SCENE XLVII

## HINC ILLAE LACRIMAE

*Cesare | Giorgianna | Cesare*

CLOUDS EVER-SWELLED, the atmosphere burdened with moisture and clinging to the nostrils. Beyond the port side, the seas raged, throbbing and bruise-dark.

"Why didn't you tell me?"

Fabio toyed with the iron band around his thumb. "What would you have done with the knowledge?"

"*Have* it," Cesare grit out.

Fabio's silver-streaked brows joined. "Listen—"

"Make me understand." Cesare motioned to the galleon. "*This*."

The captain trained his eyes on a distant skerry mounted with a lighthouse like an unlit candlestick. Somewhere afield, metal *dinged*: Giorgianna and Danilo sparring.

"My mother," Fabio began, "Melétia Spýros, was a shipwright from Salónika. My *father*, Ružan Amadi,[144] was a cenobite of the Mariano faith in Sancta Maria. Cenobites aren't *necessarily* called to a life of celibacy, but they aren't to marry or have legally-documented progeny, hence my bastard birth. *Antigone* is… a distaff venture. The old captain was my maternal grandfather, Athanásios Spýros, who is, ironically, dead.[145] I was a mate for a while, swinging between oldtown and Smugglers' Cove. That's how I met Ludovico—gambling in The Court where he tended to deal.

"There were six of us. Matìa and Durans, I'm sure you remember." Cesare did: Matìa with the cropped peach hair and Durans who could barely hear. "The latter's dead. Gobbled by the ocean's jaws. And yes, unfortunately Davide was one of us, for a time. The youngest. *I* am the reason he landed work at *The Sunrise* to begin with—I suspect employment was his motivation to get in with us." Cesare made the conscious effort to cringe, Fabio giving a look somewhere between '*I'm sorry*' and '*you're telling me*'. "Ludovico always sheltered the broken, the lonely, yet he was the *first* to express disdain for and distrust of Davide. I, in all my dumb pride, seeing Davide work the theatre sets with such ease, his intellect and charm blarneying folks, blindly relegated Ludovico's concerns to needless paranoia. And when he began *expatiating* of illusory meritocracy, how it warped my acuities, that's when he lost me. And that's when I lost at Davide's game. But that's too far off in the future, and besides the point. Fresh off the boat from Sancta Maria at seventeen, I found work as backstage crew—" *what he took* me *on as* "—and…" Fabio chuckled, mercilessly plucking the strings of Cesare's heart. "Here we are." His features eclipsed. "With De Tullia in power, all I had left was *Antigone*." His eyes braved to find Cesare's. "I am sorry, Cesare. From the bottom of my heart."

Hubris fought Cesare tooth and nail, gunning down every word of vindication. He wanted to snub Fabio for keeping secrets and telling lies

---

[144] '*Ž*' is pronounced '*z*' in Faustinian, whilst '*z*' is pronounced '*ts*'.

[145] Look up what '*Athanasios*' means at your leisure.

all those years. For leaving him. Yet, try as he might, he couldn't blame the old impresario. *Is survival a crime?* And was Cesare not a hypocrite?

He pried apart the stubborn muscles binding his jaw. "I forgive you, Pa—*Fabio*." He *tsk'd*. "That'll take getting accustomed."

Blades screeched and the melody of nearby sciamachy concluded.

The man who used to be Paolo but never really was smiled. "I'd appreciate it."

"The twins shall be elated and confounded."

"No doubt I'll receive pointed words from Lissandri."

"I'd be more worried about *Eligio*."

Fabio reached for a pack and lighter, offering Cesare. "Did you live with them and their parents?"

Cesare accepted a coffin nail, and he swore that the very moment he touched its bleached sugar paper was the first time he'd not felt like a boy anymore. "No." He didn't look at Fabio as he lit the tobacco and dragged, granting smoke a rare passage into his lungs.

"What?" Fabio's voice echoed with concern.

"It doesn't matter anymore," Cesare curtly brushed off. "We live in the theatre now."

"It meant so much to you…"

"*Means*." Cesare's tone sharpened. "That vile man will continue to bleed this city until nothing remains."

"'*Mortals are so small in the vastness of our universe that they cling to any modicum of power they can grasp*'," versed Paolo.

"And *He* has too much," Cesare sneered. "The cyclical nature of history—liberty's visage soon ossifies back to tyranny until the Republic becomes the Empire. I'd rather it be ruins."

"To put a civilisation to the pyre, one must burn those it houses. Would you be willing to live with the weight of a thousand lost souls on your shoulders?"

"I am willing to be the final one to crush this miserable edifice."

"Cesare—"

"Has that *ever* worked?"

Fabio's eyes begged desperately. But after a cloven moment, he sighed. "Why would it?"

Cesare heard a rustle, the soft drum of retreating feet. *Of course, she listened in.*

"But… *that* ancient costume?" asked Fabio.

"A curse on my forsaken bloodline," scorned Cesare.

"It was mine." *Antigone*'s captain shrugged. "When I was young. So many bàutae walked Vencenza's streets, then." Fabio's smile slipped. "Surreal to witness such antiquity. An enfleshed spectre."

Cesare sucked blood from his teeth. "How long did you know?"

Fabio chuckled. "It's *just* my rotten luck that the *one* day I braved a peek back into the óssium, I walked into a damn riot."

Cesare's heart punted. "What?"

"Just ruckus; a couple injured crows. Five years back. It's like the Saints wanted me to know."

"I've been wearing the wretched thing for six." The sky fulgurated and boomed. "I'm not willing to wear it for six more." The filter tip singed Cesare's fist as if vexed at him. He was sure the next moment he blinked, he'd awaken maimed and near-dead from Manuele's beating. "I'm glad to have you back." Cesare's throat backed up. "I didn't think I'd ever see you again…" All those years ago, he had nothing—a child who barely escaped Zargòsa alive—yet Fabio took in a runaway without a second thought, never once diminishing his pain. He owed Fabio his life and all his joys and every single drop of blood he *wasted* fighting this war. An insult to the man who granted him a second chance to live.

His sclerae stung. *Then why can't I say that?*

"And I *you*." Fabio's voice moored Cesare in reality, but light faded fast from the man's near-black eyes. "Though it's hard to feel *merry* when I can so easily lose you both."

"Not *so* easily."

"What was that about getting organs stabbed out of your body?"

Cesare flourished a blasé hand. "Peril builds character."

Fabio shook his head. "You outgrew me." He pointed to the miniscule margin between their heights. "*And* kept my cufflinks!"

A smirk crept to Cesare's lips. "Did you doubt?"

Fabio laughed, raising his arm, but halted. "Are you…?" He beheld Cesare earnestly, knowing he understood his question.

Besides the twins, Fabio was the sole person who knew the whole story. Why touch harrowed Cesare. The birthplace of his scars and burns. What horrors chased him from his shallow slumber. Why he slept on his stomach. That's undoubtedly why the old impresario dreaded learning Cesare lived alone in *The Sunrise*—at the mercy of his nightmares.

"Close enough." Cesare let Fabio wrap his arm around his shoulders, foreheads rested against one another. Sandalwood and woodsmoke enveloped him, the aromas of his only joyful childhood moments. And now, Fabio himself wasn't a mere fading memory.

Cesare's breath hitched, tears spilling unrestrained. "I put up a good fight, I'll admit." He laughed despite himself.

Fabio grasped Cesare's face, his hands worn and callused. "You better keep it that way, understand?" A tear dropped from his lashes, followed by a hundred more. "I am not burying my son."

Cesare embraced Fabio, and he hated that he could never make that promise.

ACROSS THE WHARF loomed a six-sailed dark caravel like a wing-splayed bat, a blood-red dahlia rendered upon the mainsail as if carved by a knife into a basilisk's night-nielle hide. Polished iron stamped its bow with '*Hangman's Dowry*'.

"We best be off," I said.

The captain nodded, hands hidden in pockets to mirror Cesare. "Return with tidings."

Cesare handed me an inscrutable look before descending to the berth.

"Giorgianna." Fabio's rheumy eyes hinged on me. *Here goes.* But instead of handing me a note with my father's address, Fabio unclasped his gold-and-garnet bleeding eye pendant. "I want you to have this."

"Fabio, no." My throat dried. "You cannot give me that."

"I want to," he insisted, unwilling to lower his arm.

Tears threatened as I regarded the golden chain whipped by the wind's tumult.

My fingers reached for it but faltered mid-motion, yet the request remained adamantine on Fabio's countenance when my gaze flinched to measure it, so I conceded, gently fixing the dainty thing in place. The pendant nestled between my collarbones—a third eye of my own, scarlet and furious.

Wrinkles crinkled Fabio's skin as he smiled. "I know I couldn't've recognised you in that vólto, but I reckon I had some divine hunch."

My wavering lips squeezed, tears falling. "Thank you, Fabio." I threw my arms around his neck. "*His death shall be blood-repaid.*"

Fabio's embrace tightened. "Promise me not with yours."

I sank my face into Fabio's shoulder before letting his cold hands hold mine when we parted.

A stiffened edge of folded paper touched my nerves and, as though all those years of card tricks led up to that very moment, my features yielded nothing when I spirited away the note.

"Promise not with mine." Wiping my cheeks, I squeezed Fabio's fingers and descended to the docks.

"*11 Di Vitis Lane 5/2, West Fin, Smugglers' Cove,*" I read the address inscribed in rounded print, tucking the note into Barsotti's journal hidden in my satchel.

The horizon stretched serenely against a battered sky on the brink of collapse; lightning gleamed like polished pearls in the pluvious darkling firmament.

Cesare struggled to light another sigarétta against the wind. "This pantomime is yet to play its course." He dragged smoke into his lungs, stifling a wince.

My brow strained. "Are you all right?"

"My makeup is smudged so there's room for improvement."

"And the injuries?"

"It's *liveable*," he teased.

"They say such things come in threes," I said glumly.

"Two down." His implication nudged my curiosity, but the nonchalance of his tone caught my stomach into a frore fist.

"For what it's worth, I'm glad you lived."

He scoffed. "You'll make me fear the arrival of some cataclysm."

I rolled my eyes away. Porcelain waves crested with spume shattered into fragments against the distant cliffs, against the pilings holding up the boardwalk beneath us, flecking the air with ocean's tears as they nebulised.

"The sheet music on your escritoire is in your handwriting." *Awful* handwriting.

Cesare didn't meet my gaze. "I'd rather translate my thoughts into music for only my ears to understand than leave a paper trail."

I studied his words like a stanza. "You play beautifully."

"*Saints…*" Cesare knocked his head back. "Must *everything* you say sound like a love confession?"

Irritation washed unmoored over my cheeks. "Remind me to never compliment you."

"Do forgive me if I'm not quite acquainted with your pleasantries, vólto."

My arms crossed. "You can stop calling me that, now."

A shadow flitted by the corner of Cesare's lips. "You can *make* me."

I scowled. "Lowlife."

"It's like you're *trying* to spur me."

"The feeling is mutual."

"Why did you run towards the stage?" Cesare asked strangely, tone abruptly grave.

'*Hm?*' was the only sound I could mould into corporeality as my brows gathered.

"'*A Bedlamite's Ballad*'."

Every time I heard that title, I flinched.

"I don't know," I admitted. "But I *wanted* to. And maybe that's why I did."

Cesare finally looked at me, eyes smouldering within the fuliginosity of smudged kohl, an andalusite flame each—viridian and gold and ochre. "You want revenge"

My jaw tightened. "Riddle me. When the rulers execute a man for his crimes, is that not merely revenge?" I canted my head. "Merely sanctioned vengeance?"

A cold raindrop shattered against my cheek, and the heavens soon wept a baptism unto my new flesh, rough salt wind running its fingers through my hair as I stepped towards the edge of the boardwalk.

The abyss stared into me, seas beckoning me to submerge amid billows as rageful as myself. To dissolve and become as limitless as the waters drinking the lazulum and the earth. To listen to their dialectics and veridic prosody. To know everything they know.

> *'Mortals are so small in the*
> *vastness of our universe that*
> *they cling to any modicum*
> *of power they can grasp.'*

Father always said that. I should have known.
But now I did.

TWELVE-HUNDRED-THIRTY HOURS ticked over by the time Cesare and Giorgianna arrived at The Boars' estate.

Ygal strode solemnly around her office while Isaia read Ludovico's address. By his shoulders hovered Itxaro and Chiara. On the bureau rested a revolver and a gold-plated axe encrusted with citrine and amethyst. Its blade glistened—fresh and lethal. *Dirty move, Najm.*

Sarnai rammed herself into Giorgianna's seat on a rubellite sofa, plucking a curl to toy with. "What're the chances Davide's slumming it with Luca?"

"Slim to none." Ygal rested their elbow on the axe's knob. Cesare forced himself to look anywhere but the ugly weapon. "Unlike *my* district, where all property belongs to the cadre and requires fiscal exchange by carnesíi to obtain ownership, Lucanus operates by means..." vague hand-waving, "more libertarian. Which *does* seem contradictory, but follow:

"Most property there doesn't legally belong to the cadre, so really, it's free reign. If Davide's warehouse reeks of formaldehyde and is stuffed with chopped-up cadavers, I don't imagine he'd get bugged by squatters. Head Cyclops couldn't give two fucks who comes and goes unless they interfere with his dealings."

Cesare stepped towards the centre of the office. "It's time you establish communication in the Antrum, Ygąl. Circumstances are deteriorating and we need to get a foothold while we still have our bearings."

Chiara grumbled under her breath, earning Isaia's warning glare.

Ygąl drummed the axe against the desk, Cesare's nerves jolting. "Leone and his Serpents are *tenuous* allies, but the cunt takes a month to respond *with* luck. The Cyclopes are at best unlikely, at worst: an invitation for slaughter."

An astronomical understatement. Once when a Boar was sent to offer a trade route agreement between the two cadres, Lucanus strung him up by meat hooks, removing organs and appendages from him over the duration of four days before collecting all the pieces and dumping them in Ygąl's district like mulch. The drained blood he poured into the static canals in the northeastern nook of Boar territory, and the teeth he personally mailed to Ygąl as souvenirs. All for no other reason but his own morbid amusement.

Chiara growled, freckled face scrunched.

"Words of input?" Ygąl snarled at Isaia's second-in-command.

Unfaltering, Chiara left Isaia's side. "Get your nose out of the óssium, Najm, *that's* my input. You're supposed to be the Dóminus of this district, not playing second fiddle to an *ossíi* leaching off of our cadre to serve his precious fucking 'revolution'."

Her words spurred Cesare. "Say that to my face, Chiara."

She pivoted, locking eyes with him. Gelid hatred resided in her tiny pupils. "Who the fuck *are* you? Who the *fuck* are you to embroil us into your *games* just to get us massacred?" *Games!* Isaia stood at attention,

Sarnai and Giorgianna on their feet, Itxaro's dark monobrow dented and chrysoprase eyes frisking the room for an escape route. "If you want to die, why *don't* you? But don't drag *us* into your well-earned grave."

Itxaro plucked at the khaki headscarf knotted at her nape. "Who's '*us*', Chiara?"

The silver-eyed woman didn't flinch. "You are the bringer of *death* unto this place." She spat beneath Cesare's feet, casting a hex with her silver glare as she stormed from the office.

Pulling up his cloth mask, Isaia stalked after her.

Silence thumped with Cesare's racing heart. "Well." He turned to the Dóminus. "She's a gem."

Ygąl combed her zhǐjiǎtào through her hair. "Get Ludovico's documents," she gnashed, glowering Giorgianna's way. "Since Caruana's willing to be *charitable*, you better succeed in blackmailing the Adviser." She struck her desk with the axe to startle Cesare. "I don't discriminate."

"Duly noted, Dóminus." Giorgianna smiled saccharine as poison, bowing mockingly to Sarnai's amusement. Cesare tossed Ygąl a smirk to spite them. *That's my girl.* His heart lurched. *What—?*

"And Sarnai," the Dóminus said. "Why are you here?"

"*Crescent* duty hasn't changed over yet."

Ygąl's expression voided of mirth. "Wrong answer."

Sarnai raised her palms, face screwed up.

"Are we free to *go*?" pressed Itxaro, impatiently adjusting her medusa and vertical labret.

Ygąl huffed. "Yes."

"Thank the *All*-Seer." Itxaro winked at Sarnai on her way out, exchanging a Zargòsian farewell with Cesare in solidarity.

Sarnai, blushing, tucked a lock behind her ear and cleared her throat before grumbling, "Babysitting Lucrezia duty summons." Giorgianna signed '*vestibule*' to Cesare whilst leaving arm-in-arm with her.

Silence deafened the chamber as only two remained.

The Dóminus paced behind Cesare, footfalls a rumbling brontide. "*Very* lucky, Agostini." A snort. "You'd be gutted on my floor if it weren't for Curly."

Cesare turned to Ygal, a venom-laced smile shared, and departed.

# SCENE XLVIII

## MAN IS WOLF TO MAN

*Lucrezia | Giorgianna | Lucrezia | Cesare*

A SQUALL BLAST OPEN AN ÀTRIUM WINDOW, shutters lashing on golden hinges and scraping Lucrezia's hands as she scrambled to force them shut. The sky clapped and crumbled, rain drumming on the córpus as if a million nervous nails.

*The Crescent*'s vast auditorium, eviscerated and unpeopled, drained Lucrezia's lungs the way Vencenza's grand basilica always did. Sometimes, she wondered if she was yet to heal to completion.

Clamping down on her paranoia, she ventured backstage, stalking through the ichor-painted thespian room, into the halls carrying her like arteries past the impresario's office, and out of that bloodless corpse of a theatre.

She staggered when hearing voices inside the office.

'…*onto you.*' Basilio.

A nasal snicker punched Lucrezia's gut. '*She can be* all *up on me for all I care—can't touch me for shit.*' Abramo…

Apprehension hooked onto Lucrezia's rigid shoulders, inching for her throat.

'*Inform your people.*' People? '*I'll ensure Montefiore is marked as an official dissident.*' Lucrezia watched the earth split. '*Plenty conceals beneath her supposed cluelessness, surely.*'

*I was never safe…* Anguish tore Lucrezia's chest, shook her limbs. *DAMN YOU!* All she'd ever wanted was peace. Constancy. A home.

'*Boss will be* indebted *to your contribution.*' Lucrezia's swivelling mind slowed on Abramo's bratty tones. '*Humble man, Davide.*'

Lucrezia's blood ran cold, stomach flipping over and over. *No…* Just how much was interconnected?

'*Did you know about Giorgianna?*' asked Basilio.

Abramo meandered about. '*I know* quite *the spread about our little harpy.*' His footsteps softened; voice hushed. '*You have no* idea!" The door flew open.

Abramo stood on the threshold, the gold-black uniform across his sturdy shoulders and muscular arms unclasped to bare a blouse cerulean as his beady eyes.

Lucrezia realised the jacket was Imperiáli.

His mouth gashed into a nasty smile. "Salúdi, Luce."

SHADOWS SWARMED THE PERFORATING ALLEY a block from Ygạl's estate down which Cesare and I ventured back to *The Sunrise*, wishing to collect the twins along our route to the Cove.

"I owe you my intestines." Cesare's mouth clipped into a wry smile. Fidgety fingers neatened his hair.

"Keep them," I said. "Or my trouble would be for nought." My lips squeezed, eyes shifting to peek around their corners at him. "I wouldn't wish to pry, but…" I carefully weighed my words which grew unwieldy when he beheld me with a raised brow and bemusement. "Ygạl—at the estate just now—had with him a battle-axe, gold and gem-encrusted. Its centrepiece status was interesting when she favours asiāf and peşkabz, and every time they thumped it on the table, you... seemed to flinch? Or shunned its sight." I pressed my lips together again. "Are... you all right?"

Cesare's gaze evaded mine. "If you *must* know, the scars on my abdomen were dealt by an axe."

I flinched at the revelation. "Axe..." My fingers cooled with the tenuous connections I wished to neither make nor vocalise. "And..." I gestured to my own forearm. "The burns?"

"A dropped paraffin lantern."

My eyes narrowed to slashes upon Cesare. "Does Yg̣al know something?"

"It doesn't matter," he said plainly, hands hiding away in his pockets.

"Does it not?"

A mordant half-laugh escaped him, yet my skin bled from the nick of hysteria in its undertow; the serrated edge of stifled distress. "Do you miss mine talking too much, vólto?" he quipped, reaching for his wonted nonchalance, and I wished to flip the sandglass of time and take back my every question.

My throat tied, step faltering behind Cesare before ceasing to a standstill.

"About my reasons..." When he glanced back puzzled, my eyeline fastened to the neglected cobbles circling his feet. "Two years ago..." My voice backed away in fright, but my wounds beseeched purgation. Even if it were to him—someone I'd gleaned knew pain like the lines of his palm. For once, I just wished to be heard. "In the winter solstice night, my friend, Emanuela, and I were making our way home when... three men attacked us." Panic stiffened my tongue. "Two of them grabbed me. The third man—tallest—held Ema down and..." I couldn't breathe, gulping, mouth so dry it hurt, "*h*-he beat her skull into the flagstone." My eyes watered as I saw that frost-mantled pavement, the trails of blood like crushed pomegranate, the screams ripping the sky. "Every time I tried to fight, the other two broke my fingers." I tugged my gloves off, holding up my tremoring hands. "Scars, if you don't believe me." Choosing anything above facing Cesare, I tracked the pallid rivets across my skin. "Along with those dear *mátre* graciously bestowed upon me."

I drew a broken breath. "*I*-I don't know how, but… I escaped to the nearest Guard station." My scoff came out almost a sob. "Should've known better. I spent *every single month* lodging requests to Veronesi's tribunal. All for nought. Only one of the men was punished, the others forgotten as if an innocent woman's murder meant nothing! They never even gave me their names." My chin bolted ceilingward, lashes heavy. "Emanuela looked at me in her final moments and screamed '*Run!*' at the top of her lungs…" I folded my palms over my face as tears bleared the world, "and that image will never leave me." A whimper tore from my chest with all the tears. "Her blood thawing the frost will *never leave me.*" *I wish I could drag you back from the Null…*

Pulling moisture into my throat, I blotted my face with the sleeve of my brooch-bitten blouse and let my gaze latch hold of Cesare's.

His body had locked up, horror grasping him by the ashen face. I'd almost forgotten I was sobbing at a man who asked for none of it.

"I want their names." I gathered the shreds of my voice and welded them into a blade, with all my might wishing words could be enough to murder something soulless. "I will hunt those men to the ends of the earth if I have to, and I will *tear* them and *break* them until *no* amount of necromancy could stitch them back together." My ruined heart throbbed. "There is no justice under this vile authority." I lanced Cesare's stare from mine and passed him by.

"Vólto." Slim fingertips gingerly skimmed my shoulder.

I flinched, finding Cesare's eyes roaming mine, polished with salt and starlight. "I take it back," he spoke adamantly. "If I'd known, I'd've never called you selfish. You are *not*—I need you to know that *you* will never be responsible for what happened." My gut kicked. "*You*—I cannot believe you helped me after I said something that cut so deep." Remorse traced every line of his face. "I'm so sorry."

I opened my mouth, but my voice braved no step forth, speech unformed in my throat, so I turned on my heel and left his words hanging between us.

The storm's brutality vied to break oldtown's bones as Cesare and I crossed the distance between the Antrum and *The Sunrise*, keeping to shelter.

The smiling face overhanging the rear door fulmined a presage when lightning gilded its tears.

Cesare snatched the doorknob from under my hand. "Why did you assume I wouldn't believe you?" he asked over the rain.

Thunder clapped.

"Men like the words of other men." I shooed him aside, wringing a bucket-full of water from my curls and herding them into a high ponytail once indoors.

Alchemy dripped off the hallways feeding the parlour. Within, a familiar voice mingled with the twins'.

"Sarnai?" I gasped.

She jumped. "It's Lucrezia!"

"What is?"

"Basilio summoned legionaries just as I arrived."

My stomach lunged into my mouth. "We need to go," I asserted immediately. "Relying on Ygal will take too long."

"What about the documents?" asked Cesare, tying back his drenched hair.

"Go without me." I handed to him the address. "The twins need to know."

Lissandri jolted. "Know what?"

"Cesare will explain." Heart in my throat, Sarnai and I bolted for upper óssium.

ARMOURED IN DARK SLATE, two City Guards, the very ones from the day of Giorgianna's arrest, patrolled the impresario's office, footfalls heavy to match the hands of time.

At Basilio's desk sat a slim-boned individual with a cabochon bloodstone embedded into their gold chestplate, a pearl-black braid sliding to their hip from within a graceful helm. On the inner side, their flavescent cape ran deep red as flayed skin. They had drawn blood from Basilio and Lucrezia, both phials resting beside them while they pored over paperwork. A Sánguinus. An iridite, at that.

"Is all this documentation necessary?" Basilio asked from his unaccustomed position in the armchairs. His foot tapped wildly.

Abramo perched an elbow on the back of the impresario's chair, mouth twisting into a clandestine simper at Lucrezia.

They were all one and the same. Basilio. Abramo. Davide. The state.

She scowled back at the blue-eyed pig.

She had been raised among spiders and snakes; these men held no power to frighten her. *But the men in the dungeons will...*

The older of the two officéri, eyes carved of ice, held Basilio in derision. "Your family agreed to aid the Governor in purging insurgency. All must be committed to record."

The impresario retreated into a cocoon of his own limbs. *Silent as a smart man ought to be here.*

Lucrezia glimpsed the open weave of the ceiling's plexus, the black nothingness beyond. All she could hope for was Sarnai's swift return.

"Glad this is intellectually stimulating for you, mummer," Abramo sneered at Lucrezia, the slur[146] laying effortlessly upon his tongue.

She turned away. *Keep. Mouth. Shut.*

"You don't call the shots here, Sessa," the older Guard chided. "You are a disgrace upon the Imperiálum."

Abramo grimaced. "Like the *leader's* some beacon of virtue."

---

[146] '*Mummer*' is a slur for thespians, a relic of the Empire days when the northern Salvatrici powers were highly disparaging of theatre performers—a traditional Vencenzani art form which had been banned for decades.

Both Guards lunged. The young redhead restrained Abramo's arms and shoved his face to the table. The older soldier gripped his broad pugio, bracing its glinting tip on the untarnished timber just by Abramo's mouth.

The condemned man recoiled uselessly.

The Guard levered the knife's handle downward and chopped Abramo's nose off with a sopping *crunch* of bone and cartilage.

He screamed. The pair of gaping holes perforating the centre of his face doused the desk in crimson.

The redhead prised Abramo's Imperiáli jacket off and handed it to his superior before throwing the noseless man into a wall.

Abramo's face contorted, cerule eyes shouting obscenities.

The blood on the table rippled, surged, at the Sánguinus' behest as they, never breaking focus with their paperwork, splayed their ash-grey fingers. The blood ripped into ribbons, finding a place within the decorative cavities veining their breastplate.

"Be grateful it's not your tongue," the blue-eyed Guard hissed at Abramo.

The Sánguinus signed the final document, looking up. Their eyes were white balls pierced with black pupils, no iris in sight.

The older officére turned to the rookie, and Lucrezia's stomach sank. "Remove the vítus for interrogation."

### *Boom!*

The Sánguinus dropped onto the desk, throat voiding of violet-pink blood like a cracked vase.

CESARE AND THE TWINS TRUDGED through the downpour to the fifth block on *Di Vitis Lane*—moth-eaten apartments in West Fin. On the second floor, tarnished copper embossed a lonely flat's door with '*5/2*'. A singular sheet of intercalated wood constructed the ceiling of the foyer, rain steaming through jagged rifts. *Who's to say there's anything left of Ludovico's?*

Lissandri found his lockpick and finessed the door—by far the best lockpicker of the three (something, something clockwork).

*Click.* He twisted the knob. It didn't budge.

Lissandri stiffened. "*Oh,* I hated that."

Cesare took the lockpick, handing the twins a revolver each. "Don't stand in the doorway."

The twins sidled aside whilst Cesare worked the lock.

*Click.* He twisted the knob. It budged.

He gently opened the door.

### *Boom!*

A bullet seared a millimetre by Cesare's throat, his heart bolting as the twins exclaimed.

Inside the apartment wreathed in endless star charts, beside an antique bookshelf, stood Davide.

At his hips coruscated Cesare's stilétti.

A splint bound his left arm. *Weak spot.*

His lips peeled apart to bare fangs, pale eyes glossed. "Never without my tricks, Bauta." He lifted a revolver. Aimed. "Remember what we promised with?"

# SCENE XLIX

## HAR-MAGEDON

*Giorgianna | Cesare | Giorgianna | Cesare*

SARNAI AND I RACED through the empty *Crescent*, the storm's bluster for a backdrop, ascending a ladder into the blackness of an interposed loft—for use by property masters. Ropes and pulleys bound the space like vines as we crept towards an area where a wooden framework overhanging the impresario's office filtered in light.

Two crows, a red-haired fledgeling and an older officére, circled Basilio's desk at which a Sánguinus dealt with paperwork. Basilio huddled in one of the armchairs. Lucrezia sat stiffly in the other. Abramo crouched by the streaming window, face soaked in gore.

*No crossbows*. My gun was a trump card.

The Sánguinus looked up from their final document with pin-point eyes. *An iridite*. Their magic would be stronger—iridite blood saturated easier with azoth and they were a high-ranking legionary. *They go first*.

Tracing my fingers along my eye pendant, I unholstered my revolver, savoured its weight, the coldness of its raindrop-begemmed frame and the curve of its trigger guard.

My ears attuned to the dialogue as I aimed, eyes a thin line each.

The older Guard faced the younger. '...*for interrogation.*'

***Boom!***

CESARE THREW HIMSELF FROM A BULLET'S PATH, sending a glass shard careering for Davide. The blade didn't catch him but pushed him off-balance.

The twins shot twice each, knocking Davide's revolver from his grip and puncturing his shin.

Davide clenched a stilétto in a reverse grip and speared for Cesare to avoid the twins' lines of fire. "You've walked into your *slaughter*house!" He thrust against Cesare's block.

"Three on one—I assume *I'm* the butcher." Cesare pushed hard, Davide doubling back, before reprising, breaths weak.

Davide's cast-hardened arm drove into Cesare's temple.

He lost his foothold.

Darkness petered out and pain trickled in as Lissandri steadied him. Cesare's too-rapid heart pinched. *I'm not in fighting condition.* Eligio pressed to his brother's back as the door hinges rattled and into the apartment burst a dozen people. Circular masks stamped the centre of their faces, mouthless and dark as jet. *Morettae.*

"You don't learn," taunted Davide.

"Good job, Ces," jibed Lissandri.

Cesare swallowed into his raw throat. "Takes a hoard to riot."

Morettae swarmed like black locusts.

Bullets rattled the building to its neglected foundation.

Lissandri managed to shoot down the archer but not before taking an arrow to the thigh.

Cesare's chest clenched. They needed reinforcement. *Help.* But hubris gagged his words. *Let me GO!* He stabbed a nearing Moretta's eye. Carved a gorge down their palate and mouth.

Staggering backward, Cesare grabbed Eligio by the scruff. "Get Isaia," he ripped through the pride knitting his throat.

"*But—*"

"I'll clear your path." Cesare yanked him from a Moretta whose throat he slit. "Not the time to *argue—*" The icy scorch of lòthmir sank into his shoulder.

THE SÁNGUINUS COLLAPSED, hemerythrinous blood draining across the desk. *Aim not so awful anymore, bàuta.*

Sarnai and I dove through a slot in the ceiling and into the office, landing on our feet.

The older crow drew his schiavona, Abramo nowhere in sight. *Weasel.*

I fired a trio of shots at the younger Guard lunging for the Sánguinus. Taking two bullets to his side, he pried off the Sánguinus an inaurated revolver.

We dove behind the ornate plinth bolstering a massive globe.

***Boom!***

***Boom!***

***Boom!***

***Boom!***

Sarnai squeezed my arm. "I'll distract—you'll shoot."

Fear nicked me but we had little choice.

Drawing a blunt dagger, Sarnai burst out.

I darted in the opposite direction.

***Boom!***

***Boom!***

Sarnai screamed as I released bullets.

The young red-haired crow dropped like carrion.

Sarnai half-bowed, gripping a bleeding bicep.

The older Guard hacked his schiavona for me.

I leapt back and lunged for the bloodwork phials, hurling them against a wall. Glass shattered; the humour splattered the gold-and-turquoise panels with crimson chrysanthemums.

I veered. The crow's sword stabbed an armchair. ***Boom!***

Blood rushed from a hole in his skull. His blue eyes frosted over, gibbous and seeing nothing, and I recognised him from the day of my arrest.

Unleashing my rapier, I drove it through the soldier's throat, ripped it free, leaving his head to flop on half a neck.

Haem imbued the air with hot, ferric sweetness, thinning my breath as a shiver pricked the hairs along my spine.

Lightning blinked.

"*Giorgianna!*" shrieked Sarnai.

The impresario's arms locked around Lucrezia, his pearly-hilted revolver pressed to her head. "I'll shoot!" he squawked.

"Fucking coward!" I pointed my bloody rapier at Basilio, thunder striking a hammer to the black anvil of the sky. "Tell me what I did to you!"

His lips pulled from his teeth. "You *disgraced* me, reprobate bitch! All you've *ever* done is undermine my authority—"

"And I'll undermine your rotten fucking authority until I draw my last breath!"

"I'll have that be to-*day!*" screeched Basilio. "Criminal blood just like your terrorist father!"

"Don't you see you're a puppet?" I exclaimed. "You *have* no authority at De Tullia's feet. He grants you the illusion of power because nothing is as malleable as a deceived mind."

"And *you* will *always* be a filthy slum rat dressed in velvet!"

Lucrezia dug her elbow into Basilio's rib and bolted for the documents stacked beside the dead Sánguinus. "*Giorgi!*"

***Boom!***

Basilio shot her.

Sarnai's amorphous scream surged with the lightning illuminating the bloody office.

"*NO!*" My cry was the clap of thunder.

AIR CLUNG HEAVY to Cesare's lungs as he grappled with Davide.

"You seem *drained*, Cesare," Davide cooed as their blades screeched. A mocking grin never abandoned his mouth. "*Bloodless*, perhaps?" He pushed Cesare.

Tightening the elastic that bound his hair, Cesare reprised wordlessly. Davide parried, bringing his splinted arm onto Cesare's chest, and knocked his legs, the apartment tilting as Cesare toppled.

He rolled onto his back and swiped *once*, *twice*, *thrice* at Davide who brought his heel on Cesare's chelidon, crushing it, and crouched over him.

"Spare yourself the shame." Davide's cold fingers clasped Cesare's face, palm hovering over his mouth. Nails lurched for his eyes as his hand squeezed his mouth and nose.

Cesare recoiled in frantic revulsion, fumbling for a throwing knife.

Obsidian-fletched arrows whirred past the rickety ceiling and shot down three Morettae.

Shouts rang as Davide bounced back.

Familiar faces filled the chamber: Aengus; a tall man with shoulder-length coils and brow-sweeping fringe—Etenesh's younger brother Araya; vermilion-haired Mair; contemptuous Chiara; Eligio.

"As requested." Isaia was the last to forward in, stolid face covered and head hooded.

A nasty leer snared the corners of Davide's mouth like meat hooks as he pulled out a lighter. "*I* learn, though." A flame burst out, and he tossed it at the bookshelf.

Wood and paper ignited, the stifling humidity and the structure's permitting age wrestling in a desperate tug of war, but the flames forged ahead.

Cesare groaned. "Fuck everything."

# SCENE L

## OCCHIO PER OCCHIO

*Giorgianna | Cesare*

LUCREZIA SLUMPED TO THE PARQUET. Lifeblood decanted from her abdomen.

The revolver thudded from Basilio's wan fingers. "*I-I*-I didn't—I'm not—" His tongue tripped over words and his feet tripped over nothing as he tottered, eyes bugged out at his hands, at the blood staining them no matter how clean they were. "I'm not a murderer…"

Sarnai dashed for Lucrezia and the documents.

My rapier's hilt arced the air. "*I* can be if it eases your *soul*!" The pommel smashed into Basilio's temple, claret splashing across his brow and down his face. He yowled and tumbled to the floor.

I brought the hilt crashing onto his skull, the fist clutching my dagger clobbering his face once, twice, six, seven times, hilt, fist, knuckles splitting against teeth, fingers gore-gloved, vision *red red red.*

"Psycho bitch, *stop*!" he squalled through a mashed nose and mangled lips, swatting at me to avail him *nothing!*

I gripped his purpurite vest. "Tell me everything and I'll stop." He gaped like a choking fish and I stabbed his shoulder. "*Before* I kill you!" I twisted the slit into a spewing hole.

"Sto—*stop*! Stop, I'll *tell* you!"

I ripped out my knife, sticking it to his neck where vessels bulged, *begging* to be severed.

"Davide was traced to your father, s-so he proposed using your disappearance, murder, what have you, as bait to lure him onto government premises—he'd be desperate enough!"

Recognition glinted before me like water. "'*A Bedlamite's Ballad*'." *It always circles back to that wretched pantomime!* "You *knew* there wouldn't be patrols on my journey home. That's why that crow oaf took you aside for your stupid *chat* when you should've cared for your vitae! You *knew*!" Was Ema's murder connected to this? *Guards didn't seem to patrol that night either...*

"Giorgianna..." Sarnai drawled, rustling the documents.

"I needed to aid Davide in killing you," Basilio slurred, "which would help the Governor liquidate your father. When legionaries searched your apartment, they found those outlawed books—traced their purchase to Ludovico." My chest caved. "The Bauta shouldn't't've gotten in the way..."

My lip twitched. "You were never a snake." I hammered my knuckles hard into Basilio's face. "Snakes have *spines*." Blood spurt from his shredded flesh along with the stream of screams from his gullet. "At De Tullia's feet is where you belong, you miserable *worm*!" I beat my rapier's hilt into his skull; blood sprayed into my mouth and I spat it in his face. "*Dead*!"

"Giorgianna, *stop*!" Sarnai seized me under the arms.

"*Blood* is all I will *leave* of you!" My blade grazed Basilio's rib, buried in his arm, waist, thigh where it ripped a gushing defile from Sarnai dragging me back. "Let *go*!" My throat purged a growl as I floundered in blind fury.

Sarnai restrained my forearms, squeezing my sides between her knees. "Giorgi, *please*!" I faltered, lungs heaving. The crimson-slathered room came into juddering focus. "You need to go to the others! I have a bad feeling!"

My gaze trained on Lucrezia. *No.* I rushed for her, pawing her shoulder with my bloody, bloody hands.

She winced, eyelids barely splitting.

Sarnai palmed Lucrezia's brow and palpated her pulse with unstained fingers before slinging her arm over her shoulder with my help. "I'll get her to Etenesh—she's less than my size and I'm strong enough."

I embraced Sarnai tight, "Thank you," and bolted.

FLAMES GAINED GROUND.

"*Break the roof!*" bellowed Isaia.

Eligio shot holes in the ceiling above the fire.

"Isaia!" Chiara shouted from the desk. "Bolster me!" Bloodied dagger between her teeth, she lunged, Isaia's fingers laced into a ledge for her, and sprung for the armillary sphere of Genaris hanging within a golden hoop above the bookcase. *A trapezist.* Grabbing hold, she sliced off the four-ringed planet, snatching it as she hoisted herself fluidly into the hoop in its stead and smashed the ceiling fissure into a larger hole with the model.

Water warred with flames, quenching them slowly.

Chiara gripped the hoop, swinging her legs spear-straight at— "*Cesare!*" Lissandri's shout grabbed Cesare's attention seconds before the trapezist's feet knocked breath from his chest.

"*Fool!*" She jabbed the bulbous pommel of her dagger into the base of his throat before knocking the underside of his chin. Cesare's head thrust back, a bright taste of copper bursting in his mouth as he bit his tongue.

She raised her dagger to stab. He shoved her off. Chiara somersaulted and leapt upright. Cesare flipped into a crouch stance and, in smooth momentum, swung his extended leg across, barging her ankle and knocking her over. Legs wheeling in the air and almost kicking Cesare's face as he stumbled upright, Chiara bent like elastic and flung herself effortlessly to her knees, daggers gripped in reverse.

"You are *all* fools!" She pounced.

Cesare parried. "It was *you!*" *Chiara* was how Davide found his way here. How he remained safe in a place for good measure threatening his life.

Chiara sliced for Cesare's head.

"Do you realise what you've *done*?" He reeled back, shoulder blades stabbing the narrow stairs leading to a trapdoor to the roof.

"I'll kill *you* before you kill *us!*" Chiara thrust for his heart.

A shriek erupted from her as Davide yanked her backwards by the hair.

"*Ah-ah,*" he crooned, "not *yours.*" He hurled Chiara. Her head slammed the door. "*My* kill." Slaughter glinted in his eyes as he attacked Cesare with a stolen stilétto. "As promised by *blood.*"

Cesare's step teetered, Davide pushing him with every mutually-parried strike up the stairs. *Burn for this, Manuele.* He shoved open the trapdoor, rain pelting hard as hail.

His foot collided with Davide's throat.

Davide tumbled across the flat roof but sprung up in moments. "All I've ever wanted was freedom." He advanced, "Just like *you,*" striking.

Cesare blocked, passing back to regain lost balance. "So you can go back to fucking corpses and little kids, you disgusting fuck?"

Davide's lips pursed. "Your judgemental nature wounds me."

"*Does* it now?" snapped Cesare. "Does my judgemental nature *wound* thee?" He lunged at Davide. "Traitor and *coward—*" he cut Davide's chest, mealy flesh splitting with a vermeil gash "—is all you *ever* were!" He thrust.

Davide faded, stepping across, slashing Cesare's elbow and pushing him.

Cesare's dagger skidded from his grasp; Davide kicked it off the building's side and knocked Cesare down, tall enough to restrain his legs.

He pinned his cast into his neck, Cesare ramming his right arm into Davide's chest to guard his throat from caving.

Cesare went to punch Davide with his left hand, crying out when he crucified his palm with a stilétto to the rain-drenched roof.

Davide's head angled. "Do you know how they make your defected mind better?"

"They chop my head off," gritted Cesare.

"You'd *wish* they did." Davide freed Cesare's hand and pressed the blade under his chin, pricking skin so he couldn't swallow without driving it deeper. "We've known one another for *so* long." Davide's splinted hand locked around Cesare's chin as he traced the blade around his jaw to his cheekbone. "Seems almost... full circle."

Lòthmir glimmered, and Cesare's worn mind wasn't quick enough as the tip of the stilétto carved deep through the centre of his right eye.

His lungs emptied a scream.

Every blink gored his cornea, half his field veiling red where it didn't entirely eclipse.

Davide hovered the blade a nail's breadth from Cesare's left eye. "You were always so gamine to me." Bile filled Cesare's throat. "How I *yearned* to clasp your slim neck. To feel your sinuous tendons struggle against my grip as I squeezed air from your delicate throat." Davide pressed harder.

Cesare grabbed the rain-cold blade of the stilétto, arm trembling as he steered the dagger away from his face. Flesh squelched and spat blood between his anguished fingers.

Davide's eyes bulged, veins protruding from his forehead.

"*A noose'll save you the trouble in due time.*" Cesare dropped his arm from Davide's chest. The splinted elbow drove into his larynx, the weight of the fucker's entire frame cutting his airways.

Cesare snatched the second stilétto sheathed at Davide's hip, braced uninjured fingers around its familiar hilt, and crashed the encrusted tanzanite into Davide's face.

He faltered with a cuss.

Cesare kicked him off, straddled him, punched him with a bloody fist. *My kill. As promised by blood.* He buried his dagger in Davide's chest, mazarine cotton staining as if with wine. "I *hope* my judgemental nature wounds thee."

Davide's shrivelled lips rouged with ichorous funeral shrouds. "You never struck me where it hurt." An abhorrent smile gashed his face, eyes pale and glassy as death glazed them, and Cesare's guts turned cold. "I don't know what pain is," croaked Davide. "You killed me, but you lost. Because I have nothing for you to take... and I will *always* know how to hurt *you*." He swung the stilétto for Cesare's head, grabbing his collar and hoisting himself onto Cesare as he reeled away from the weapon. A slash landed on his shoulder.

Cesare drove his dagger into Davide's neck, crawling backwards.

Heartbeat jumped to his throat as he plummeted through the tear in the roof into the apartment, pulling Davide with him.

Screams sparked on his impact.

Davide barely broke his painful fall.

The pallid deadman twitched.

Cesare's heart rattled as he gripped his knife and blindly stabbed Davide's head, distress forcing his hand.

Arms pulled him across the floor. "Ces, he's *dead*!" shouted Eligio.

"*Don't touch me!*" Cesare recoiled. Heaves tore his chest as the ruined apartment came into corporeality through a singular lens.

The fire had extinguished, the right third of the bookshelf charred.

Where Davide lay with his face caved in smashed chunks as if watermelon, Moretta corpses too littered the floor.

Araya clutched a wound at his ribs. Isaia bled from cut-up ankles and calves. Mair leaned on a broken-nosed Aengus and nursed their severed hand. Lissandri's side oozed blood. Eligio's mouth bloomed with a purple-red bruise.

The hideous pain in Cesare's eye plunged through to his brain like a knitting pin inserted into his socket, a trickle of blood tracing his right cheek. *All these people...*

Lissandri screamed.

Into the back of his knee had lodged an arrow.

Cesare whisked the twins behind him and plucked his second stilétto from Davide's cooling husk, Hounds drawing their weapons.

Morettae clogged the apartment, a man and two women at the navel. One woman, an archer, stood tall and dark-skinned, snake bites in her lips, coily hair trimmed tight to her head and eyes sitting like pieces of bright turquoise within monolids. The other was shorter, blonde and fair, gaze blazing hatred. Shocks of dust-brown hair coated the gangly man's head, muddy orbs scowling as much as his mealy face.

"Cadres!" exclaimed the ocean-eyed woman.

The blonde glowered. "Nettlesome busybodies!" Her glare shot to Cesare.

He stopped. She stopped. Recognition struck them both at once. *Saints…* The rounded curve of her cheek, the pert nose, the honey eyes poured between thick lashes and sun-gold hair tumbling to her collarbones. The Salvatrici accent. Everything he remembered from *The Sunrise*. But older.

Cesare stepped brazenly around Isaia. "Vivinna?"

A breathy '*no…*' rustled behind him.

"*Lorita* to you, *Cesare*," she hurled. Where he thought the detestation in her tone might cut, it didn't, and he realised he no longer cared if it might.

"You killed Davide!" The man pointed a blaming finger at Cesare.

"Who was on the Governor's payroll," sniped Cesare.

"*Liar!*" spat Lorita.

A Moretta sprung forth as if upon the blonde's order, revolver cocked at Cesare.

**Boom!**

# SCENE LI

## OF DEALS AND MADMEN

*Giorgianna | Cesare*

THE POUNCING MORETTA DROPPED LIKE A SACK, their skull's innards minced with my bullet.

Morettae lurched back.

My middle twisted when I beheld Cesare. From a cut through his right eye, blood trailed down a face bleak as a deadman's. My gut only tightened when I saw Eligio's bruise, the arrow in Lissandri's knee and the blood at his side.

A Moretta streaked for me with a swinging shortsword.

**Boom!** I shot them through the chest. "*Listen!*" I roved an unfaltering gaze among The Morettae as I waited for silence to preside. "They are telling the truth." My voice donned a commanding cadence, my Shadow speaking through me. "The state held Davide at ransom due to past connections with my father, dissident Ludovico Damiani—the man whose home you stand in. Davide's sole motivation was regaining his gang's independence, which the Governor promised him *only* upon the compromise that he could lead him to The Bauta."

A lanky white man with murky eyes grimaced. "I don't believe a word of hers."

"Lapo," reproved a soft-voiced woman with snake bites.

I produced the purloined paperwork.[147] "Ascertain for yourselves."

The swarthy woman cautiously approached me to peruse the documents. "*No...*" Lapo and a blonde flocked near as her euclase eyes bulged. "*All* this time...?"

Her cheeks dulled at my nod, murmurs reverberating among the Morettae. "Davide led you to a massacre at the assembly with the aim of decimating your ranks." My heart weighed despite it all. "How many did you lose?"

The woman's eyes dimmed like clouds drawn over a sea. "Half. M- my sister, too—"

"Why are you telling her this?" snapped the blonde with glowers my way.

"Davide didn't care for you *or* your cause," I pressed on. "You were wanted out of the way because, to De Tullia, you are merely pests distracting from whom he perceives as the true threat."

"I *did* wonder how he knew so much," the ocean-eyed woman mused. "So... *this...*" She spun towards the blonde. "Lorita, this is perfect!" Her voice sparkled. "They can help us!"

Lorita's full lips pulled from her teeth. "We won't accept *help* from Antrum cadres!"

"Do humour me how *your* plot is faring on its own," Cesare opened his big mouth and started talking again. "I've gathered you don't appear intent on proceeding further than killing De Tullia as if that alone will change anything."

"And what of *your* plot?" snarled Lorita.

"We have dirt on Adviser Clario Barsotti's dissenting sentiments," I reclaimed my right to speak. "*Unwashable*. With it, I intend to infiltrate the ministerial house. Ignorance is servitude—the more Vencenzanii are

---

[147] All Vencenzani ink is impervious given the waterfaring culture.

unaware of, the stronger a hold De Tullia keeps on his throne. *But,* if we heedfully disseminate incriminating information among the populace, we will aid in dispelling state propaganda, thus stirring an undercurrent of discontent." I glimpsed askew at Cesare. "And what is anger and vengeance if not a tyranny's reckoning?"

Lapo ambled circles, throwing me slighting leers. "Why should we trust a cheap skank taught to craft bewitching words? They'll pick you off like an annoying louse in that deathtrap. And what's to say she's not a sympathiser—that *all* of them aren't? I'm with Rita. Kill them and avoid the grief of their lies."

Karambits and stilétti glinted.

I held up a halting finger, grasping Lapo's behold as we circled each other. Grim mirth crooked my lips as I roamed a hand down the length of my high ponytail. "Look around." A gesture to the Moretta corpses, to the floorboards smeared in guts, the skyscape carpet soaked alizarin. "How little *you've* accomplished, and yet..." Flourishing a hand, I attuned to the diamond thrum in my blood. *A second try?* "You talk too much." Between my fingers, I observed Lapo's insolence wobble and fall. His hand rested on his neck, brows ducked. "And if it so *pains* you to cooperate, lest you learn you were wrong all along," my veins seared, frosted; blood curled around my organs and bones and suffused all my flesh, "I'll put you out of your misery." Azoth burned in the spirals of my fingertips, Lapo's breath catching on my nail and seeping out as his neck *twisted* with the passage of my hand through space.

A rush rose up my throat, whirled behind my retinae in swells of vertigo.

Gasps and squeals shook the edifice at the sight of Lapo convulsing, his tongue flailing around throttled words as vertebrae in his neck *pop! pop! popped!* like firewood.

Dread wrenched my innards, my fingers spasming only to wring his neck harder. I strained to gulp. Iron perfume sharpened with the trickle of blood from my nostrils. An ache engorged my skull. "Don't ever imply I won't survive a deathtrap." My fingers locked. Lapo seized, twitching grotesquely. "Don't *ever* imply I don't wish every filth on that high council *dead!*" I yanked my fist towards my shoulder.

Lapo's throat snapped like levin.

Blood surged up my oesophagus.

He crumpled misshapen, a chorus of gasps and screams for accompaniment, claret vesicating through exposed pits of his flesh twisted like pale clay.

My lungs glutted on air. "Don't... *ever*... imply I won't come collect my debt." I swallowed the blood on my tongue, lifting fluttering lids to behold the Morettae. Their visages blenched—a row of petrified mannequins.

Silence reigned.

The aquamarine-eyed woman jumped forward. "I want to help!"

Lorita, nasty smirk donned, swaggered closer. "Intimidated by Curly's witchery, Kel-Kech?"

I twirled my fingers at her, licking blood off my lips. She pressed two fingers either side of her heart in succession.

"I'm *intimidated* by the *state*," Kel-Kech threw back before holding forth to The Morettae: "Our plans were squandered when we allowed Davide to lead us. These people may be our chance."

"Who exactly are *you*?" Lissandri hoisted a questioning brow as he and Eligio flanked Cesare.

"Lower ossíi," replied Kel-Kech. "Some smugglers: mostly factionless but we had a Hydra before he vanished."

I glimpsed Cesare.

"I'm with Kel." A swart Naambe[148] man, head wrapped in a manganese-violet moussor, walked himself over to the larimar-eyed woman.

My chest tightened as more Morettae followed until only a Gilmylvetlan[149] woman with a pair of black braids remained by her lonesome.

Lorita's wide eyes pleaded with her.

---

[148] *NAAHM-bheh*; '*bh*' is pronounced like a breathy '*b*'/'*v*' hybrid; the people of Naangdi.

[149] *geel-myyl-VEHT-lahn*; people of Gilgyčurmyn (*geel-GYY-choor-myyn*).

She fingered the beaded strings suspended by her forehead-circling band, "Sorry, Rita," and joined Kel-Kech, the Naamбe man draping his willowy arm around her deer-skin-arrayed shoulders.

Lorita's shoulders shook, knuckles white. Her jaw welded shut against words, jerking, tight as overwrought hinges in keeping with her limbs. But, expelling a taut breath, she yielded. "Fine. But I *won't—*" her eyes flashed at Cesare and me like a warning lighthouse "—make this pleasant for you."

Cesare strode across the room's centre, features held by contempt. "Believe me when I tell you I'm *well* acquainted with *pleasantries*." He turned to address everyone with fire in his voice. "The situation is dire. I'm unwilling to believe Davide informed the Ministry of nothing, even if he wasn't bargaining on their victory, which places us *all* in danger of decimation without even considering where his supposed accomplices could hide. We plan to waylay the Adviser soon, the outcome of which will be pivotal to determining our subsequent course. Reconvening is necessitated."

"We squat in an abandoned armoury in The Court," said Kel-Kech. "Not too far from the entrance to Smugglers' Cove." She shook her head. "But he never informed us of any accomplices he may have." *Surely another bluff.*

I drew my baselard. "Blood is worth diamonds."

Cesare sighed a quiet '*for fuck's sake*' as metal sang its unsheathing.

Yet more blood anointed the floorboards.

Yet more promises sealed in scars.

Wiping my blade on my pants, I faced The Morettae. "You have no right to any of these documents. Just as you have no right to be in this house."

Lorita seethed. "Who are *any* of you to command us?"

I riveted to her eyes my unbending glare, pacing near, watching her brace as if confronting a demon. "De Tullia executed my father. I do not *care* about your pride." I pointed my dagger to her chest. "This is bigger than *you*, than *me*, and all of *we*." I launched my eyeline for Kel-Kech. "We shall speak again."

She held her palms open skyward. A soft smile found her lips, her brow serene.

The Morettae picked up their fallen siblings and trooped out, Lorita muttering prayers under her upturned nose as her departing eyes snicked me like a last word.

I beheld the ruination. The gore-slicked floors and riven ceiling of my father's forgotten home. The peeling chars and filling puddles. The munted sky charts and orreries and armillary spheres. So much of *him*. Of his restless soul.

"Davide set the place on fire, so we broke the roof to put it out," explained Lissandri. "But—"

"Not right now." My heart launched into horrified bating. "Come."

THE STAIRCASE skewering the apartment building streaked by as Cesare fought to keep himself blinking as seldom as possible.

Giorgianna's recount of *The Crescent* echoed with the patter of rain, but he could hear only fragments amid the storm of his own thoughts.

This was good—*better* than good! Their one-step-forward-two-steps-back hobble shifted and with every misstep, by fortune or divinity, they gained shaky ground. And yet… *what was she thinking?* She had no clue as to the luck she'd land with Kel-Kech, no idea what those people would do when Lapo fell at her hand.

They emerged on *Di Vitis Lane*.

The vault wailed, seas tossed, a saturnian haze thickened the atmosphere.

Cesare latched onto his senses as rain sluiced his face and bound hair, at last whirling to meet Giorgianna's blood-moon eyes.

Their radiance faltered. "Your eye…"

Cesare wanted to grab her shoulders and shake sense into her like the hypocrite that he was. "You're a *lunatic*!" Instead, his hands slipped around her jaw, and he kissed her for a brief and reckless second.

She expelled a sharp breath, warmth bleeding from her skin into his coldness.

Even beneath the downpour, she smelled of bitter rose petals. And she tasted of divine retribution.

Cesare reeled back. His stomach keeled when sanity came to vanquish the ephemeral instant of his madness.

Blood marred Giorgianna's cheek where his mauled hand had touched her, raindrops running the crimson proof of his momentary folly down her neck.

Their eyes mortared together. Equally wide. Equally stunned. Their tongues equally deserted of words. *Why did I—?*

"Lucrezia got shot," Giorgianna burst out, hands smacking over her mouth in time with exclamations of shock. "In the abdomen. Sarnai took her to Etenesh but…" She gaped for words, eyes flooded. "I don't want to fear the worst."

Eligio folded his hands over Giorgianna's. "We're with you."

"I'll keep watch here in case," Isaia said. "Araya: get Mair help. Aengus: see if Sarnai's had Ygal informed."

"Yes, boss." Aengus bowed a blood-smudged smile despite his mangled nose, cupping Isaia's face and kissing his lips.

Everyone dispersed.

Cesare reined in his heartbeat.

The four ascended the abandoned lighthouse in the cliffs, Giorgianna and Cesare aiding Lissandri where needed. The wound on his side oozed slowly, though held fast and threatened no haemorrhage, but undeniably pained him.

Shame ate at Cesare all the same.

As they crossed the rope bridge into lower óssium, a flustered woman zipped by, Eligio limping on his sprained ankle from her path. Cesare steadied him.

His half-eclipsed eyes trained on Vencenza's skyline.

Unwavering against the rain, the horizon bleared in smog and cinder, effulgent light converging into a singular nucleus among the rooftops like a rising sun. *Like flames…*

"Wait, that's…" Cesare heard Giorgianna.

Until he heard nothing at all.

# Scene LII

## Memento Mori

*Cesare*

*THE SUNRISE* BURNED.

The twins clutched each other. Giorgianna's shaking hands lay laced over her heart. All stared speechless as a vicious conflagration devoured without abandon those drapes stitched from the aquarelles of celestial dawn, the dressing room chiming with ghostly melodies and glittering dust, the musical instruments forgotten and untuned, the fading frescos gilding wood-spun halls. Every memory buried beneath thaumaturgy and tyranny. All that was left.

Cesare couldn't breathe the torrid air. Couldn't *breathe*.

*The Sunrise* had meant everything to the twins. To Fabio. To *him*. Maybe it meant something to Giorgianna. *And yet that cursed bàuta survived!* Safely forgotten at Etenesh's apothecárium.

Glass shattered from inside an àtrium window, boards collapsing.

"*Rosa?*" Eligio's scream broke.

Giorgianna bolted for the girl who stumbled from the window, hissing and throwing her head from the flame's spit. She pulled Rosalia into the half-courtyard where limestone sheltered them to brush her free of fire. "Why did you go in there?" She went to palm her face.

Rosa shrunk back with a shriek.

Dread took root in Cesare when he saw the burns devouring the length of Rosalia's left arm, shoulder, neck, all the way to her face where her cheek seethed the lurid pink of intestines. Her sclerae branched with bulging vessels, pupils freakishly dilated. *Drugged.*

"I went home from the *Curios*—"

"Why did our parents let you?" Anguished rage sharpened Lissandri's tone.

"*They didn't!*" Rosalia shouted. "I snuck away for the kitties! One moment I was there, and the next I woke up woozy in the parlour with everything up in flames and so was I." She gestured to her iridescent dress wrecked with burns like eschar. Her face crumpled. "It really hurts."

Giorgianna wrapped her arm around Rosalia's uninjured side. "We have to go."

The twins aided one another as Eligio wiped away welling tears. Yet Cesare couldn't budge from the despair chaining him down. Couldn't tear his ruined eyes from the glow upon the gold tears of the smiling faces haloing *The Sunrise*'s main door, the cataclysmic blaze unconquered by the downpour. Fire in his blood, under his skin, his flesh, his soul. A destroyer. *A death-bringer.* Like him.

'*…I will always know how to hurt you.*'

Cesare's cuff yanked sharply. "*Cesare!*" Giorgianna yelled out to him as if she'd been shouting for epochs already, eyes nitid, begging.

He did not want to walk away—with all his might wished he did not have to flee another home.

But there was nothing left.

# SCENE LIII

## TITHES

*Giorgianna*

I BARGED THROUGH THE APOTHECÁRIUM DOOR.

Gathered around a stretcher holding Lucrezia, Ygal joined Sarnai and Etenesh. Her large fingers wrapped around Lucrezia's tiny hand as she knelt by her side, head bowed, fingertips kneading the sleeping woman's nazar ring like a bead upon a prayer rope.

Sarnai bolted to crush me in an embrace. "She's alive and so are you!"

Tears beaded as I embraced her tighter. "*And you.*"

"*Holy Three!*" Etenesh gawked at our battered company. "What happened?"

"*The Sunrise*," Eligio choked out, eyes riddled with sorrow. "It's burning." My heart tore.

"Your eye!" Etenesh exclaimed at Cesare. "What is going on?"

"Davide. Ignore it," he dismissed. *Why do you always do that?* "Check Rosa, I suspect she was drugged and left in the burning parlour."

The thought clutched my guts into cold irons.

"Right, sit," Etenesh ordered, ushering Rosalia to a wooden reclining chair.

I took to tending to the twins' injuries alongside Sarnai whilst Etenesh threw on her netela, sanitised herself, and set up a glass tube rack. Ygąl didn't dare leave Lucrezia, didn't speak.

"Did you see anything?" Lissandri questioned, lifting his chiffon shirt to bare to me the clotting laceration on his left side.

Etenesh voided a vial of azurean liquid into a tube. "There *were* Imperialíi about." Dampening a cotton swab with saline, she swabbed Rosalia's nose, dipping the implement into the test tube. Gloom limned her eyes, crevices sunken between her drooped brows. "I am so very sorry."

The knife in my heart turned as I met the vìtae's eyes.

Rosalia's burn-born pain trumped all else in her lukewarm gaze. Every muscle in Lissandri's face angrily fought tears. Eligio's eyes swam, wet cheeks flushed red as his sclerae. Cesare didn't look up from his vigil near the desk, teeth clenched so tight around his cheek he surely bled.

> *'There is soul in every*
> *performance, thousands of*
> *dazzling pictures in every*
> *word. Storytelling is a force*
> *of life—its own magic.'*

*The Sunrise* was their haven within a world gambling on their deaths. Their home. *Mine.* The corner of a forgotten realm which harboured me when I had nothing and nobody.

My hand shot to my face, tears pouring. They, *The Sunrise*, Ema, my father and those executed alongside him. *The Arum* lavìri. The people forsaken to the slums and the camps. So, *so* many more. *Is it worth this?* How could freedom be worth losing all you love? How could freedom be worth such aching loneliness? *Was Mother right?*

My teeth screeched, a horrible ache pushing on my heart.

"*You never deserved this pain…*"

While I wrapped Lissandri's torso in the finest Dīmarḍi gauze, Etenesh watched with erudite eyes as the eddying azure within the tube bled into fuchsia. She slotted it into the rack. "Morphera."

Rosalia craned her neck. "What's that do?"

Etenesh disposed of the used equipment. "A mild soporific brewed from the leaves of *Scelestum morphera*, a summer shrub endemic to southern Maanaat but found all over." She trawled through hosts of bottles with vitreous *clanks*. "When boiled, the resulting tincture acts as one ingredient for apozems, while the *vapours* possess elevated tranquilising faculties—knock a dozen people out in *seconds* if concentrated enough." Etenesh pulled out a corked flask, round as a bubble. Moonstone wisps of adularescence whirled in gaseous ribbons through its vacuum. "In a pressurised receptacle, the steam can be deployed as a biological weapon. Once in contact with oxygen, it's undetectable, unless through nose swabs or nasopharyngeal aspirates." She faced Cesare. "I reckon that's what did it, but a large space like your parlour dispersed it enough that Rosalia thankfully awoke." She plucked an amethystine vial. "I can unfortunately offer only katō-apozem." Her face wilted. "It will scar quite significantly."

My stomach sank.

Rosalia puffed her cheeks, swishing air side to side before wincing. "It's only skin." Her focus roamed to Etenesh. "I don't want it to hurt anymore." *She's so unmoved...*

"I'll do it." Eligio stood, face drawn. "Tend to Ces."

Lacing his stays back up, Lissandri thanked me, cracking his knuckles, leg jerking wildly.

Etenesh reached for an angelite flacon of eyedrops. "I'll need to administer Torpor.[150]"

---

[150] An aqueous solution made from flowers of *Prasinum accidia*, literally 'green-leaved torpor', found across Isatōnia. Causes complete motor and sensory paralysis. Two other species exist in this genus: *Prasinum angustia*, literally 'green-leaved harrowing' (*Harrow*) which causes complete motor paralysis, slowing of the eyes, but no sensory paralysis (*i.e.* one can still sense touch). *Prasinum goldarus*, literally 'green-leaved smite' (*Smite*), causes motor paralysis from the neck down and no

I sat down with my pounding head lolled, Sarnai leaning her cheek on my shoulder. *Tailoring takes it out of you monumentally.* It was a wonder how much damage I'd dealt to myself.

Etenesh inspected Cesare's paralysed optic with a miniature flashlight. "Open globe penetrating laceration through the iris and pupil. Massive pupillary tearing. Lamellar laceration of the sclera."

A horrible realisation seemed to wash through Cesare, emptying him of colour. "I'll lose my vision."

I beheld Etenesh with bated breath. *Please say no.*

"…Most likely." The apothecary's quiet words silenced the edifice.

> *'Must keep the eye sharp for the revolution.'*

Every day Cesare honed his aim like a weapon to unmake the world. As much aggravation as awaking to a hammering in the walls spurred, I knew why he did it. Why his vision mattered.

Etenesh's behold bounced along the rafters. "I'm receiving an apozem shipment in the coming month." She toyed with her disk-shaped gold earring, expelling a ponderous *'hm…'* "If I inject the eye with Bloodletter,[151] it'll hamper the bleeding but keep the wound fresh —ano-apozem cannot function on scar tissue. You'll need to come in daily for upkeep *and* use Torpor drops, otherwise you'll be in agony. Chances are, you *will* lose a degree of your sight, but at least you'll retain some." Etenesh sanitised her hands. Cesare remained tomb-silent. "For *now*, I'll patch your eye up." She pulled supplies from some drawers. "Alas, I've no surgical skills besides needles." Through a phial's orifice, Etenesh suctioned liquid—Bloodletter—into a syringe.

Cesare tipped his head back, and I couldn't look away as she pulled taut his brow and slid the glinting steel needle into the gash goring his eye, depressing the plunger.

---

sensory paralysis. Effects are localised if topically applied, and systemic if ingested or injected.

[151] An aqueous anti-healing drug derived from the seaweed *Illince thiocea* native to the coral reefs around Ayangumida and Kamōtu. A misnomer, as Bloodletter does the opposite of encouraging bleeding, instead impeding scar formation by forming a gel plug over the wound.

I now owed so much more to Etenesh. We all did.

With an ever-crestfallen countenance, Eligio stepped away from Rosalia.

The seething burns sweeping her arm and cheek curdled to scars, webbing like spidersilk all the freckles once swarming her skin. Flesh whorled and drooped from a razed brow around her golden orb.

The knots in my chest refused to yield, every passing minute hailing a new reason for them to stay in perpetuum bound.

Etenesh secured a pad of oval gauze over Cesare's eye, passing him a protective eye patch—a square piece of black cloth with loops hitched to each of the four corners.

He hooked the straps over his ears, rising. "Thank you." He pressed clasped hands to his chest, and I could swear they trembled.

"Ces..." Eligio murmured quietly. His fearful eyes lifted, and my blood ran algid. "I have a bad feeling."

Cesare stared back, gaze darting to Lissandri. To me.

*Eighteen hundred hours.*

We rushed for our weapons and tore out.

# SCENE LIV

## CADAVERA VERO INNUMERA

*Cesare*

*THE SUNRISE* A HARROWING BEACON in the sobbing vesper sky, Cesare traversed oldtown towards *Commegnos' Curios*, heart in his throat.

The shopkeeper bell jingled a jeer at them.

And Cesare's heart stopped.

The furniture Lâlẹn and Micheletto broke their backs to restore lay shattered once more. Cabinet doors and damask curtains hang in shreds. Gemstones and serrated glass clogged the floor, the moon rifling her thread-thin fingers through the glistering wads of torn necklaces. Through the blood slicking *everything*.

Screams and gasps thronged the too-small space.

On a mangled shelf, Lâlẹn and Micheletto sat side by side. Poised and tranquil.

Blood disgorged by the paunched orifice of their guts saturated their sumptuous clothing, entrails spewed across the floor at their folded feet. Slits opened their throats, baring the mould-white cartilage, tongues yanked out through the gaping lacerations. Their bruised fingers twisted grotesquely, death a cold stench soaking the static air.

"No... *no!*" Eligio's anguished wails thrust Cesare back to horrible reality. "Mạti, ạbậ, *NO!*"

Lissandri grabbed his own hair, babbling madly, eyes flinging in every direction until he stumbled into a broken vitrine and cut himself on the bladed glass.

Tears scorched Cesare's remaining eye. "*I'm so sorry...*"

Something plopped at his feet with a slosh.

An... *organ?*

*Crunch!*

Shrieks scattered as a corpse plummeted from the ceiling into the ruin: gutted, throat cut, fingers broken just as the Commegnos. Gouged pits festered in the corpse's sockets, and ribs, severed off the spine, protruded like grisly wings from inside the ragged muscle of their back, lungs pulled out and stretched over the slippery bone into membranous wings. *A Hound.* The one Cesare requested to watch the *Curios.*

Eligio doubled over, emptying his stomach.

Lissandri kicked an upturned chair, picked up a nacre snuff box and flung it into fragments.

"*Nonononono*—" Eligio reeled back, head clutched in screwing fingers. "This can't be this can't be this *CAN'T!*" He screamed and screamed in helpless despair. "They did nothing! They were so *kind* and *good* and they were *punished* for it! They were *guiltless!*"

"Eligio!" Giorgianna grasped his cheeks. "*Look at me!* We cannot stay here."

Eligio kept shaking his head. "I can't—"

"I *know!*" Giorgianna's voice shattered. "I know how much grief hurts and devours you. But little by little, drop by drop, every single day, that awful anguish will ebb. And one day you will wake up and the pain will be liveable."

"I don't want to wake up," muttered Eligio.

Lissandri embraced his older brother.

"*They* would want you to," implored Giorgianna. "*Please*, Eligio."

Within the slick cavity of Micheletto's gutted stomach glinted a silver pin, a scrap of blood-softened paper skewered onto it. *Déjà vu...*

Cesare tugged the pin free. The scrawl across the note turned his stomach worse than the fetor of cooled flesh:

'*Walk carefully, Bauta.*'

'*...I will* always *know how to hurt* you.'

"*Why them?*" Cesare heard Eligio breathe his own thoughts into being, and tears broke from his eye, singeing stigmata into his cheek.

He doubled back, almost tripping over a broken amphora.

Torsion twisted his jaw.

'*...you lost.*'

Cesare would drag the fucker back from Hell just to murder him again and *again and again!* But he couldn't. He couldn't do anything. *There is nothing left.*

"Ces?" It was Lissandri's voice. Or it could've been nothing at all.

If not for him, the Commegno family would never have been embroiled in this calamity. If not for him, all these innocent lives would not sever short so fast.

*You never deserved this pain...*

But he did.

# SCENE LV

## PLEROMA

*Giorgianna*

CANTILLATING ILLUTÈRI CHOIRS haunted the manifold halls of the basilica like eerie spirits.

Scarlet silk sashes caressed my arms as I nestled in a niche within the soaring walls of a dormitórium[152] just beneath the ceiling, an air foramen behind me and ornate colonnettes below, sheltered from the glinting fangs of lightning under the auspices of shadows.

Rain endured since *The Sunrise*'s burning five turns prior. Some days a drizzle. Some a tempest. Weeping ceaselessly, nevertheless. Levin barely illumed the sky to-night, but once in a while, the dark sphere fractured.

I trained my ear on the dialogue below.

---

[152] Dormitorii serve as segregated sleeping quarters for áni (*siblings*) of the Order of Illutère. The High Priest and their Clergia are granted bedchambers elsewhere in the colossal cathedral.

'*…neophytes disappearing,*' a sóra fretted, goading my ever-nagging curiosity.

'*More?*' another gasped. Young.

'*Horrific and worsening,*' the first confirmed. '*Three newly-ordained were reported missing just this auróra—two rúvae and an áne.*'

'*What does Domínie speak of this?*' a third asked, tremors spraining her voice.

'*They made contact with the General, but nothing has come of it.*'

'*Aísne Faciáe, praemùnivit am no 'áltri potíri.*[153]'

Light and the oragious tumult drained as the window shut, gilded alchemy pooling across the sandstone floor carved with faces and stars in feeble trickles from the sun-shaped apertures in the vaulted ceiling. The Thinker's visage embossed the window doors, eyes shut and pensive, a third eye open in place of a mouth.

I counted passing minutes on my breaths like coins in a gambling house.

Once shuffling settled, the fourth sóra pronounced, '*Dél'ì lùtius e vísus benedétti.*'

'*Mèa sóra,*' all sórae intoned.

'*Sánguinem del'èa,*[154]' she replied.

Silence vanquished all but the ghostly psalms and the whispering patter of unrelenting rain.

With the ecclesiastical silks I'd filched from a shrine secured on a pillar through the other end of the foramen, I wound the two swathes around my thighs, locked my feet, gripped hold, and pushed from my hiding spot, letting go and twisting as I plummeted.

My loose braid skimmed the floor as I hung upended, spine arched. None of the sisters stirred.

Looping my arms, I manoeuvred my feet free, tracing circles in the air as I unwound my thighs. I paused before the final coil, shaking as every muscle ached, and wheeled through the air, tucking in my freed

---

[153] '*Divine Faces, may we be protected.*'

[154] Literally '*blood of I*'. There is no 'I' vs 'me' distinction in Faustinian.

legs and letting the silks hoist me upright to step onto the tiles in my stockings. *Flexibility begs improvement.*

Half-masks adorned the sórae, rubious, eye openings occluded by gentle domes, clinquant gold lunes rendered upon the brows like bowls to hold celestial light. A somnátta.

Gulping a crimson capsule of Thalem,[155] I unpinned from my corseted waist two bulbous flasks of Morphera, opening and setting them tactically around the dormitórium before retreating to the shadows and slipping through the foramen.

I draped the silks to the marble hallway, shutting the vent.

Ankles crossed and unbound waves curtaining his face, Cesare leaned against a golden pilaster, one hand pocketed and the other perpetually fiddling with a loop of his eyepatch.

'*Executed,*' I signed when he looked up, and swung to the floor.

Floating the silks down, I shoved them into the corner of a lavabo where my boots waited for me, unlacing my hair.

Cesare passed me my rapier along with a cynical smile. '*Let's hope this little ambuscade doesn't land* us *in a matching predicament.*'

Rolling my eyes back, I routed for the basilica's minor dome. Inside was housed The Limbus—a shrine slotted above the chancel, a gold-circumscribed oculus opening in its front wall to gaze down through the apse. Chryselephantine colonnades within, wreathed in stucco, held up a vault sprawled with frescos of sparkling luminaries and abstract cognition—faces welded with faces, suns wrought of moons, false windows embellished with plate tracery and soft jewel stain. A sanctuary just beyond the Gods' totality where the fragment of a soul they bestowed upon the hylic was most acutely aware of its incongruence.

Watery light filtered through glass slits in the dome like portals within the sanctum sanctorum of ancient temples, moonlight rippling along the ouro-veined marble.

---

[155] A gel to counteract Morphera, made from the berry of *Mulleum ophthalmos* found across Faustina, Shpokë, Očuva, and Themistóklis (literally '*crimson eye*', named on account of the engorged, crimson vessels in the sclera resulting from Morphera dosage—a symptom Thalem dispels first).

At the omphalos stood the Minister of Emissaries, Clario Barsotti, clothed in an opulent umber robe and black biretta, vólto doffed to bare his visage to the Divines. *"Heaven's tears cleanse all,"* he whispered the conclusion to his prayer.

I dragged my rapier's tip along the marble with a banshee's shrill screech, shedding the shadows.

The Adviser groped his heart and swivelled with a gasp.

We locked eyes, his dark as timber, the left shot through with a pale blue streak.

*"Guards—!"*

"Are visiting the Land of Nod." Cesare's voice reverberated through marble as he paced from the darkness unhurriedly, catching shards of nocturnal light on his stilétto.

Shudders coiled around the Minister's ankles as he fumbled to assume toothless defiance. "What do you want?"

"We have something *you'd* want." From his jacket, Cesare pulled Barsotti's journal, and the Minister's breath ceased to stir the air. "Displeased, are we? Saints *forbid* this little book ends up on the Governor's desk by some unfortunate turn of chance."

Each fibre binding Barsotti stiffened. "I shall ask again what you want."

"For this empire to crumble into the dirt where it belongs," declared Cesare plainly, counterfeit Vencenzani accent falling away like a theatre curtain. "But, to attain my victory, I require passage inside the ministerial abode."

The Minister's face bleached, recognition gripping his voice reeds along with the words—*"The Bauta…"*

Cesare's furtive smirk tilted into a grin, eye ignited. "I appreciate a man with deductive skills." Glee slipping, he unsheathed his second stilétto. "It *is* entirely within your power to refuse, but understand that your life is a gambling chip I'm under no obligation to hold on to."

The Minister of Emissaries held Cesare's gaze—unable to sever himself free, rather than undaunted—and stole half a step back.

Dragging my rapier, I scraped the floor.

The marble shriek jolted Barsotti.

He whirled to me with wary eyes and unmasked dismay, fists close to his trunk, but considered, greying brows scrunched to his lashes. "…Very well." The hands of time stuttered at the moment his hesitant words struck the clock's glass, fracturing the cyclical continuum. "I can devise means to aid you, but require time and consultation with my Centúrion.[156]" The Minister held up slender palms when Cesare's teeth bared. "An ally! Ioana De Rege. I trust them completely."

"Your word is worthless to me when I know the kinds of spiders you crawl among," sneered Cesare.

"Do you *want* passage into the government house, or *not*?" Barsotti's brusque question did well to startle me and muzzle Cesare. His comportment donned bona fide authority, and the moment his gaze pierced through each of us, Clario Barsotti truly looked like a Governor's Adviser. Perhaps, upon him dawned the realisation that *we* could be *his* key *out* of The Bone King's domain. "If you demand my aid so uncouthly, then I shall make use of every loophole and lifeline you cannot touch. You will never hold absolute ascendancy over me." His eyes stalled on mine. "And *I* shall have your names. *Full*."

We observed each other as I weighed my options, realising there *were* none if I wished to collect my dues. "Giorgianna Damiani."

Barsotti's face dropped. "Ludovico's daughter…"

My heart turned but my mouth called forth a humourless smirk. "Debt collectors."

The Adviser's gaze flinched away, awaiting Cesare's answer.

Cesare's filthy, *filthy* pride grappled with him, his jaw flickering, shoulders rigid as a statue.

Catching his overwrought gaze, I brandished my fingers, '*Do it.*'

His eyes shunned me, chin born aloft, lips twitching as he clung to his guns, stubborn and uncompromising. But, no matter how vehemently he might wish otherwise, he and I both knew we ran out of alternatives long ago, and *this* was more unlikely than finding the same speck of azoth in the cosmos twice. So, Cesare unwound the coiled muscles of his jaw, eye disdainfully slitting for Barsotti. "Cesare Ramiro Agostini."

---

[156] *chehn-TOO-ree-ohn*; leader of the Guárdia, the Adviser's guards.

The Minister sighed wearily. "Know that I cannot make promises. However, if it buys my life, I will grant you passage inside by whatever means."

Cesare clicked his tongue, looking to me. "Her."

Barsotti peered my way, body drawing like a bow with no arrow as I circled him, my boots echoing through marble.

"I am rather the apologist of retributive justice." I pointed my rapier at Barsotti's chest. "And I'm unsatisfied with your bargain." He paled. "Is your life not valued higher, Minister? Are you not willing to pay what*ever* it takes?"

"What more could you want?" the Adviser breathed.

Ribs clenched my burning heart. *This is it.* I would finally know. "Two years ago, a woman named Emanuela Vehanush Airaldi was killed by three men on a winter solstice night. Familiar?"

Barsotti considered his words. "…Yes. It's… known among the Ministry."

The grip around my hilt trembled. "I see." It took *everything* to not run him through. "You know the perpetrators?"

Eyes eluding mine for a split beat, the Adviser nodded slowly.

My vision shuddered and I drove my blade forward.

Barsotti fell, whimpering as deep red blossomed into a rosette on his chest.

"My companion has more mercy than I." Rage drank my blood. "One man killed Emanuela and two assaulted me. *One* of those two was executed. I want *all* their names. Who was the man your *chums* bothered to put to the blade?"

The Minister scrambled to search his memory. "Erminiu Matracia.[157] *A*-a City Guard."

"Of course," gritted Cesare.

*Good riddance to worthless scum.*

"The second," I demanded. "The one who helped him."

"Abramo Sessa."

---

[157] *ehr-MEE-nee-oo maht-RAH-chah*

My stomach lurched. And yet, the picture pieced itself together a little more. Was that why he reviled me from the start? *Is that why he came into employment at The Crescent?* Did Basilio know?

"He too was the bird sort?"

"An Imperiálus. His position graced him with a suspension over death."

    *Corrupt.*

        *To.*

            *The.*

                *Bone.*

                    "And the third?"

The Adviser's lips wobbled.

I thrust the blade deeper, forcing him to crawl back as darkness striated his torso. "Cough it up, Barsotti, before it's *blood* your gullet is spewing!"

He struggled to swallow, to piece together his breaking voice. "General Manuele Dioli."

For a tick in time, I didn't feel my heart beat. Didn't hear the choirs.

Drawing back, I glimpsed Cesare, but I couldn't look long at the illimitable horror upon his face.

*The Minister of Blades...*

Manuele... Emanuela... *Gods, why must you be so cruel?*

"Dioli..." I looked down at the Adviser who braved to meet my behold. "Several months back, officéri arrested a neighbour of mine for alleged treason and conspiracy. He was executed alongside my father, but that day, his sentencing included *murder*. His name was Arturo Dioli. That was intentional, wasn't it?" Horrid astonishment clutched my heart. "Manuele's crimes were pinned on *him*, weren't they?"

"Yes," Barsotti confirmed. "Easy to feign a transcriptional error."

I couldn't breathe. *An innocent sacrificed... for me.* "It's all entwined with the plot to execute my father." The Adviser's eyes begged me for his life. A life built on the graves of so many of *Us*. "Correct?"

Barsotti gaped like a choking salmon. "Y-yes... b-but I d-don't know w—why... your friend..."

My teeth creaked, eyes blistering. "So much *justice* that Emanuela was never granted it. *I* was never granted it. I am *owed* it! And you *all* will pay your dues in blood." The words became my prayer to the Gods, a furious psalm to rip open the firmament and carve itself into the walls of the indomitable church. Chrysopoeia for my putrescent ichor.

I wiped my blade on the embroidered hem of Barsotti's silk gown, flicking corkscrews over my shoulder as I snapped back to my striking height, snideness curling my lips. "Many thanks!"

Cesare slashed the Adviser with a devious smile. "A pleasure to meet you, signór." Tipping his tricorn, he sauntered for the exit.

Barsotti's hands tremored as he inspected his bloodied regalia.

"Hold it up to the rain," I sniped. "Don't heaven's tears cleanse all?"

# SCENE LVI

## LA LORO STORIA
## È LA NOSTRA STORIA

*Giorgianna*

VENTURING BACK THROUGH THE DORMITORÍI, I collected all the Morphera flasks and headed with Cesare to the hypostyle halls encircling the basilica's vast piazza: erected from eburneous marble and travertine, innumerable columns rising like lacquered ribs.

The waning moon waded through turbulent midnight seas as if a clumsy boat, raindrops jumping to suicide from the gloomy spume of lachrymatory clouds and smashing themselves open on the cosmatesque stonework, the cityscape afield a swathe of fuligin gossamer strewn with lights like glitters.

An inscription etched a stone ridge below eaves embellished with acanthus and ivy scroll mosaics:

ILLUTÉRO AD'DÉL PRAEVARICÁTORI.
BENEFÁCIO AD'DÉL IMMÚNDUM.

*ENLIGHTENED BE THE TRANSGRESSORS.*
*BLESS'ED BE THE TARNISHED.*

My lips curved. "Fortune favours fools."

"You *must* be joking about Manuele," said Cesare.

A mordant laugh twirled in my throat. "Au contraire, signór." Even with the reason for Emanuela's murder yet to be known, with Davide's potential troop missing, my father's fabled discoveries unknown and so much remaining to be pieced together, I *finally* held my key, *finally* had those coveted names. Now, came my time to carve them with a bloody knife into gravestones—those men's soulless husks deserved no grace of immolation.

"You *saw* what he did to me," insisted Cesare.

*All the more incentive.*

"I will do worse to him." I headed for the stairs.

"There are…" Cesare halted me, hand jerking away from my elbow as quickly as it touched me, "*rumours* about him…" his head shook slowly, "but I don't for a second believe they are merely that." The chatoyance of hatred illustred his eye. "He is a rapist."

"I know." Notwithstanding, revulsion sewed my muscle, nausea bubbling in my core. "And so," my voice softened to death, "I will drain him of blood and drown this wretched world."

"*No!*" Cesare burst out.

Nails sank hard into my palms, my eyes searing a warning into him.

"I want him equally dead." Cesare fidgeted with a loop of his eyepatch, perusing the ceiling of the cloister before matching my gaze. "Let *me*—"

A flick of the wrist and I stuck my dagger to his throat.

He backed up with a sharpened breath.

"I. Will kill. *You*. If you get in my way," I sneered.

His pupil pulled its iris like a dying galaxy. *Fear*. Of *me*.

*I* was the one worth fearing now.

"*But*." My observation slid to the garnet eye encrusted beneath my baselard's pommel, like caramelised ichor glinting. "Our aims align as stars upon a blood moon sky screaming for apocalypse." Mine and

Cesare's eyes interlocked. "Your enemies are mine also."

He tracked my circling saunter, gaze never breaking step with mine. "Basilio Lanuza."

"Abramo Sessa," I scorned.

"General Manuele Dioli," he sneered the name.

My footfalls reversed, blade dragging down the length of Cesare's neck, skin unbroken. "Grand Judge Giordano Veronesi."

"Governor Crescenzo Zuane De Tullia," with a flourish of an elegant hand, Cesare mused that forsaken moniker like a sonnet's closing line.

I halted, dagger poised between Cesare's collarbones. "Men like They don't deserve to live, and shall have no peace so long as *I* do." I drew the blade away at long last. "And if *you* help me decimate a bloodline..." Lighting streaked the darkness as I resumed my tread.

"...*You* will help *me* topple an empire." Cesare's sharp lips cut into line so wicked, and thunder cracked the firmament asunder. "Crush into dust that skull the rulers dwell within."

"Etch into their skin the names of every soul they stole." I drew closer.

"So you may drown this wretched world." He mirrored my motion.

"And you may *eat the flesh of kings*." My voice dropped to a whisper when I ceased close enough to clutch Cesare's breaths between my canines, peering into the chasmic blackness of his pupil, his iris coruscating with nebulae. Abyss calling unto abyss. And some wayward splinter of mine wanted him to kiss me like he did beneath the rain before the sky fell. "How much is blood worth?"

My question thinned his eye.

I stepped back, tugging my sleeve and holding out my forearm wordlessly.

He considered me for a beat in time, countenance strange and unreadable, before steadying my hand and slicing my wrist. I shivered as azoth thrummed ardent through my bloodstream.

Cesare shed his jacket and pulled up his cuff, wrist bared to me, the same upon which burn scars glistened like splashed oil. "You dance well."

My gaze flinched at him. His fervid scrutiny knocked me off-kilter, as if every scintilla of inferno his flesh entrapped converged like a supernova in his singular one.

Setting my teeth, I slashed Cesare's wrist.

Crimson starlight washed my blade, droplets spilling beneath my nails.

A blood promise—scabs to stitch us together. Indissoluble.

I never thought my nemesis in every possible world would be a projection of me. That I would begin to see something akin to myself when I looked at my most beloathed. That he would *gnaw* at me.

I brought my hand to my lips and sipped his blood off my finger, its iron tang sipid and untouched by the diamond frost of azoth. So rawly human.

My eyes lifted.

Cesare blinked mutely, closing his parted lips.

I shrugged and gazed upon the twinkling city. "What did you mean by calling yourself an instrument?"

Sheathing his stilétto, Cesare draped his jacket over his shoulder, weighing up my query. "I am only as useful as my cause." The words jolted me, yet he watched the rainy nightscape with near-jaded aplomb, arms crossed. "Nothing is quite as daunting as the endeavour of bringing about a revolution. But De Tullia has... grown too steadfast in his unchanging ways. And if the world, by shifting tides or apt machinations, as you said, becomes discordant with him, then he'll come plummeting from his throne. *That* is what I'm an instrument of." Cesare's eyeline fell to the staircase. "Even so, this revolution grows more self-sufficient by the day, and soon, its existence will no longer be contingent on mine."

"But why does that make your 'use' finite?" I countered hurriedly. *After everything, he cannot truly believe himself to be disposable...* "You are a *linchpin*, but not a mere object. To reduce yourself to rule—to something which can outlive its purpose and be done away with—is fallacious at best but *ludicrous*, in truth." I looked at him until he looked back. "So many people want you to live irrespective of whether *any* of this comes to fruition. You are a person before a martyr."

"There are things more immense than the Self; more pertinent to preserve. The Self *is* finite, Giorgianna."

I disregarded the twinge in my chest at my own name, contending, "The *Self* is *transcendent*. The material world is finite." I gestured to the church, to Vencenza. "This—*all* of this. We live for such a blip in this cosmic cycle."

*So,* is *it worth it, after all?*

"We *exist* in this world," Cesare cut back. "We aren't separate from it and thus are tethered to its materiality."

I opened my mouth to argue, but my voice wouldn't yield words.

'*Has that* ever *worked?*'

Why would it?

My heart turned unbearably heavy. *Prideful bastard.*

"I've been trapped in this limbo for so long," Cesare went on darkly. "I had nothing but the theatre and that spider took it and left me with only spite which I was no longer allowed to express. I suppose there's humour in that." He pocketed his hands. "I would throw rocks at the walls of the senators' homes and the windows of the rich out of toothless protest because that's all I could do to purge that spite without taking it out on myself. Aged seventeen, I stuck needles into my arms for a *modicum* of reprieve from this Hell. And so, I started to waste away. It was enough to give me pause, but not enough to seek escape. That shoe dropped when I began to *forget*. It's a wonder I scraped out of that pit at all." Cesare lifted his eye to the government house, its carcass agleam like polished cartilage beneath rain-flecked obumbration. "*He* is the pestilence killing this body." Such *hatred* honed his voice, and in that moment, I believed words *could* kill, soulless or not.

"Blood does not wash off," I mused.

"I don't want their blood." Cesare scoffed without an ounce of mirth. "I want this rotting fucking corpse to burn."

I studied his face. The scrying-crystal curve of his eye blazing with fallen empires. The dim alchemy tracing his sculpted features like candlelight.

"Our lives are stories written with washable ink," I heard myself speak.

Cesare peered at me with a creased brow.

My gaze slipped to the shoulder I shot, resting for a heartbeat before finding the moon, now an eerie, pale beacon drowned within distraught clouds. "If we are destined for ruination regardless, we are not without reason to put to the pyre the pages confining us." Leaving Cesare's scrutiny unreturned, I stepped into the baptising rain.

Across the óssium, my eyes fastened to that white-boned acropolis crowned in aqueducts. A corrupted civilisation, this twilight of a decaying empire emanating from its eyeless godhead.

I wondered what it would be like to watch it burn.

To stand beneath and gaze upon the afterglow of its collapse.

# EXEUNT

# DUES STILL OWED
# BLOOD YET TO BE REPAID

And so we come to the end of this bloody pantomime's first half.

In the intermission between now and the second novel's publication, if you enjoyed *Non Serviam*, it would mean the world to me to receive your reviews on Goodreads, StoryGraph, Amazon, or other retail sites on which the book is listed. Word of mouth is the best way to support independent creatives, and the royalties earned from all English copies of *The Hypostasis of Dissent* duology will be donated to *Doctors Without Borders*, the *Kurdish Red Crescent*, and *All for Armenia*.

If you decide to post about my books on your social media, including photographs and the like, feel free to tag my publisher (at) *lacrimose.and.righteous*. I would be honoured.

Until we meet again, reader.

SCAN TO GO TO
GOODREADS

SCAN TO GO TO
AMAZON

SCAN TO GO TO
STORYGRAPH

# ACKNOWLEDGEMENTS

So many golden hands were put to the creation of *Non Serviam* that I fear I mightn't be able to do it justice in a measly couple pages, but trying my best is the least I can offer.

I want to firstly thank the brilliant artists I commissioned for a number of illustrations. Ayşe-Mira's work is a slice of an ancient matriarchal time and was my first choice when thinking of whom to commission for the mask chart. *Çok teşekkür ederim, canım*; I couldn't be happier with the outcome. Nadia's gritty, metal-like linework so perfectly brings the military emblems into being, and her attention to detail is outstanding. *La ringrazio molto, mia cara amica.* The taṭrīz and key illustration on page 12 of the paperback is done by the wonderful Sophia; the authentic touch of a Palestinian-Lebanese artist on iconically Palestinian symbols is beautiful and I value it so deeply. شكرا جزيلا.

It must be noted here that most of the chapter titles are references to popular culture, literature, music, Gnostic scripture, and famous Latin phrases which I do not claim as my own. Notable are *SCENE V* (a play on *To Kill a Mockingbird*, the title of a novel by Harper Lee); *SCENE XVIII* (Italian translation of the title of John Milton's epic poem *Paradise Lost*); *SCENE XIX* (famous line from Emily Brontë's *Wuthering Heights*); *SCENE XXV* (Revelation 17:6); *SCENE XXXI* (line from Cassandra by Florence + the Machine); *SCENE XXXVII* (line from *L'infinito*, an Italian poem by Giacomo Leopardi); *SCENE XXXVIII* (line from *Ptolemaea*, by Ethel Cain).

Of course, I cannot overstate my gratitude to my editor, Belle Manuel, herself the author of the *Twisted Fates Trilogy* and the *Soul Stealer Saga* who put invaluable time and effort to helping polish *NS*.

These acknowledgements wouldn't be complete without thanking the beta readers and critique partners who kept my faith burning: Nelita for being there since the very beginning and having read the roughest of drafts (*and somehow enjoyed them...?*) along with just about every iteration since. R. E. Levy, author of queer gothic horror novella *Rivers of Eden*, for providing immense feedback as a beta reader, and whose kind words helped reignite my confidence as an author. Celina جان of *Qafiyah Review* who not only provided wonderful feedback for the first two chapters of *Non Serviam*, but held space for me as a fellow [mixed] minority SWANAn by accepting my poetry in the inaugural issue of her SWANA-centric literary magazine.

Lastly, yet arguably most importantly, my wonderfully diverse online space, full of radically-leftist activists, poets, artists, culture enthusiasts, and the kindest, most dynamic, and interesting people I have ever come across, is something I hold so incredibly dear and sacred. Not least of those people are Sila, Maryam, Daniel—poet and author of *A Casket Full of Poems*, Lilly, Raina, Stefano, Edelneria, Ellis—author of *Saturnalia*, Megan, Hydrawi—Italian author of *Infesto*, Ross and, very pertinently, Arev, Armenian-Persian-Jewish artist, activist and owner of art boutique *Mulberry Jaan* whose SSWANA-and-Central-Asian solidarity group I met countless wonderful, likeminded people through. Ճատ շնորհակալություն, ջան.

So, *so* many more could be named that I'd be here for another book's-worth of pages. I see all of you and I'm so grateful for your presence.

Thank you.

~*Sfar*